"MOMMA!"

Kate looked around.

"Momma, help me!"

A little girl stood far off in the distance, dressed in a green plaid smock with a white collar. Dressed the way Kate's daughter, Laura, had been on a class trip with her nursery school six years ago, a trip from which she had never returned.

"Mommy? They want to hurt me! Make them stop!"

And then Kate could see the child clearly, a little girl with long dark braids standing stiffly, with her arms opened. "Laura!" Kate screamed, running toward her.

Kate's daughter was alive. Kate's dream had come true—but her nightmare had just begun. . . .

HEAR THE CHILDREN CALLING

HEAR THE CHILDREN CALLING

Clare McNally

AN ONYX BOOK

NEW AMERICAN LIBRARY

A DIVISION OF PENGUIN BOOKS USA INC.

ONYX
Published by the Penguin Group
Penguin Books USA Inc., 375 Hudson Street,
New York, New York 10014 U.S.A.
Penguin Books Ltd, 27 Wrights Lane,
London W8 5TZ, England
Penguin Books Australia Ltd, Ringwood,
Victoria, Australia
Penguin Books Canada Ltd, 2801 John Street,
Markham, Ontario, Canada L3R 1B4
Penguin Books (N.Z.) Ltd, 182–190 Wairau Road,
Auckland 10, New Zealand

Penguin Books Ltd, Registered Offices:
Harmondsworth, Middlesex, England
First published by Onyx, an imprint of Penguin Books USA Inc.

First Printing, July, 1990

10 9 8 7 6 5 4 3

 REGISTERED TRADEMARK—MARCA REGISTRADA

Printed in Canada

PUBLISHER'S NOTE
This is a work of fiction. Names, characters, places, and incidents either are
the product of the author's imagination or are used fictitiously, and any
resemblance to actual persons, living or dead, events, or locales is entirely
coincidental.

Prologue

August 21, 1969

WHENEVER PARENTS DESCRIBE THE PERFECT BABY, the item that always tops the list is sleeping through the night. After a day of meeting the demands of even the most complacent infant, Mommy and Daddy want nothing more than a solid eight hours' sleep. Babies who sleep through the night at a few weeks old are rare. Babies who sleep through the night from day one are almost impossible.

But Lincoln and Georgina Adams had such a child. Lincoln Jr. never uttered a sound, not even at the moment of birth. Georgina, looking down over her suddenly flattened tummy at the glistening body of her firstborn son, did enough screaming for both of them.

From the neck down, he was perfect. But there would be no bothering to count ten little toes and fingers on this child. For the face on the slightly misshapen head was almost nonexistent. There was no nose, two piglike black eyes, and only the tiniest slit of a mouth.

Georgina screamed, and screamed, and screamed.

September 2, 1969

"I want you to kill him."

Georgina's voice was like that of an automaton. She sat up in bed with pillows propped behind her, a tray of untouched breakfast straddling her legs. She'd been here for the last week, ever since her husband put her to bed at the first signs of labor.

Lincoln poured her coffee, sighing deeply. "You know I won't do that," he said. "He's our son."

Georgina's eyes were clear as she looked up. She'd finished crying days ago.

"Look at it, Lincoln," she said. "What the hell kind of life is it going to have?"

"With therapy—"

"Therapy can't rebuild its face, for Christ's sake," Georgina snapped.

"You don't know that, Georgina," Lincoln said. "Plastic surgery can be miraculous."

Georgina regarded her cup of coffee for a few moments before picking it up and taking a long sip. "The trouble with you doctors," she said, "is that you think you're God. Nobody can reconstruct a face like that. It's cruel to let it live."

Lincoln slammed his fist against the headboard behind her, making her dishes rattle. Her eyes went wide.

"Stop calling him 'it,' " he roared. "His name is Lincoln Junior! Why don't you try being a mother to him? He's a baby. He has needs."

"He never cries," Georgina said, going back to the same faraway voice she'd used moments earlier. "He never makes a sound."

"Then you feed him on a schedule," Lincoln said. "That special bottle I brought, the one for kittens, is the perfect size for him. He may be ugly, Georgina, but he needs love. I can tell that when I hold him, the way he relaxes in my arms, so content. He's just a baby!"

"He's a *freak!*"

Georgina's scream was accentuated by the sound of her tray crashing to the floor. She threw aside her covers and pulled herself up from the bed.

"Georgina, no," Lincoln cried. "It's too soon. You shouldn't get up—"

"Leave me the hell alone," Georgina seethed, limping on water-bloated legs to the door of the bedroom. She didn't even glance at the bassinet when she passed it. Instead, she stumbled down the hall to the dining room, where she pulled open the liquor cabinet. She'd get drunk. She'd get drunk and she'd forget and she'd pretend it was all a nightmare.

Lincoln grabbed the whiskey bottle before she could pour a second drink.

"This is no way to handle our problem, Georgina," he said sternly.

She glared at him. "Oh, you cold-hearted son of a bitch. Who are you to tell me how to handle our problem? I carried that child for nine months. I prayed to God through six years of marriage to get pregnant. I was so happy when the doctor told me the news. And then this . . ." She leaned her head forward, empty tumbler in her hands, and began to cry.

Lincoln sat down and took her in his arms. He knew better than to say another word. He knew how much she hurt, because his pain was just as deep. But wasn't a mother's love supposed to transcend all boundaries? Why didn't she love Lincoln Jr.?

He realized suddenly that she had stopped crying. Her breathing was slow and even. Somehow, she had fallen asleep. Gently, Lincoln picked her up and carried her back to the bedroom. He thought about her pregnancy and how it had come about. The medicine she'd taken . . .

No, that was impossible. Anything that had gone in her mouth had been thoroughly tested. He knew that for a fact, because he worked as a research biologist for Georgina's father. Neither man would ever hurt that woman. ·

As he tucked her covers around her, he thought for a moment of laying the baby down next to her. Maybe physical contact would bring out her maternal instincts. But he thought better of it and turned to check on little Lincoln.

The baby lay on his side, just as Lincoln had propped him, a rolled-up towel set behind his back to keep him from rolling. His breathing was raspy but steady. Lincoln covered the small body with a little blue blanket. Georgina had crocheted it in anticipation of a perfect child. What she got was a monstrosity that they kept well hidden from the world. Nobody, not even Georgina's father, knew the child had been born. Lincoln had to take his time making the announcement, preparing just the right words. He wasn't even sure if it would be a birth, or a death, announcement.

He left the room.

Georgina fell deeper and deeper into sleep, and finally began to dream.

The baby was crying. No, no, that can't be. It doesn't make any noise at all. It doesn't have a mouth.

But it was crying. And Georgina suddenly had the irresistible urge to get up and go to him. It was almost as if the baby was pulling her toward him with an invisible magnet, pulling her out of the bed, across the floor.

She didn't want to look in the crib. Oh, God, she hadn't looked at the baby since the moments after its birth. She couldn't take it.

Please, no!

The baby commanded her to look at him. Not with words or cries, but with such incredibly strong emotions that Georgina felt a burning pain throughout her body. She could not resist. She looked in the crib . . .

And saw a perfect, blue-eyed baby boy.

No, Lincoln Jr. is a freak!

He smiled at her, a smile like sunshine. She smiled back, reaching down to lift him gently into her arms. It was all a nightmare, a mistake! Lincoln Jr. was perfect, perfect, perfect . . .

Lincoln, come and see our baby boy. Lincoln, you have to come see him! Lincoln . . .

"Lincoln!"

When Georgina cried out in her sleep, the sound awakened her. She was sweating on one side of her body. No, not sweating. Her milk had let down. Milk that should have dried up already. She felt an odd tugging at her breast. A cold chill washed over her as she slowly pulled back her covers.

The baby was there, latched to her, sucking away contentedly.

She knocked him aside with one swift arc of her arm, sending him to the floor. Her screams brought Lincoln running.

"Georgina, what . . . Oh, God! What have you done?" He hurried to the baby and picked him up. Georgina watched with wide-eyed horror as he kissed the child over and over again. "Thank God you're okay," he said to the baby. "Thank God we have a thick carpet in here."

He began to pace the floor as a father might do with a crying baby. Except that Lincoln Jr. wasn't crying.

"Why did you do that?" Georgina demanded.

"Do what?"

"Put it in bed with me," Georgina cried. "I told you, I don't want it near me. How can you be so insensitive?"

"Georgina, I didn't put the baby in bed with you," Lincoln said.

"Well, he sure as hell didn't get here by himself."

"But I didn't move him," Lincoln said, a look of worry passing over his face. "I swear it!"

Georgina was pensive for a while. The dream came back to her, only now that she thought of it, it was more vivid and real than any dream she had ever had.

"He made me do it," she said softly.

"What?"

"He made me pick him up," she said. "He used his mind and he tricked me into thinking he was beautiful."

"Georgina, you're crazy."

"I want him out of this bedroom, Lincoln," Georgina said. "Either he goes, or I do."

"I don't think—"

"I want him out of here!"

Lincoln breathed in a deep sigh. "Very well." He lay the baby down in the bed. Lincoln Jr. stared at nothingness with pig eyes. Not for the first time Lincoln wondered if he was blind.

He wheeled the bassinet out into the hall and down to the guest bedroom.

"Sorry, little guy," he said. "Life's giving you the short end of the stick, isn't it? But I'll make it up to you. I'll research day and night until I find a way to help you."

She hates me.

The voice was so loud and clear that Lincoln swung around to see if someone was standing behind him. The doorway was empty.

He was tired, that's all. Hearing things.

My mother hates me. Why does she hate me? Why? Why?

No, this was impossible. He could hear a child's voice in his mind. But how? He turned back to the baby's crib.

I want her to kill herself. Kill herself before she kills me.

"This isn't happening," Lincoln said. "You can't be using telepathy on me. You're too young, and you don't even know words. I'm imagining things! I'm going as crazy as Georgina."

"Lincoln, will you come here?"

Not understanding why he was grateful to get away from the baby, Lincoln hurried down the hall to his wife.

She was sitting up in bed, her hands tucked under her covers.

"My mother hates me," she said, her voice a strange parody of the childlike one Lincoln had heard in his mind. "I want her to kill herself. Kill herself before she kills me."

"Georgina, how did you know?"

He saw the pistol, too late. A single shot aimed at her neck took Georgina's life.

Down the hall in his bassinet, Lincoln Jr. shed his first and only tear.

1

A CHILD WAS CRYING, BUT NOT ONE OF THE ADULTS who stood around him could hear. The sound didn't come from his mouth; his lips were pressed together in angry protest. It came from deep within his mind, a scream sounded for the thousandth time in hope that someone would listen. But no one did.

"You're doing fine, Tommy," a young man said as he taped wires to the boy's forehead.

"Just a little blood sample, Tommy," said a woman in white.

A pinch. The boy winced, but didn't say a thing. He knew there was no use in it. No one would hear.

"Now, you know what to do, son," his father said from somewhere behind the big green chair where the boy sat, wired to machines he didn't understand. "It's just like all the other times. Bring the toy tiger to life, Tommy."

Tommy wanted to shake his head, to cry out "No!" But when he moved, the electrodes pulled hard at his skin. And he knew any protests would go unheeded now and he would be punished later.

He fixed his eyes on the stuffed tiger. It was a cub, big green eyes luminous in the bright, clinical lights. The boy stared hard at him.

I don't want to do this. I'm scared!

"Concentrate, Tommy," a woman said. "Don't be afraid. You can make him do whatever you want."

I can't make him! It never works right.

The tiger began to move.

11

"Keep going, Tommy," the woman said. "You were so close the last time. Maybe today . . ."

No! No! NO! I don't like this!

The green plastic eyes thinned. The head turned. The embroidered mouth opened to reveal long teeth that couldn't possibly be there.

"Send it to the dummy, Tommy," a man said. "Make it attack the dummy."

The toy tiger, an adorable plaything moments before, had turned into a miniature version of the real thing, no less vicious for its size. Tommy's eyes moved to a battered store mannequin that sat on the other side of the room. But the tiger didn't follow his gaze. Once contact was broken, the beast seemed to gain a mind of its own. It leapt toward the chair where the child sat confined by straps and wires.

Tommy screamed.

"Nnnnnooooo!"

One of the adults jerked Tommy's chair out of the way, wheels screeching on the tile floor. The tiger flew past the child and struck a technician, teeth sinking into her neck. She screamed, grabbing at it.

"Tommy, make it stop!"

Stop! You're a toy. Just a toy.

Instantly, the tiger fell to the ground. The woman touched her neck and brought back fingers tipped with blood. At her feet, the tiger was once again a plaything.

Tommy's father's face came into view. "I thought you were going to try harder today, Tommy."

He sounded disappointed. Tommy hung his head, silent again. He tried so hard to please the grown-ups. He'd been trying for as long as he could remember. But he was afraid of the things he could do, and that fear kept him from being in complete control. He closed his eyes and remained quiet as the electrodes were disconnected.

But in his mind, he cried pitifully. And for the first time since he was a small child, someone heard him. His thoughts carried out of the building, beyond the iron fence that surrounded the center and all the houses within it, beyond the mountains that formed a natural barrier between the boy's home and the neighboring city.

As she was driving up a mountain road, on her way to a picnic with her niece and nephew, a woman suddenly experienced a flash of head pain so intense she had to slam the brakes. The children begged her to say what was wrong, but she couldn't. She could only stare up into the trees, listening to the cries of a child, a little boy whose brain was on the same wavelength as her own. The cries were so pathetic that tears began to form in her own eyes.

Ignoring the dismayed protests of her passengers, she sent a thought message back to the child.

Tell me where you are, little one. Tell me who you are, and how I can help you.

In his chair, free now of the wires, the boy finally relaxed. He had stopped screaming inside his mind, for somehow he sensed that he finally had been heard.

2

ON THE NORTH SHORE OF LONG ISLAND, NEW YORK, Jill Sheldon was busy readying the Science and You Museum for an annual fund-raiser. The building was closed to the public tonight, in order to welcome important and well-to-do guests. Exhibits in physics, biology, astronomy, and the like were set up in Plexiglas booths spread throughout four rooms. Nothing was encased, and PLEASE TOUCH signs decorated the brightly painted walls. In this, the largest room, several exhibits had been moved aside to make room for a long buffet table.

"Maybe we need a few more carnations," Jill said, pointing. "There, next to the seafood platter."

Her assistant, Virginia Dreyfus, shook her head. "It looks fine," she said. "Everything is perfect."

"I hope so. How well this museum runs for the next year is going to depend on the donations we take in tonight."

"We'll do great," Virginia said. "Just let our guests run through the exhibits and they won't be able to resist pulling out their checkbooks."

Jill wished she could share her assistant's confidence. "Look at me," she said, holding out her hands. There was a faint rattling of onyx and lapis bangles. "I'm shaking like a leaf. I'm so nervous!"

"Don't be," Virginia encouraged. "The museum will sell itself. Everything looks great—especially you."

Jill looked down at herself, feeling just a small wave of confidence despite the butterflies in her stomach. She had spent weeks looking for just the right dress. She finally chose a strapless, turquoise satin gown. Rhinestone danglers sparkled in the shoulder-length fall of her brown curls. She wore a small amount of makeup, just enough to bring out the green in her eyes and the faint shadowing of high cheekbones.

"There's our first guest," Virginia said, tapping Jill's shoulder. "He looks familiar."

A silver-haired man approached, dressed in a dark suit and red tie. He held a notebook in one big hand, and two pens stuck out from his breast pocket.

"Oh, it's Patrick Cameron," Jill said. "He writes a science-and-math column for the *Suffolk County Chronicle*. He's given the museum more publicity than any other journalist." She smiled, holding out a freshly manicured hand to greet him.

"Jill, don't you look wonderful," Patrick said. He helped himself to a glass of champagne from a passing tray. "To continued success," he said, lifting the stemmed goblet. "I know you'll attain it, Jill. Ever since you started working over in Centerport five years ago, I knew you'd be doing something of your own someday."

"Well, maybe we aren't as big as the Vanderbilt Planetarium," Jill said, "but I think we offer an important service to the children of Long Island."

A few more people came through the door, then another group, and soon Jill was busy moving from one guest to another. Some clustered in chattering groups; a few wandered through the exhibits, trying them out. After a while, Virginia tapped Jill and whispered that everyone had arrived. Jill lifted a rubber baton and tapped it against a series of chimes, clear tones filling the room. Her guests turned to her.

"I want to thank you for coming tonight," Jill said. "I didn't prepare a speech, because I know these exhibits will speak for themselves. There will be two tours, one to be led by my assistant, Virginia Dreyfus, and one to be led by me."

While Virginia led her group into the adjoining hall, Jill remained in the front room.

"You heard the chimes I played a few moments ago," she said. "It's part of our Sound and Hearing Exhibit. You'll notice this particular room is dedicated to the five . . ."

She felt a sudden flash of heat across the back of her eyes, and for a moment the sentence was lost. Jill blinked and quickly regained her composure.

Stage fright, that's all. Take it slow!

". . . dedicated to the five senses," she went on. She led them to a table laden with variously sized brandy glasses. "The kids get a big kick out of this one."

She dipped her hands into a bucket of soapy water, then dried them. Gently, she ran her fingertips over the rims of different glasses, producing a bell-like rendition of "Twinkle, Twinkle, Little Star."

Her guests laughed and clapped.

"When my hands are clean and dry," Jill ex-

plained, "my fingers rub over the glass and shake it
ever so slightly. This produces the musical tones you
hear, according to how much water is in the glasses or
how big the glass is. If my hand was oily, it would
only slide over the rim and no sound would come out."

Her guests moved about, trying out tuning forks and
old gramophones.

"Let's move on to the next exhibit," Jill said. "Here
we have Sight, and in this particular instance, color.
Color comes from light, and the colors we see are
those that bounce from the object to our eyes. A red
apple looks red because all colors but red are absorbed. But how we see color also depends on its re-
lation to the colors around it."

She scanned her guests, her eyes resting on the name
tag worn by a woman in a blue-green suit. Deliah Provost. Jill couldn't remember her from the guest list,
and when she met her dark eyes, that strange burning
sensation shot through her skull again.

"With . . . different accessories," Jill said, steadying herself, "Miss Provost's suit might look either
green or blue."

She led them on.

"Here are some color panels," Jill said. "The kids
love looking through these, seeing things in different
colors. And please try the kaleidoscopes."

For the next thirty minutes, Jill showed off her exhibits, growing more confident with each presentation.
Worry about stage fright passed quickly, and when the
tour was over, she stood back and watched her guests
with a satisfied smile.

Someone touched her arm, the fingers warm against
her chilled skin.

"I've come with a message, my dear," a voice
whispered. "Ryan is alive. You must go and find him,
for he is in terrible danger! I can't stay . . ."

Jill felt herself falling, lights whirling over her head
like the vortex of a tornado. Voices, music, and footsteps all blended into one confusing mess. The walls
began to move, to close in on her. She grew feverish,

sweat forming on the top of her quivering lips. Jill's chest constricted, her heart pounding as if struggling to make more room for itself.

It was all over in a matter of seconds. Jill's eyes snapped open and she looked around herself. Whoever had spoken to her had already disappeared into the crowd. On legs that seemed boneless, Jill turned and hurried from the room. Busy looking over the displays, none of the guests noticed her. A short flight of steps took her into her office, where she sank into a leather swivel chair and forced herself to breathe deeply. After a few moments, the dizziness passed, and she was able to lift her head to stare at the door.

"How the hell did you know?" Jill whispered.

With her eyes closed, Jill could still imagine the last time she saw her child alive—a three-year-old in ticking stripe overalls with a red shirt and high-top sneakers. With his blond hair tousled by the warm summer winds, he turned at the end of their walkway to say good-bye.

"See you, Mommy!"

"Keep an eye on him, Jeff. Don't let him eat too much, okay?"

"He's still my kid, Jill. I wouldn't let anything happen to him."

"Good-bye, Ryan. I love you."

"I love you, too, Mommy."

"Good-bye, Ryan. I love you," Jill whispered now. They were the last words she had ever spoken to him.

That evening, a policeman had appeared on her doorstep. He was a young man, with bright-red hair shaved close to his head and a small scar that ran along his hairline. Funny, Jill thought, how she could remember that particular detail: "I'm sorry to inform you that there's been a terrible accident . . ."

And he'd gone on to describe how witnesses saw Jeffrey's car fly over an embankment, bursting into flames at the bottom. There was no way to get to it, and by the time the fire was put out, the bodies inside were burned beyond recognition. Two bodies—a man and a child.

"No! No! You've made a mistake! They can't be Ryan and Jeff. It's a trick. Jeff's kidnapped our son. *It's a trick!*"

But everyone else involved finally convinced her that the bodies had, indeed, belonged to her little boy and ex-husband. For weeks after the funerals, Jill had walked around in a fog, sleeping little and eating less. She became like a zombie, not caring about anything. Her mother came to check on her one day and gasped to find an emaciated shell where her daughter had once been. She had bodily lifted her and carried her to the hospital, where Jill was treated for anorexia. Therapy had followed, convincing her she had to get on with her life. And that meant getting away from people who stared or offered stupid, sympathetic comments. She finally made use of her science degree from Michigan University and moved to Long Island, where she had worked in various labs and museums until finally earning enough to open up her own. And in all that time— six long years—she had never told anyone about Ryan.

So how, she wondered, could anyone have known?

"I'm damned well going to find out," she said, pushing back her chair and rising. She dried her eyes, checked her mirror to be sure they weren't red, and returned to the party. Everyone was buzzing, and no one seemed to notice she had gone. Looking them over, Jill was more confused than ever. She knew all these people and had never taken one of them into confidence. Who, then, had been the one to open up a still-painful wound?

3

KATE EMERSON HELD FAST TO HER LABRADOR'S leash, the leather strip snapping taut each time the dog saw a squirrel or a rabbit. She pulled back on it, commanding him to heel, but Boston Blackie had other ideas.

"I know, fella," Kate said. "You've got fall fever. I'd like to run through these woods myself."

She breathed deeply, taking in the scent of damp leaves newly colored red and orange. Though it was early morning, she could already smell the cinnamon aroma of pumpkin pie wafting through the cracks in a nearby kitchen door. The air was crisp, the wind tickling the back of her neck where skin showed between the rim of her cable-knit sweater and her bobbed brown hair.

"Sweater weather," her sister Diane called it. It was Kate's favorite time of the year, so relaxing after a busy and hot summer. And this summer, the coastal New England town of Gull's Flight, Massachusetts, had been particularly busy. They'd just celebrated their tricentennial, and the little curio shop where Kate worked had done booming business.

Boston Blackie was yelping at something. They were nearly to the end of the woods, coming upon a roadway that would lead them to the house Kate shared with her husband, Danny, and their two children.

"B.B.," Kate scolded. "'Will you please stop this yanking?"

But Boston Blackie's yelps grew more frantic.

"What is wrong with . . ."

19

As Kate stepped out of the woods, the crisp autumn air suddenly rose in temperature about thirty degrees. The multicolored trees that should have been across the road had disappeared, leaving only a long stretch of barren ground.

"What on earth?"

Kate gazed across the roadway, lined now with sagebrush instead of chrysanthemums and asters. Somehow, she was standing on a desert roadway, looking toward a row of flat-topped mountains. Mesas, her subconscious told her, pulling out a file from her school years.

Mesas, in New England?

Kate let Boston Blackie's leash drop. The dog cowered next to her, its tail between its legs, making pathetic whining noises. Kate turned a complete circle, confusion contorting her face.

"I must be sleeping. That's it. I fell asleep on the couch. I was so tired after raking leaves and . . ."

She bit her lip and felt pain.

You don't feel pain in a dream, do you? And you don't smell pumpkin pie and you don't feel the hot wind on your neck . . .

"But there is no hot wind here," Kate cried. "It's autumn in New England."

Suddenly hot, she tore off her sweater, letting it dangle at her side. She could feel the warm sand tossing against her face as she undid the top buttons of her blouse.

Then she heard the child's voice.

"Momma!"

Kate looked all around.

"Momma, help me!"

A little girl stood far off in the distance, dressed in a green plaid smock with a white collar, and green twill shorts.

Dressed the way Kate's daughter, Laura, had been on a class trip she'd taken with her nursery school six years ago, a trip from which she had never returned.

"Laura?" Kate's voice was no match for the hot, whistling wind.

"Mommy? They want to hurt me. Make them stop."

And then she could see the child clearly, a little girl with long dark braids standing stiffly, her arms opened.

"Laura," Kate screamed.

It wasn't an illusion. It couldn't be an illusion. Her daughter had come back to her. Everyone had said Laura must have drowned when the boat capsized, that the strong undercurrents of Great Gull Bay had dragged her out to sea. But Kate had never believed that, and here was her daughter now, calling to her. Laura was alive!

"Mommy?"

"Oh, Laura," Kate squeaked, racing toward her daughter with tears streaming down her face. "Oh, Laura, you're safe!"

Laura stood her ground, waiting. But Kate began to notice that no matter how much she ran, her daughter was always the same distance from her. Something was keeping her from getting to the child.

"Laura," she shouted, stopping. "Come to me."

Laura didn't move.

"Laura, *please!*"

But now the child turned around slowly and walked away from her mother. Kate ran after her, one arm reaching forward to grab the retreating child. She cried out her name, begging her to come back. Her feet wove themselves into a knot of tumbleweed, and she flew forward, smashing her head on a jagged rock. Kate burst into tears, pounding the desert floor angrily. Sand flew up, stinging her eyes.

Then the sand stopped flying and the desert floor seemed harder, and it was no longer so terribly hot.

Kate felt arms around her and turned to see her husband's concerned face. She wasn't outside anymore and she wasn't dressed in her cable-knit sweater and corduroy pants. She was wearing a nightgown, and she was crouched down on the bathroom floor.

"Kate, you had a nightmare," Danny said, hugging her. He touched her forehead and brought back a finger dotted with red. "You must have woke up when you fell against the tub."

"I hit my head on a rock," Kate choked.

Danny smiled reassuringly. "There aren't any rocks in here. You had a dilly of a nightmare, that's all."

Kate stared at him. A nightmare. She had only dreamed her baby girl was alive.

Danny helped her to her feet. "Let me put a bandage on that," he said. "Then I want you back in bed."

Kate didn't say a word as Danny gently dabbed at the wound to clean it, covered it with antiseptic cream, and bandaged it with gauze. Danny was so much like Laura, as if she'd only inherited her father's genes. Dark eyes and hair, big bones. Even at three Laura had been an exotic child. But in the dream, she had appeared much older. As old as she might be today . . .

The dream had been so real Kate could still feel sand scratching the back of her neck. She reached back there and felt something gritty. Her hand came around so fast she almost struck her husband. Tiny brown crystals sparkled beneath her nails. Sand.

"I—I saw Laura," Kate stammered. "She was in a desert, calling to me, and I couldn't get to her. Danny, Laura is alive. She's alive and she needs us."

"No, Kate," Danny said. "Laura was killed. She's been gone for six years."

Kate shook her head. "No, she's alive," she said. "She's alive and she's sending me messages to come for her. Danny, we have to find our daughter. She's alive. I know she is."

She threw herself in her husband's arms, sobbing uncontrollably. Danny rubbed her back, staring at his reflection in the door mirror. His wife seemed so small against his massive football player's chest. Kate's nightmares had stopped about eighteen months after Laura's death.

Why had they come back?

4

WHEN THE SCHOOL BUS PULLED UP TO THE STONE steps of the Thomas Jefferson Grade School, in the San Francisco suburb of Sandhaven, ten-year-old Elizabeth Morse was the first one out. She held her books close to her small frame and scurried through the drizzling rain, yards ahead of the next child.

"Good morning, Elizabeth," Mrs. Bettany greeted.

Beth nodded and slipped into her seat. Usually, that would have been the extent of the attention Mrs. Bettany paid to the child. She was so unassuming it was easy to forget she was there. But because of the rain, the children would not be playing in the school yard, and Beth had come into the classroom before the others. It gave Mrs. Bettany a rare few minutes to wonder about her. Beth was so pretty. Her thick, wavy red hair could have been the envy of the other fifth-grade girls, if only Beth would do something with it. She had those kind of thick eyelashes that would never need mascara. And Mrs. Bettany had no doubt the child's complexion would always remain peaches-and-creamy.

But there was a sadness about her that overshadowed her sweet loveliness. It wasn't because of an abusive environment, the reason other children she'd met had that haunted look. Beth's father was a prominent real-estate tycoon, and her mother an illustrator, Mrs. Bettany had met them and knew they were kind. She had been with Beth from the time she was a young child, when her twin brother, Peter, had died in a plane crash. Sick with the flu, Beth had missed the trip. And because she had survived when her twin hadn't, she

23

carried an unfair burden of guilt on her small shoulders.

But the small desks had filled with children and it was time to get on with the business of teaching fifth grade. The morning went on, and Beth Morse simply blended into the background.

As Mrs. Bettany discussed the atmosphere of Jupiter during a science lesson, something made Beth turn her eyes toward the window. It had grown dark outside, storm clouds blocking the sun and bringing night to the morning. Rain pattered on the window, but Mrs. Bettany's voice was louder.

Then Beth heard another voice. It was familiar, and yet she couldn't quite place it. It seemed to be coming from outside, as if someone were calling her from the school yard down below. Slowly, she rose from her seat and walked toward the window. Mrs. Bettany, busy drawing on the board, did not see her. But one by one, the children began to notice. They exchanged glances and giggled behind their hands.

Beth stopped at the radiator, placing her hands gently on the frosty pane of glass. She gazed into the school yard, her eyes drawn toward the swings. There was a boy sitting there, looking up at the windows. He had thick red hair like her own. Even though it was raining, he wasn't wearing a coat. He reached up toward her with both arms.

Help me, Bethie. Please help me. They're going to kill me.

Beth began to scream.

Mrs. Bettany swung around from the board and gasped to see the little girl standing at the window, banging so hard on the glass that cut-outs of pumpkins worked loose and fell to the floor. "Elizabeth!"

The teacher hurried through the desks, reaching to take hold of the child. "Beth, what's wrong?"

The class went wild, laughing and talking all at once.

"Stop this noise," the teacher ordered, as much for

the other children as for the little girl in her arms.
"Mary Swenson, get the nurse."

Beth kept screaming.

"Elizabeth Morse, you stop this!" Mrs. Bettany
turned her around and looked directly into the child's
wild green eyes.

"It's Peter," Beth cried. "It's Peter. He's down
there and he needs me. Let me go! Let me go!"

The nurse appeared at that moment, and together
the two women led the hysterical child from the room.
"It's Peter!"

Mrs. Bettany gazed over the top of Beth's red hair
and shook her head at the nurse. In her office, nurse
Dora Lamb sat the child down and gave her a drink of
water. She spoke soothingly to her until at last she had
calmed down.

"Can you tell me what happened?"

Beth shook her head, staring at her lap. The animated child they had just seen was gone now, replaced
by the quiet little girl Mrs. Bettany had always known.

She beckoned the nurse from the room, where Beth
now lay quietly on a cot.

"I knew it would come to this someday," Dora said.
"Can you tell me what happened?"

Mrs. Bettany described the earlier scene as she remembered it. "She kept crying out about someone
named Peter," she said.

Dora's gray eyebrows went up. "That was her twin's
name," she said.

"She said he was in the school yard," Mrs. Bettany
said. "What could have made her act like that?"

Dora shook her head sadly. "I don't know. But losing a sibling, especially a twin, is an awful thing for
a child to live with. Maybe something happened at
home this morning to set the child off."

"You call Mrs. Morse," Mrs. Bettany said. "I'm
going to the principal's office to report this." She left
the room, wondering as she walked along the hallway
why a little girl would suddenly begin crying out for
the twin she had lost almost six years earlier.

5

KATE WATCHED DANNY POUR HER MORNING CUP OF coffee, staring at the steaming brown liquid as she rested her chin on her fist. Outside the French doors, the early-morning fog rolled thickly over the pine deck. She could hear the faint sound of a foghorn on Great Gull Bay, like some melancholy cry for help. Like Laura crying for help . . .

"I saw her," she said, taking the cup and leaning back with it.

"You dreamt about her," Danny said, buttering English muffins. "Although I don't know why, after all these years."

Kate looked around at him, blue eyes wide. "Don't you think of her?"

"Most every day," Danny said. "But I've accepted the fact that she's gone, much as I hate it. Kate, you know what an exhaustive search took place after that boat capsized. Laura's body was dragged out to the ocean by a strong undercurrent."

Kate shuddered, the hot coffee not warming her. "I could never really accept that," she said.

Danny sat down, too, and handed her a plate. "It's been years since you had a nightmare." A request for an explanation remained unspoken, and somehow that made it all the more obvious.

"If you're worried about me having another breakdown," Kate said, "that's not the case. I'm perfectly fine."

She was gazing at him in a way that seemed both innocent and defiant. Kate's roundish face was child-

26

ish, and behind wire-framed glasses her large blue eyes gave her an almost angelic look. Though her shoulder-length, light-brown hair was usually impeccable, today it hung in limp strands.

"It's such a strong feeling, Danny," she said. "As if I actually did see Laura last night—as if I were actually standing in that desert."

Danny's brown eyes reflected the concern in her own. Before he could respond, the sound of a door opening signaled them to be quiet.

"The boys are coming down," Danny said.

Four-year-old Chris and his two-year-old brother Joseph came running into the room, their little bare feet slapping the cold tile floor. With giggles and grins they jumped into their mother's lap.

"Hi, Mommy," Chris cried.

"I want cereal," Joseph lisped.

"Don't I get a good morning?" Danny asked, pretending to be insulted.

The boys giggled and shook their heads, cuddling deeper into their mother's arms. With blond hair cut Dutch Boy style, they both looked exactly like Kate.

"Go on, boys," Kate said. "Say good morning to Daddy."

In unison, they jumped down and went to hug their father. Danny still had the build of the linebacker he'd been in college, and the children seemed lost in his arms.

"Joseph, you're wet," Danny said.

Kate pushed her chair back. "I'll take care of him," she sighed.

"Let me," Danny said. "This is why I love the weekends. I get to be a hundred-percent daddy." He picked Joseph up and left the room.

Chris climbed into his booster seat and waited for breakfast. "Mommy, what day is it?"

"Saturday, Chris."

"When's Halloween?"

"About three more weeks."

"How long is three weeks? How many days is it?"

"Finish your breakfast, Chris," Kate said, standing up. The four-year-old never stopped asking questions. "I've got to get dressed for work."

In the upstairs bathroom, she brushed her bangs aside and lowered her glasses to have a better look at the small cut on her head. It had a V shape, surrounded by a small purplish bruise. Kate looked over at the tub, wondering what could give her a cut in such a shape. It didn't make sense.

Kate washed up and dressed in brown wool pants and a quilt-lined flannel shirt. Though it was only the middle of October, it was already nippy cold in the coastal Massachusetts town. She tied on a pair of black high-top sneakers, then walked down the stairs to the kitchen. The fog had burned away and the morning sun shone brightly through the windows. Danny and the boys were on the patio, watching Boston Blackie romp on the grass. She gave all three of them a hug and kiss, then turned and left. As she was passing the mantel in the living room, something made her stop short. She went to it, lifting a picture of her daughter that had been taken just a month before her death.

Disappearance, Kate corrected herself. She just disappeared.

"Laura," Kate whispered.

She heard Danny and the boys coming into the house and quickly shoved the picture into her handbag. Then she turned and hurried from the house. Her mind was so full of Laura that it was pure instinct that brought her into downtown Gull's Flight that morning. Trim Cape Cods with sparkling white fences, older homes weathered by the salt air, trees brilliant with yellow and orange, all flew by her unseen. Kate had wished them all away, trying to bring back the desert where she had seen her child last night.

Laura had sent her a message. In spite of anything Danny thought, and no matter how hard she tried to think his way, Kate could not believe the incident had been just a dream. It had been too real. Kate could feel her daughter right down to her corpuscles. Somehow, her daughter was trying to tell her she was alive. And it was up to Kate to find the child.

As was usual on Saturday morning, the downtown area was alive with people. Kate pulled into her reserved parking space, right behind the little gift shop she had been working at for the past four years. But she didn't go directly into the Baby Bear Boutique this morning. Instead, she walked through the parking lot to the side street. Elserman's Drug Store took up most of it, having been expanded twice in its hundred-year history.

Sol Elserman was standing at the doorway with a broom in hand, dressed in a white apron and looking like he belonged in the nineteenth century. He greeted Kate. " 'Morning!''

"Hello, Sol," Kate said, not stopping.

Sol scratched his head and watched her, wondering what her hurry was on such a beautiful fall day.

Kate crossed the boulevard and sidled between a park bench and a fiery-red gum tree to get to the brick walkway. She pushed open the door to Walter Suskind's Photography Shop.

"Hello, Wally," she said.

"Good morning, Kate," Wally said, his eyes sparkling behind round glass frames. "Come in to buy film for Halloween?"

"I haven't really thought about it," Kate said. She opened her purse and pulled out the picture of Laura she had taken down from the mantel. What would Walter think of her when she made her request? She thrust the picture forward. "I need fifty copies of this."

Walter took the picture. He frowned up at her, then looked back down at it again.

"That's Laura," he said.

"I know who it is."

"Something happening?"

Kate shook her head. "I'm not sure. Maybe. But please, Walter, not a word about this to anyone."

Walter looked doubtful.

"Sure, Kate," he said. He slipped the picture into an envelope, then ripped off the top and handed it to Kate. "I'll have them sent to your shop in a few days."

Kate thanked him. She turned and walked from the store, somehow feeling more at ease than she had in days. No matter what would happen, at least she knew she had taken the first positive step in the search for her daughter.

Walter Suskind stood in the door of his shop, watching Kate Emerson's retreating figure. He rubbed a thumb behind his ear, wondering what Kate planned to do with fifty pictures of a dead child.

Unless, of course, Laura wasn't really dead. Unless Kate knew something and was doing some sort of amateur investigating.

Walter turned and hurried to the phone, dialing Sol Elserman's number.

"Elserman's Drug Store," a man's voice answered.

"Sol, it's Wally," Walter said. "You ain't gonna believe what Kate Emerson just asked me to do."

6

TOMMY BIVERS SAT AT THE KITCHEN TABLE, STUDYING his mother as he ate. She was so absorbed in some technical manual that she seemed oblivious to him. Tommy had been watching his parents a lot lately, though he wasn't sure why.

Well, he thought, maybe it's 'cause I'm mad at 'em.

Parents could be such pains sometimes. Until a few months ago, he had never questioned the weekly visits to the clinic, even though he hated them. The word of his parents was law, and all it took was a stern look

to silence him. Gosh, they were strict. Tommy wished
for a nice guy like Michael Colpan's dad—poor Michael's mom had disappeared a few weeks ago, but
they weren't supposed to talk about that. He would
even like to live with Billy Randolph's mother and father, who were always playing games and telling jokes.
Candy Kilmer's mother was a great cook.

But all his parents did was read books with big
words and numbers. When they did talk to him, it was
to tell him how important he was and how he had to
try harder at the clinic to control his powers.

Powers. What a funny thing to call this gift that
frightened him so much. He didn't like bringing ob-
jects to life, or making living things behave like other
things. His earliest memory of the clinic stayed with
him, like a waking nightmare.

Suddenly, the kitchen was forgotten and he was six
years old again.

*Good, Tommy. Very good! You made the little don-
key open his mouth and bray.*

*That's the first time you got a sound out of them,
Tommy. Good work!*

Let's try something new, Tommy. Something fun . . .

Something fun . . . Tommy snapped out of the reverie, afraid to let himself remember what had happened that day. But it pushed itself into his mind,
unbidden. He saw an image of the wooden donkey, an
articulated creature that stood about waist-high to him.
It was cute, and it was even funny to see it bray. But
what they made him do next wasn't funny at all.

Make him walk over to the cat, Tommy.

Tommy had made him walk, easily as imagining it
in his mind.

Now make him kick the cat.

Kick the cat? Why? It'll hurt the cat.

*Just a gentle kick, Tommy. Nothing to hurt the kitty.
Just a nudge to wake her up.*

I can't! What if I hurt her?

Make it kick the cat, Tommy.

No!

The cry had been so loud that even today Tommy winced at the memory of his own voice. His mother didn't even look up at him.

Tommy, do we have to threaten you? You know you must do as you're told.

I don't want to hurt her.

You won't hurt her. But if you don't do what we tell you, we'll have to punish you. There's a cage of snakes in the back room, Tommy. We could lock you in there, open the cage—

I'll do it!

And he had tried to have the wooden donkey push the cat very gently with his hoof. But he was so frightened that he lost control, and instead of a gentle nudge, the wooden donkey's leg kicked hard.

So hard it crushed the poor cat's ribs. Tommy had screamed and screamed until Dr. Adams gave him a shot of something. The next thing he knew, he was lying in a bed at the clinic. A whole day had gone by. Shock, they told him. Dr. Adams had apologized for the mistake. They had been so excited about his ability to bring sound from an inanimate object that they had pushed him too far. They'd give him a few weeks to rest and then they'd try again.

They'd been trying for three years now, but Tommy had never given in to them. Sure, he made things move and even had stuffed animals attack an occasional store mannequin. It scared him, but thoughts of snakes in the back room scared him even more. Tommy didn't know why he was afraid of snakes, but the very thought of them made him break out in a cold sweat.

The worst part was that he couldn't talk to anyone about it. He'd seen the way Michael Colpan's daddy hugged Michael all the time, and how even Jenny Segal's mom—strict and mean-tempered as she was—sometimes had a kiss for her daughter. Maybe he had no right to be loved. His mind had cried out for caring. And somehow, a few days ago, someone had answered him. He'd heard her voice in his mind, and for the first time in years he felt comforted. The voice had spoken to him a long time, a nice lady telling him he didn't belong here, that there were people outside the center who really did love him.

Tommy wished he could know who they were. He tried to send thought messages to the woman again, but he couldn't contact her. He sighed, finishing the sandwich. Maybe it was just his mind playing games. His brain did funny things like that sometimes, playing tricks on him. He was stuck here forever, with parents who didn't love him, going to a place he hated to do things that terrified him.

"I'm finished, Mom," he said, carrying his plate to the sink.

Her book closed with a thunk. She tucked it under her arm and stood up. "Then let's be going," she said, pulling on a sweater. There was a black name tag on it, with Helena Bivers engraved in white.

They walked out to the car, an unnecessary luxury since the clinic was less than a mile away. Helena worked at the clinic, as did Tommy's father, Martin. Many of the adults here worked at the clinic. Jenny Segal's mother was one of the nurses and Bobby Hocson's parents were both doctors.

The closer they got to the clinic, the more nervous Tommy became.

"You will do as you're instructed today, won't you?" his mother asked. "You won't embarrass me like you embarrassed your father the other day? Because I won't tolerate it, Tommy. This is nothing new, coming here for tests. You know it's necessary. The only way you'll ever be able to use your talents to the fullest is to test them out now, when you're young."

"Uh-huh," Tommy mumbled, fidgeting in his seat.

Helena turned her eyes back to the road. "Tommy, Dr. Adams has so many wonderful plans for you children," she said. "It's so important that you listen to him and follow his orders. You're too young to understand how important this all is, but you must trust us."

"I don't like to hurt things," Tommy said.

"Someday you may have to use your powers to hurt," Helena said, pulling into her parking space. "If you ever need to defend yourself, you must learn now how to do it."

"But I—"

Helena took hold of his shirt, twisting it in her fist. "You'll do as you're told, Tommy. Don't forget about the snakes." With that, she hurried ahead of him, into the building.

Slowly, reluctantly, Tommy followed. Well, it would all be over in an hour. They'd wire him up and ask him to make something come to life and then they'd let him go.

The wooden donkey was sitting next to the green chair.

Tommy gasped, freezing in the doorway. His eyes went wide at the sight of the carved animal, something he hadn't seen since the day the cat was killed.

"Come in, Tommy," Dr. Adams said. He was smiling, his light-blue eyes sparkling. The doctor had a perpetual sunburn that was a weird contrast to his snow-white thatch of hair. His teeth were just as white and he was always grinning. Most of the kids at school liked him. Some of the girls even had crushes on him. Tommy thought he was a creep, though he couldn't explain why.

Tommy stood his ground.

"Come in, Tommy," Helena urged, a hint of unspoken threats in her voice.

"Don't be afraid of the donkey," Dr. Adams said. "You see, I had a long talk with your father. We think we know what the problem is. We think you're suppressing your gifts because of that unfortunate accident with the cat."

It wasn't an accident.

Tommy didn't dare speak the words aloud. He walked to the chair and sat quietly while the electrodes were fastened to his skin.

"Now, Tommy," Dr. Adams said, "we're going to

try something. We're going to reenact the scene of that
day three years ago.''

Tommy gasped.

"Oh, not with a real cat this time," Dr. Adams
reassured. "Only with a toy. But you'll make both
animals come to life. This time, the donkey will kick
the cat, but it won't hurt it. It can't hurt something
that isn't alive, right?''

Tommy nodded slowly.

"Good," Dr. Adams said. "Now, concentrate,
Tommy. You know what you have to do.''

Dr. Lincoln Adams stood back from his subject, his
face a mask of cool, scientific detachment. But inside,
he was churning with excitement, as he always did
when he watched these children in action. He never
grew tired of comparing them to the monstrosity that
had been Lincoln Jr. Who could have known, back in
the late 1960s, that his life would be dedicated to great
work like this? Who would have thought the tragedy
of his first child's death would make him a man hon-
ored in all medical and scientific circles? It hadn't happened yet, not in years of work, but one day it would.
Provided none of these little guinea pigs screwed
things up. He'd noticed some changes in the older
ones, most notably Jenny Segal, Michael Colpan, and
Tommy here. He'd keep a close watch on them. Nothing, not even the children he'd created, must stand in
his way.

He wondered what Tommy was thinking of right
now. He imagined the thrill of studying one of those
brains. But that would come later . . .

Tommy was staring hard at the wooden donkey.
Where had they been keeping it? he wondered. He had
hoped it had been destroyed. That poor kitty.

The monitors around him went crazy for a few seconds.

"Concentrate, Tommy," his mother said.

Tommy pushed the memory of the cat from his
mind, and the monitors calmed down.

Within a few seconds, the donkey began to walk, stiff-legged, toward the cat.

"Now, the cat, Tommy."

Tommy turned his eyes to the stuffed feline. Slowly, slowly, its back arched up and its tail went straight and puffy. Lips that should have been sewn shut curled back. Spit came from a mouth full of stuffing.

One of the lab technicians was whispering in the background.

"Wow, wait until we try this on a hu—"

"Shh, you idiot!"

Tommy pretended he hadn't heard.

On a human? They want me to hurt people?

The monitors skittled wildly.

The donkey made its way toward the cat, but the cat didn't move. Though it had come to life, Tommy did nothing to make it walk.

They want me to use this on people!

"No! No, I won't do it!"

The cry broke his concentration and the animals became toys once again.

"I won't hurt anyone! I won't!"

Dr. Adams rushed toward him, his previously expressionless face full of grandfatherly concern. "Tommy, settle down," he ordered. "Calm yourself. No one asked you to hurt anyone."

Tommy glared at him. "But you're gonna do it, aren't you? Someday, you're gonna make me hurt a person. I know it. I know it."

"Thomas Bivers, calm yourself this instant," Helena commanded.

"You go to hell!"

Tommy could hardly believe he'd just said that, and the shock of his words silenced him. He tried to take them back, to apologize, but he just couldn't speak.

"No one is going to ask you to hurt anyone, Tommy," Dr. Adams reassured. "But you must go on with these tests. It's so important, Tommy. You know what would happen if you left the center? The Outsiders would get you, and God only knows what they'd do to you. You heard what happened to Michael Colpan's mother. You don't want that to happen to you, do you?''

Tommy shook his head.

"Then we can go on with the tests?''

Tommy remained motionless. What could he do? He didn't want to go on, but there was no one here to help him. He suddenly remembered the voice he'd heard the other day, that nice woman's voice. If only he could get her back again . . .

What am I going to do? Please help me! You said you'd help me!

Faintly, like a bad telephone connection, the voice came to him.

Don't let them hurt you. Get away as fast as you can. I'm trying to find the people who truly love you, who truly belong to you. But you must wait and give me time. You must not let them hurt you.

She said something else, but her words were lost.

Setting his teeth on edge, Tommy looked Dr. Adams straight in his blue eyes and said, "No way.''

"Tommy! Shame on you, talking to Dr. Adams that way,'' his mother cried. "Dr. Adams, you have my permission. If a small dose of that back room is what Tommy needs . . .''

Tommy felt heat in his groin. He squeezed his muscles to keep from wetting his pants. They were gonna lock him in the room with the snakes. They were really gonna do it this time.

Dr. Adams nodded gravely.

"I'm sorry,'' Tommy cried. "I won't do it again, I promise. I'll be good. I promise.''

"I'm sorry, too, Tommy,'' Dr. Adams said, "but you don't seem to understand how important this is. You'll have to be punished so you never forget again who's in charge here.''

He cocked his head toward the back room. One of the men came to take the boy by the arm. Tommy opened his mouth to cry out, but his mother cut him off.

"One word, Tommy," she said, "one cry, and I'll have Dr. Adams increase your time in there. You deserve this for being disobedient."

I hate you! I wish you weren't my mother, 'cause you hate me, too. I know you do.

Tommy walked reluctantly toward the door. The technician reached for it, started to open it.

"Stop," Dr. Adams cried.

Tommy turned to look at him, his eyes pleading.

"Let him go," Dr. Adams said. "Tommy, have you learned your lesson?"

Tommy's muscles relaxed instantly. "Yes, sir."

"And next time you come here, are you going to be good?"

"Yes, sir."

"Then go on home, Tommy," Dr. Adams said. "But remember, there won't be another chance. Disobey my orders next time and you'll spend an hour in there. An hour, Tommy. Remember that."

"I—I'll remember."

"Go home, Tommy."

The young boy ran as fast as he could. Far ahead, he could see the gates leading from the center. He longed to go through them, to keep running. But he knew it was impossible. All the children had been taught from early on that the fence was electrified and that no one left the center without permission.

Instead, he rounded the corner to his own house. Once he was inside, he went to the kitchen and poured himself a big glass of soda. He gulped it down fast, then poured another. Like an adult unwinding with alcohol, Tommy felt himself relaxing. Nothing had happened, he reminded himself. He hadn't been punished, after all, even though he had refused to listen to the grown-ups.

Maybe that lady he kept hearing was making him stronger. Maybe, he had a chance of winning, after all.

7

JILL SHELDON ROSE EARLY THE NEXT MORNING, grateful for the sunshine that washed away her nightmares. Her dreams were always the same, seeing Ryan hurrying toward her with his arms outstretched, embracing nothingness as he vanished into thin air. Jeffrey was there, too, laughing at her in a strange, mocking way.

But in the daytime she could concentrate on other things. After a light breakfast, she dressed for work, combing her hair to fall in loose curls over the cowl neck of her teal-blue dress.

The question about the stranger's knowledge of Ryan needled her. Jill thought she might have slipped one time, mentioning the tragedy to someone who eventually told Deliah Provost. But the more she thought, the more she was certain she had never told anyone what happened in Michigan. And this morning, she was determined to confront the woman and find out what she knew.

At the museum, Jill could see evidence of last night's benefit in bits of crepe-paper streamer curling from the ceiling and forgotten balloons on the floor. She smiled, thinking what a success it had been. They had tallied nearly twenty thousand dollars.

Her phone began to ring as she headed upstairs to her office.

Who'd be calling me at seven-thirty in the morning? she wondered.

The caller introduced herself as Deliah Provost. Jill recognized her name from the byline over her syndicated horoscope column. She hadn't been on the guest list last night, and yet it turned out she had been there.

"I'm the one who told you about Ryan," she admitted. "I was afraid to talk to you last night. Even now, this conversation is—"

Jill cut her off impatiently. "That was a cruel thing you did."

"I know, dear," Deliah said in a sympathetic voice. "And I can't begin to apologize. Please believe that I had no intention of hurting you. But I have been receiving messages from a child named Ryan."

Jill leaned forward, resting her head on the heel of one palm. "I never told anyone about Ryan. How could you have known?"

"I wish I understood," Deliah said. "Thoughts come to me unbidden. I've seen other images of you, with a little boy. Ryan is your son? A child with light-brown hair?"

"He's my son," Jill said, her voice quiet. "But he died six years ago."

"Oh, no," Deliah said. "The images I get are of a boy who's very much alive. Jill, we must talk about this."

"I know my son is dead," Jill said. "I saw proof of it six years ago. Why are you tormenting me like this?"

"Jill, you must believe that I'm sincere. Please, if we could meet and talk—"

"I don't want to talk to you," Jill snapped. "Don't call me again." She slammed the receiver down and wrapped her arms around herself, rubbing away the cold sensation that had enveloped her. Deliah was crazy, saying Ryan was alive. It was impossible!

Abruptly, Jill pushed back her chair and left her office. There were things to do before the museum's day began, and there was no time to think of a strange woman who might be either vicious or insane.

Virginia appeared at precisely nine o'clock, followed close behind by a busload of kids from a nearby

Children's Shelter. Their laughter and delighted questions helped Jill to forget Deliah.

The day passed quickly as Jill welcomed dozens of visitors. When the museum was finally closed for the night, she locked the doors and leaned against them with a sigh of exhaustion.

"What a day," she cried. "I'm beat!"

Virginia walked through the rooms with her, turning off switches and picking up bits of litter. "Me, too," she said. "I'm going to sleep well tonight, for certain."

Jill didn't answer, unsure whether she'd be able to sleep herself. She went into her office and sat for a long time behind her desk. Now that the museum was so quiet, the thoughts that had been fighting to surface in her mind came out loud and clear. Slowly, like a teenager taking out a secret pack of cigarettes, she opened her desk drawer and lifted out the false bottom. Ryan grinned at her from an eight-by-ten portrait taken at a department store shortly before his third birthday. He hadn't lost the baby roundness of his cheeks, and his green eyes sparkled merrily.

"Oh, Ryan," she whispered. "What I wouldn't give to believe that woman!"

But there had been evidence, and witnesses. Deliah was wrong. Ryan couldn't be alive!

But what if he is? Don't you want to be absolutely certain?

"I'm not falling for some crazy woman's trick," Jill said. "She probably just wants money, and then she'll pretend to look for my son only to tell me she failed."

She never mentioned a fee, did she?

"I hung up too fast," Jill said.

What if the whole thing was a lie? One of Jeffrey's tricks? Ryan might need you, Jill. He might be in trouble, or perhaps Jeffrey told him you don't want him anymore. You have to be sure, Jill. You have to be sure, be sure, be sure . . .

Before she could stop herself, Jill reached for a phone book and looked up Deliah's number.

"I knew you'd call," Deliah said when she answered.

"Did you?" Jill asked coolly. "I thought I made it clear this morning that I'm not buying your psychic routine."

"But you're calling me now," Deliah pointed out. "Have you changed your mind? Do you want me to help you?"

Jill leaned back in her chair, ready to offer the bait, expecting Deliah to reveal her true colors. "How much do you want?" She heard a sigh over the other end.

"Jill, I make my money through my newspaper column," Deliah said. "My powers are a God-given talent, and I never ask money when trying to help someone. The only thing I ask from you is time, so we might clear things up together."

"I—I don't know what to say," Jill stammered, hardly believing the woman didn't want money. "You really do want to help me? You really do believe Ryan is alive somewhere?"

She realized she sounded like a small, hopeful child, and she forced herself to remain objective. She was merely giving Deliah the benefit of the doubt, only because she couldn't explain the woman's knowledge of her son's death.

"Can we meet for dinner?" Deliah said. "I'm free now."

"The museum is closed," Jill said. "Do you know where the Landing Restaurant is, near Cow Harbor?"

Deliah said she was familiar with the place and agreed to meet Jill there in an hour.

After making a last-minute check of the museum, Jill went out to her car and drove home. She changed out of her work clothes into a blue-and-white sweater and slacks, then headed out to downtown Port Lincoln.

Deliah was already waiting for her at the Landing, seated at a table nearest the window. In the setting sun, the boats that bobbed up and down in the water were almost dreamlike. She didn't look like someone who dabbled in the occult. Her neck wasn't laden with chains bearing amulets and charms; she didn't dress in black or have long red fingernails. Deliah wore a simple brown suit with silver seashell earrings and a matching silver necklace. She smiled at Jill and offered her hand.

No poison rings, Jill thought.

"I'm so glad you've decided to talk with me," Deliah said. "Someone or something is frightening your child."

Jill sat down, glancing at a family of ducks that swam just a few feet from her table, disappearing under the building. A waitress came to leave menus, and she scanned the bill of fare. "I'm very skeptical," she said. "When Ryan and Jeffrey died, I didn't want to believe it. But dental records were traced and proof was given that the victims of that terrible car accident were my son and ex-husband."

"Tell me exactly what happened," Deliah said.

"You mean you don't know?"

Deliah smiled, closing her menu and setting it aside. "Visions come to me in bits and pieces," she said. "You see, I came to your museum as any other visitor might. But as I walked around, I kept getting feelings that brought the voice of a little boy to my mind. Wondering if it might be the child who called me for help, I took something of yours to strengthen the contact."

She pushed a small plastic dog toward Jill. It had been sitting on the shelf in her office, and she hadn't even noticed it was missing.

"Holding the dog helped me see that Ryan was once a bright, happy boy. A child of remarkable talents."

Jill stiffened. "How did you learn his name?"

"From your own thoughts, Jill," Deliah said. "There was no effort in that. Even when you aren't actively thinking about him, he remains on the brink of your subconscious. You often picture him looking back over his shoulder, waving to you."

Ice formed in Jill's chest. Deliah had just described Jill's last image of her son!

No! Don't give in to her. It can't be true.

"I see," Jill said, steadying herself. "This is all very coincidental. How is it you just happened to find me? I don't live where I used to, and out of all the people in the United States—"

"Maybe it would be better if you told me the story from the beginning," Deliah interrupted. "If I knew what circumstances led to the boy being in this dangerous predicament, I might be able to help put a stop to it."

Jill stared at the woman for a few seconds, then shrugged. What did she have to lose? "All right, I'll tell you what happened. Ryan and Jeffrey were killed six years ago. Jeffrey drove his car over an embankment, and it caught fire. There was nothing anyone could do."

"Did you see the bodies?"

"What was there to see?" Jill asked, looking up. "The police told me they were burned beyond recognition." She felt tears rising. "Can you imagine such a thing happening to a little boy?" she asked, her voice high. "Ryan was only three!"

"Jill, I'm certain your son is alive," Deliah said. "For some reason, the police lied to you. It's some kind of conspiracy."

"How can you say that?" Jill asked, wiping away her tears. "The police had dental records traced. No two are alike."

The waitress returned to take their orders. Deliah did not speak again until she had left.

"You keep saying 'records' in the plural," she said. "But tell me, what sort of dental records would be available on a three-year-old? Had Ryan even been to the dentist at that point?"

"He—he went when he was two and a half," Jill answered, unsure what Deliah meant.

"Were X rays taken?"

Now Jill's mouth dropped open as a thought occurred to her for the first time. Ryan's teeth had never been X-rayed! How could there be dental records for him?

"But Jeffrey's matched," she cried. "And there was a child in the car with him, strapped in Ryan's booster seat."

"Then it was another child," Deliah said, her voice low. "I heard a name mentioned in my thoughts—Dylan? Does it mean anything?"

Jill shivered. "He was the detective in charge of the case. He was very helpful. But then, he stopped calling on me."

Deliah nodded. "He is a friend," she said. "You would do well to contact him." She reached across the table and took Jill's hand. "There's something else I must tell you, Jill. It's about other messages I've been receiving. Evil messages, warning me to be silent about your child. These people are dangerous, monsters. They murdered one child and kidnapped another. God only knows what else they've done. But I know your son needs you, Jill. He's terribly frightened."

"Do you—do you know where he is?" Jill asked hopefully, ignoring the logical part of her brain that still insisted this was impossible.

Deliah nodded. "The day I heard him calling to me—"

Suddenly, a deafening roar filled the air, and mallards swimming on the water outside the restaurant shot up into the sky. Jill turned to see a huge boat barreling toward the picture windows of the restaurant, a white rooster's tail shooting out from behind it. Deliah's mouth froze, her words lost.

People screamed, knocking over chairs and pushing at one another to get out of the way. Jill was on her feet in an instant, running with the crowd. When she reached a safe distance, she turned to see where Deliah was. Jill gasped in horror. The woman hadn't moved from her chair!

"Deliah!"

Deliah seemed not to hear her. She was staring, as if in a trance, at the speeding hulk.

In truth, she *had* pushed her chair back when Jill did. But then a voice reached her mind, a voice so malevolently powerful it locked on to her like a vise.

You won't stop us, Deliah. You won't ever save the child!

The shock was so complete she was frozen solid by it. There was no time to fight back.

Seconds later, before Jill could make a move, the boat came crashing through the windows. Glass flew everywhere, water sprayed like a wave over the tables and chairs. With a great, short *thunk,* the boat came to a stop, its bow striking a column and cracking it almost in half.

For a moment, everyone was frozen in stunned silence. Then, slowly, a waiter made his way through the carnage to the front of the boat. He stared in disbelief at something no one else could see, his face growing pale. A few seconds later, he began to retch, covering his mouth and running from the room.

Others went to the boat, but Jill stood where she was. She knew what they were looking at. She heard them crying out in horror. Jill could see the ring on Deliah's hand as it hung limply at her side, the only part of her visible from behind the column.

"Let's help her," someone insisted. "Maybe she's still alive."

"Don't be an idiot," a man growled, "that boat cut her in half. Where the hell is its captain, anyway?"

The maître d', trying to bring order to his demolished restaurant, pushed a table over and used it to climb into the boat. He turned the ignition off, bringing merciful silence to the room. Then he went below, appearing a few minutes later shaking his head.

"You aren't going to believe this," Jill heard him say. "But it's empty. There's no one on board."

And Deliah knew that, Jill thought, sickened, thinking how the woman hadn't moved from her seat. She knew they were coming for her!

Outside, the parking lot was already splashed red with the lights of an ambulance.

8

AS THEIR DAUGHTER SLEPT UPSTAIRS, STUART AND Natalie Morse held each other close. The house was so quiet now it seemed impossible that just a short while ago they had had to call a doctor to calm their hysterical, screaming child.

Elizabeth had told them about the boy in the school yard, the one who looked like Peter.

"But it didn't just look like Peter, Mommy," Beth had protested. "It *was* Peter. He was crying out for me to help him."

"Beth, you know Peter is gone," Stuart had said. "Why are you talking about him now? Why today?"

"Because I saw him."

"You saw a boy who resembled your brother," Natalie insisted. "Honey, it couldn't have been—"

Beth's head swung back and forth. "No," she yelled. "It's him. I saw him. I saw him like I used to do when we were little and we weren't even in the same room. And he called me Bethie. Peter's the only one who ever called me Bethie. Peter's in trouble. Peter needs us."

Beth's voice had become so shrill that her parents finally decided to call her pediatrician, a close friend of Stuart's who agreed to come to the house. Finding the child hysterical, he gave her a shot and recommended she be kept in bed for a day or two.

So now, sitting on the couch in their quiet Victorian house, a distant view of the Golden Gate Bridge visible through the picture window behind them, Stuart and Natalie tried to make sense of what had happened.

"Beth says he was calling to her," Natalie reported. "She said it was like when they were little and used to 'talk' from different levels of the house."

"We called it Channel Twin," Stuart said with a nostalgic smile. "Funny how each one always seemed to know what the other was doing or thinking."

Natalie sighed. "Beth hasn't talked about Peter in years," she said. "I just can't understand how it happened today."

"Because someone played a trick on her," Stuart said darkly. "Someone asked a young boy to play a role, to call out to our daughter as if he were her long-lost brother."

"But why, Stuart?" Natalie asked. "Why would anyone play such a cruel joke?"

"Unfortunately, I do have enemies," Stuart said. "People are jealous of my success as a builder. The environmentalists hate me, and I'm sure there are a lot of people who don't want to see me build that office complex just outside of town."

"But to torment a disturbed child!"

"Nobody's going to torment Beth again," Stuart said. "We'll keep her home for a while, like the doctor says. If someone is using her to get at me, I won't let them near her."

They heard the faint rattle of mail being shoved into their box. Natalie got up off the couch and went to open the front door. There were art-supplies catalogs, a packet of coupons from local merchants, a few charity pleas, and a brown manila envelope. Natalie's eyebrows went up, disappearing under a thick curtain of auburn bangs. She put the other mail on a mirrored table and walked back into the living room with the large envelope. The address was written in grease pencil, in carefully printed block letters. There was no return address. She opened it and pulled out what seemed to be a drawing. She took one look at it and let out a gasp. It fell from her hands, sailing to the floor in slow, back-and-forth motions. Stuart was on his feet in an instant to retrieve it. He picked up the paper and studied it with a frown.

"Natalie, what's wrong?"

"This is sick."

It was a pastel portrait of a young boy, gazing out from the paper with wide green eyes. A spattering of freckles lay across his pug nose, and tousled red hair framed his round face.

"It looks just like Peter," Natalie whispered.

"It's not Peter," Stuart said. "It's a sick joke, like the boy in the school yard—"

"But it's what he would look like now," Natalie said. "If he'd . . . uh . . . " Nervously, she ran her fingers through her hair.

"If he'd lived through that plane crash," Stuart said. "But he didn't, so we know this can't be him. I'm sure it's the same people who played that trick on Beth."

He looked around the rug and found the envelope on the floor behind his wife. "No return address," he said.

Natalie pointed to the postmark. "Stuart, it says Santa Fe," she said. "Someone sent this from Santa Fe! We don't know anyone there."

Stuart frowned. "Your parents live in Albuquerque," he reminded her. "Could you possibly have relatives in Santa Fe?"

"No one that I know of," Natalie said. "What's the sense of it, Stuart? Why make us think our boy is alive?"

Unable to answer, Stuart put his arms around her. Inside his chest, his heart thumped hard and his lungs seemed to constrict. There was just a glimmer of feeling, just a tiny bit of hope that this wasn't a hoax, after all. Maybe Beth really had seen her brother this afternoon—or an image of him. And someone had gone to a lot of trouble to send them a picture of what their little boy Peter might have looked like today, at age ten. He tried to fight the hope, but it was growing stronger.

Maybe, by some miracle, Peter was still alive.

9

A DARK-HAIRED CHILD HUDDLED IN THE SPACE BE-tween her bed and night table, her knees pulled tightly into her chest. Her nightgown was soft, smelling of lavender soap, but she found no comfort in it. The shouting outside her room made her feel very afraid, and she wished her parents would stop their fighting.

Maybe, if she'd been a good girl at the clinic today, Momma and Daddy wouldn't be arguing. But ever since the dream she'd had a few nights ago, she had begun to wonder if the people at the clinic were really her friends.

In the dream, there was a lady with glasses walking a big black dog. She seemed very kind, but when the little girl tried to talk to her, some people she recognized from the clinic came to stop her. They waved burning torches at her, threatening to punish her severely if she ever spoke to the woman again. If the people at the clinic were her friends, why did she have such a bad dream about them? And why did she still feel, days later, that they really would hurt her with fire?

At that thought, Jenny Segal looked up and glanced quickly around the room. Everything was okay. She knew there would be a price to pay for fighting the doctors this afternoon, and she prayed it would have nothing to do with fire. Fire would be the worst thing they could do to her.

Maybe they'd burn her favorite doll, or all her books . . .

Jenny bent one foot up and started tearing off a too-long nail, remembering this afternoon. It had started out like all the other visits to the clinic, which had been going on for so long that the child could not even remember not going.

"Here's my best girlfriend," Dr. Adams had greeted. "You get prettier every time I see you, Jennifer. How old are you now—ten?"

He always asked a lot of questions, all the while taping things the grown-ups called "electrodes" to her. She liked Dr. Adams, who was almost as handsome as her daddy. But she didn't like the wires. And she hated the needles. More than that, she hated the scary things they were always asking her to do.

Still, she had only protested once before.

"Why do I have to go there?" she'd asked her mother as they'd walked to the low, brick building that housed the clinic.

"You know why," her mother had said. "It's to help find out why you have people talking inside your head. The doctors are trying to find out a way to make them stop."

But years of tests and treatment hadn't made them stop at all. If anything, they'd grown louder as she'd grown older. For some reason, the doctors were always asking her to try to talk to some of the people. But the little girl never could, no matter how hard she tried.

That was until this afternoon. As Jenny was sitting there in the big chair, wires poking out in every which way, a voice came to her that was louder than all the others. And among the strangers that surrounded her— unseen by others in the room but clear to the little girl with her eyes closed—she spotted the kindly woman with brown hair and glasses. The woman had reached out to her.

Don't let them do this, baby.

The child had cried out, grabbing for the wires and ripping them away.

"Who's talking to you?" Dr. Adams had demanded. "Tell us, Jenny."

But Jenny had only thrashed about in the big chair, knocking shiny metal instruments from a tray draped with a white cloth, kicking at Dr. Adams. It was as if something else was in control of her body and she couldn't stop the tantrum.

They'd stopped it for her, with a sharp pinch of a needle. Next thing she knew, she was in her bedroom, slowly awakening to the sounds of angry voices. She touched her head, but realized these voices were on the outside.

At the sound of her mother's angry voice, she nervously grabbed hold of the lamp cord dangling over the edge of the night table. It crashed to the floor. A moment later, her door opened and her parents came rushing to her.

"What happened, Jenny?" her father asked, the hall light making his blond hair glimmer like a halo.

Her mother picked up the lamp and set it right again. She was dressed in a silky red robe that hugged her tightly, her dark hair falling free to her waist.

"I—I fell out of bed," Jenny said, sniffling. "I had a bad dream."

"Another one?" her father asked. He looked at his wife. "Why is she having so many nightmares these days?"

"How should I know?" her mother demanded.

Jenny's father smiled, holding out a hand to help her to her feet. At ten, she was nearly as tall as he was, and when she gazed at him, her eyes met his.

"Well, everything's going to be okay now," her father promised. "You're Daddy's big girl; you'll be okay."

Jenny smiled. She hated it when other people called her a big girl, knowing they were making fun of her large bones and long legs. But when Daddy said it, she knew it was out of love.

"Well, get back into bed," her mother said. "You've got a busy day at the clinic tomorrow."

Jenny's mouth dropped open.

"Tomorrow?" her father said, protesting for the child, who couldn't. "Isn't that a bit soon?"

"She's got a lot to make up for," her mother said sternly. "After the nonsense she pulled today—"

"I'm sure that wasn't Jenny's fault."

"Oh, and whose fault was it?"

Another argument was brewing, and her father turned quickly away to stop it. He pulled Jenny's covers up and leaned down to kiss her good night. "Don't you worry," he said. "There'll be no clinic tomorrow if I have anything to say about it."

Jenny smiled, but the smile faded as soon as her door closed. She didn't want to go back to the clinic. Not tomorrow, not ever!

She closed her eyes and tried to sleep, but all she could think of was that big chair and all the weird machines around it. And the grown-ups' voices asking her to send thought messages to someone in another room. And demanding that she tell them what voices she was hearing.

Jenny tried to think of the woman with the dog. After a short time, she saw her again. This time she was sitting on a couch. There were two little boys to either side of her, leaning toward a book she held open in her lap. In her mind, Jenny walked closer to the couch.

The woman looked up at her and the book dropped to the floor. She cried out with such fright that Jenny backed quickly away, opening her eyes and ending the dream.

10

KATE EMERSON WAS SITTING WITH A PICTURE BOOK
on her lap, her boys tucked warmly to either side of
her, when the little girl appeared to her. She noticed
movement in the doorway and looked up to acknowledge Danny's presence. Instead, a child with long, dark
hair stared at her from the shadows.

"Laura!"

The book crashed to the floor, and in that instant
the child vanished. Kate shot to her feet, knocking the
boys away in her haste. She ran toward the now-empty
doorway.

"Laura! Laura, come back!"

"Mommy, where're you going?" Chris demanded.
He climbed from the couch and followed his mother
into the hallway.

Joey tried to keep up, stumbling forward on chubby
toddler legs.

"Mommy, stop," Chris yelled. "Come back and
read our book."

"Mommy, stop," Joey echoed.

They caught up with her in the kitchen, where they
watched in confusion as she spun circles. Her eyes
were enormously round. At the sight of tears streaming down her cheeks, Joey burst out crying.

Chris went to her and tugged at her robe. "Mommy,
what're you doing?" he demanded loudly.

The back door opened now, and Danny came in
with Boston Blackie. The dog ran to Joey and began
to lick the tears on his face.

Danny looked from his wife to his sons, then back to Kate again. "What's going on here?"

Kate waved her hands in front of her, as if she didn't know what to do with them. With his big, strong hands, Danny took hold of her smaller ones and held them steady. "Oh, Danny," she whispered. "She was here. I saw Laura. I saw Laura standing in the doorway of the living room."

For a moment, Danny just gazed at his wife, uncomprehending. Then he pulled his hands away and turned quickly to the boys. "Hey, it's getting late, you guys," he said. "You should have been in bed an hour ago. Let's go."

Despite their protests, he took them firmly by the shoulders and steered them out of the kitchen.

"But I wanna know what's wrong with Mommy," Chris yelled. "Why'd she throw the book on the floor? Why'd she run away? Why's she crying? Why—"

"I don't know, Chris. You go on to bed and we'll discuss this in the morning." Danny went upstairs with the boys. A few minutes later, he returned, to find Kate sitting on the living-room couch.

"She was standing right there," Kate said softly.

"Kate, what the hell is this?" Danny said. "You scared the crap out of those boys, you know. It's been years since you even mentioned Laura. Why now? And why, for God's sake, in front of Chris and Joey?"

Kate looked up at him, her teeth set hard. "Because she was there," she said defiantly. "Laura was standing right there in that doorway."

"Kate, that's impossible," Danny said, sitting beside her. "Laura's been gone for nearly six years. She's dead, Kate. I thought Dr. Lee helped you come to grips with that."

Kate slid away from him. "I could never come to grips with my child's death! I've never felt right about it. Why didn't anyone see her fall overboard? Why didn't anyone ever find a body?"

"We live near the ocean," Danny said, in a patient

tone used for repeating the same information for the umpteenth time. "Strong currents—"

"No, there were no currents," she said, shaking her head vehemently. "Danny, I know Laura is alive. I've seen her . . ."

"You've seen dreams!"

"I've seen Laura," Kate said. "She's sending messages. Just like the ones she used to send me years ago. Don't you remember, Danny, how she could do that?"

Danny picked at a loose thread on the couch, saying nothing.

"I can remember one time she did it," Kate went on. "It was when she was three and a half, when Mrs. Ginmoor first started sitting for us. I was driving home from the boutique and I saw Laura running down the block crying. By the time I swung around to catch up to her, she was gone. But when I got home, Mrs. Ginmoor said she had never left the back yard."

"You saw a child who looked like Laura," Danny said.

"It was Laura," Kate insisted. "I know my own daughter, for God's sake. And I found out something: a big stray dog had come into our yard just moments before, and it frightened Laura so much she started crying out for me. Her physical body was in that back yard, but she sent her spiritual body out looking for me."

Danny sighed. "Kate, I remember that incident. I still say it was just a child who looked like Laura. The whole thing was coincidence."

"Like the time I saw Laura crying at the foot of our bed, only to find she was still in the throes of a nightmare in her own room?"

Kate's eyes challenged Danny for an answer. He didn't respond.

"Like the time Mandy Seacoff's mother called to say Laura was comforting her sick daughter when all the time Laura was sitting right on this couch, watching television? Like the time—"

Danny shot up from the couch. "All right," he cried. "There were strange incidents. But they mean nothing now, because Laura is dead. And no amount of hoping is going to bring her back."

"Danny, I don't think she is dead," Kate said. "I think something happened to her and she's trying to send the same kinds of messages to us. She's in trouble, Danny, and I can't ignore her."

Danny bowed his head, looking like a forlorn little boy despite his size. "Dear God, Kate," he moaned. "You were doing so well these past years. I thought, after we had Chris and Joey, that everything would be all right."

"It won't be all right until I find Laura."

Danny went back to the couch again, taking Kate in his arms.

"I know you wish our little girl was still here—"

"I'm going to bring her back again."

"Oh, Kate . . ." He said nothing more. Danny knew his wife was a stubborn woman, and if he pushed her, there was no telling what she would do.

"Danny, help me?"

"You know I will," Danny said, kissing her softly. "Come up to bed, Kate. Come and rest. In the morning you'll be thinking differently."

"No, I won't."

"It's late, Kate," Danny said. "We've had a hard time."

"I'm not crazy, Danny."

"I never said you were." He stood up, leading Kate with him.

Upstairs in their bedroom, Kate went to the window and pulled back the priscilla curtains. The full moon illuminated the beach below, where the dark rim of the bay rippled gently along the sand. Kate followed the sparkles of moonlight on water as far as the horizon.

"She's out there," she said. "Somewhere, our little girl is out there waiting for us."

She let the curtains fall and shuffled over to the four-poster. She climbed in next to her husband, cuddling close to him.

Danny reached to flick off the light, then turned in the blackness and embraced his wife. He wished at that moment that he could hold her like this forever, to protect her from the demons that toyed with her mind. For it had to be demons, even the psychological kind, that had brought about this renewed interest in Laura. And Danny didn't want anything to hurt his beloved Kate.

In a short time, hugging tightly, the two of them were fast asleep. And Kate found herself in the desert again.

She was walking along a seemingly endless highway, dust kicking up around her feet. Sagebrush dotted the landscape about her and the glaring sun made her squint. She stopped abruptly when she came to the bleached skeleton of a long-dead animal. Slowly, the dream-Kate bent down to pick it up.

The few tufts of fur that still remained tickled her hand as they blew in the desert wind. Kate dropped the skull. The dull thud reverberated endlessly, thumping noises that sounded like . . .

. . . like running feet.

Kate looked up, and there was Laura racing toward her.

"Laura!"

Kate began to run, faster and faster, down the long stretch of road. Laura ran toward her, her sleeveless dress fluttering around her, arms stretched out. But a few feet away, the child stopped.

"Laura, come here," Kate cried. "It's Mommy. Come here, Laura. Let me help you."

Laura shook her head vigorously. "I'm not Laura," she cried. *"I'm not Laura!"*

She turned and ran away from Kate with a scream so loud it broke through the barriers of Kate's subconscious, forcing her awake.

For a long time, Kate lay trembling, staring at the stripe of moonlight that shone through a gap in the curtains. She wanted to wake Danny, to tell him she had seen Laura again, and that she sensed more than ever that their little girl was in danger. But Danny wouldn't listen to her. He had made that very clear.

So Kate cried silent tears for her daughter and made silent vows she would work on her own to find her little girl.

Danny said nothing of the previous night at breakfast. The boys seemed to have forgotten all about it and were as wiggly and giggly as usual as they downed bowls of hot oatmeal with strawberry preserves on top.

Kate thought that all was forgotten until Danny went to kiss her good-bye before leaving for work at the car-repair shop he owned.

"I'll call you this afternoon at the boutique."

He said good-bye to the boys and left.

"Is Mrs. Ginmoor coming today?" Chris asked.

"Yes, she is," Kate said. "It's a work day for me."

"I wish you could stay home." Chris pouted. "I miss you when you go to work."

Kate went to Chris and hugged him. "I'll come home early," she promised.

Before she could finish, the doorbell rang. A UPS man in a brown uniform greeted her. He handed her a large yellow envelope. It was from Walter Suskind's Photography Shop. Kate opened it and pulled out a thick pile of eight-by-tens. From each, the black-and-white visage of her daughter smiled out at her. Kate carried them back to the kitchen.

"Tell you what," she said to Chris. "I've got some paperwork I can do at home today. I'll tell Dorothy I won't be in."

"Oh, boy," Chris cried. "Joey, Mommy's staying home today."

"Mommy," Joey cried.

Kate waved a hand at them. "But Mrs. Ginmoor is still coming," she said. "I have to do work at home, so I'll need her help."

Chris climbed down from his chair and went to hug

his mother. "I'm just glad you're home today," he said.

"Finish your breakfast, boys," Kate said. "I'm going to be in my bedroom. You can just let me know when Mrs. Ginmoor arrives."

When the elderly sitter showed up, half an hour later, she was surprised when Chris answered the door.

"Where's Mommy?" she asked Chris.

"Upstairs," Chris said, frowning. "I knocked on her door, but she told me to go away."

"Oh, dear," Mrs. Ginmoor said. "I hope she isn't sick. Let me go up and check." She went up the stairs, Joey and Chris tagging behind her. At the door to the master bedroom, she knocked and called out to Kate. "Kate, dear, are you ill?"

"I'm fine, Mrs. Ginmoor," Kate called back. "Just very busy."

"The boys are worried about you." She heard Kate groan, then a shuffling of papers.

A moment later, the door opened. Kate grinned sheepishly. "I'm sorry," she said. "I was so caught up in paperwork. I'll be staying home today, Mrs. Ginmoor. But I still need you to keep the boys out of my hair."

"Of course," Mrs. Ginmoor said doubtfully. She had never known Kate to reject her children this way. She glanced at the pile of papers Kate held in her arms. No, not papers. Photographs. She wondered what was on the other side of them.

"Well, I've got to get back to work."

"Yes, Kate," Mrs. Ginmoor said. "Come along, boys. Let's get out the play clay."

Joey followed her obediently, but Chris stayed behind. He threw his arms around his mother and, in doing so, knocked the photographs from her arms.

With a gasp, Kate fell to the floor and started gathering them up. Mrs. Ginmoor came rushing back to help her. "No, it's all right," Kate cried. "I can handle it myself."

"Oh, Chris, look at the mess you—" Mrs. Ginmoor

stopped short. She picked up one of the photographs, then met Kate's guilty eyes. It was an old picture of Laura, but it had been altered. The soft baby curls had been lengthened, the brows darkened, the face shadowed along its edges to look thinner. All the pictures were altered in different ways, dozens of them, to look like Laura might if she were still alive.

11

JILL PACED THE BLUE CARPETING OF HER APARTMENT, following the same path through her living room, bedroom, and kitchen over and over. The hair she had clipped back so neatly that evening hung loosely now. There were dark circles beneath her eyes, mascara blended there by tears. She ached all over; she was exhausted, but she couldn't sleep.

The police had escorted her back to the station for questioning, but after a time had finally determined she was just a casual acquaintance of Deliah's and that the woman's death was probably a freakish, tragic accident. Drawing her strength back together, Jill had managed to get home safely. After a weary climb up the flight of stairs to her apartment, it took three tries to unlock her door.

Jill flopped into an easy chair and began to swivel it back and forth. It was so hard to believe: one moment, Deliah was alive; the next, she was gone. Worse, she hadn't even tried to save herself. Why? What was going on in her mind when she saw that boat racing toward the dock?

"She never finished talking to me," Jill whispered. She wondered, with some shame, whether she was

more upset about the accident or about the fact that
Deliah was no longer around to answer questions. Now
what was she supposed to do? She jumped from the
chair, moving with newfound energy into her bathroom. The bright light stung her eyes, but when she
had splashed cold water on her face, her weariness
vanished. Whatever reason there was for Deliah's
death, it wasn't the end of her hopes. Someone would
answer her questions, and she had a good idea where
to start asking them.

Jill returned to her bedroom and opened the drawer
of her night table. She pulled out a green leather address book filled with names of friends she'd made on
Long Island, and then she finally unearthed an an-
cient, battered directory. Jeffrey had given it to her
their first Christmas together, and in it she had listed
all the people she knew in Wheaton, Michigan. There
was a final entry listed, just a few months before she
left for New York—the number of her local police station.

If there was anyone to set her mind at ease, it would
be Craig Dylan, the detective who had been in charge
of investigating Jeffrey and Ryan's accident. As Jill listened to the phone ring, she closed her eyes and tried
to steady her nerves. The detective was going to think
she was crazy.

The line clicked.

"Wheaton police."

"Hello, may I speak to Detective Craig Dylan,
please?"

"I'm sorry, Mr. Dylan is no longer at this precinct," the woman's voice said.

Jill rubbed her eyes wearily. She should have known
it would be a waste of time. "I really need to speak
with Detective Dylan," she said. "Has he moved to
another precinct?"

"Are you a friend?" the woman asked chattily.
"You're a little late. Mr. Dylan moved away about,
oh, five or six years ago."

Jill shot to her feet, her eyes opened wide. Six years ago—about the time of the accident!

Calm down, Jill! It's just a coincidence.

"If you give me your name and number, I can have him call—"

"It would be easier for me to call him," Jill interrupted, quickly fabricating a story. "You see, we're having a class reunion, and I'd like to invite him. He'd be terribly disappointed if he didn't receive an invitation."

She heard the woman mumble something. "I've got a crowd here at the desk," she said. "Trouble at the local gin mill. Here, I'll give you Craig's number. Just don't say where you got it from, because I'm not sure I was supposed to give it out." She rattled off the number.

"That's not a Michigan area code," Jill pointed out.

"It's Florida," the voice said. "Fort Lauderdale, Florida."

Jill hung up and dialed Craig Dylan's new number. After just three rings, a woman's weary voice came over the line. "Yes?"

"May I speak to Detective Dylan please?"

There was a pause.

"Who—who is this?"

"My name is Jill Sheldon, and I—"

"What do you want from us?" the woman cut in.

"I need to speak with the detective," Jill said, confused by the woman's tone. "I'm sorry to call so late, but it's urgent."

She heard a man's voice in the background and the woman saying who was on the line. There were words that sounded like an argument and then a man's voice came over the line.

"Mrs. Sheldon," Craig Dylan said. "How did you find me?"

"From your old precinct," Jill said. "Please, Detective Dylan, something has come up regarding Ryan's accident. It's important that I talk with you."

"What—what's wrong?" There was an uneasy tone in the detective's voice.

"I have reason to believe Ryan is alive," Jill said. "There's a very strong possibility that he wasn't the child they found in my husband's car. I remember you saying there were some questions about the case, but you never elaborated. I need to know now what you meant by that."

"I don't remember saying anything like that," Craig replied. "Mrs. Sheldon, what makes you think there was a mistake?"

Jill told him about Deliah, ending her story with the woman's accident.

"Maybe I'm crazy to believe someone like that," Jill said, "but I've got to find out for myself. And I don't know of anyone else who can help me."

"You're not crazy," Craig answered. "Look, Mrs. Sheldon, there's only one piece of advice I can give you: forget about Ryan. Forget whatever it is this Deliah person told you. Maybe Ryan is alive—I don't know. I had doubts myself. But I can assure you the people responsible for the accident will not let you get to him. You want him safe? Forget about him. Because even if he is alive, they'll kill him before they give him back to you."

"Who'll kill him?" Jill demanded.

"Forget about it, will you?" Craig said. "You don't know who you're dealing with. These are terribly dangerous people. If they find out you're looking for Ryan—"

"Then he is alive," Jill gasped. "Where is he? You've got to tell me where he is."

"I can't," Craig answered. "I just can't!"

Now Jill was screaming, tears running from her eyes. "You bastard! You can't keep my little boy from me. Where is he?"

It was Craig's wife who came back on the line.

"My husband doesn't know a thing," she said, her voice cold. "Please don't try to call us again."

There was a click. Jill called into the receiver, but no one answered. They had hung up on her.

"No, you don't," she said. Her hand was trembling as she redialed the Dylans' number. This time, she reached a busy signal.

She couldn't let it go at this. The detective had indicated Ryan was in danger—and that meant he was alive. There was only one way she would ever get a straight answer: she would have to go to Fort Lauderdale to confront the man in person.

It would be the only way to find out what he was afraid of.

12

THE SMALL SCHOOLHOUSE, TUCKED AWAY IN A REmote mountain community in the Southwest, had room for only fifteen children. They were all about the same age, between eight and ten. Jenny Segal sat in the second-to-last row, right behind Tommy Bivers. She often stared at the curls on the back of his head and tried to send him thought messages. Ever since her own experience at the clinic, when unseen voices told her not to do what the grown-ups said, she had wanted to talk with Tommy and ask what made him fight back.

"Pay attention, Miss Segal," the teacher snapped.

Jenny sighed and went back to work. She didn't understand why she had to learn a lot of things, like calculus and physics. It was easy enough, but she didn't understand what a kid was supposed to do with all this information. Still, the grown-ups in her life kept insisting it was important, and she had learned not to argue.

Until the other day.

What had given her the strength to cause such a scene? What had given Tommy his strength?

At last the bell rang and school was let out. As usual, Tommy took off with all his friends. Jenny's own friends sidled up to her. As they headed down the sand-dusted main road that branched off into their own streets, Cissy Critchfield nudged Jenny and pointed to a lone figure up ahead. Jenny followed her gaze and saw one of the maintenance workers leaning against a lamppost. She never paid much attention to the workers at the center, but all the children knew this man. Well, he really didn't seem much older than any of them. Fifteen, Jenny guessed. No one knew his name, and no one was brave enough to ask him. Jenny thought he had the scariest eyes she'd ever seen, blue so pale they seemed transparent. He often leered at the younger children, as if he knew his eyes were frightening.

"Look at that creep," Cissy said. "Look at those sloppy clothes. He's always hanging around, staring at everyone."

"I wonder what he does here?" Jenny said.

Another girl, Bambi Freed, put on a grin that was downright feral. "Do something to him, Cissy," she urged.

Cissy's eyes gleamed. She focused them on the scraggy young man up ahead. A moment later, he threw back his head and let out a loud noise that sounded very much like a duck's quack.

"Stop it, you guys," Jenny scolded. "How mean! Leave him alone."

"We're just having fun, Jenny," Bambi said.

Jenny grumbled. "Well, have fun with someone else. Just 'cause you can make people do things . . ." Her eyes went very round suddenly, and she pointed at something over Cissy's shoulder. Bambi started screaming, backing away. When she felt the tickling on her cheek, Cissy started to scream, too.

"Get it off! Get it off of me!"

Other children came running to see what was happening, and screamed and yelled at the sight of a huge, multilegged thing crawling over Cissy's back. Its odd colors told Jenny where it had come from.

A moment before, it had been Cissy's pink-and-apple-green backpack.

"Get it off!"

"Who did that?" someone shouted.

"Cut it out, you're scaring her," a boy yelled.

Cissy went on screaming and screaming. The spiderlike creature moved with watery slowness, and at this point it was almost up to her shoulders. Finally, Michael Colpan came to his senses. He took his own backpack and swung it hard at Cissy's back, sending the monster flying to the pavement.

Instantly, it turned into a backpack again. And as if on cue, several grown-ups came running. Among them was Dr. Adams.

"Cissy," he cried, concern in his blue eyes. "What happened, sweetheart?"

Cissy was too hysterical to answer, so Jenny came forward. She told him how the backpack had suddenly changed into a monster, but she left out the part about teasing the maintenance man.

"Who did this?" Dr. Adams demanded, swinging around to glare at the children in the crowd.

They all took a step back from him.

"We don't know, Dr. Adams," Bambi said. "None of us kids would hurt one another."

Jenny's mind replied to her: No, you little jerk, but you'd hurt a defenseless worker.

Then Jenny wondered if he was so defenseless. She looked toward the lamppost, but he was gone.

"No, I suppose you wouldn't," Dr. Adams agreed. "But I don't know how this could have happened. You children must be in control of your thoughts at all times. This is what the clinic is all about, for those of you who seem to have developed a distaste for it." He looked directly at Jenny when he said this. Then he put his arms around Cissy's shoulder and led her away.

The other children walked off and Jenny was soon standing alone. She still stared at the lamppost, wondering about the strange maintenance worker. Well, not quite alone . . . She felt a tap on her shoulder and turned to see Michael Colpan. She smiled shyly at him.

"That was a brave thing, knocking that monster off Cissy."

"Whoever did it to her," Michael said, "she probably had it coming."

Jenny frowned. "That's mean!"

"Sorry," Michael said, "but Cissy Critchfield's a snob."

He dropped the subject. "Can I walk with you?"

"Sure," Jenny agreed.

He looked at Jenny and smiled. Strangely, in spite of his crazy red hair and zillion freckles, he was kind of cute when he smiled. And he didn't seem to mind that Jenny was a few inches taller. It was Jenny's turn to stare at her own shoes.

"You're nice," Michael said. "You think the same way I do, sometimes."

Jenny squinted at him. "I know we can talk with our minds, but stay out of mine. I don't like that."

"But sometimes I can't help it," Michael said. "Sometimes you think words so loud that they come right to me. I know you have dreams about a lady and a dog."

Jenny's heart started thumping.

"You—you won't tell, will you?"

" 'Course not," Michael said. "I hate this stupid place as much as you. I know you wonder what's on the other side of the big fence and what the Outsiders are really like. I was thinking that maybe—maybe someday we could find out."

"Maybe, someday," Jenny agreed, nodding slowly. "But I don't want to talk about it now. This is my street. Good-bye, Michael."

She turned and hurried away, leaving the scrawny red-haired boy alone. Thoughts raced through her mind as she headed home. Imagine, sneaking away from the clinic and seeing what was on the other side of the mountain. The thought both excited and terrified her. What if the Outsiders really were cruel? What if the woman she saw in her mind was as evil as the others?

"She can't be," Jenny cried. "She's nice. I know she is."

"Who is?" her mother asked.

Alice Segal was standing in the front yard, taking pictures of a flower that had budded on her cactus. Jenny hadn't realized she'd been speaking out loud. She thought of a quick response.

"A girl at school," she said. "Some of my friends don't like her."

Jenny's mother made a noise behind her lips. "We'll have to work on you kids getting along together," she mumbled. "Can't have the project ruined with bickering."

Jenny felt her stomach tighten. Her mother had caught her in a lie. What if she tried to investigate further?

"I—I have homework," she said quickly. She rushed into the house.

In the front yard, Alice Segal let her camera fall on its strap. She walked into the house herself, determined to find out who Jenny had been talking about. The girl was being entirely too recalcitrant lately. She would not allow her to misbehave. She would not allow the child to ruin what she and others had worked so long to achieve.

When she got to Jenny's room, the young girl was sitting at her desk, her nose in an astronomy book. Alice stopped. It amazed her that a ten-year-old could breeze through subjects she had had trouble with in college. The child's education was important. Alice turned and walked away, deciding to let the matter drop.

In her room, Jenny let out a long-held breath. She put down the astronomy book and picked up a mystery story. But as she read, the words began to swim on the page, until she finally closed the book and put her head down on her desk. She could not stop thinking about what Michael had said. She wanted to see what was outside the center. More than anything, she wanted to find the brown-haired woman with the two little boys. Somehow, she knew they meant something to her.

"I know you," she whispered, her head still tucked into the crook of her arm. "I'm sure I know you."

Maybe, if she let herself relax, she could conjure up the woman's image again. It was so easy to call people to her—"from another dimension, perhaps the afterlife," the grown-ups in the clinic said. Jenny didn't always like the people who came to her. Sometimes, she was afraid. As she rested her head on her desk, she thought back to the first "encounter" she could remember.

There had been a woman, a blond-haired woman, standing on a boat. Jenny had never seen a real boat, but knew them from pictures. And yet somehow, in her memory, she could smell salt air and hear gulls crying.

There had been other children, too. Little children. Jenny looked up at the woman, watching the wind blow her wavy blond hair.

"Now, class, we must all stay seated," the woman had said. "The ferry will take us for a ride to Blair Island and we'll have a nice picnic. Won't that be fun?"

All the children had shouted and clapped their hands. They had been led to rows of wooden seats. Jenny had started into one, but a man had held her shoulder and guided her to the next row. She had been happy, because this meant she got to sit on the end . . .

Jenny's mind went blank at that moment. What a strange memory, she thought. She really had no idea what it meant, because her parents insisted she had never been on a boat in her life. But it was this very memory that had conjured up one of the first images her mind created while seated in the big green chair at the clinic.

She had seen the blond-haired woman running every which way, crying out a name, her eyes wild with fear. Jenny had called to her, and the woman had turned to answer. Jenny had spoken aloud while in the chair, "Don't be afraid. I'm here. I'm here and I'm safe."

Someone had spoken roughly, a woman. "Don't let her make contact. She's trying to make contact."

"Who are you talking to, Jenny?"

Jenny had shaken her head. "Teacher."

"No, you must not speak to her," a man cried. "She will hurt you, Jenny. She has fire with her."

And something had burned her arm, searing through the thin fabric of her sleeve.

"Put her out of your mind, Jenny. Make her stop burning you."

Jenny had screamed and screamed . . .

She sat up straight now, staring at the pair of small pottery birds that sat on the back of her desk. She had wanted to call up the woman with the brown hair, not remember that horrible time when the blonde had tried to hurt her.

Slowly, she pushed up her sleeve and looked at the scar on her arm. It had grown faint over the years, only a hint of it remained, but the fear of being hurt like that again had kept her from calling back the blond-haired woman. She had called her "teacher," but did not know why. Mr. Sarth was the only teacher she had ever known.

There had been other "fire-carriers," as Jenny had come to call the bad people who hurt her through her thoughts. There had been a policeman—Jenny only knew policemen through pictures—a great big bear of a man with sad eyes. Both times, the grown-ups at the clinic had commanded her to push them out of her mind.

"They're going to burn you, Jenny. They have fire."

At first Jenny had accepted all this. But in time she

began to wonder how they knew which ones had fire. She had felt no threat herself from the images and had not felt any pain until the grown-ups in the clinic actually commanded her to drive them away. Even in her young mind, Jenny sensed the grown-ups were trying to keep her from making contact with certain people.

Just the way they kept most everyone in the center from ever making contact with the Outsiders. Only a select few had gone beyond the electrified gates. Michael Colpan's father was one. He worked in one of the center's big buildings, designing things he was not authorized to talk about. He would take his blueprints, and those of the few other engineers, and bring them into the nearby cities.

No wonder Michael wanted to see what was on the outside, Jenny thought. His father must have some wonderful stories.

She breathed in deeply, setting her mind straight again. It kept wandering off, and she wanted to call up the brown-haired woman again. Jenny wondered, If I ever tell the grown-ups of this woman, would they say she was going to burn her? The woman seemed so kind that Jenny could never believe such a thing.

"Jennifer!"

Jenny groaned. "Yes, Mom?"

"Jenny, there's someone here to see you," Alice said.

Jenny was surprised to see Tommy Bivers standing in her living room. Alice shot her a look of disapproval, but left the pair of ten-year-olds alone in the living room.

"Hi, Tommy," Jenny said, unsure of herself.

Tommy only gazed at her. "You've been thinking about me," he said.

Jenny looked down at the floor, blushing. When would she learn most of the other children were able to read her thoughts?

"It's all right," Tommy said, "because I've been thinking about you, too." He stepped closer to her, and lowered his voice. "I know what happened to you at the clinic."

Jenny gasped, looking up at him.

"It's okay," he said. "I won't tell anyone. But your thoughts have been so loud in school I couldn't help it. Jenny, I'm confused, too. Something's really wrong here. I never thought it before, but now I'm certain of it. A couple of weeks ago, I was sending out thought messages, hoping someone on the outside would hear."

"The Outsiders? Is that safe?"

Tommy shrugged. "Who knows? I don't care. I only know I hate the clinic; I always have. I've hoped ever since I was a little kid that someone on the outside would make contact with me. Jenny, I never told anyone, but someone did. It was a woman. I couldn't see her, the way you can see people, but I could hear her voice. She told me that there was danger and that these people were not what they appeared to be. Jenny, I know you've seen others, too."

Jenny looked back over her shoulder. "We can't talk here," she said. "But my mom would be suspicious if I left with you. She knows what happened to you at the clinic."

"Of course," Tommy said. "She works there, with my mother. That's why I told her I came by to ask about the homework assignment. I can't stay any longer, Jenny. But we've got to talk. Just you and me."

"And Michael Colpan."

Tommy frowned. "That weirdo? Why?"

"Because he knows what I've been thinking," Jenny said.

Tommy nodded.

At that moment, Alice came back into the living room. It was as if she did not want to leave her daughter alone with Tommy any longer than necessary. "So, have you gotten the assignment?"

"Yes, Mrs. Segal," Tommy said. "Thanks, Jenny. I'll see you at school tomorrow." Waving his fingers at Alice, he turned and left the house.

"I don't like that boy," Alice said. "He's a troublemaker."

Jenny did not say a word. She had come to distrust the grown-ups here in the center. Even her own mother.

13

EAGER TO MEET WITH CRAIG DYLAN, JILL HAD CALLED in a reservation on the next available flight to Florida. She left the museum in Virginia's care, promising she'd be back in a day or two. Because she did not want to involve her partner in what might be a dangerous venture, she made up a story about researching a laboratory equipment company's newest experiment kits.

Jill had thought a lot about this trip, through a night of little sleep. The part of her that had thought this was a waste of her time, that accused her of being an overly hopeful mother, had diminished to almost a whisper. Craig Dylan's fear was no illusion. And when you're a scientist, you ask as many questions as you can until you find the answer you want.

The answer I want, Jill thought, is that Ryan is alive somewhere.

She didn't have time to wonder what would happen if that answer wasn't possible. Her flight number was called and she followed a group out the door to the airplane.

The autumn wind tossed her hair into her eyes as she walked up the steps. The stewardess smiled and welcomed her on board. Jill found her place and tucked the overnight bag under the seat in front of her. She watched people filing onto the plane: a man in an army uniform, several business types, a mother with a girl of about three. Jill's heart caught in her throat and she felt her eyes grow moist. She blinked away her tears before they could rise, and she gave the little girl a smile.

How lucky you are, she thought of the mother, you have your child with you.

"Hi, lady!" The small child had noticed her staring.

"Hello," Jill said. She closed her eyes, settling herself for a nap. Ryan had been like that when he was little, chattering away to everyone. As sleep wrapped around her, an image of Ryan at age two came to her dreams.

He was sitting in front of the couch, his legs tucked beneath the coffee table, walking his toy elephant across the table.

"Look what I can do, Mommy!"

The elephant's trunk began to grow. It snaked across the room, but even when she felt its plush tickling her neck, Jill could not move. Even when the trunk wrapped around her throat, she stood frozen.

"No, Ryan."

"Elep'ant loves you, Mommy!"

Choking, choking . . .

Jill gagged and blood stained the front of her sweatshirt.

The gag had become a gasp as she sat up with a jerk. The stewardess had wheeled a cart next to her seat. Shakily, Jill bought herself a white wine. She sat back with the plastic tumbler and let the alcohol steady her nerves. Combined with the steady hum of the airplane's engines, it lulled her, and she let it wash away the remains of the dream. She wouldn't let herself analyze its possible meaning.

She busied herself with her inflight magazine for the rest of the trip; the articles that should have been trivial fluff to her scientist's mind became no more than a jumble of words. When at last the plane touched down in Fort Lauderdale, Jill was one of the first out of her seat, eager to disembark.

She found the car-rental desk and chose a Ford Tempo. Half an hour after landing in Florida, she was checking into the hotel. After checking in, she went to the gift shop and bought a local map. It was lunchtime, but she only stopped in the coffeeshop long enough to drink an iced tea while mapping out the route to the Craigs' place.

September had tempered Florida's heat to a comfortable warm, and she drove with one elbow propped on an open window. In her mind, Jill conjured up an image of Craig Dylan.

He had been in his mid-thirties back then, with brown hair he wore parted down the middle and blown back from his boyish face. Jill recalled that he stood a few inches taller than her, with good posture. It was the confident way he had carried himself, along with brown eyes that seemed full of caring, that had made Jill trust him when the others had let her down. He had worked hard for her, and she hoped he would do the same now.

Jill found his street. It was a fairly new development of attractive brick-and-fieldstone ranches, with lawns trimmed just so and brilliant flowers surrounding mailboxes. Many of the homes had ornaments, such as birdbaths or the ubiquitous pink flamingo.

There were no decorations on the Dylans' lawn.

Jill pulled into the driveway. As she got out of the car and walked toward the front door, all the doubts she had been fighting these past few days began to rise again. She pushed them back down, firmly reminding herself that Dylan had indicated he knew something about Ryan.

She took a deep breath and knocked at the door. Moments later, a frail, dark-skinned woman answered. She was attractive, but Jill immediately saw the tense way she held fast to the doorknob.

"Yes?"

"Is Mr. Dylan home?" Jill asked a little nervously. "I . . . My name is Jill Sheldon. I called yes—"

The sentence was never completed. The woman gasped, her eyes growing wide, and backed away a step.

"Go away," she commanded. "Leave us alone." She tried to slam the door shut, but Jill's hand shot out and grabbed the frame.

"Please, don't be afraid," Jill begged. "I really do need to talk to your husband. It's my little boy, don't you see?"

There was a squeaking noise from somewhere behind the woman.

"Let her in, April."

April looked back over her shoulder. Then, with a shake of her head, she pulled the door open and beckoned Jill to come in. Whatever greeting Jill had planned caught in her throat when she saw Craig Dylan. The squeaking noise had been a wheelchair. Craig reached out a hand to take hers, smiling warmly. The hand was shaking slightly. His hair was more gray than brown now, and the full cheeks that had made him seem so boyish were sunken in. His eyes still had a glint of caring about them, but they had a dull cast now.

He had aged twenty years in less than a decade.

"M-Mr. Dylan?" Jill stammered.

"It's me," Craig said. "I knew you'd be coming." He swung the wheelchair around and wheeled himself into another room. Jill followed him. Shaking her head, mumbling, April took off in another direction.

"I apologize for my wife," Craig said. "She's afraid."

They had entered a solarium, bright sunlight pouring in through glass walls that curved up across the ceiling.

Jill found a seat on a pink flowered chintz couch. "Why is she afraid? And you? What's happened here? You said you knew something about Ryan."

Craig shook his head. "Only what I learned six

years ago. And what I learned cost me a hell of a lot."
He opened his arms and looked down at the wheelchair.

"I don't understand," Jill said.

"I was suspicious about the whole thing from the
start," Craig said. "The accident, I mean. I've never
seen a report processed so quickly. If you could get
hold of the autopsy report, I wager you wouldn't find
a whole heck of a lot. The whole procedure was
sloppy, rushed through as if no one wanted to get involved."

"But you got involved," Jill said.

"I started asking questions," Craig went on. "I
went to those friends your husband had been with the
day he took your boy to the zoo. Strange people. They
didn't seem to really care what had happened. Oh,
sure, they expressed concern. But I can spot a phony
a mile away. They didn't really care!"

His hand curled up into a tight fist and he pounded
his armrest. Jill waited until he calmed down, his fingers stretching out again.

"I told my captain how I felt," he said, his voice
even now, "and he told me the case was closed. Usually, if I was suspicious about something, he trusted
my instincts enough to let me go at them on my own
time. But for this case, it was weird. For this case, he
told me to drop the whole thing. He didn't exactly say
I'd be sorry if I didn't, but the insinuation was there."

"Obviously, you didn't drop the case," Jill said.

"How could I?" Craig answered. "I'd gotten this
far. The whole thing smelled funny. Your husband had
some pretty strange friends."

Jill nodded. Those strange friends were one reason
their marriage had ended.

"I tracked down a few of them," Craig said. "I
had this idea that maybe one of them sabotaged the
car, to make your husband pay off a debt."

"He owed a lot of money to friends," Jill said,
shivering to think how much the detective knew about
her family's personal secrets.

He looked at her, with enough of a smile to put her at ease. It faded quickly. "I'm not going to tell anyone what I learned," he said. "Anyway, I finally came to the conclusion that it wasn't money anyone wanted. It was your kid."

Jill gasped, a hand flying to her mouth. "Then Ryan was kidnapped!"

Craig shrugged. "I don't know," he said. "But it's amazing what a gun can do to perk up a conversation. I caught one of those guys off-guard, and when I threatened to put a hole through his head, he blabbered off like crazy. He said the accident had been a setup, that they had killed your husband, but that it was a dummy in the car seat."

"But people saw—"

"People thought they saw a child," Craig went on. "The car was in a deep ravine when it blew up. Who's to say what was in there? I know something for certain. My captain, the medical examiner, maybe some of my fellow officers—they're all a bunch of lying bastards. Someone's got your son, Mrs. Sheldon. And it makes me sick to think what kind of people they are."

Jill sank back into the overstuffed cushions of the couch, her fingertips stroking her lips. Ryan was alive!

"Oh, I don't know . . ." She burst into tears, bending forward to bury her head in her folded arms.

Craig left her that way for a few minutes, then wheeled himself closer to her. "You don't know what you're getting yourself into," he said. "I know in my heart that wasn't your kid in that car. But I also know that you're risking your life, and his, if you go after this. Leave it alone, Mrs. Sheldon. As long as they don't know what you know, they won't hurt him."

"You keep talking about 'they,' " Jill said. "Who the hell are 'they'? Who are these monsters?"

"Monsters," April Dylan said. "That's not the right word for them." She was standing in the doorway, fidgeting with the corner of her apron. She came to stand behind Craig's wheelchair.

Jill returned her gaze to Craig. "You said you got

one of my husband's friends to talk," she said. "Who was it?"

"His name was Ronald Preminger," Craig said.

An image came to Jill's mind, a clean-cut young man with wire-framed glasses and blue eyes cold in a chiseled face.

"I remember him," she said. "Although I never knew him well. Jeffrey kept his business life separate from his home life, and I never became acquainted with his friends. What else did he tell you? Did he say where they took Ryan?"

Craig shook his head. "No, he didn't answer that question."

"Why not?" Jill asked. "Didn't he know? You had a gun on him, for heaven's sake. Why wouldn't he talk?"

Now the detective frowned, staring down at his lap. "I—I don't remember," he said. "We were talking— I mean, Preminger was talking. We were in the bedroom of his house. I had the phone off the hook. Didn't want any interruptions. And there was this weird moaning sound—"

"The receiver?" Jill asked.

Craig shook his head. "I remember something happened. I don't know. I can hear him begging me not to shoot. And then, that moaning got louder, and louder, and louder . . . ."

As if he were reliving the moment, Craig cupped his hands over his ears and squinted his eyes as if in pain.

"Stop it," he cried out.

"Craig?" April's voice was shrill.

The retired detective bent forward, crossing his arms over his head. "Let me down!"

He began screaming unexpectedly, seeming as if he didn't know where he really was.

Jill watched him, confused, frustrated that she couldn't do anything to help him. But she couldn't get inside his mind, to know the terror that spilled forth now, as real as the day it had happened.

Something came from the phone. Not just a sound, but something ugly and foul-smelling. It started as a wisp of acrid smoke, curling out of the receiver, undulating in time with the strange moaning noises.

"What the hell is that?" Craig demanded.

"They've come to help me," Preminger answered, smiling. "You're a dead man, Detective."

Then the smoke snaked toward Craig, who stood momentarily frozen as it wrapped itself around his hand.

His wrist was snapped in two before he even had time to react.

The gun fell to the floor as he cried out in pain.

Then the smoke began to take form, a gelatinous substance that smelled like death and rotted food. Shock forced Craig into action, blocking out the pain of the broken wrist. He knocked aside the jelly snake that slithered over his body, leaving a blackish-red trail.

"Get it away from me!"

Preminger only laughed at him.

Craig dived for his gun, shooting at the snake-thing. It had coiled itself up like a cobra, the head wavering back and forth. The bullet split it into a dozen pieces, offspring that looked like creatures from the darkest depths of the sea.

"No!"

Craig fell to the floor, covering his head, trying to make it to the exit. The monsters latched on to him, covering his body, teeth as thin and sharp as needles digging into his flesh. They began lifting him, up, up, up . . .

Suddenly, he was swinging upside down from the ceiling.

"You'll be sorry you interfered," *Preminger had cried.* "This doesn't concern you, Detective. We are more powerful than you would ever believe."

"Put me down."

"Gladly, Detective."

Preminger snapped his fingers. The moaning on the phone stopped. The monsters disappeared.

Craig Dylan landed headfirst on the floor, snapping his neck.

"Nnnnnooooo!"

"No! No! No!"

"Craig! Craig, it's April. You're safe, darling. You're safe here with me."

Craig, who had been screaming for the past ten minutes, became suddenly quiet. He sat up straight, looking at his wife through wide eyes that were brimming with tears.

"I felt it all again," he said. "April, I thought the nightmares had ended."

April glared at Jill, seething. "Do you see what you've done?" she demanded. "You brought out a memory that is very painful to him. Get out of here, now. Get out of our house."

"I'm sorry," Jill cried. "I didn't know."

"*Get out!*"

"Please, I—"

April came at her in such a way that Jill was certain the woman meant to hurt her. She backed away quickly, turning to run toward the front door. By the time she reached her car, she was crying herself, shaking so badly she couldn't get the key in the ignition.

Craig Dylan had remembered something horrible, so terrifying that it made him scream even today. And if they could do that to a grown man . . .

Jill's car screeched out of the driveway. She bit her lip, trying to calm herself.

Trying not to think what they could do to a little boy like Ryan . . .

14

EVERY MORNING AFTER BREAKFAST, NATALIE WOULD climb to the third floor of her house, where she had set up an art studio. Her drawing table was set up in front of a big picture window, facing a postcard view of Victorian houses. The house sat on the edge of Sandhaven, a small suburb of San Francisco, and from up here Natalie could just make out the uppermost cables of the Golden Gate Bridge. She was staring at the bright-blue sky, rubbing a pencil eraser over her lips, when the creak of the door brought her out of a daydream.

Beth approached her, her arms cradling a large stack of mail. "Sure is a lot of stuff for you today, Mom," she said. "Can I look at this catalog? I see some nice T-shirts."

"After I've gone through it," Natalie said. "I illustrated a few ads in there."

As she took the mail from her daughter, Natalie surreptitiously looked her over from head to toe. Stuart's idea to keep her home from school had been a good one. The rose had come back to Beth's cheeks, and she even managed an occasional smile. Happily, there had been no further mention of the previous day. While Stuart was trying to find out who had pulled the trick, Natalie was just glad that Beth wasn't dwelling on her "vision" of Peter.

Beth leaned over her mother's shoulder and eyed the top of the drawing table. "What're you drawing today?"

"A necklace," Natalie said, picking up a strand of

83

gray-and-blue beads. "It just came in from Snyder's and Company. I'm sketching it for *Little Extras* magazine. But I've been daydreaming all morning and I'm not getting much work done."

Beth reached toward the beads and fingered them gently. "Pretty," she said.

"I wish I could afford them," Natalie joked.

Beth shifted from one foot to the other, tilting her head. "When Daddy sells his big building, we'll have lots of money," she said. Without looking at her mother, she added, "How come some people don't want him to build?"

"What do you know about that?" Natalie asked.

"I heard you talking," Beth said with a shrug. "I heard Daddy say somebody must have dressed up like Peter to make me so sad Daddy would forget all about the office building."

Natalie felt an uncomfortable knot of guilt twist inside her. She picked up a ruler and pretended to sketch in lines for copy.

Beth spoke again before she could conjure up an answer. "Do you think I should go live with Grandma?"

Natalie put the ruler down and swiveled her chair. "What on earth for?"

"Maybe if I go live with Grandma," Beth said, "then nobody will stop Daddy from doing his work. It's 'cause of me, I know it. Everyone thinks I'm weird. The kids at school must have told their parents, and I guess those parents don't want Daddy putting up buildings. I guess they think he's weird, too."

"Oh, Beth," Natalie cried.

She took her daughter into her arms. In that moment, years of reports from the school came back to her, reports that said her daughter was painfully shy, unwilling to participate. Well, they'd finally done it! They'd crushed this child's self-esteem so badly that Beth just wanted to run away and make things right.

"Elizabeth," Natalie said, "don't ever say that again. You are not weird."

"But I hear things, Mom," Beth protested. "And I see things no one else does."

"You have daydreams," Natalie corrected.

"I saw Peter."

Oh, God, not that again!

Natalie pushed her daughter gently away, holding her at arm's length. "You didn't see Peter," she said. "You saw someone who looked like him. We've already discussed this, Beth."

Beth jerked away. "You talked about it before," she cried. "You and Daddy. But not me. No one listens to me." With tears streaming down her cheeks, she turned and raced from the room. She slammed the door shut with such force that a pencil holder on Natalie's drawing table fell to the floor.

Natalie started after her, but stopped herself. No, Beth needed time to sort things out for herself. She needed to face the reality of Peter's death.

Much as she wanted to run to her daughter's aid, Natalie knew she had to give Beth some space. And so, with shaking hands, she started sorting through the pile of mail Beth had just brought up. Bills, a welcome check, more bills, advertisements.

And a manila envelope postmarked Santa Fe, New Mexico.

For a few moments, Natalie stared at the carefully printed address. She knew the right thing to do. Tear the envelope without ever opening it. As Stuart would say, don't give 'them' the satisfaction of seeing how startled she was. Seeing . . .

Quickly, Natalie looked up at the window. Was someone seeing her right now, spying on the house? She glanced up and down the street, and only sat back when she realized there was no one out there. Not only were these monsters tormenting her daughter, she thought, they were making her paranoid.

She tore open the envelope. Out slid a crayon sketch of a boy with red hair, a thin boy whose green eyes were rounded in terror. Terror of what?

"Stop it," Natalie told herself. "You're falling into

their trap.'' She started to stuff the picture back into the envelope when she noticed writing on the back. The words cut through her heart.

YOUR BOY IN DANGER. MORE TO COME.

Natalie shook her head vigorously, driving away the fears and hopes that were starting to surface. Someone was sending her a message about Peter. Someone thought he was alive . . .

The emphatic ''No!'' that came from her blended perfectly with the muffled sound of her daughter's screams. Natalie jumped from her chair, racing down one, then two flights of stairs until she reached the kitchen. Beth was at the back door, banging on the frame and screaming.

''Beth! My God,'' Natalie cried, rushing to her.

''It's Peter,'' Beth screamed. ''He's leaving. Oh, Mommy, he's leaving. Make him stop!''

''Beth, it can't be—''

Beth pointed a shaking hand.

Natalie looked up to see a figure retreating toward the gate behind their house. She reached to open the door. Now she'd apprehend the culprit.

''It doesn't open,'' Beth said.

Natalie twisted the handle, but it wouldn't budge. She checked the lock, all the while glancing up at the slow-moving figure. The door wasn't locked, but somehow she couldn't get it open. She couldn't let him get away.

''Beth, the window,'' she cried. She hurried over to the sink, climbing onto a stepladder to unlatch the window lock. It, too, was jammed shut. It was as if someone had glued them.

Natalie went back to her daughter, crying out herself. ''Please, stop. Why are you doing this? Please!''

The boy had been walking so slowly that it had taken him nearly two minutes to reach the back fence. Now he turned, even more slowly. When Natalie saw his face, she sank straight down to her knees, so shocked that no sound came from her mouth.

It was Peter. Peter, who had died in a plane crash six years ago.

The boy opened his arms wide, waving both hands toward himself in a beckoning motion. Then he opened the gate and left the yard.

At that precise moment, the back door swung wide open. Natalie, still on her knees, stumbled forward. Beth clambered over her, racing toward the fence. Natalie pulled herself up, running.

But by the time they reached the alleyway, the boy had vanished.

"Did you see, Mommy?" Beth cried, tears streaming down her face. "Did you see?"

Natalie nodded her head, unable to speak. She hugged her daughter close.

"It—it certainly looked like Peter," she mumbled.

"It was," Beth cried. "He needs us, Mom. He's in danger."

The words scribbled on the back of the picture came to Natalie's mind. More and more, the hope that Peter might be alive somewhere was turning into reality.

"Mommy, what're we going to do?"

Natalie did not answer. She didn't know what she could do.

15

KATE STOOD IN THE DISPLAY WINDOW OF THE BABY Bear Boutique, arranging pumpkins, paper leaves, and corn-husk dolls to welcome the arrival of fall. She thought of the previous day, when Mrs. Ginmoor saw all those pictures of Laura. The sitter had been kind, not asking any nosy questions. But the look in her eyes told Kate she felt great pity for a mother who was so obsessed with a lost child.

"I hope she doesn't tell Danny," Kate said, lifting up a huge pumpkin. She noticed a little girl standing across the street, perfectly still, facing the window of the boutique. The pumpkin Kate held smashed to the floor.

The child was Laura.

"Kate?" Dorothy Williams came running through the store, weaving around the merchandise tables. The proprietress of the boutique still held the tape from a box she'd been unpacking. "Kate, what happened?" she asked. "Oh, look!" She frowned at the mess of smashed pumpkin.

Kate blinked, and the child across the street disappeared into the crowd of passersby. "I'm so sorry," she said. "I don't know what happened." She got on her knees and began to pick up the biggest pieces, fumbling with the slippery mess.

"Well, let me get the mop," Dorothy said.

Kate carried the pumpkin pieces to a trash can. When she came back to the window, she gazed across the street for a few moments, as if she could bring the child back again. Of course it wasn't Laura. It only looked like her.

"Here," Dorothy said, thrusting the mop at her. "If you ask me, Kaitlyn Emerson, you are a woman in need of a vacation. You've been so edgy these past few days."

"I haven't been sleeping well," Kate admitted. "I'm having nightmares."

Dorothy's brown eyes rounded with concern. "You poor thing," she said. "Are you eating right? If you eat the wrong thing, it can have a negative effect on your brain."

"Oh, Dorothy," Kate sighed, stepping down from the display to carry the mop back to the supply room. "Who would believe we're the same age? You sound like my superstitious old grandmother."

"But you do look tired, Kate," Dorothy insisted.

"Why don't you take the afternoon off? Things are a little slow today, anyway."

"Dorothy, I don't know if—"

But her boss was cutting her off with a quick wave of her hands. "Oh, I know," Dorothy said. "Borgman's Craft Emporium has received the most adorable collection of costume patterns. Have you made the boys their Halloween outfits yet?"

"No, I haven't," Kate said.

"Then go on over there and take a look at their selection," Dorothy said. "Maybe concentrating on getting the boys ready for Halloween will put whatever other problems you have out of your mind."

Kate stared at her. God, how she wished it were that easy. But Dorothy was right. She'd been a nervous wreck all day, and she wasn't much help to Dorothy at all.

And if I make them something special, it will help them forget the scare I gave them the other night.

Kate went into the back room and pulled her coat off an antique wooden rack. Slipping her arms into it as she walked to the front, she said, "Thanks, Dorothy."

"You're welcome," Dorothy said, opening the door for her. Soft notes blew into the store from seashell chimes. "Just stop over at Stephen's Vegetable Mart and get me a new pumpkin."

Kate laughed. She strolled along State Street, looking everywhere for a sign of the little girl. She again thought of the possibility she had only looked like Laura, but only for a moment. She knew her own child, and that little girl across the street had been Laura. Maybe not Laura in the flesh, but an image sent to her as a cry for help. If only she could communicate with her . . . Somehow, something was preventing Laura from sending her complete messages.

When she reached Borgman's, she forced herself to stop thinking of Laura for a moment. She had two other children at home whom she loved dearly, and she couldn't let her dedication to finding her daughter get in the way of her obligation to Chris and Joey. She paused to admire the craft shop's window, where child mannequins had been dressed as witches, scarecrows, and mice. Inside, Kate went to a chest-high table laden with pattern books. Choosing one, she flipped open the huge tome to the costume section and tried to find one that would work for both her boys.

Laura wanted to be a bunny on her last Halloween.

Kate shook her head abruptly and realized she had been staring at a picture of a little girl with dark hair and eyes, wearing a bunny costume and looking very much like Laura. She quickly turned the page.

She was shaking now, but she was determined to find a pattern and get started on Joey's and Chris' costumes. She finally chose a pair of dinosaurs, knowing how much her children loved the prehistoric creatures.

Kate found the pattern in the files, then carried it to a row of brightly colored knits to pick out her fabric. Down the aisle, she could see a woman cutting yardage at a low table, chatting with another customer. There was no one else in the store.

She found a perfect shade of green and with a moan managed to pull out the heavy bolt of fabric. It left a space on the rack about ten inches thick. Something made Kate glance at the opening, and with a cry of dismay she dropped everything to the floor.

There was a little girl standing there, her round, dark eyes overflowing with tears. She spoke in a soft voice, "I'm scared."

"L-Laura?" Kate choked out her daughter's name.

The little girl reached toward her, over the double width of tables. Shaking, Kate tried to take her hand.

Laura dissolved into thin air when Kate's hand touched her. There was nothing left of her but a sense of icy cold that shot up Kate's arm and grabbed at her heart, pulling her into blackness as she collapsed to the floor.

16

Unable to get any more information from Craig Dylan, Jill Sheldon had despondently moved up the date of her departure. She was certain the detective was hiding something. What had those people done to him, to make him such a whimpering, terrified shadow of the man she remembered?

Dozens of questions whirled in her mind as she sat on the flight home the next morning, staring out the window at the marshmallow puffs of clouds below. She would call Ronald Preminger and demand that he tell her what really had happened six years ago. On the logical side of her brain she knew he wouldn't reveal a thing, but her heart told her she had to try everything she could in her search for Ryan. Craig had hinted at one hell of a coverup, and Jill wondered just how many people in Wheaton were in on it.

When at last the plane bumped down in McArthur, Jill stood up and pulled her overnight bag from the compartment above her seat. Other people were standing, too, retrieving their own belongings. But from the corner of her eye Jill noticed one man sitting perfectly still in his seat. That in itself wasn't unusual—many people waited patiently for the plane to stop completely. But there was something about him that bothered her. He seemed young, his hair light brown and neatly combed, his face clean-shaven. If Jill had been asked to describe him, though, she would have faltered at his eyes. He was wearing dark glasses.

Even so, Jill had the strange feeling he was staring at her.

Ridiculous! Keep thinking like that and they'll have you hallucinating just like poor Detective Dylan.

She tucked herself into the line of departing passengers, exiting the plane as quickly as possible. She did not see the man take out a pen and jot a few lines down in a small notebook.

In fact, he was completely forgotten once she drove onto Veteran's Highway. Though it was night, Jill was too full of adrenaline to go home. Instead, she decided to head into Port Lincoln, to the museum. She decided she would call Ronald Preminger from there. If he had anything to tell her, she wanted to know it now.

Jill often stayed after hours, able to think better when surrounded by the exhibits she had helped to design herself. She loved this place, set up in an old house just south of the town's park. Putting all her energy and resources into it had been therapeutic, helping to fade out the horror of Ryan's death, even if nothing could erase it completely. Jill always felt more at home here than in her small apartment.

But tonight, an unfamiliar nervousness crept over her as she closed the museum's front door behind herself. Something seemed wrong, out of place. She stopped and looked across the floor, her eyes scanning neat rows of exhibits softly illuminated by night-lights. Jill reached for a switch near the door and flicked it on. With the room brightly illuminated, she could see that nothing was out of place. Shaking her head at herself, she walked toward the small flight of stairs that led to her office.

Jill could have teased herself all she wanted, but nothing would take away the odd feeling of dread that enveloped her. As she hurried by them, tubular bells jangled from their invisible strings, making her gasp. A hologram of a cat followed her movements, three dimensions trapped within two, and Jill wondered if someone else might be watching her. She went up the stairs, passing the closed door of the supplies closet and finally reaching her office.

Jill sat for a moment and collected herself. Virginia

had left a note on her desk saying the day had been very busy and telling Jill there were eleven tours booked for the next week. Jill put these aside, then reached to open the largest door in the old desk. She pulled out a false bottom and removed a locked file. It contained all her important papers, including the accident report, newspaper clippings, and Ryan's death certificate. Armed with the new facts she'd obtained in Florida, Jill had wondered if there might be some clue here she had missed when she had read these as a grieving mother. Turning the combination lock, she opened it and spilled out the contents. She found the lease to her apartment; the deed for the museum; a copy of her own will; however, there were no papers on the accident.

Jill reached quickly for the drawer, pulling it out far enough to see to the back. She had misplaced them, of course. But the desk was empty.

"You didn't misplace anything," she told herself firmly. "You always put things in their proper place."

So, logically, this meant someone had gotten into her desk. But who? Jeffrey was the only other person who knew of its secret compartment. He had been the one who gave the antique desk to her, long ago when their marriage had been a happy one. But now she was the only person who knew the combination.

The strange feeling of being watched overwhelmed her, and it took all her strength to beat it back down again. She took a few deep breaths and forced herself to think clearly. If anyone was in here right now, she would have been jumped already. There had been plenty of opportunity. Still, she was unwilling to stay here alone. Deciding she could phone Preminger just as easily from home, she stood up and slipped her jacket back on, entering the hall.

The supplies-closet door was open.

Jill stopped short, trying to remember whether it had been open just a moment ago.

You're tired, Jill. Of course it was open! You just can't remember.

She was almost to the stairs when she heard a sweet, childish voice.

"Mommy, help me!"

Jill froze. It seemed her insides had vanished in an instant, leaving an icy, dark void within her frame. She grabbed the banister, holding tightly.

No! You're hearing things.

"Mommy! Mommy!"

"Ryan?"

Jill turned around, racing toward the supplies closet on legs that seemed made of lead. Through the darkness, there on the back wall she saw an image of her little boy. Ryan was there, hiding in the closet, cowering in fear.

"Oh, God," Jill screamed. "Ryan!" She ran in to him, flicking on the switch at the same time.

Ryan was gone.

In his place, there stood a young boy of about fifteen years old. His hair was ash blond and curly as Ryan's might have been, but his eyes were dark and his face was marred by acne scars.

"You bastard," she growled, barely able to get the words out. "You bastard! Who the hell are you?"

She was screaming now, rushing toward the intruder with her fingers curled like talons.

He stepped aside, sending a jar of mercury to the floor. The silver globbed together, shining in the light above. "Lady, don't," the boy cried. "Please!" He grabbed a beaker and held it up like a weapon.

Jill stopped herself. "Who are you?" she asked again. "How could you be so cruel? Do you have any idea what kind of scare you've given me? I thought— I thought you were my son."

She covered her face, bursting into tears. The boy saw an opportunity and tried to rush out past her. But in a moment of fury, when her mothering instinct replaced all sense of logic, Jill reached out and grabbed the teenager. At the same time, her other hand curled around a dark, amber bottle. She threw him to the floor, surprised at how lightweight he was. Then she quickly uncorked the bottle and held it, at a forty-five-degree angle, right over his face.

"You know what sulfuric acid does?" she asked.

The boy's mouth dropped open. "Oh, God, lady . . ."

"It'd make a pretty big mess of your face, wouldn't it?" Jill teased cruelly.

"Please!"

"You tell me something, kid," Jill went on. "You tell me who sent you here and who told you to call me Mommy."

"I—I can't!"

"It'll burn your face pretty bad . . ."

"I'm afraid!"

Something about his words brought Jill's sense of decency back to her. With a sigh and a shudder, she righted the bottle again and replaced the cork.

"It's only peroxide," she said, her voice free of the almost-demonic tone it had taken on a moment earlier. "Listen to me. I'm sure someone paid you to break into this place. They kidnapped my little boy and now they're trying to stop me from finding him."

The teenager bit his lip, still sprawled on the floor. "I'm sorry," he whispered.

"Tell me who paid you to do this," Jill begged.

"Can't."

"What was the money for? Drugs?" Jill asked. "You're in a lot of trouble. If I call the police . . ."

The word "police" brought out the same reaction as the threat of being doused with acid. The boy shook his head wildly. "Okay. Okay. I'm a janitor's assistant at the hospital. Some guys came in talking about a job they needed done. They took one look at me and said, 'He's just right.' Then they told me some things to say when you walked by the closet. I guess it was supposed to scare you. I don't really understand it. But they paid me fifty bucks—"

Jill cut him off. "How did you get into my desk?"

"They told me about the false door," the boy said. "And the combination."

"Who?"

"I don't know," the boy cried. "Just some guys at the hospital."

"Guys?" Jill echoed. "Doctors?"

"Looked like doctors to me," the boy said. "I—I think I remember what it said on one of the name tags. If I tell you, will you let me go?"

Jill could tell he was a boy who had already had many brushes with the law. Still, in spite of the cruel thing he had done, she felt pity for him. He was being used, much the same way she was certain Ryan was being used.

"They'll never know you botched up," she promised. "Tell them I went a little crazy when I saw you, but don't tell them I turned on the light. You can say you got away first."

The boy seemed to relax, his shoulders sinking back a little. "I can go?"

"Tell me the name," Jill ordered.

"Sure, sure," the boy said, standing at last. "I'm not one hundred percent certain. But it was something like Sampson, or Safson."

"I can find out for myself," Jill said. "Get out of here, kid. And please, try to think who you'll be hurting next time you try to earn money this way. You can't begin to know what pain you've caused me tonight."

"I'm sorry," the teenager said. "Really sorry." He raced down the stairs on sneakers that made no sound.

Jill sank to the floor, burying her head in her knees. She had no desire to go home now. The exhaustion and hunger that had claimed her earlier had vanished, replaced with a need to make sense of what had just taken place. Someone had paid a young kid to act like Ryan. It was pretty easy to see why: they wanted to scare her out of trying to find him. But a question repeated itself in her mind: who could have known about the secret door and the lock combination?

Jill ran over the name the boy had given her. Sampson, Safson . . .

Something familiar about it.

"Safson," she whispered. "Saf . . ." She slapped the tile floor with the palm of her hand. "My God, I don't believe it," she cried, leaping to her feet.

Safton was the name! And Ken Safton had been one of those friends from Jeffrey's med school.

17

WHEN STUART MORSE CAME HOME FROM HIS OFFICE, Beth always greeted him at the front door and led him back to the kitchen. There, he would find Natalie fixing one of her fabulous meals, a ruffled apron tied over her jeans and sweater. It had become a tradition, and Stuart looked forward to it as the signal his busy day had ended.

But tonight when he came home, the front hallway was dark. He pulled off his trenchcoat and hung it in the closet, looking up the staircase, then down the hall. "Beth?" he called. "Nat?"

There was no answer. Because there was no smell of cooking food in the air, he did not walk back to the kitchen. Instead, he hurried upstairs to the second level. Maybe Beth had had a relapse, and was in bed.

He opened her door. Light from a streetlamp illuminated her covers, laid carefully over her mattress. Stuart closed the door and went to his own room, knowing that Natalie sometimes let Beth crawl into their bed when she was upset. But the king-size platform bed was neatly tucked in.

Now he was beginning to worry. Natalie would never go off without leaving a message.

As he passed the door leading to the upper floor, he

heard voices. A sigh of relief passed through him as he realized Natalie and Beth must still be up in the studio. But still he wondered how Natalie could have lost track of the time. She'd never missed a meal before, and knew what it meant to him to sit down with his family when he came home.

He opened the door and headed up the stairs. "Hello!"

There were scrambling footsteps and a busy rustling of papers. Then the door opened wide.

"Stuart," Natalie cried. "What time is it?"

"Six-thirty," Stuart said. "Same time I get home every night. What's going on up here?"

Beth had a look of guilt on her face. She bent her head and stared down at her shoes. It was Natalie who answered. Stuart thought she spoke a little too quickly.

"I was just so busy," she said. "With Beth sick at home, I haven't been able to get much work done."

She turned and hastily began putting caps back on her marker pens. "Just let me clean up," she said. "I have something ready to go in the microwave. I'll only be a minute. Beth, you go downstairs and put on a pot of water for noodles."

"Okay, Mom," Beth said. She glanced at her mother as she walked to the door, not acknowledging her father's presence.

"Where's my kiss, Elizabeth?" Stuart asked, feeling a little hurt. Beth had never rejected him before.

She gave him a perfunctory kiss and hurried out of the studio.

Natalie came to her defense. "She's been upset, Stuart," she said.

He nodded. "I understand."

He went to put his arms around his wife. "Something's wrong," he said. "What happened today, Natalie?"

"Nothing," she insisted.

"Come on—"

"Stuart, nothing," Natalie cried. She couldn't tell him about the boy they'd seen in the back yard. He'd start ranting that it was a prankster again, and Natalie didn't want to hear that. But she could also tell he wouldn't let things go so easily. So she grabbed for an answer. "Well, we did get another picture," she said.

Stuart rolled his eyes. "Did Beth see it?"

"No, thank God," Natalie said. "It's there on my desk, in an envelope."

Stuart did not move. "From New Mexico?"

"Yes."

"Then I know what I have to do," Stuart said, his shoulders heaving up and down in a sigh. "I have to hire someone over there to keep a watch on the Santa Fe Post Office and learn who's been sending these."

Natalie touched his arm. "Oh, that would be something," she said. "Then we could find out who has our . . ." She stopped herself. "I mean, who has been tormenting us."

Stuart gazed at her. "Natalie, you aren't starting to believe this?" he said. "You don't really think Peter is alive?"

You can't, because I suspect it myself, and one of us has to keep his head.

"Stuart, I don't know what to—"

Before she could finish, she was interrupted by her daughter's ear-piercing shriek, a scream so loud it carried up two flights of stairs.

Hundreds of miles away, in a remote community tucked away in the Rocky Mountains, another child screamed. This was a boy, Michael Colpan. He sat strapped into a big green chair, wires taped to different parts of his body. The chair faced a one-way mirror, and through its glass the adults in the room could see one of their colleagues standing near a stove. On it, there seemed to be a pot of boiling water.

They had asked Michael to force the woman to put her hand in the pot.

"But she'll hurt herself," the boy had protested.

"What do you care?" one of the men had said. "You don't know her. She means nothing to you."

"I don't want to," Michael had cried. "Can't I make the monkey jump up and down like the other times?"

"We already know you can do that," a woman said. "Now you must move on to more difficult tasks. Concentrate, Michael. Make her put her hand in the pot."

"No!" He turned to his father for help.

Ralph Colpan only shook his head sadly. He gave his son a helpless look that seemed to say "Do as you're told, son. Do it, or they'll hurt you."

The other grown-ups were exchanging worried glances. They might have expected defiance from a kid like Tommy, maybe even from a frightened little girl like Jenny Segal. But Michael Colpan had always been so cooperative, so quiet.

"Michael, you don't want to disobey, do you?" someone asked. "We could turn out the lights in here—"

"I'll do it," Michael cried.

He was more terrified of the dark than of doing harm to a complete stranger.

And so he closed his eyes, concentrating on her image as he had concentrated on monkeys and rats and other lab animals over the years. He pictured her hand moving toward the pot . . .

But somehow, the image changed. He no longer saw a strange woman, but a young girl who was somehow familiar. He had seen her face before, but he couldn't place it. What was she doing in his mind? What happened to the woman in the other room? Now a young girl was standing near a stove, watching a steaming pot. She moved her hand toward the pot, oblivious to danger.

Michael realized she would hurt herself, and he tried to stop it. But it was too late. The command had somehow been given from his thoughts, and she plunged her hand deep into the water. Her mouth opened in a silent scream. Michael's own scream filled in the sound.

"Michael, wake up."

He felt the tapes being pulled away as wires were hastily removed.

"Michael, it's okay! Look!"

Michael opened his eyes. The woman held up her wet but uninjured hand.

"The water wasn't really hot, Michael," someone said.

Michael blinked and stared at the woman. Only his father noticed the single tear that ran down his cheek.

Ralph went to the child and hugged him. "I'm sorry," he whispered, so close to the child's ear that no one else could hear. "I'm going to find a way to stop this, I promise."

Michael didn't hear him. He could only think of the young, familiar girl he had seen in his mind.

In Sandhaven, California, Stuart and Natalie burst into the kitchen to find their daughter holding up her arm. It was bright pink up to the middle of her forearm. She looked at her parents with wide eyes.

"Someone told me to put my hand in the pot," she cried. "I couldn't stop."

"Oh, dear Lord," Natalie said, rushing to her daughter.

Stuart quickly turned on the cold water. "Put it under here," he said.

He and his wife helped move the trembling child to the sink. As she ran her arm under the ice water, she seemed to relax.

Stuart finally asked for an explanation. "What do you mean, someone told you to put your hand in the pot?"

Beth did not look at her father.

"It was a voice in my head," she said. "A boy's voice. Like Peter when I heard him the other day."

"Beth, you know you didn't—" Stuart began.

Natalie shushed him with a tap on his arm. "But, Beth," she said, "Peter would never make you hurt yourself."

"Oh, no, Mommy," Beth cried. "It wasn't Peter's

fault. When he realized what was happening, he tried
to stop. But it was too late. Mommy, some bad people
are making Peter do terrible things.''

Her mother and father didn't say anything.

Beth moved her eyes back and forth between them.
''It's why he's sending me messages,'' she said. ''He's
scared. Mommy, Daddy, we have to help him.''

Stuart flicked off the water. ''I don't want to talk
about it,'' he said. ''I'm more concerned about you,
Beth. How does your arm feel?''

''It doesn't hurt anymore,'' Beth said.

''Look, no blisters,'' Natalie said.

''The water didn't have time to boil,'' Stuart said.
''Thank God you're okay. But I can see we better not
leave you alone, Beth. Not if you're going to be hurting yourself like this.''

''But I didn't do it myself.''

Stuart ignored her protests. ''I'm going to get our
coats,'' he said. ''We'll go out to dinner tonight. I
think we all need a break.''

When he left the kitchen, Beth turned to her mother.
''Mommy, we have to tell him,'' she said.

''Daddy needs time to sort things out,'' Natalie said.
''He wants Peter alive as much as we do, but he doesn't
dare believe it.''

''It's true,'' Beth insisted. ''My twin is alive, and
we have to help him.'' She frowned at her mother, her
eyes seeming to ask why Natalie wasn't helping bring
Peter home again.

18

THE WAITING ROOM OF THE PARAPSYCHOLOGIST'S OF-
fice was darkly paneled, table lamps giving off a warm
glow that was meant to relax nervous clients. Kate
held fast to Danny's big hand as they sat together on a
comfortable wooden bench. To either side of them,
end tables held scattered stacks of outdated maga-
zines. Kate put her head on Danny's shoulder and
stared at the faded Houdini poster that decorated the
opposite wall.

Danny gazed ahead himself, silent. Any protests he
had about his wife's seeing a parapsychologist had been
used up in an argument they'd had the previous night.

When Kate had fainted in the crafts shop, another
customer recognized her and called the garage where
Danny worked as head mechanic. He arrived just minutes after she came to, and had insisted on taking her
to their family doctor. The physician had found nothing wrong with Kate and attributed her collapse to
nerves. He had recommended a mild sedative. Kate
had refused to have the prescription filled.

"Drugs won't solve my problems," she said. "The
only thing that can do that is finding our daughter."

"Kate, you know in your heart our daughter is
dead."

"She can't be," Kate had argued. "The messages
I've been receiving are too clear. She wants to contact
me, but something is preventing her from coming
through. So I know what I have to do, Danny. I have
to contact her myself."

She had gone to their overstuffed magazine rack,

103

pulling out issue after issue until she found an old article on a study being done at Boston University on paranormal phenomena. While Danny roared protests in the background, she called up Dr. Alec Tavillo and explained her situation. Intrigued, he had agreed to see her at once.

So now they were sitting in his waiting room, in a small building just off the campus, Kate twisting her fingers nervously and Danny trying to control his emotions. The opaque glass door opened and a young woman beckoned them inside.

"Make yourself comfortable," she said to Kate as she led her into a small room. It was like a den, complete with an easy chair, family photographs on the walls, and a chess game set up on a pedestal table. There was even a kind of monitor that could have been mistaken for a television set.

Dr. Tavillo walked in a moment later. Kate was surprised to see how young he was, somewhere in that range between twenty-five and thirty-five when age is impossible to guess. She took a quick side glance at the diplomas on the wall and noted he had graduated from the Boston School of Psychiatric Medicine just four years earlier. He shook Danny's hand, then extended his arm to Kate.

"I'm Alec Tavillo," he said. "How are you, Mrs. Emerson?"

"I don't know," Kate said, honestly. "Scared."

Alec smiled. "No doubt," he said. "It isn't every day one goes under hypnosis. In fact, I wouldn't be jumping into it this quickly if Dr. Lee hadn't explained the situation to me. The idea of your daughter trying to communicate with you is intriguing. Has she made contact with you, Mr. Emerson?"

"No," Danny said simply. "I want you to know I'm here under protest. I don't believe in this mumbo-jumbo, but if it will help Kate realize the mistake she's making, I'm willing to go along for a while."

Kate started to say something, but Dr. Tavillo spoke up first.

"Your attitude is common," he said. "And understandable. I could give you arguments why it makes sense to believe the unbelievable. But we are here foremost to help your wife."

Danny nodded, then took a look around himself at all the framed degrees on the walls. "I see you have a degree is psychiatry," he pointed out. "What made you switch to parapsychology?"

"It's something that has always fascinated me," Alec said. "In med school, I studied the mind as we understand it. But, along with many others in my field, I believe there are mysteries just beyond our grasp. I'm a strong believer in the paranormal."

"In the supernatural?" Kate asked.

Alec held out a hand, as if offering something. "If you want to call it that," he said. "I'm hoping that studies will prove that these things are possible, and a time will come when they are no more unusual than the idea of the sun at the center of our solar system. But I'm rambling, and I know you are eager to begin." He indicated the easy chair. "Please, sit down," he said. "Mr. Emerson, if you'd take a seat back there on the couch?"

Kate climbed into the chair, her small frame somewhat lost in its big cushions. She let out a long, slow breath. Already, the comfortable furniture was making her relax.

"What will you be doing?" she asked.

"Nothing that will hurt you," Alec insisted. "Since you have already communicated with your daughter through your mind, I'm hoping that hypnosis will break down any barriers that are keeping her from contacting you now. First, I'm going to take you back to the first time you saw Laura appear. There may be a clue as to why she chose this time to contact you. Then, we'll go over each episode. I want you to look for details, anything that might help you find out where Laura is being held."

"I feel," Kate said softly, "as if I'm finally doing something constructive."

"Are you ready?"

"I suppose," Kate sighed.

"Kate, I'm going to help you relax totally," Dr. Tavillo said. "Remember, I can't force you to do or say anything that goes against your basic morals. Don't be afraid of embarrassment. And most certainly, you will not feel any pain. You are only looking at images. Okay?"

"Okay." Kate took one last look at Danny, who managed a slight smile for her. Then she turned and fixed her eyes on Alec's.

"Close your eyes," he said. "Good. Now, think about your toes, Kate. They're going to start feeling tingly, and that tingling is going to go up into your feet."

In a few minutes, Kate's feet tilted away from each other. By the time Dr. Tavillo reached her neck muscles, her entire body had relaxed so much that it seemed she was in a deep sleep. He nodded to Danny, who leaned forward in amazement.

"How do you feel now, Kate?"

"Scared. So scared."

The words were dull, monotone.

"You don't need to be afraid," Alec reassured again. "Kate, I want you to think back to that first dream you had of Laura. Can you remember it?"

Kate nodded.

"Now, go back just a little bit more," Alec said. "To dinner that night. What were you talking about?"

"Christopher's birthday is coming up," Kate said. "He wants a Galaxy Blaster." She sat up, the same way she had straightened herself at the dinner table weeks earlier. "No, you can't have that, Chris," she said. "You can't have everything you see on TV. Don't whine. I will not have guns in my house." She turned her head. "Danny, you talk to him . . ."

"Kate, come back again," Alec said.

Kate settled back.

"Yes?"

"Did you talk about Laura at all that night?"

"We don't talk much about Laura," Kate said. She tilted her head, seeming to consider something. "Not that night."

"Did you see a picture of her?"

"Pictures of her everywhere."

"Tell me about going to bed."

"I have a headache," Kate said. She put her fingers to her temples. "Haven't had such a bad headache in a long time. Must be my period coming up. And I feel cold, too." She snuggled into the chair as if getting comfortable in bed. A few moments later, she was breathing evenly.

"Kate?"

No answer.

Danny asked, "Is she asleep?"

Alec held up a hand to silence him. "Kate, have you fallen asleep?"

"Yes."

"Let's move to the dream, Kate," Alec said. "Are you there yet?"

"Walking Boston Blackie," Kate said. Her eyebrows furrowed. "What on earth? What happened to the trees? Isn't that a mesa over there?" She shook her head.

"Crazy. There are no mesas in New England. How can I be in a desert?"

"Tell me what you see?"

"Flat-topped mountains," Kate reported. "Tumbleweed. It's so hot! Oh, someone's waving to me . . ." She bolted upright, arms reaching forward. "Laura! Oh, my God, it's my little girl!"

"Tell her to come to you, Kate," Dr. Tavillo urged.

Tears started down Kate's round cheeks. "She's trying," she said. "But she can't. She keeps running, but she doesn't get any closer."

"Tell her to stop running," Alec ordered.

"No, she wants me."

"Tell her, Kate," Alec commanded. "It's doing no good. You have to talk to her. Ask her where she is."

Kate brought her fingers to her lips. "Oh, baby,

stop running," she said. "You wait and I'll come get you."

"Where is she?" Alec pressed.

Kate froze suddenly, fingers still to her lips, leaning slightly forward.

"Kate?"

"She's gone," Kate said dully. She sank back into the chair.

"Think about her, Kate," Alec said. "Think about the next time you saw her. What were you doing?"

Kate frowned, then nodded. "I was decorating the store window," she said. "She was across the street."

Suddenly, Kate's eyes snapped open. She jumped from her chair and went to the window of the doctor's office. But instead of the highway below, Kate saw the street outside the Baby Bear Boutique.

"Laura!" Her arms opened wide, and, unseen to Alec or Danny, a pumpkin smashed to the floor. "Oh, what a mess!"

"What happened, Kate?"

"Dropped a big pumpkin," Kate said. She looked back up at the window. "Laura's gone."

Alec came to stand beside her. "You saw her again at the crafts store."

"She was in the next aisle," Kate said.

"Reach out to her," Alec said.

Kate turned toward a floor lamp and reached out. When she touched it, she screamed so shrilly that Danny jumped to his feet.

"What's happening?" Alec asked.

"Oh, she's back," Kate cried. "My baby is back." She wrapped her arms around nothingness.

"No, you're not Jennifer," Kate cried. "You're Laura!"

Laura pressed her hands over her ears. She began to speak in a babyish tone that only Kate could hear.

"I not Jenny. I Loh-ra. I Lo-rah Em'son. I want my mommy!" She doubled over, screaming.

"No! Don't you do that to me. No fire. It hurts. It hurts."

"Laura, please! It's Mommy! Tell me where you are so I can stop them!"

Laura calmed down, looking up at her with dull eyes. "I'm Jennifer," she said. "My mother is Alice Segal and I don't know you. I'm Jennifer."

And then she was gone.

Kate sank to the floor, screaming.

Alec dropped down beside her.

"I'm going to bring you out again, Kate," he said. "It's over. Listen to me. One-two-three!"

The screaming stopped. Slowly, Kate straightened herself until she was sitting cross-legged. She looked up at Alec, then at Danny. Her husband had tears in his eyes and she knew he had come to believe as she did that Laura really was trying to reach them.

"I feel horrible," she said softly, reaching up to her face. She felt tears and brought her hand away to look at them.

"You saw Laura again," Danny said.

Kate nodded. "Yes—I did. But there was something wrong."

She held up a hand. Alec brought her to her feet.

"Laura was so frightened," she said, shivering. She rubbed her arms. "She said they were going to hurt her."

"But she wouldn't say where she was?" Alec asked.

"No," Kate said. "She pulled away from me and kept insisting her name was Jennifer. Suddenly, she acted as if she didn't know me." Kate's lower lip began to tremble, but she bit it hard.

"What now?" Danny asked.

"Most important, at least we were successful in contacting your daughter," Alec said. "But someone is stopping her. We have to call her again, to let her know we can help."

Danny came to put his arms around Kate. "My wife has been through enough today."

"Danny . . ."

"No, your husband is right," Alec agreed. "I

wouldn't risk putting you under again. We may not even connect with Laura. Or Jennifer.''

Danny shook his head.

"Why Jennifer?''

"No doubt the name she was given after she was kidnapped," Alec guessed. "For whatever reason these people took her, they wanted to erase the memory of her earlier life. That wouldn't be hard to do with a child as young as three.''

Kate looked up at her husband.

"Oh, Danny," she said. "I think they were going to burn her. She was crying about a fire.''

"Brainwashing," Dr. Tavillo speculated. "It's more effective when accompanied by the threat of physical harm.''

Danny's teeth set on edge. "Those bastards," he hissed. "I'm going to kill them.''

"First," Alec pointed out, "you have to find them. Kate, next time Laura appears to you, you're going to remain calm. You'll ask her where you can find her. Most important, you won't call her Laura. Apparently, she was threatened with severe pain if she used that name. Call her Jenny. Ask Jenny where you can find her.''

"I'll try," Kate said. "But I don't know if . . .'' She turned to hug Danny, not letting herself imagine the torment her daughter might be suffering at that very moment.

19

RALPH COLPAN WORKED LATE MOST NIGHTS, HUNCHED over a drawing table with one of the thousands of blueprints he'd created rolled out before him. Unlike other working drawings that might have depicted houses or skyscrapers, these prints did not carry easily recognizable numbers along the dimension lines. Everything on the print, from the material identification to the draftsman's initials, had been written in a code known only to Ralph and his few immediate superiors. For this was the secret work of a project so immense, so potentially threatening, that only a select group knew of its existence.

Ralph had designed many buildings in his years at the center. The very building where he now worked, along with eight other architects, was his own creation, the first he constructed for Dr. Lincoln Adams. Now, as he sat contemplating a blank sheet, his pencil eraser pressed against his lower lip, he thought back to the first time he had met the doctor.

Lincoln Adams had gone to a lot of trouble to find the designer of a small theater in Silverton, Colorado. The building was unique in that, in addition to structural makeup usually found in theaters, it also boasted underground passageways that allowed the actors to perform mystifying illusions such as disappearance and bodily projection.

"You have ideas," Adams had said, "qualities that I seek for an important project."

Those were the doctor's very first words to the architect. No "hello," no introduction. Adams had al-

ways been a man of few words, among adults. With
the children, however, he was completely different. He
really opened up to them, chattering away as he probed
their minds and guided their powers. The children,
Ralph thought, were very, very special.

It had been a child who had brought him, along with
his wife, Risa, from their home in Silverton to this
isolated mountain community in New Mexico. Adams
had promised him an astronomical increase in salary,
executive status, and all the benefits to go with it. But
it was not until Michael's arrival that he finally con-
sented.

Adams had arrived at the Colpan house holding the
hand of a big-eyed, freckle-faced little boy. Michael
had run immediately to Risa, hugging her tightly and
calling her Mommy. Risa looked over at the doctor
with surprise, then knelt down to the child's level and
hugged him tightly. Michael returned the embrace with
such intensity it seemed he was terrified to let go.

"He is the son you have always wanted," Adams
had said. "The son you shall have if you join me. I
need your abilities, Ralph Colpan. Join me, and give
your wife the child that God has denied her."

There had been much discussion over the next days,
many tears and arguments. Ralph had wondered if it
was a legal adoption that Adams planned. Where had
he gotten Michael from? But Risa was emphatic in
her insistence that this child was meant to be theirs.
All the while that Michael remained with them, he
called them Mommy and Daddy as if he had been born
to them. In the end, Ralph knew what he had to do.
For Risa's sake, he had to accept Adams' offer, no
matter what it entailed.

It wasn't until a few months later that he realized
what Adams had in store for Michael, and for the other
children brought into the center. Though Ralph knew
it was ethically wrong, the fact that the children never
seemed to be hurt by their sessions in the clinic caused
him to accept what was happening. And the realization
that he had been part of something illegal for several

years now, without turning himself in to the proper authorities, quieted any protests he might have had.

Protests. He could hear Risa's protests regarding Michael's twice-a-week visits to the clinic.

"Can't they leave him alone? Can't he have a normal childhood?"

"He isn't really normal, Risa."

"He's a ten-year-old boy!"

Ralph shook his head. Sad that his last full conversation with his wife had been an argument. She'd left for Santa Fe the next morning, nearly a month ago, and he hadn't seen her since. Adams' refusal to do anything about it had prompted Ralph's decision to end his son's torment. Someday, Michael would have to be told the truth. He was growing up, and soon he'd no longer be the innocent boy who accepted everything the adults around him said as unquestionable law. Ralph had seen the first signs of it at Michael's last visit to the clinic.

But there was no time for such thoughts. The sky outside his window was glowing red-violet, and the setting sun meant Michael would be sitting on the roof of their house, watching for his father's arrival from work. Ralph put his pencil down and left his blank paper. There was no need to lock his office door. Any important prints were taken the moment they were finished.

As he left the building and headed down the dusty road that bisected the community, Ralph removed a small penlight from his breast pocket and flicked it on and off. Moments later, a similar pattern occurred in the distance. Ralph laughed. He had sent the message, "I'm on my way," in Morse code, and Michael had returned with "Emilina's got dinner ready."

Sure enough, he found the cook filling a huge bowl with noodles as he entered the house.

"You get that boy down from the roof," the elderly Mexican woman ordered. "He went up there right after school today and has not been down since. His head is too full of thoughts, Mr. Colpan. A niño like that should be playing in the sun . . .''

Ralph nodded wearily, thinking that Adams did not allow the children enough free time. He opened a door at the back of the kitchen and walked around a spiral staircase until he reached a dark storage room. The flick of a switch found a ladder, and he climbed up through a rectangular patch in the roof. He found Michael sitting near the chimney, his knees tucked under his chin. He looked very much like Risa, who had also had thick, wavy red hair. It was as if Adams hadn't chosen him only for his ability as an architect, but for the fact his wife happened to resemble this orphan.

But he had learned in time that Michael was no orphan. He wished with all his heart that he could right the wrongs that had been done to the boy. Ralph loved Michael so much. He felt tears rising in his eyes, tears of frustration from not knowing what was to become of this brilliant, shy little boy.

He cleared his throat. ''What're you looking at, son?''

Michael stared off at the silhouettes of the nearby Rockies.

''I'm thinking,'' he said simply. ''Something weird's happening in my mind, Dad. It's been happening ever since Mom ran away, and I don't know what it means.''

Your mother didn't run away, Michael. They did something to her, crushed her attempt to escape this prison.

Michael turned suddenly to his father, his green eyes flashing.

''If Mom was dead,'' he snapped, ''I'd know it. I'd feel it. But I don't feel anything at all.''

No matter how often Michael read his mind, Ralph could never get used to it. He stiffened a little to suppress a shudder.

''Maybe because there is nothing of her to feel, Michael,'' Ralph said. ''When she left the center, carrying those papers for delivery from the main post office in Santa Fe, her return was expected by the end of the day. She dropped off the packages, but no one knows what became of her after that. If she had tried to run away . . .''

Michael's small hands clenched into fists. The cool autumn air tousled his red curls, throwing them into a disarray.

''Someone betrayed her,'' he seethed. ''One of the mind-reader children was forced to tell where my mother really went. They make us do things like that, you know, Dad. They make us do bad things at the clinic. They are planning to use us for something horrible.''

Ralph had to turn away from his son to hide the stricken expression on his face. The words were far too mature for a ten-year-old, even one as brilliant as Michael. He rubbed his arms and listened to the echo of Michael's words in his mind.

They are planning to use us for something horrible.

In his subconscious, there was a vague answer: And I am one who is helping them.

But Ralph never allowed it to surface, knowing that Michael could easily pick up his thoughts. He needn't worry. Michael had returned his attention to the mountains.

''There's someone out there, Dad,'' he said. ''I keep feeling that someone outside the center is very important to me.'' He looked down at the red shingles on the roof, looking like a child about to make a confession. ''Something weird happened to me the other day, Daddy,'' he said. ''I was playing on the swings outside the school, and I looked up into a window and saw a little girl with red hair like me. She was banging on the window and screaming, but when I went up into the classroom to find her, she was gone. Then, the other day when they were trying to get me to put that lady's hand in the hot water?'' He fell silent, waiting for encouragement.

''Yes?''

''The lady wasn't there anymore, Dad. It was that

little girl again. I couldn't let her hurt herself, I just couldn't. I was so scared." He turned and buried his face in Ralph's muslin shirt.

Ralph patted his son's back. "I know," he said. "I'm trying to find a way to put a stop to all this."

"I just wish I could find that little girl," Michael said. "It's like I should know her, but I don't. And you know something? Laura says she feels someone from the outside calling her, too."

"You know what you have been taught about the Outsiders," Ralph reminded.

Michael nodded. "They hate us all. They don't understand us and would have destroyed us all if Dr. Adams hadn't built this shelter for us."

"That's right," Ralph said.

Lies, all lies. Don't think, he'll hear you.

"Maybe it was Outsiders who took my mother," Michael said thoughtfully.

Ralph struggled to swallow a lump that was forming in his throat.

"Maybe," he rasped.

"I don't think so, though," Michael said. "But when I find this person who keeps entering my mind, I'll find out."

"You might," Ralph agreed. He patted his son's thin shoulder. No athlete, this boy. "Emilina sent me up here to tell you dinner is ready. We don't want to keep her waiting."

When they had descended into the storage room, Ralph put an arm around his son's shoulders and leaned down to whisper to him, "These thoughts you've been having about someone entering your mind," he said. "You must be sure to keep them to yourself. Tell your friend Laura this, too. Speaking out loud about things like that could be very dangerous."

Before Michael had a chance to respond, Ralph threw open the door at the bottom of the spiral staircase and entered the kitchen.

20

ORDER AND LOGIC. THAT WAS THE WAY A SCIENTIST was supposed to tackle any problem. One step at a time, trying out all possible leads until an answer was found.

Except that it was damned hard to be logical when your child's life was at stake.

Still, Jill Sheldon had forced herself to go home after the incident in the supplies closet, to sit and think about all the information she had. Ken Safton was just another clue, and it didn't take much effort to figure out what he was doing in Port Lincoln. No doubt he'd been assigned to keep an eye on her, setting up his practice on Long Island, a doctor inconspicuous among thousands of other doctors.

After finding the boy in the supplies closet, Jill had given up the idea of confronting Ronald Preminger. If he was involved in all of this, no doubt he'd already been warned about her investigation. She could imagine the conversation the two "doctors" had had over the phone with each other, discussing ways to curtail Jill's search. She realized that Ken Safton had paid the teenager to frighten her, thinking it would stop her from continuing her investigation. Maybe she was in the dark about a lot of things, but they were downright stupid. Because the trick they had pulled in an attempt to frighten her had only rubbed away the last shadows of doubt she had that Ryan was alive.

She had dreamed all night, seeing Ryan playing happily, sometimes seeing his toys come to life to play with him. When the alarm woke her the next morning, she lay staring at a beam of sunlight that stretched across her ceiling. In the night, in her dreams, another question had been answered.

Now she knew why they wanted Ryan.

"Because he can create hallucinations," she whispered. "Because he can move things around without touching them."

But acquiring an answer to the question had only created other questions. Just what were they going to do with Ryan? Just what had they done with him? Who were they?

Jill rolled out of bed, full of nervous energy. She wanted to find Ken Safton. She wanted to shake him, kick him, beat him, until he told her the truth about Ryan. But first, she had to find out how to approach him. She didn't even know what kind of medicine he practiced.

"The chances of Ken Safton talking to me are zip," she told her reflection as she washed her face and applied her makeup. "He'll probably deny ever having lived in Wheaton, Michigan."

And worse, if she did confront him, he'd get back to Ronald Preminger, who might see to it that Ryan was hurt. No, first she had to find out where Ken Safton was practicing and then, somehow, she had to get the information she needed.

Though she usually ate a good breakfast to get her through a hard day of work, she had no appetite this morning. She went into her room and took a scarf from her dresser drawer, wrapping it around her head. Outside in her car, she unhooked a pair of sunglasses from her visor and slipped them on. Satisfied she could not be recognized, Jill headed toward the local hospital. She had been able to get information on Craig Dylan through trickery. Now, she would try the same approach to find Ken Safton.

"Let's hope this works," she said as she pulled out of her space in the apartment complex driveway.

Just as she turned onto the road, another car pulled from the lot, moving in the same direction. Jill did not even notice it until she stopped for a red light and happened to look into her rearview mirror. A cold chill brushed her skin.

It was the man from the airplane.

She thought of her broken desk and the boy in the closet. They were really keeping an eye on her, weren't they?

"Well, forget that," she said out loud, strength in her voice.

Jill watched for a gap in traffic, then sped quickly onto Jericho Turnpike, to the sounds of an angry truck horn. She accelerated, driving a few miles per hour over the speed limit. When she finally slowed and looked into the rearview mirror again, the car following her was not in sight. At least she could be certain no one would see her going to Shoreline Medical Center.

Early in the morning, long before visiting hours, it was very easy to find a place to park. When Jill entered the lobby, decorated with pumpkins and ghosts for Halloween, she was the only nonstaff person in sight. Nurses and interns, doctors and maintenance workers crisscrossed paths as they began a new shift. The receptionist, busy behind a computer terminal, seemed oblivious to Jill.

"Good morning," Jill said.

The woman looked up and smiled. "Good morning," she said. "May I help you?"

Jill placed her hands gently on the countertop. She really wanted to wrap her arms around herself, because suddenly she felt very cold. But a study of body language had told her open arms were often equated with honesty. She knew that taking off her sunglasses would enhance the illusion, but she didn't dare. Eye color, hair color, these were traits that were easily remembered should she be caught. She smiled herself.

"I have an appointment with Dr. Kenneth Safton," she said. She had no idea that Safton worked here, but he really hadn't been out of med school long enough to set up private practice. "I'm Jane Selden, from the

Suffolk County Chronicle, and he's agreed to do an interview. Can you direct me to Otorhinolaryngology?''

"Let me tell Dr. Safton you're on your way up," the woman said politely.

Jill suppressed a smile. Bingo! Luck was on her side this morning, leading her to the right place.

The woman punched a few buttons on the computer.

"Oh, I think you're a little confused," she said. "Dr. Safton isn't in ENT. He's working in Ob-Gyn."

I should have guessed!

Jill rubbed the back of her neck, trying to think quickly.

"Yes, he is," she said. "But my article is on the study of ear, nose, and throat problems in unborn babies. Dr. Safton has agreed to introduce me to some of his colleagues."

"I see," the receptionist answered. She picked up a telephone and punched in a four-digit code. A moment later, she hung up. "Dr. Safton doesn't seem to be answering. Perhaps he's with a patient. If you'll wait over there on the couch, I'll try him again in a few minutes."

"Thanks," Jill said.

She walked to the waiting area and sat down on the red leatherette couch, picking up a magazine and pretending to be busy with it. In a short time, the opportunity she had been awaiting walked through the doors—a group of hospital volunteers armed with tiny plastic pumpkins full of candy. Jill stood up and mingled into the group, unnoticed. When they got off at Pediatrics, she stayed on the elevator until she reached the third floor.

The nurse's station was the hub of a wheel with spokes that branched off in four different directions. Bold letters identified the floor on a sign that hung from the ceiling—OBSTETRICS/GYNECOLOGY. The front panel of the station bore a notice with big, black letters: VISITORS: 2–3:30 P.M.; 7–8:30 P.M.

Without even looking up, the nurse behind the desk said, "Visiting hours are listed below."

Jill walked right up to her, putting on her most professional smile.

"I'm not a visitor," she said. "I'm Jane Selden, of the *Suffolk County Chronicle*. I have an interview with Dr. Safton this morning."

"No one told me about it," the nurse said, peering suspiciously through thick-lensed glasses. Jill knew she would not be swayed as easily as the woman at the front desk.

"Well, I do have a deadline to meet," Jill said, "and I can't come back today. Dr. Safton would be quite upset if he wasn't included in the article I'm writing."

Now the woman nodded. "That's probably true," she said. She mumbled something about Safton being egotistical, then raised her voice to say, "His office is down that hall, second to last on the right. But I didn't even see him come in this morning." She sniffed disapproval, as if annoyed that someone had upset the hospital's schedule.

"Thank you," Jill siad. She hurried toward the hallway before the nurse could stop her, more important, before the front-desk receptionist called upstairs. The door was clearly marked: DR. KENNETH SAFTON, in white block letters on a red plastic plate. Jill knocked, but there was no answer. She knocked again.

Jill looked over her shoulder and watched a woman in a bathrobe shuffle toward a sign marked SHOWERS. On the other side of the floor, a newborn baby set up wailing. The intercom called "Dr. Nicholas to labor."

Slowly, she turned the knob on the door, surprised to find it unlocked. Jill knew she had only a few minutes, but she hoped that in that time she would be able to find something of value. It was unlikely Safton kept anything incriminating here, but while she had the opportunity to spy, she had to take the chance.

The office was attractive, simply furnished in grad-

uated shades of brown. Posters depicting forest and
mountain scenes decorated the walls, and a cross-
sectioned model of a pregnant torso sat on an end
table. There were books lining the wall behind the
desk, and a skull set on a post on top of a black file
cabinet.

But there was something wrong. In spite of the ste-
rility of the atmosphere—not a speck of dust or a paper
out of place—in spite of the magazine-photo layout of
the office, Jill sensed something that made her uneasy.
There was an odd smell in the air, a mix of smoke and
. . . something.

"Nonsense," she whispered. "You don't have time
for this."

She started toward the file cabinet, pulling open the
top drawer. Manila folders gave the names of dozens
of patients; categorized articles clipped from the *Jour-
nal of the American Medical Association*; receipts for
purchased items. Jill took a step back to open the next
drawer down, and something crunched beneath the
heel of her shoe. She looked down at the rug and saw
a half-dozen white slivers. Jill bent to retrieve them,
turning them carefully in her hands. Bone.

She swung around quickly. Kenneth Safton was lying facedown behind his desk, one arm extended with
his fingers curled around a shotgun. At right angles to
him lay a skeleton, a huge chunk of its skull shattered
by the impact of a bullet.

Safton had shot at a skeleton.

Jill stared down at the body, unmoving, unsure what
to do. If she called for help, they would question her,
and they would know she had lied about her identity.

She took a step toward the corpse and felt her gorge
rise. She pressed her hands hard into her stomach to
fight the queasiness therein.

Safton's neck was gripped in the jaws of the skeleton, long-dead teeth sunk deep enough to sever the
doctor's jugular vein. It was the other smell she had
noticed—stale blood.

Jill found her legs and hurried from the office. When

she got to the end of the hallway, she nearly slammed into two patients and forced herself to slow down. She stopped at the desk.

"Dr. Safton wasn't in yet," she said, surprised at the calm in her voice. "But I left a note on his desk. I'll call him later."

She sped toward the elevators even as the woman was asking her again about her name. By the time she reached her car, she was shaking so badly that she had to sit for a few minutes until she was relaxed enough to drive.

Kenneth Safton had been murdered, in a bizarre and horrifying way. How could a skeleton come to life, to sink its jaws into a man's neck? Safton must have been trying to defend himself when he shot at the skeleton. The fragments of bone Jill had found on the carpet were bits of the thing's skull. But Safton couldn't defend himself against something that was already dead. Somehow, someone had brought it to life long enough to commit murder.

Almost the way Ryan used to bring his animals to life.

"They must know that he tried to scare me," Jill said, cutting off the thought about Ryan. "Somehow, they found out the kid goofed up and revealed Safton's name to me."

A sick feeling passed through her as she imagined what they had done to that poor, frightened teenager. She was so lost in thought that she nearly ran a red light on Jericho Turnpike and slammed her brakes to avoid a collision. The man in the car she almost hit gave her the finger.

"Screw you," Jill growled.

When the light turned green, she forced herself to drive at a steady pace until she reached the museum. She had to let the day go on as usual, so as not to arouse suspicion. It was certain they were spying on her, and if they knew she had found Safton's body, they would surely kill her.

When she entered the museum, Virginia was busy

unpacking a box of magnetic marbles. She pulled up a string that seemed magically connected.

"Aren't these fun?" she asked. "The kids are going to go wild with them. By the way, we have another school group scheduled this afternoon."

"Call me if you need help with them," Jill said. "I'll be upstairs in my office."

Virginia watched her partner hurry up the stairs, wondering what was wrong with her. Jill's face was white as a sheet and there had been a slight tremor in her voice.

"Come to think of it," she said, letting the marbles fall back into the box, "she's been weird ever since the gala." She went upstairs herself and walked through Jill's open door. Jill shoved something quickly into her desk drawer, but not quick enough for Virginia to miss that it was a photograph. She walked toward her partner's desk.

"What is it, Jill?" Virginia asked gently. "You've been so edgy lately. Is it that family problem you were telling me about?"

Jill nodded.

"Want to talk about it?"

Jill shook her head. How could she tell Virginia the truth, knowing what these people were capable of doing? Knowing they had murdered at least two people, had crippled another, and had kidnapped a child? She sighed.

"No, it's something private," she said. "There's really nothing you can do for me." She stood up and forced a smile on her face. "Come on," she said. "We've got to get ready for the troops."

When the group of schoolchildren arrived, they were so enthusiastic that Jill was almost able to forget what had happened an hour earlier. But she walked through the tour in a fog, introducing the exhibits by rote. She signaled to Virginia, who came quickly and took over. Jill went upstairs and got her jacket, slipping out of the museum without being seen.

Where was she to go from here? Every time she

came a step closer to finding Ryan, an invisible ax chopped away the next step. If only Deliah were still alive . . . If only she were able to tell Jill how she came to be privy to the thoughts in Ryan's mind . . .

Jill started driving through Port Lincoln, down streets lined with orange and yellow and red trees, past houses decorated with pumpkins and Indian corn and an occasional hanging sheet-ghost. She drove nowhere in particular, just needing the steady hum of the car's engine to steady her own nerves.

Somehow, Deliah had to have been near Ryan. But where? If she had been in Michigan, why hadn't she told Jill this in the first place?

Because she was murdered before she could do it.

The more she drove, the more clearly Jill began to think, and an idea occurred to her that had not come up previously. One way to find out where Ryan might be was to learn where Deliah had been on her most recent trip. She couldn't very well call the woman's family, who had had enough grief. But hadn't Virginia said the woman wrote a syndicated column? As another reporter, maybe Patrick Cameron could help her out.

Jill turned a few corners and headed south. Twenty minutes later, Route 110 took her into Melville, and the parking lot of the *Suffolk County Chronicle*. But no sooner had she rounded the back of the building than she saw three police cars with their red lights blaring. It didn't take her long to figure out what they were doing there.

Someone had found Ken Safton's body, and the police were looking for Jane Selden.

21

Lying in bed the night after Beth's accident, Stuart had racked his brain trying to think of an answer to all that had happened. If it had been a political enemy, they certainly had a roundabout way of protesting his work. Besides, how could anyone have gotten near to Beth? The older the night grew, the less he was convinced it had anything to do with him and his buildings. Natalie had mentioned the way the twins had been able to communicate through their thoughts. Maybe that's what was happening now . . .

He flipped onto his side, bunching up his pillow in anger. How could he let himself be drawn in by this spell? He had to remain strong, for Natalie and Beth.

But he had to do something to help them. Somehow, he had to convince them it was all a hoax. He fell asleep thinking of this . . .

. . . and woke up with an idea.

"Natalie, if I can show you once and for all that Peter was on that airplane, would you accept the fact that he's gone?"

"Of course," Natalie said. "But it's Beth you'll have to convince."

"I can do it," Stuart said. "I'm going to call in a very big favor."

Beth walked into the kitchen then, dark circles under her eyes. She shuffled over to the table and sat down. Natalie put a glass of milk in front of her.

"Are you okay, Beth?" Stuart asked gently.

She shook her head. "I want my brother home."

Stuart looked up at his wife, but Natalie had turned

126

to the stove again. "I wish I could make that happen, Beth," he said. "But Peter is gone."

"No!"

Natalie came back to the table with a platter of bacon and eggs. "Let's not discuss this during breakfast," she insisted. "Beth, Daddy says he's going to look into the matter. He's going to find out what really happened to Peter."

Now Beth's eyes lit up. "Oh, Daddy," she cried. "Thank you."

Stuart held up his hand. "I can't make any promises," he said. "But I'll try."

Stuart was as good as his word. When he arrived at the office, he asked his secretary to look up an exchange in Albuquerque, New Mexico. When the party came on the other end, he heard, "Sunflower Airlines."

"I'd like to speak to Philip Dositt."

Moments later, the president of the airline was on the phone. Pleasantries were exchanged, for these were two men who had known each other for years.

"I need a favor, Phil," Stuart said.

"And I owe you dozens," Phil said. "When I think of what you've done for me over the years, how you helped me when this airline was nearly bankrupt—"

Stuart interrupted him. "This is a big one. Just listen, Phil." He explained what had been happening with his daughter and just how he planned to put a stop to it.

Hearing the story, Phil whistled softly. "It'll take some doing, Stu," he said. "But I'm sure I can dig it up. I'll get back to you as soon as I can."

In fact, he was back to Stuart by late that afternoon. Stuart listened carefully, asked Phil to repeat what he had said, then thanked his old friend for all his help. Armed with this new information, he headed home. As he drove, staring at the road through a gray curtain of rain, he could feel the muscles in his body growing more and more tense. How could he have let this slip by? Why didn't he ask questions at the right time, six years ago? He clenched the steering wheel so hard the tensed muscles of his forearms began to quake. By the time he arrived home, he felt so horrible inside that all he could do was hold Natalie when she greeted him in the foyer.

"Stuart, you're white as a sheet," Natalie cried, tucking back a lock of wet hair that had fallen over his forehead. "What's wrong?"

"Is Daddy sick?" Beth asked.

Stuart pulled away. He took a deep breath and told his family what he had learned from Phil Dositt.

"Peter wasn't on that airplane."

Natalie gasped.

"I knew it," Beth cried, triumphant.

"Stuart, how . . . ?" She helped him out of his coat.

With his arms around his wife and daughter's shoulders, he went into the living room and sank down on the couch before answering. "I called in an old favor," Stuart said. "You remember how I lent Dositt money about twenty years ago, when his airline was going downhill?"

Natalie nodded, but she was eager to hear what had happened.

"I knew they took films of people as they passed through security," Stuart said. "So I asked Phil to look up the film shot the day Peter supposedly got on the plane." He pulled Beth closer to himself, but turned his gaze fully in his wife's direction. "Peter wasn't on the film," he said. There were tears brimming in his eyes, but he took a deep breath to keep them from falling. "Phil said he looked at the movie over and over. He knows what Peter looked like. How could you miss him, with that red hair? But no one at the airport knew the child's description. Natalie, they put another little boy on the plane. Some other child had Peter's ticket, with Peter's name."

"But that doesn't make sense," Natalie cried. "Remember, Stu, when I had to stay home because Beth was sick, I hired Peter's nursery-school teacher to take the trip with him. Agatha would never have gotten on that plane without him. And surely my parents took him right up to the gate—''

"Nevertheless," Stuart said, "Peter was not on that flight. Someone must have gotten him after your parents left.''

"But what about Agatha?'' Natalie asked.

Beth's eyes rounded. "Maybe she's alive, too.''

Stuart shook his head. "No, Beth. I thought the same thing, but Phil checked into it for me and said that Agatha was definitely on the plane. He called a friend in Records who said her body had been positively identified. Somehow, someone was able to get to Peter between the time Grandma and Grandpa left him and the time the plane took off. More strangely, they even substituted another child for him.''

"Then they took Peter away,'' Beth said. "But why? Who are they, Daddy? Are we going to get Peter back?''

"We're damned well going to try, Beth,'' Stuart replied.

Natalie closed her eyes and shook her head. She was full of feelings: dismay, anger, hope, and a strange sadness for the nameless little boy who had been murdered in Peter's place, because . . .

"Someone wanted Peter,'' Natalie said, opening her eyes again. "I don't know why, but they went to a lot of trouble, so it can't just be an ordinary kidnapping. I have a bad feeling, Stuart. These people are evil, I'm sure of it.''

Beth bounced up and down on the cushion. "Peter's in trouble,'' she cried. "I know it. He's been calling to me, but you guys wouldn't listen.''

"We'll listen now, Beth,'' Stuart said. "Do you think you can contact him?''

Beth shrugged. "I've been trying ever since that day I saw him at school. But it's like he can't hear me. He keeps appearing to me, but he always looks so scared. But when I call to him, he never answers.''

"Maybe we have to wait until he makes contact again," Stuart said.

Natalie pulled Stuart's hand onto her lap and started to rub the back of it. "What do we do first, Stuart?"

"First, we have dinner," Stuart said. "I can't think straight on an empty stomach and we've got a lot of planning to do."

"Planning?" Beth said.

"We're going to visit Grandma and Grandpa Blair," Stuart said. "They may have answers to some of our questions."

22

JILL HAD SAT IN THE PARKING LOT OF THE *SUFFOLK County Chronicle* for just a few minutes before backing out and driving away toward downtown Port Lincoln. Dazed, unable to decide what she should do, she had wandered around for nearly an hour. She passed boutiques decorated for Halloween and Thanksgiving; she strolled through the small park and finally sat down on a bench at the end of the dock, watching the sailboats go by.

There was no doubt the police had come looking for Jane Selden. She was grateful for the fact she'd had the sense to hide her hair under a scarf that morning and that she'd worn sunglasses. Why would anyone connect her with Ken Safton? In fact, once the coroner's report came in, they'd know she couldn't have committed the murder. The paleness of Safton's body and the coagulated blood would tell them he'd been killed some time in the night. Jill imagined the lab technicians questioning one another about the skeleton, wondering why Sufton had shot at the thing. And wondering about the mysterious woman who had rushed from his office this morning, only to disappear.

Disappear. That's what she had to do. A breeze blew off the water, chilling her. Who was she escaping from? The police? Or some dark, powerful force that thought nothing of killing one of its own to keep its secrets?

But she couldn't just take off. She'd have to give Virginia some kind of excuse—"family problems," she'd say—she'd have to go somewhere that would help continue her search for Ryan. And though she didn't like the idea of returning to the paper, she knew there was only one way she would find out where to go: she had to talk to Patrick, as she had planned earlier, to find out what Deliah's last assignment had been.

Jill sat for a few more minutes, convincing herself that the police had no doubt left by now. Then, determined, she got up and went to her car. When she arrived at the newspaper, Patrick was busy at his typewriter, plunking away with one hand while eating a bagel with cream cheese with the other. When he saw Jill, he put it down and made a welcoming noise.

"Hello," he cried after swallowing the mouthful. "What a nice surprise. Come to thank me for the column I wrote on the gala?"

"It was wonderful," Jill said.

Patrick stood up and cleared a pile of *Scientific American*s from a chair. "Sit down, Jill," he said. "You look a little pale. Is it that cold out? You want some coffee or hot chocolate? I've always got water boiling, and those envelopes—"

Jill shook her head. "No, thanks," she said.

"So, what can I do for you?"

"Patrick, I need a favor," Jill asked. "You know I was the last person with Deliah Provost, don't you?"

Patrick nodded, looking sad. "Poor woman," he said. "I never thought much of her column. All that horoscope and stargazing stuff is balderdash when you consider the wonders of real science. But she was a decent person and didn't deserve to die like that. I always wondered what you were doing with her, Jill. You don't seem the superstitious type.''

"Not at all," Jill insisted. "But Deliah said something to me the night of the gala that made it necessary to meet with her.''

"What was that?''

Jill sighed deeply. She hadn't told Virginia the truth because she didn't want her friend to get hurt. And she didn't want Patrick involved in this, either. But Patrick was an intelligent, strong person who could take care of himself. And without him, she might never find her son.

So she told him the whole story. Most of the story, anyway, with the part about Ken Safton deftly removed.

"Meeting with Craig Dylan convinced me my son is alive," she said. "But I don't know where to go from here.''

Patrick whistled. "I never would have guessed," he said. "You always seemed so cheerful. It must have been horrid for you, losing your son like that and having no one to share the grief with.''

"When I came here from Michigan," Jill said, "I had made up my mind to get on with my life. And I was doing fine until Deliah came along.''

"So, how can I help?'' Patrick said.

Jill leaned forward, her hands opened out as if the theory she had was something she could offer physically. "My son was a telepath," Jill said. "Now, I know you don't believe in that sort of thing, but it's true, I swear. I figured that the only way Deliah could have gotten a message from him was if she'd been near him. So I was wondering: can you find out if she took any trips before she died? If I knew the last place she visited, I could look there for my son.''

Patrick rubbed his lower lip with his index finger for a few moments, taking this all in. "It's amazing,'' he said.

"Can you help?''

He shrugged, standing. "I can sure try. Wait here a second, Jill. I'll see what I can dig up."

After he left, Jill picked up a two-year-old copy of *Scientific American* and thumbed through it while she was waiting. Patrick was back within ten minutes. "It was easy," he said. "Deliah has a sister in Albuquerque, New Mexico. She went to visit her last month and came home the night before the gala."

"New Mexico," Jill cried.

"That's right," Patrick said. "If Deliah was in contact with Ryan just before the gala, maybe it was there."

Jill stood up. "Then I have to go there."

Patrick reached out quickly and took hold of her arm. "Whoa! Do you have any idea what a trip to New Mexico is going to cost you, especially with such late notice?"

"I know," Jill said. "But we're talking about my son."

"Who may not even be there," Patrick said. "Are you going to spend hundreds of dollars each time you have even the slightest clue as to Ryan's whereabouts?"

Jill looked annoyed. "Then what do you expect me to do?" she asked. "Sit around and wait while my baby is in the hands of murderers?"

"At least look into it further," Patrick said. "What was that detective's name? Dylan? Call him and ask if there's any chance Ryan was taken to New Mexico."

"He won't talk to me," Jill said. "His wife made it very clear I wasn't to bother them again. And after what happened at his house that day, watching him freak out like that, I could never call him. No, Patrick. If Deliah was in Albuquerque before the gala, then that is where my son contacted her. I'm going." She stood up, zipping up her jacket. "Patrick, thank you for your help," she said. "Wish me luck?"

Patrick sighed. "There's no arguing with you," he stated matter-of-factly.

"If I can, I'll be on a flight tomorrow morning," Jill answered.

Patrick smiled and shook his head. Then he opened his arms and gave Jill a bear hug. "Maybe you'll be buying an extra ticket," he said. "A child's, one way back to New York."

Jill hugged him back. God, how she prayed he was right!

23

IN THE DAYS FOLLOWING KATE'S FIRST SESSION WITH Dr. Tavillo, Laura did not make any new appearances. The parapsychologist suggested that, perhaps, she was too frightened to do so after coming so close the other day.

"And she saw you in unfamiliar surroundings," Alec pointed out during a phone conversation. "I think our next session would be best held in your home, where Laura will feel safe."

Danny had made arrangements for the boys to stay with Mrs. Ginmoor at her own house, and both he and Kate had relinquished a day's work to their partners. Dr. Tavillo arrived at the house shortly after lunch, dressed in a tweed jacket, corduroy trousers, and turtleneck sweater. Mist from the nearby water twisted strands of his hair into tight little curls. Danny stepped back and let him into the kitchen.

"Kate's in the living room," Danny said. "We're very eager to get started."

Alec smiled. "You, too? I wasn't sure if I had you convinced the other day."

Danny's shoulders rose and fell. "It's sure as hell

something happened to Kate. I just want to find out what's really going on here.''

Kate was sitting on the living-room couch, facing the entrance, her arms wrapped around a soft-sculptured doll. It was the size of a small child, with dark braids made of yarn that fell to the waist of a pink pinafore. Dressed in a pink blouse and faded blue jeans, Kate looked very much like a child herself.

"Dorothy Williams, my boss, made this for Laura on her third birthday," Kate explained. "I thought— if Laura came today—that it would help.'' There were tears rimming her green eyes. She reached behind her glasses and rubbed them away. "Please help me get her back, Dr. Tavillo," Kate implored. "I haven't seen her in days and I'm afraid we've lost her."

"Then let's get started," Alec said. "Kate, I want to try a different approach today. I want to try to have you remember something very pleasant about Laura. Some memory that she may be able to pick up, wherever she is, and feel comforted.''

"How about her third birthday?" Danny suggested. "The day Dorothy gave her the doll?''

"That was a long time ago," Kate said.

"You'll remember," Alec said. "Kate, I'll bring you under the same way as we did the other day. Are you comfortable?''

Kate nodded. She wasn't comfortable at all, but she was ready. Danny sat on one side of her and Alec sat on the other. The doctor took her by the hands and told her to close her eyes. Within moments, she was completely hypnotized.

"That was fast," Danny whispered.

"She's eager," Alec replied softly.

He let one hand go, but stroked the back of the other with his fingertips.

"I want you to go back in time, Kate," Alec said. "Back to Laura's third birthday. Can you remember what happened when your friend gave her the doll?''

A smile spread across Kate's face, though her eyes

were still closed. And in her mind she saw tiny Laura
sitting on a stool in the Baby Bear Boutique.

Aunt Dorothy's comin' soon, the child had said. *And
she's bringin' me a dolly.*

Oh, how do you know that? Kate had asked.

*My brain tells me. Mommy, it's a big doll. Big like
me! It has brown hair and eyes and it's wearin' a pink
dress.*

Chubby arms shot up into the air.

The chimes on the door jingled and Dorothy entered
with a huge package. Dorothy and Kate smiled at each
other.

*I'm aching to see this myself, Dorothy. You've been
talking about this "surprise" for weeks! What could
it be?*

*You'll see, Kate! Here you go, Laura. Happy Birth-
day, precious!*

Laura had torn open the packaging and squealed
with delight to see the huge doll. She hugged it tightly
and kissed it. Then she went to kiss Dorothy. Kate
smiled, but inside she was shaking. Not only had Laura
guessed the present was a doll, but she had described
its appearance perfectly.

In present time, Kate frowned.

Alec squeezed her hand. "Is something wrong?"

"Laura knew about the present," Kate explained.
"Even when I didn't know myself, even when Dorothy
had been working in secret, Laura knew."

"That frightens you?"

"It—it confuses me," Kate admitted.

"You must drive the confusion away," Alec said.
"You must concentrate on the joy of the moment. Can
you call to Laura now, Kate? Can you remind her of
her doll?"

Though he knew he wasn't supposed to do so,
Danny cut in. "You told her to call Laura Jennifer."

Alec nodded but didn't look beyond Kate. "If necessary," he said. "But let's try Laura first. Can you
do that, Kate?"

"I don't know."

"Can you try?"

Kate breathed deeply. "Laura?"

Danny looked around, half-expecting his daughter to appear out of nowhere. He caught himself and forced his concentration on Kate.

"Laura, it's Mommy," Kate said. "Can you hear me?"

"Call her with your mind," Alec suggested.

Kate's head bent forward, and her eyes squeezed tighter. She called to her lost child, not only with her head, but with every cell in her body and every fiber of her soul.

Laura, please hear me! There's someone here who wants to see you. Do you remember Maggie? She was your favorite doll, honey. She's waiting here for you to come home. We're all waiting for you. Laura?

Kate breathed deeply, shuddering. Danny rubbed her arm, but she didn't feel his touch.

Laura, don't be afraid. Please, please answer me. I want to help you.

"I can hear you."

Kate sat up straight suddenly, her eyes snapping open. "Laura?"

The child stood before her, wearing a plaid dress and holding a book in her hands.

"Where are you, Laura?"

Laura replied in a voice only Kate could hear.

"I'm at school," she said. "Who are you? I keep dreaming about you, but I don't know who you are."

"Oh, honey," Kate cried. "I'm your mother. Don't you remember me?"

The child, standing in the doorway, shook her head vigorously. Danny and Alec saw the pictures on the wall behind her, but Kate could see a barren yard and the back of a brick building.

"You're not my mother," Laura said. "My mother is Alice Segal. But I wish you were my mother. I like you. I always feel happy when you're in my mind."

"Laura, that's because I really am your mother," Kate insisted. "Who is Alice Segal? Laura, something's happened to you. You've been trying to contact me with your thoughts, asking me to help you. But I can't do that if you don't tell me where you are.''

''I'm at school.''

''I know you're at school,'' Kate said. ''Where is the school? How can we find it?''

''It's in the center.''

''The center?''

Alec cut in. ''Ask her the name of the nearest city.''

''Laura, what city are you living in?''

''We're not in the city,'' Laura said. ''We have our own special place. Dr. Adams says it protects us from the Outsiders, from the people who don't understand us. I don't get it. You're an Outsider. So how come you're so nice?''

''I'm nice because I love you, sweetie,'' Kate said. ''Laura, please help us. Does the center have a name?''

Laura's head bobbed up and down.

''Sure it does,'' she said. ''It's called the LaMane Center. It's in the mountains.''

''What mountains?''

Abruptly, Laura turned to her side.

''Someone's coming,'' she cried. ''Oh, I can't stay! If they heard me . . .''

''Laura!''

''I wish . . .''

''No! Don't say that to me. No fire.''

''What fire?'' Kate pleaded. ''Laura, who is hurting you?''

''I'm not Laura. My name is Jennifer! Jennifer! Jennifer!''

She was gone.

Kate sat back, her eyes closing again as tears fell down her cheeks.

''Get her back out,'' Danny ordered.

''Right away,'' Alec replied.

When Kate was fully conscious again, she related what Laura had said.

"She's in a place called LaMane Center," she said. "In the mountains, somewhere."

"That could be anywhere," Danny said. "The Adirondacks or the Poconos, or—"

"What was she wearing, Kate?" Alec asked.

Kate looked at the doctor, bringing an image of Laura back to her mind.

"Short sleeves," she said. "Which means she can't be anywhere around here."

"Warm climate," Alec said. "That narrows it."

"Not much," Danny said. "What about this LaMane Center? What do you suppose it is?"

Kate, who had been hugging the doll all this time, put it aside and sat chewing on her lip. Something about the word "LaMane" was terribly familiar.

Before she had time to think about it, the telephone rang.

Kate went to the kitchen and lifted it from the receiver. She expected to hear one of her friends. Instead, she was greeted by someone speaking in a deep, whispering tone.

"We know what you're doing, Mrs. Emerson."

"What do—"

"Don't try to find Laura, Mrs. Emerson," the voice said.

Kate looked around the doorframe and called down the hall. "Danny? Danny, come here." She spoke into the receiver. "Who are you?"

"Laura belongs to us now," the caller went on. "If you try to get her back, we'll hurt her. Just like we're hurting your little boys, right now."

"No!"

Danny grabbed the receiver from her. "Hello? Hello? Is anyone there?"

His demanding tone was met by silence.

Kate had backed against the counter and stood staring at the telephone with her arms folded tightly. "He said he was hurting the boys."

Danny didn't stop to question her. He hung up the receiver and dialed Mrs. Ginmoor's number. In the meantime, Alec put his arm around Kate's shoulder and led her to a chair. As she gazed up at her husband, her eyes were full of inquiry and the color was slowly draining from her face.

"It's ringing," Danny said.

There was a click, and then, "I'm sorry. The number you have dialed has been disconnected. Should you require Directory Assistance—"

Danny hung up the phone. "It's dead," he said. "I don't understand. Kate, what happened? What did the caller say?"

"He told us to stop looking for Laura," Kate said. "He said if we tried to find her, they'd hurt her. Then he said 'just like we're hurting your little boys, right now.'"

"I better get to Mrs. Ginmoor's," Danny said, grabbing for his car keys. "Dr. Tavillo, can you stay with—"

"I'm coming, too," Kate cried. "They're my babies."

Danny saw no point in arguing with her. Joined by Dr. Tavillo, they climbed into Danny's car and sped off toward the West end of Gull's Flight. As they pulled onto the gravel road that led up to Mrs. Ginmoor's modest bungalow, Kate grabbed the waist of her seat belt and squeezed it tightly. The house had taken on a sinister appearance, like a dilapidated mansion haunted by malevolent spirits.

"All the shades are drawn," Kate whispered.

"Maybe Mrs. Ginmoor took the boys out for a walk," Danny suggested.

Kate shook her head vehemently. "No! She never pulls her shades. She loves the sunlight. Danny, something's going on in there."

No sooner had the car stopped than Kate jumped from her seat and was running toward the front steps. The front door stood slightly ajar, and Kate pushed inside without knocking. Danny and Alec followed close behind.

"Mrs. Ginmoor?"

Kate's voice bounced through the house as if all the rooms were completely empty. She went back toward the kitchen while Danny and Alec took to the upstairs. Kate found the remains of lunch on the table—two half-eaten bologna sandwiches and empty cups that had held milk. The warm smell of pumpkin pie, which should have comforted her, made Kate feel queasy. It took her just a moment to realize why. The filling was smeared all over the table and chairs, the crust smashed to bits on the floor.

"Kate, Kate, come up here."

Kate left the mess in the kitchen and ran upstairs. She found Danny and Alec in a bedroom. They supported Mrs. Ginmoor between them. The woman was staring down at her trembling hands, her lips moving as if in speech, but without sound. Kate hurried and knelt down before her. Mrs. Ginmoor stared at her through strands of gray hair that had come loose from a hairnet.

"Mrs. Ginmoor, what happened?" she asked. "Where are the boys? Where are Chris and Joey?"

Mrs. Ginmoor shook her head.

"Please," Kate cried. "Where are my babies?"

"She's in a state of shock," Alec said. "I'm going to call an ambulance."

"N-no," Mrs. Ginmoor croaked. "I'm so sorry, Kate. So sorry. The pie exploded. I—I guess there was an air bubble that popped, and it sprayed the filling all over. The boys were a mess, so I put them in the tub."

"Where are they now?" Kate demanded.

Mrs. Ginmoor burst into tears, burying her face in her hands.

"Oh, my God," Danny groaned, jumping to his feet.

Kate ran after him, following him to the bathroom.

"Chris? Joey?" Danny's deep voice penetrated the walls, but there was no response. He stopped short in the bathroom doorway, his bulky frame blocking the light.

Kate tried to get around him.

"Oh, no," Danny gasped. "Oh, my dear God, nnnooo!"

Kate ducked under his arm. Her knees buckled, but Danny instinctively caught her before she hit the ground. And then, even as his cries of dismay turned to silent, disbelieving tears, Kate began to scream with all her might.

The boys were sitting in the tub with their arms around each other. Their eyes were closed and their lips blue. A long black cord dangled over the edge of the tub, leading to a smoldering wall socket.

24

FOUR PEOPLE, THREE MEN AND ONE WOMAN, SAT ON folding chairs that faced a giant television screen. Bright video images bounced off their white coats, the reflections like ghosts. They sat perfectly still, studying the tape carefully.

On the screen, a young boy sat in an overstuffed lounge chair, tilted back so that he faced up to a big overhead light. He might have been a child cuddling up to take a nap in his daddy's favorite chair. But any semblance of comfort was eradicated by the presence of multiple wires and machinery. The four people—Dr. Lincoln Adams, his nurse Alice Segal, and two technicians—were unmoved by the wide-eyed look of fear on the boy's face. One by one, the wires were taped to his head and chest. A metal clip encircled one of his fingers, and a soft, thin rubber tube was tied around his upper arm.

"I don't want that shot," Tommy Bivers said.

The nurse in the film, a gaunt young man with a

face marred by acne scars, grinned. "It's just to keep you calm," he said. "After the seizure you had the other day, the doctors are afraid to take chances. Now, turn away and let's get this over with."

Tommy glowered at him.

In the screening room, Jenny's mother leaned forward. "Look, you can almost read his thoughts," Alice said.

On the screen, Tommy went on staring at the nurse. The young man blinked and a moment later jabbed the needle into his own arm. Realization of what he'd done hit him almost immediately, and he began to shout in anger. "You little brat," he cried. "You made me do that."

"Isn't that what you guys want?" Tommy asked. "For me to hurt people?"

The nurse had raised his hand to strike the boy, but it was stayed by a firm grip. Tommy looked back over his shoulder, then made an annoyed face. Dr. Adams' image appeared on the screen. With sunlight shining through the window behind him, the picture recorded by the hidden camera was distorted, giving the doctor a surreal appearance.

"There's no need for that, Mr. Vinton," Dr. Adams said soothingly. "I'm sure Tommy will cooperate today. After all, he's had time to think about his bad behavior the other day and how close he came to spending a few hours in the dark with our pet rats."

Everyone in the screening room saw the look of terror that passed over Tommy's face. And they saw it quickly disappear, replaced by an unexpected look of defiance.

"I don't want to do this," Tommy cried. "Not anymore. You want me to hurt people. I heard that guy the other day. I heard him say, 'Wait'll we try this on a human.' I heard!"

In the darkened room, one of the technicians squirmed uncomfortably as he watched the film. His big mouth had gotten him a stern reprimand from the doctor, and now he was on probation. One more stupid remark like the one he'd made near Tommy, and he was out. He didn't let himself think what "out" might mean—not after the rumors he'd heard about the Colpan woman.

"Oh, I'm sure you were mistaken, Tommy," Adams said in a congenial, almost-patronizing tone. "We would never hurt anyone. Only the Outsiders hurt people."

"Not all the Outsiders are bad, I think," Tommy answered. "I think you made that up."

"Are you contradicting me, Tommy?"

There was a threat in the doctor's tone that immediately silenced the boy. Dr. Adams nodded and beckoned to someone off-screen. A moment later, the wooden donkey was brought in. Tommy stared at it, but when a cat was brought in—a real cat this time—his mouth dropped open.

"No! No! I won't do it."

The boy started ripping at the wires, looking like a child trying to throw snakes from his body. He leapt from the chair, landing on the tile floor with a soft slap of bare feet and ran toward the door. "I'm getting outa this place," he cried.

The nurse moved swiftly, grabbing Tommy by his upper arms. Vinton struggled to keep hold of him, dodging the boy's kicks.

"Tommy, calm yourself," the film image of Adams commanded.

"No."

"Tommy, you must do this," Adams insisted in a firm but soothing tone. "It's the only way you'll be in control of your powers. Are you afraid?"

"You're using us," Tommy cried. "You want us to hurt people. But I won't do it so you better let me go."

"Calm down."

"I want to go home," Tommy seethed.

In the darkened screening room, Adams sat back and tried to comprehend what he was seeing. In the midst of it, it had all been too confusing. But now that he could observe it as if he were an Outsider, he tried to understand what had gone wrong with his project.

What in the hell had started this rebellion? Although they probably resented the sessions at the clinic, the children hadn't been mistreated there. He shook his head, unseen in the dark. Correct that, he thought; they hadn't been mistreated in years. In the beginning, punishment had been necessary to keep them in line. He had to erase any earlier memories, so that the children's minds became blank slates upon which he could write out his brilliant plan. And it had been brilliant, moving along smoothly, until this Bivers kid started up. It was Tommy's fault, being threatened with rats. Served him right for being disobedient.

Again, Adams asked himself where the rebellion had come from.

And then he told himself it didn't really matter. He was the master of all around him and nothing would stop him from seeking his goal. From the first time his experiment worked successfully, he knew greater things were in his future. He smiled, thinking of that first experiment. The young runaway had been so gullible, right up to the day she gave birth to what Adams referred to as "the result of my latest experiment." But there was too much going on on the screen to give that much further thought.

On screen, his image had been soothing the hysterical Bivers boy. Adams looked up to see himself signal for Vinton to let him go. And suddenly two bigger men appeared out of nowhere, grabbing the child and dragging him back to the chair.

"I can't let you go without the shot, Tommy," Adams said. "You are far too hysterical."

"No, please."

"I promised you could go," Dr. Adams reminded. "But first, you're going to take your medication. Unless you want to be punished, Tommy. The rats?"

Tommy shook his head, his expression wild with fear. "No rats!"

"Then do as you're told," Tommy was admonished.

Tommy said nothing and Adams nodded at the nurse. "Hold him down."

Tommy cried softly, but did nothing in protest. The threat of rats was enough to silence him for the moment. He didn't even whimper when the shot was administered.

The video went fuzzy.

Dr. Adams turned to the technicians and sighed. "I've watched that film three times," he said, "and I still can't understand where the boy's gumption came from, after all these years. We've had protests from the children before, but reminding them of the things they fear the most has always stifled any of that. So, what the hell happened this time? Why did Tommy Bivers fight us even when he knew he'd be punished?"

"It's not just Tommy," Alice Segal reminded. "My own Jenny and Michael Colpan are also giving us trouble. Just the other day Carl Mendolez blew up one of the machines. There have been other, minor incidents. It's like a mutiny."

The third man in the room spoke up. "Maybe the things we put in their minds when they first came here are wearing off," he suggested. "Maybe we ought to educate them again."

All eyes turned to Dr. Adams. Everyone in the room knew "educate" was a euphemism for "brainwash." But the doctor shook his head.

"We did that only because it was necessary for the project," he said. "The children's minds had to be erased of all memories of their pasts. But we can't fool with them now, not this far along. It might ruin everything we've been working on."

Adams stood up, walking to the video machine. He stopped it and pressed the rewind button.

"There are worse problems," he said. "Someone in the center has turned traitor and is sending information to the outside."

"We've been working on that, sir," the male technician who was on probation said. "I'm sure there won't be any real problems."

"Make sure there aren't," the doctor said. "We haven't been working on this experiment for the last fifteen years for you to screw up now. I want you to find the traitor, and I want him stopped."

"Stopped?" Alice said, not quite certain what he meant.

The doctor nodded. The two technicians looked at each other.

"We'll start a search at once," one of them promised.

"And I want more emphasis placed on tailing the families," Adams said. "They'll be the ones to lead us to the traitor. Make sure no harm comes to them until we find out who he is. But when we do, I want them all dealt with." He went to the door and opened it. "Within the week!"

25

THE SUN HAD JUST DISAPPEARED BEHIND THE ROCKY Mountains when Jill exited the main building of Albuquerque Airport. She stopped and breathed deeply, taking in the clean, thin air. She had left the pollution, noise, and crowds of New York three thousand miles behind her. It seemed now, as she walked toward her rented car with her keys dangling from her fingers, that the life she had built for herself on Long Island was just an illusion. The science museum; the few friends she'd made were all part of a world created because she thought she had lost the only thing that had ever really mattered to her: her son, Ryan. But now she was going to find him. He was here, somewhere, held captive by people who wanted to take advantage of his extraordinary gifts.

Jill unlocked the car and tossed her one suitcase into the back seat. She hadn't packed for a long stay. She was certain she'd find Ryan quickly and bring him home.

As she was about to get into her car, she became aware of a nearby presence. She couldn't have explained it, but something made her turn around and look back toward the doors of the terminal. Of course there were other people there, passengers who had been on the flight with her. But that wasn't what was bothering her. There was a man standing offside, and though he wore dark glasses, Jill recognized him at once. She had seen him on the airplane from Ft. Lauderdale and just outside her apartment building. She gazed at him for a moment, then caught herself and quickly slipped into her car. Well, she had lost him once; she could do it again. Still, she was relieved when he did not follow her out of the parking lot. She watched his figure in the rearview mirror as far as she was able, but he never moved once.

Jill followed the road signs to Central Avenue. The brilliantly lit sign of a shopping mall stood like a beacon against the purple sky, indicating a landmark she had been told to look for at the Rent-a-Car desk. At the next road, she made a sharp left and pulled into the parking lot of the hotel.

Jill parked under a lamp and exited the car. Carrying her suitcase in one hand and a manila envelope filled with pictures of Ryan in the other, she entered the lobby and checked in. Her room was luxurious—not because she'd asked for first class, but because, at such late notice, there was nothing else available. There were two double beds, two low bureaus, and a round table decorated with a flat terra-cotta pot of cactus. When she kicked off her shoes, her aching feet sank into the pile of the carpet. The television set offered a choice of movies, and there was even a refrigerator stocked with ice.

Jill entered the bathroom. When she hit the switch, she was immediately bathed in red light. She realized it was a heating lamp, and flicked another. This time, the room was washed fluorescent. It made her skin look pale; she could see dark circles under her eyes. In the six-hour airplane ride, she'd rubbed off all her makeup and lost the blown-in wave of her hair.

"God, Ryan, if you could see me now," she mumbled. She turned on the faucet and splashed her face with cold water. Then she glanced at her watch and realized she hadn't adjusted the time. In her mind, it was after seven. Mountain Time made it just after five.

"Early enough to get started," she told herself.

She put the glass down and went to the bed, sitting on the edge. She picked up the receiver and waited for the front-desk clerk to answer.

"I was wondering if you could get a phone number for me," Jill said. "The name is Maureen Provost. She lives in Albuquerque."

"Just a second, ma'am." The clerk was on the line again in a few moments. "There's a Maureen Provost on Bryn Mawr. And at University Place."

"University Place—where's that?"

"Near the campus, of course," the desk clerk said. "Mostly students in that area."

"Then let me try the first number," Jill said. "If it doesn't ring through, I'll get back to you."

It did go through, and Maureen Provost was only too happy to speak with Jill.

She had a dish of hot sopapillas and a pot of herbal tea ready when Jill arrived at her home. It was an adobe-style house, the wood floors left bare except for handwoven Navajo rugs. The furniture was wood-framed, softened by thick muslin pillows. There was a long, battered table in the dining room, underneath a wagon's-wheel lamp. At the back of the room, three niches had been dug out and each was filled with an exquisite Indian sculpture.

"How lovely," Jill commented.

"Steven, my husband, purchased them in Nevada many years ago," Maureen said. "He wanted them to have their own special places. Since he's a teacher like myself, he had time one summer to cut through those walls. It took days. This house was built thirty years ago, but the mud and grass used for the bricks are still as sturdy as ever."

As she spoke, Jill studied her face and thought how different she was from her older sister. Where Deliah had been dark and somewhat matronly, Maureen's hair was a rich brown and hung in waves over her small shoulders. Jill guessed her to be much younger than Deliah had been, maybe not much older than Jill herself.

"Please, sit down," Maureen said. "My husband has taken our children out to pick up their Halloween costumes. We won't be disturbed. The sopapillas are hot. Would you like some honey for them?"

"Thank you," Jill said. She accepted one of the airy pastries and savored a few bites before speaking again. "Mmmm. I've never had these before. You really didn't have to go to such trouble."

"It was no trouble," Maureen insisted. "I knew you were coming. I've been waiting for you a long time."

Jill set the pastry on a blue spatterware dish and looked across at her hostess. "You were?" she said. "You have the same talents as Deliah?"

Maureen smiled. "To a lesser degree. It wasn't psychic powers that told me you'd be here. It was my sister. You see, she told me she planned to contact you. After I learned of her death, I knew it would be only a matter of time before you came to me."

"If you knew about Ryan," Jill said, "why didn't you pick up where your sister had left off?"

"And how was I to know where that was?" Maureen asked. "You saw what happened to Deliah, Mrs.

Sheldon. The police told us there had been no one on that boat. They chalked it up to a weird accident, but we knew better. My sister was murdered. Do you think I'd chance my own death—as well as yours and that of an innocent child—by contacting you?''

Jill sighed. "I understand. You're right. It's been terribly dangerous. This whole thing is a nightmare."

"But you're almost at its end," Maureen said. "That's why you've come to Albuquerque. You finally learned where Deliah picked up her feelings of Ryan's existence."

"That's why I'm here," Jill said. "Deliah never finished telling me what happened. I'm hoping you can fill in the gaps."

"I'll try," Maureen promised. "But first, pour yourself some of that tea. You're shaking, and it will warm you."

Jill realized suddenly that she was cold. She filled her cup and sat drinking while Maureen relayed what had happened.

"Deliah had been camping in the Sandias with my children," Maureen began. "She told me that, as they were driving home the next morning, her mind was suddenly filled with a voice so loud, so full of terror, that she was forced to stop the car. That was Ryan calling her, Jill. A frightened little boy begging someone to put a stop to his torment."

Jill gasped, her breath sending a cloud of steam up from the tea.

"She tried to communicate with him," Maureen went on. "She tried to find out where he was, but as suddenly as the voice came to her, it stopped. Deliah was convinced there was a child in trouble. She pursued the thought connection and was able to ascertain that the child had something to do with a woman named Jill Sheldon."

"If she was able to read that in Ryan's mind, why didn't *he* know me? Why didn't he contact me?"

Maureen shook her head uncertainly.

"Perhaps fear of the memory forced the knowledge

into his subconscious. She made a connection with Florida, too.''

"Where we used to live," Jill explained.

"Deliah could not let it go," Maureen said. "She worked hard until at last she traced you to Long Island.''

"Someone else knew what she'd picked up," Jill guessed. "And they murdered her for it, before she could give me more information. But I've been stronger. In spite of everything they've tried to do to stop me, I've come this far.''

"No doubt they know you're in Albuquerque," Maureen said. "Please be careful, Jill. I'm sure they'll be watching your every move.''

"I know," Jill said, and went on to tell about the man who had been following her. "But now I'm on the lookout for them. Just let them try to stop me. But I need to know where to go now. Did Deliah say exactly where she heard my son's voice?''

Maureen nodded. "She was driving past a community that was built ten years ago in the mountains. It's a strange place. No one is allowed within its gates and few people ever leave it. The entire community is self-sufficient, right down to its medical care. It was built by a doctor named Lincoln Adams as a respite for families with handicapped children.''

Jill shuddered. Did these people consider Ryan's talents a handicap, something to be overcome—or corrected? "What's it called?" she asked finally.

"The LaMane Center," Maureen said. "If Ryan is being held anywhere, my guess is that it's there.''

Jill frowned thoughtfully. "LaMane? Why does that name sound so familiar?''

"I wouldn't know," Maureen said. "I'd never heard it before. But I've already drawn you a map how to get to the place.''

"LaMane," Jill said again. She shook her head. "It doesn't matter. I'm sure it will come to me. But I'm tired. It was a long plane ride and I have an early day tomorrow. I'm going to have to find a way to sneak into that place, to see if Ryan really is there.''

"What will you do when you find him?" Maureen questioned. "You can't just pick him up and walk out of the place. Not when it's been his home for so long."

Jill sighed. "I don't know. I just want to find him, then I'll take it from there." She stood up.

Maureen escorted her to the front door. "Good luck, Jill," she said.

She could hear Maureen Provost's voice as clearly as if the woman were standing right next to her.

And then her own voice in reply: "Just let them try to stop me!"

Something snapped, and Jill came to her senses. She had to defend herself. But how, standing naked, dripping wet in the shower? God, this was like some horror movie. Did he have a knife? Or maybe he planned to electrocute her while she was wet, make it look like an accident . . .

The shadow moved slowly. Jill backed up and felt the metal coil of the Shower Massage like a snake against her back. Quickly, she unhooked it and stepped out of its path.

The door started to slide open.

Jill turned the cold water off completely and turned the hot on full blast.

A gloved hand reached in.

With a shaking hand, Jill twisted the dial to pulse speed. A body leaned into the shower stall, a man dressed in the uniform of a hotel worker. Jill held up the massage nozzle like a gun and blasted him full in the face.

Her screams mixed with his cry of dismay. Still holding the shower head with one hand, she pushed the doors toward him with all her might, wedging him in. Then she dropped the nozzle, jumped out of the bath, and stumbled toward the door.

"Help me! someone, help me!"

She kept on screaming as she slammed the bathroom door shut. Jill could hear the shower doors squeaking open and the shuffling footsteps of her assailant as he slipped across the wet floor. Moving with a speed brought on by survival instincts, she grabbed a chair and wedged it under the doorknob, making it impossible for the attacker to escape.

By now, someone was pounding on her door. Jill grabbed her robe and wrapped her dripping wet body with it. Then, gasping for breath, she yanked open the door. A small crowd had gathered in the hall, summoned by her screams.

"Someone—someone get security," Jill breathed. "A man tried to attack me."

Murmurs of dismay rushed through the group. One man pushed his way forward and took Jill by the arm. He was a young man with red hair that curled down over his ears. Something about him was familiar . . .

But everyone seemed familiar these days. It seemed any face could belong to Jill's enemies.

"I've already contacted them," he said. "They should be up momentarily. You poor girl! Is he in there now?"

Jill nodded. "I—I used hot water to stop him."

The man walked toward the bathroom door. Through it, Jill could still hear the sound of water rushing from the hanging shower head. The man knocked at the door, but there was no answer. He turned back to Jill with a questioning glance.

"He's in there," Jill insisted. "Just get the police."

"Here they are," someone in the doorway cried.

Two uniformed guards ran into the room, an elderly Hispanic and a freckled teenager. Jill noted that neither one of them was carrying a gun. What in the hell would they use for defense against a would-be murderer?

"Aren't you going to call the police?" she asked.

"Let's just get the situation in hand," the older man said. He went to the door and knocked. Still, there was no answer. He looked at the redhead, then at the teenager.

"Maybe he got out already," the teenager suggested.

"How?" the red-haired man demanded. "We're on the fourth floor and there's no window in the bathroom."

The Hispanic guard turned to Jill. "Could he have slipped out as you were running?"

Jill shook her head. "He was caught in the shower door when I shut this one. He's in there. Don't let him trick you. He must be waiting for you to open the door. Maybe he has a gun. Why don't you call the police?"

The redhead patted her on the shoulder. "Calm down," he said. "You're becoming hysterical."

A red film seemed to come down over Jill's vision, but she fought to keep her temper in check even as she reprimanded the man. "Hysterical?" she echoed. "Why shouldn't I become hysterical? Some maniac just tried to murder me. Just stop being so damned patronizing and call the police."

The guards ignored her. The older man removed the chair and stood to the side of the door. Then he reached carefully to turn the knob.

The room and hallway became silent as everyone stopped breathing in unison. Only the splash of water could be heard, from the bathtub hidden somewhere in the steam. Jill watched the door open wider and wider . . .

The older guard stepped into the bathroom.

"No, don't," Jill cried.

Moments later, he came back out. "There's no one in there."

"What?" Jill cried. "He has to be. He couldn't have gotten out."

The red-haired man entered the bathroom himself, reaching to turn off the shower. He came out, shaking his head. "It's empty," he said.

Jill looked from the security guards to the red-haired man to the people standing in her doorway.

"It can't be," she cried. "I saw him. He opened

the shower and—and . . ." She sat down hard on the edge of her bed, shaking her head in dismay. "He was there," she said, more softly now. "I know he was. I'm not crazy."

"Well, there's no one there now, lady," the older guard said. "Come on, Ramón. We go off duty in five minutes."

Jill opened her mouth to stop them, but they were already gone. The crowd in the hall dispersed, mumbling to one another about the crazy people you meet when you travel. Jill was left alone now with the red-haired man.

"Why don't you leave, too?" she asked. "Everyone else thinks I'm off my rocker."

"I don't," the man said. "But I can tell when someone's stressed out. You've been working too hard, haven't you? Pushing yourself? You're probably so tired that you fell asleep momentarily in the shower and dreamed someone was in there."

"That's impossible," Jill said. "I'm not given to an overactive imagination." She stood up, tightening the belt of her robe. "Please leave now," she said. "I don't want to talk to anyone."

"Sure," the man said. "But if you need me, I'm in Room Four-fifty-eight." He turned to leave the room.

Impulsively, Jill reached out to touch his arm. "I don't know your—"

He turned so abruptly that his hair swung back, revealing a scar that ran from his hairline to his ear. Jill felt her knees grow weak as memories came flooding back to her.

"What was that?" he asked.

"I—I said I don't know your name," Jill managed to gasp.

I know him! God, I remember now.

"Adam Scott," was the reply. "Room Four-fifty-eight, if you need me."

Jill nodded slowly, trying hard not to let her shock show through.

When he finally left the room, she staggered to the

bed and threw herself down on it. First, her would-be murderer vanishes completely from a locked room. And then the man who comes to help her turns out to be the very same man who, as a trim young cop, came to tell her about the accident that had apparently killed both Jeffrey and Ryan.

26

THE FIRST THING KATE WAS AWARE OF WAS THE steady ringing of a bell. She stirred, her legs rubbing against cool cotton sheets. She breathed deeply and smelled pine cleaner. Danny was such a love, she thought, letting her sleep late while he cleaned the house. No doubt he'd make it sparkle from attic to cellar. And she so needed sleep, warm and comforting and protective sleep.

"I love you, Danny," she croaked.

Her throat was dry, and when she tried to open her eyes, she found they were too heavy. She rolled to her side and wiggled until she was comfortable. She could sleep late today, Dorothy would watch over the boutique and Danny would take care of the boys.

The boys.

Kate jerked out of her twilight sleep with a shudder and a gasp, leaning on one elbow until she could catch her breath. Chris and Joey. Something had happened to Chris and Joey.

Blinking, she gazed at her surroundings in bewilderment. Three shining bars made a railing on both sides of her bed. There was a little box clipped to her pillow, attached to a wire that led to a panel on the wall behind her. A hospital. What was she doing in a hospital when Joey and Chris were the ones who had been hurt?

She rolled onto her back, rubbing her head in an effort to bring herself to complete wakefulness. She could remember Dr. Tavillo coming to the house, even some of the hypnosis session. And she could remember someone calling her on the phone, saying terrible things about Joseph and Christopher. But beyond that, the day was a blank. She knew something had happened to her boys, but what?

Desperate for answers, Kate leaned to one side and unlatched the bed rail. She swung her feet over the edge of the bed and grimaced when they landed on an icy linoleum floor. There were no slippers in sight. Kate shuffled to the closet and opened it, but it was empty. No robe, no slippers. The nightgown she wore was hospital-issue. Whoever had brought her here hadn't expected her to wake up right away.

"Well, I am awake now," Kate said out loud. The sound of her own voice gave her a feeling of control.

Determined, she opened the door to her room. But instead of a hospital corridor, she walked onto an endless length of desert roadway. It was happening again.

"I'm not dreaming," Kate said, firmly. "I'm awake. I know I'm awake!"

She heard sobbing and turned in its direction. There, sitting on a rock not four yards away, was Laura.

"Oh, Laura," Kate cried. "You've come back again."

She started toward the little girl. But Laura held up one hand in a "stop" gesture. "Don't come any closer," she said.

Kate stopped in her tracks. "Laura, what do you mean? It's me—your mother. I've come to take you home again."

Laura's dark eyes thinned. "You are not my mother. You are an evil woman who keeps sneaking into my mind and telling me lies."

"No."

"You are," Laura snapped. "And my name is

Jenny, not Laura. Stop coming into my dreams. Go away and stay out of my mind.''

"Laura, please," Kate implored. "Tell me why you are doing this? Who is making you do this?" She started toward the child again, but Laura got down off the rock and went to seek shelter behind it.

"Don't come near me," Laura cried. "You're bad and you're trying to hurt me! You're an Outsider."

"A—a what?"

"An Outsider," Laura cried. "Everyone outside the center wants to hurt us because we're different. Because we're special."

"Laura, I'd never hurt you."

Laura covered her ears, dark hair falling around her arms. "You're not my mother! You're a devil! A devil! Go away. Go away. I hate you!"

Kate covered her face and began to cry. What had happened? Who had turned her little girl so vehemently against her? What had those monsters done to her precious Laura?

Someone tapped her on the shoulder. She uncovered her face and found herself standing outside her hospital door. A round-faced nurse looked down at her, her eyes full of sympathy. Kate recognized the look. It was the kind she'd seen most at funerals.

"Oh, my boys," she choked. "Did something happen to my boys? I wasn't with them, and—" Kate stopped herself, bewildered. What had happened?

"Your husband will discuss that with you when he comes back," the nurse said, the harsh edge of her brogue seeming to bounce off the smooth white walls.

Kate looked over her shoulder and tried to find some clue that the desert had really been there. There was nothing in sight but a dozen doors lining the hallway to the nurse's station.

"I—I saw my daughter."

"You must have been sleepwalking," the nurse said. "Come back to your bed, Mrs. Emerson."

Kate looked at her with wide eyes. She followed the nurse into the room like an obedient puppy, letting the nurse help her back into the bed. But she couldn't sleep. It frightened her not to know that her boys were okay. And the daughter she thought she was so close to finding had denounced her with hatred beyond the child's years. It was more than a terrible day. It was a day created in hell.

Far away, in an isolated village in the Rocky Mountains, someone else was experiencing her own personal hell. Jenny Segal stared through tear-filled eyes as a technician removed the electrodes from her, one by one.

"If you had told us at once about this woman you have been seeing," Dr. Adams said, "this might not have been necessary. But you let yourself be drawn in by her, Jenny. In spite of all my warnings about the Outsiders, you believed this woman."

Jenny sniffed loudly. "She—she seemed so nice."

"All Outsiders seem nice until they find out what you really are," Dr. Adams said. He gave Jenny a hand and helped her down from the chair. His smile was the same as usual, but even though she was only ten, Jenny had the feeling he used the same kind of smile when he talked to one of his pets.

"Well, she won't be bothering you any longer," her mother said. "That woman is gone from your mind, I'm sure."

Alice looked over Jenny's head at Dr. Adams. The little girl gazed up at the adults, reading a message between them but unable to comprehend exactly what it was. She only knew this: her mother had heard her talking in her sleep and had found out about the woman with brown hair and glasses. Right after breakfast, she had taken Jenny by the arm to the clinic, where the little girl was forced to call on the woman. Where she was forced to call her horrible names and tell her never to come back again.

Jenny cried all the way home, ignoring her mother's commands to stop. She felt as if a good friend had been torn from her, and for the life of her she couldn't understand why it was necessary. . . .

27

IF ANYONE HAD QUESTIONED WHERE BETH GOT HER incredible mane of dark-red hair, the answer would have come within seconds of meeting her grandmother. Lillian Blair's carefully permed hair was still rich in color, her red curls tipped just here and there by white strands. She was standing on the sidewalk in front of her house, wearing a yellow linen suit and a blouse embroidered with brilliantly colored flowers when Stuart, Natalie, and Beth climbed out of their taxi. Beth's grandfather, Oscar, stood just behind Lillian, his hands on her shoulders. Stuart thought, as he paid the driver, that Natalie was the perfect blend of her parents: her mother's eyes and cheekbones, her father's mouth and complexion. And when they embraced, he tried to fight the suspicions he'd been harboring that, somehow, Lillian and Oscar Blair had placed their grandson in the hands of kidnappers.

"It's so good to see you," Lillian cried. She was a jovial woman who never seemed to speak softly. Every word, every gesture was full of emotion. "Come in. Come in. I have a little snack ready." She put her arm around Beth's shoulders and hugged her tightly. "And, of course, hot chocolate for you."

Beth smiled. Tired from the plane trip, she didn't say anything.

"We certainly were surprised to hear you were coming," Oscar put in, coming up alongside Stuart. He tried to take one of the suitcases, but Stuart shook his head. Inside the house, he set them down near an antique brass coat rack.

"As I explained over the phone," Stuart said, "something urgent has arisen. But we can talk about that after Beth has gone to bed tonight."

Before Oscar had a chance to question him, Stuart moved quickly into the dining room. Lillian had set the oak pedestal table with orange and red stoneware, painted to resemble sunflowers. There was an apple strudel and a chocolate layer cake as well as an assortment of cookies.

"This is a little snack?" Natalie asked. "We only called you last night. Where did you find the time to bake?"

"It was my pleasure," Lillian insisted. "How often do I get to see my precious granddaughter?"

Stuart looked around, leaning a little to glance into the kitchen.

"Where is Beth, by the way?"

"The bathroom," Natalie said. "I don't think she's feeling well, Stuart."

There was a look in Natalie's eyes that told Stuart she meant something more than jet lag. He gave his head a slight shake and quickly changed the subject—so quickly, in fact, that Lillian and Oscar gazed across the room at each other. Stuart had said something urgent had come up. Both grandparents wondered if something was wrong with Beth.

As the grown-ups were talking, the little girl had already left the bathroom and was exploring the bedrooms. She went back to the one she knew would be hers for the stay, the room where she always slept when she visited her grandparents. Grandma Lily had laid a handwoven serape over the four-poster bed. There was a big stuffed cat sitting in the rocking chair. Grandpa Oscar had bought it for the twins when they were babies. Even though her father said it was impossible, Beth was sure she could remember them playing tug-of-war with its long, striped arms and legs. She picked it up and held it close, trying hard to remember Peter as he had been when they were together.

"Oh, Peter," she whispered, a single tear falling from her closed eyes, "please tell me where you are."

Someone tapped her shoulder. Beth opened her eyes, expecting to see one of the grown-ups. Instead, a boy stood in front of her. He had red hair and freckles, and his eyes were brilliant green.

"Peter!"

The boy's head tilted to one side. "Who are you? Why do I keep seeing you? Please, can you help me?"

"Yes, Peter. Yes, I can—"

"Don't call me Peter. My name is not Peter. I am not Peter! My name is Michael Colpan! Michael! Michael!"

He was screaming so loudly that Beth was certain the adults would come running. She reached out to him, to touch and comfort him.

Her hand grabbed thin air. Beth took a quick step forward, turning quickly in search of the boy. How could he have just disappeared like that? There was no sign of him, but as if from a great distance, she could hear him calling out to her.

Please help me. Please, I don't want to hurt anyone. Stop it! Please stop!

Beth ran to the window and unlocked it. As she pushed it up, the crisp mountain air rushed into the room. But now she could hear Peter's voice more clearly. She looked toward the dark silhouette of the mountains. Resting her hands on the windowsill, she leaned out and screamed into the night, "Peter! Peter!"

Her shrill voice had raised a barking of dogs before strong hands took her by the shoulders and pulled her back into the room.

Beth gawked up at her father, her eyes wild. "Daddy, I heard him. Peter is very close, I know it."

Stuart nodded. "Yes—yes, Beth. That's why we're here."

"But you don't want everyone in Santa Fe to know our business, honey," Natalie put in.

Beth swallowed hard, then spoke in a voice that was only slightly more controlled. "He's in those mountains, Mommy," she said. "He was calling to me. He's scared. I think someone's trying to hurt him."

Oscar and Lillian, who had been watching all this from the doorway, came to join them. Oscar wore a dark frown, but for the moment he kept his thoughts to himself, trying to make sense of what Beth had said. Lillian, on the other hand, had no intention of fading into the background.

"Natalie, what the hell is going on here?" she demanded. "What's this talk about Peter? Why is Elizabeth talking in such an insane way? To say that Peter is in those mountains—"

Oscar shushed her, irritably. "Lillian, let the children explain themselves in their own good time," he said.

"The time is now, Dad," Stuart said. "I think we should sit down, don't you? Some of that hot chocolate might calm Beth down."

Lillian opened her mouth to say something, but Oscar was already steering her back to the dining room. No one spoke again until they were all seated, with cake and beverages set out before them. Beth rested her chin on her hand and stabbed at the layer cake, a dessert that, a few weeks earlier, she would have polished off in seconds.

"I think you'd better prepare yourself for a shock," Natalie began. She looked over at Stuart, trying to think how to begin. He picked up the hint and tried to explain what was happening.

"Mom, Dad," he said, "some things have come up. Circumstances—bizarre circumstances—have led us to believe that Peter is alive."

Lillian's gasp filled the room.

Oscar sat up straighter, reaching quickly for his coffee cup. He took a long gulp and choked. "How can that be possible?"

For the next hour Stuart and Natalie took turns relating the events of the past few weeks. Occasionally, Beth would fill in information they did not have, all the while toying with her uneaten cake. When at last they finished, Oscar sat thinking quietly, shaking his head. Lillian pushed her chair back and got up to walk around the room.

"My grandson—alive," she cried. She looked up at the ceiling, the tears on her cheeks glistening in the light of the chandelier. "If only it could be true."

"It *is* true," Beth insisted.

"But why would anyone take him?" Oscar asked. "I could understand something like this happening today—now that you're a big-shot real-estate tycoon and a prominent political figure. But six years ago? What would be the point?"

"We're not sure," Natalie said. "But we do know this: Peter has been trying to communicate with his twin—with Beth. Maybe they wanted him for his gift of telepathy."

Lillian tossed a hand. "Oh, Natalie. Lots of people have telepathy. My own mother did. And no one kidnapped her. It must be something more than that."

"No matter what the reason," Stuart said, "we have to get our son back. And that's where we think you can help us. You were the last people to see him alive. Can you remember the day you took him to the airport?"

"Oh, well, hell," Lillian cried, "that was six years ago. We couldn't possibly remember every detail."

"Anything," Stuart cried. "Can you remember walking him up to the security check? Can you even remember going into the airport?"

Oscar looked down at his empty plate, as if the crumbs of apple strudel could jar his memory. He certainly remembered helping Peter pack his suitcase. And there had been an argument . . .

He turned to Lillian. She was standing behind Beth now, rubbing her shoulders. "We had a fight," he said. "About Peter's flying home with a baby-sitter.

You said you thought it was disgraceful that neither Stuart nor Natalie could take the time to travel with a little four-year-old.''

"You said that?'' Natalie asked.

Lillian shrugged. "He seemed so helpless.''

"For heaven's sake, Mother,'' Natalie said. "He was flying with one of my best friends.''

"Who managed to get onto the plane without him,'' Stuart put in. "That's the gap here. Agatha Braun was killed on that flight. How she could have walked on board with the wrong child is beyond me. Try this— can you remember leaving him with Mrs. Braun?''

There was a pause, then Lillian held up one long red fingernail. "Oh, I do recollect something,'' she cried. "We took him into that little gift boutique. Don't you remember, Oscar? He wanted to buy something for his sister. I can even hear him saying, 'Poor Beffie'—he always called her Beffie—she's got a sick tummy.'' And then he picked out a little road-runner for her.''

"That's right,'' Oscar said. "It was in a running pose on a piece of wood, and there was a little sign that said: 'Souvenir of the Land of Enchantment.' ''

Stuart finished pouring himself another cup of coffee. When he set the pot down again, he said, "Okay, you got him into the airport. Who exactly was with you?''

"Just the two of us and Peter,'' Lillian said.

"What happened to Agatha?'' Natalie asked.

"Who?''

"Agatha Braun,'' Natalie said. "The woman who took Peter on the trip.''

Lillian shrugged. "Oh, I think she was off checking in their luggage.''

"And when did you meet up with her?'' Stuart asked.

"With whom?''

"Mother, with Agatha Braun,'' Natalie said, growing impatient.

Oscar let out a slight, breathy laugh and Lillian

tossed her hand again. "Who in the world are you talking about?" they both said.

"There was no Agatha Braun with Peter," Oscar insisted. "He got on the plane all by himself. We took him up to the gate and watched him get on."

Natalie stiffened, but Stuart reached across the table and took her hand.

"Something's going on here," he said. "Somehow you've blocked the memory of Natalie's friend escorting Peter. A minute ago, you said she was checking in the luggage. Now you say you don't know who she is."

Oscar bowed his head and began to rub his eyes. Lillian sank into a chair, looking forlorn, quiet for once in her life.

"I'm sorry," Oscar said. "It's all a jumble. I don't know why I said there was no Agatha Braun. Of course there was. I don't know where the thought came from."

"Someone put it into your head," Stuart answered. He got up and walked around the room, shaking a fist. "Somehow, between the gift shop and the security check-in, someone got hold of you and Peter. They took Peter, but planted false memories in your brains so you'd remember watching Peter get on the plane."

Oscar whispered, "We were brainwashed?"

"Brainwashed," Lillian gasped. "Of all the ridi —"

"It's not ridiculous, Mother," Natalie said. "Nothing in regard to finding Peter is ridiculous. And if there's any way you can help us, any way at all . . ."

"Of course we'll help," Oscar insisted. "I just don't see how."

Stuart came back to the table, sitting again. He finished his coffee and started on a third cup.

"Did anyone come to visit you during Peter's stay?" he asked. "Anyone out of the ordinary?"

"Not that I can remember," Lillian said.

"There's a lot you can't remember," Natalie grumbled.

"What about the pictures being sent to us?" Stuart went on. "Do any of your acquaintances dabble in art—specifically, portrait work?"

"Of course some of our friends are artistic," Lillian said. "How can you live among such natural beauty as the Rocky Mountains and not feel creative?"

"But portraits?" Oscar added. "Sorry."

Natalie sighed. "If only there was some way we could jar your memories, some way to break through the wall they created six years ago."

There were a few moments of silence as the adults pondered the idea. Then Lillian gave her hands a quick clap.

"I have an idea," she cried. "Why not recreate the scene of the crime? They do it so often in mystery novels. We could all go to the airport, visit that gift shop, and see if anything comes from that point."

Natalie and Stuart nodded in unison.

"Great idea," Stuart said. "Let's all get our coats and—"

Natalie tapped his shoulder, then pointed at Beth. She had fallen asleep, her head rested on her arm and a strand of red hair lay across her cake dish.

"Not all of us," she said. "I don't think Beth could take it."

"Then I'll stay with her," Lillian said.

"Oh, no, we need you at the airport," Stuart said. "The combination of both your memories is vital. No, Natalie can stay here with Beth."

Natalie nodded. "You'll call as soon as you think of anything."

"Of course, darling," Lillian insisted.

As Lillian got out the coats, Stuart picked up his daughter and carried her to her bedroom. As he tucked the serape in around her, she opened her eyes halfway and mumbled, "Peter's waiting."

Stuart kissed her forehead. "I know, honey," he whispered. "We'll find him." He exited the room and joined his in-laws in the foyer.

"I hope this works," Oscar said.

"It's worth a try," Stuart said. "Come on, before it gets too late and the gift shop closes."

In fact, the shop-owner was beginning to turn off his lights just as the three entered. The old man eyed them with the disdain he reserved for people who bought last-minute gifts. Stuart and his in-laws paid no attention to the stares as they headed toward the display of knickknacks. They were also completely unaware that, from a phone booth across the lobby, they were being carefully observed. The pale-faced young man, who seemed much younger than his fifteen years, was dressed in a fringed suede jacket and faded dungarees. His eyes were the strangest blue color, so pale they seemed almost white. He leaned deeper into the phone stall and spoke in soft but clear tones.

"They're here, Father."

"Don't call me that. Someone might be listening."

"I'm sorry . . ."

"You know what you have to do. Use your powers to the fullest, boy. Use them, and destroy our enemies."

"Understood."

Carefully, the boy hung up the phone. To anyone observing, he looked like a late-model hippie visiting New Mexico in search of a new, peaceful life. He hoisted his big satchel up over his shoulder and strolled over to a water fountain. He noticed the older woman holding a small replica of a road-runner. He wondered what had taken them so damned long to find it. From the moment the Morses had arrived in Albuquerque, he had expected them to end up back at that gift boutique. After all, it would be the last definite memory the Blairs would have had. So he had waited patiently in the terminal, the position assigned to him ever since his father learned the kid's family was flying into New Mexico. And now they were back, on the verge of remembering what had really happened.

"Destroy them," he repeated. He tucked himself

into another phone booth and began to unzip the
satchel. It was stuffed full of laundry, except for one
glimmering, diamond-shaped crystal. The teenager
held it up and let the overhead lights refract through
it into small rainbows. His years of training at the
center had led up to this moment, when he could prove
the worth of his talents. When he got through with his
targets, his father would be so proud of him. He would
prove that because he was the oldest of the children at
LaMane—older than the next child by five years—he
was also the most powerful.

He imagined himself in the gift shop, just behind
the display of bric-a-brac. Slivers of blue light ema-
nated from his fingertips, an electrical current travel-
ing directly into the road-runner statue held by the
woman. Electricity to bring life . . .

In the gift shop, Lillian let out a scream and dropped
the road-runner.

"Did you remember something?" Stuart asked, eagerly.

"Lady, don't break the merchandise," the shop-
owner snapped.

Lillian looked at the two men. "It burned me," she
cried.

"How could—"

Before Stuart could finish his sentence, there was a
sudden rumbling, like the shock of an earthquake. The
display case in front of them began to wobble.

Cursing, the shop-owner came running from behind
the counter. "Get outta my shop, you troublemakers!
Out! O-U—"

He never finished spelling the word. Suddenly, a
stuffed mountain lion that had been set in the window
came to life. It sprang forward with a might roar, claws
ripping into the shop-owner's chest. As the man
screamed in dismay, its sharp teeth sank deep into his
neck, sending a great gush of blood to the window.
All around the shop, dozens of innocent toy animals
began to come to life, howling, screeching, roaring.
Road-runner statuettes zipped around the room in a

bizarre, almost comical way, smashing into walls and chattering noisily. Armadillos rolled up into balls and badgers showed sharp teeth. Hissing, one of them raced toward Stuart.

"Let's get out of here," Stuart cried, grabbing Lillian by the arm.

"What's happening?" Lillian demanded.

"I don't know," Stuart cried over the din. When the badger was within range, he gave it a swift kick and sent it across the room. It smashed against the wall and landed to the floor in a plush, lifeless heap. "Oscar!"

Oscar did not answer. Stuart turned to urge him out of the store. When he saw his father-in-law, his stomach turned flip-flops.

Oscar had collapsed against a display of gum and candy, his face striped by bloody claw marks. Something long and brown was hanging from his lip. Stuart realized to his dismay that it was a rubber rattlesnake. But this toy had somehow gained the poisonous qualities of the real thing.

"Oscar," Lillian cried out, rushing to him.

"No, get out," Stuart said. "Someone is doing this to us. Don't you see the people in the terminal? None of them hears us. None of them sees the blood on the window. You get out and call Natalie. Let me help Oscar."

Lillian had turned white as a sheet, but somehow she managed to stumble toward the doorway. An armadillo, only an inch long and made of glass, skittered across the floor. Lizards jumped from the shelves, landing in her hair. Lillian screeched and slapped at them, but continued on to the door.

Then, just as she was about to reach it, a steel gate rolled down from its recess in the ceiling and slammed shut. They were locked in.

"Help us," Lillian cried to the people walking by. A flight had just come in and a large group was heading toward the baggage area.

"Please! We're trapped! Help!"

As if she didn't even exist, not one of the people turned her way. Lillian went on begging for help until at last she caught the look of a bedraggled teenager staring at her from across the room. His eyes were so full of malevolence that all fears created by the animated toys paled in comparison to the dread that suddenly arose in Lillian's mind.

He knows who we are. He knows why we're here, and he's going to kill us.

She pulled away from the window, kicking at the road-runner puppets that were pecking at her ankles, drawing blood through her stockings.

"Stuart, what will we do?" she asked, her voice shrill.

"The window, Lillian," Stuart said, hooking his arms around Oscar's chest. He had managed to rip the rattlesnake away, and now trickles of blood poured from two puncture wounds in Oscar's lip. The unconscious man was impossibly heavy, and Stuart had to muster every ounce of his strength to drag him toward the display window. It was free now of animals, who were either flying or crawling wildly. But the mountain lion that had attacked the store-owner lay on its side, inanimate. The lizards that had jumped on Lillian and the road-runners that had pecked at her were also strewn about the floor, motionless. A quick thought flashed through Stuart's mind that, once the toy had been used, it was rendered lifeless again. But there was no time for that. He had to get them out of the store, fast. Whoever was doing this had already killed one man and seriously injured another. He lay his father-in-law down and picked up a magazine rack. Hoisting it like an awkward javelin, he threw it through the display window. Shards of glass flew everywhere.

And still the people in the terminal moved on, oblivious.

Stuart helped Lillian through the opening. Then he went to drag Oscar out, stepping carefully over the broken glass. He stepped backward through the window, his arms hooked around the unconscious man's chest. Just as he was about to hoist Oscar through the opening, he heard Lillian let out a gasp. Following her gaze, he looked up at the window frame. Impossibly, like a movie running backward, the glass of the window was flying back into place.

With a grunt of effort, Stuart tried to move on. But somehow, his feet were frozen to the ground. He let go of Oscar and tried to pull himself out. But his body was frozen, held in the window by some force. The glass was fusing itself together and he could not get out of its way. As it neared his chest, he cried out in dismay, begging for help.

"Lillian, for God's sake, pull me out!"

The older woman just stood frozen, unable to comprehend the madness of what she was witnessing. It was all a dream, just a horrible nightmare.

"Help me! God, hel—"

The last words were followed by a loud gulping sound as the windowpane fought to heal itself in spite of the obstacle in its way. Molecules reconstructed themselves, created new glass where there was nothing, pushed the glass through Stuart's waistline . . .

Behind him, Lillian screamed and screamed.

28

MICHAEL COLPAN WAS DOING HIS SCIENCE HOMEWORK when something like a balloon blew up in his chest. It suddenly felt as if his insides were being pushed away, leaving only empty space. The sensation was so painful that he tumbled out of his chair, holding himself across his stomach.

"Dad?"

He barely choked out the word. Then he remembered that his father was working late tonight and that Emilina had gone home. He was alone. The terrifying feeling that something very bad had just happened to someone who cared about him washed over the boy like scalding water.

He heard the little girl's voice again, the same one he'd heard in a dream a while earlier.

They're killing our father. Help him, Peter. They're killing Daddy.

"Where are you?" Michael called.

But there was no answer.

The pain across his abdomen heated up to such an intensity that Michael sprawled across the floor and screamed. He doubled up, his eyes squeezed shut, crying out desparately for help—from his father, from the little girl, from God.

Then, just as suddenly as it had started, it stopped. Michael stared up at his ceiling, unmoving and dazed. If only his father were there . . .

She had said something about someone "killing Daddy." No! Michael thought hard and felt that his father was still very much alive. But that horrible feeling, the sense that someone had been hurt very badly, was inexplicable. Michael tried again to call the little girl with his mind, but with no luck.

He had to talk to someone. Grabbing his hooded jacket from the end of his bed, he slipped it on and left the house. The children were forbidden to walk around at night, but Michael didn't care. He needed to be with his father, and even if they threatened to lock him up in the watch tower, they couldn't stop him.

He shivered and zipped up his jacket. The watch tower. It stood at one corner of the LaMane Center, where a guard kept vigilance to be sure no one broke in. Dr. Adams said it was to protect them from the Outsiders. But he never explained why no one was allowed out of the center, either.

Nightmares about that tower had haunted Michael for most of his life. Alone on the darkened road, with only the wind to speak to him, Michael was unable to resist the memory of his most recent dream.

He was dangling in midair, a sharp pain firing from the top of his head. Someone had him by his thick crop of hair and he was being held arm's distance from an open window in the tower. The wind slapped him hard, and the ground below spun in circles.

"What's your name?"

"Mommy, Mommy, Mommmmeeeeee!"

"Tell me your name or I'll drop you, kid. What is your name?"

"Peter . . . Pete-er Morse."

"No!"

And suddenly he was falling free, down, down . . .

Michael shook his head hard to free it of the horrible dream. How many times had it come to his mind over the last years? It seemed so real, like something that had really happened. But he knew it couldn't have. His name wasn't Peter, it was Michael Colpan.

So why did that little girl keep calling him Peter?

He started to cut across the road to the main street, but he noticed a light on at Jenny Segal's house. Jenny had heard voices too, he remembered. Maybe she could help him figure this out.

But Jenny's mother wasn't very nice, and if she knew he'd come here alone, she'd call Dr. Adams on him. Jenny's father was okay, but Michael was certain the best thing to do was sneak into Jenny's room through her back window. It was on the ground floor, the middle window of three. Michael hurried over to it and stood on tiptoes to peer in. Jenny was sitting on her floor, dressing a doll. She started when Michael rapped at the window, but smiled when she realized who it was. Hurrying to close her door, she came and let him in.

"Are you crazy?" she demanded. "If anyone finds out you're out alone—"

"Jenny, I need to talk to you," Michael said. He was shaking all over.

"Are you cold?" Jenny asked. "Want my comforter? You could sit in the chair."

Michael shook his head. "Listen to me, Jenny. Those voices you hear. Do they ever make you hurt or feel scared?"

Jenny looked confused. "Not at all. I always feel safe and happy when I hear from that woman."

She sighed, bending to retrieve her doll from the floor.

"Except now I'm forbidden to contact her. Our teacher heard me talking to nobody he could see, and he told my mom. She said if she ever heard of me making contact again, she'd—she'd—"

Jenny's eyes squeezed shut and Michael watched helplessly as she fought with some unspeakable terror. Was it the same kind of feeling he had when he thought of the watch tower? He wondered.

"She said she'd stick my hand on the flame of the stove," Jenny blurted.

"Ugh!" Michael's eyes slitted. "She didn't really ever do that, did she?"

Jenny shook her head. "I don't know. I dream about it sometimes, and I'm really scared of fire, so I wonder if it could have happened. But I don't remember."

The way I'm scared of the watch tower, but can't remember ever even being up there.

"Jenny, something bad happened to me a few minutes ago," he said. He went on to describe the terrible pain and the feeling that someone he loved had been torn away from him.

"That girl I keep seeing said it was our father," Michael said. "But my dad is alive, I know it. And what did she mean our? I don't have a sister."

"Maybe you do," Jenny suggested.

"What do you mean?"

"When I see that woman," Jenny said, "I sometimes see her with two little boys. And I keep thinking they should be my brothers. I keep thinking maybe they really *are* my brothers.''

"But you're an only child, just like me," Michael poitned out.

"So's just about everyone else in this place," Jenny said. "Did you ever notice that? There's only one of us with a brother, and that's because Ronnie and Ricky Gautier are twins. How come none of our parents ever had any more children?''

Michael shrugged. "Beats me. But what do I do about the little girl, Jenny? And what do you do about that lady? 'Cause I know you'll contact her no matter what your mother says.''

"We'll find them," Jenny said without hesitation. "Go on back home, Michael. Start making plans. We'll try to find a way out of here in three days.''

Michael backed away from her, looking at her as if she were crazy. "Out of here?" he echoed. "But, Jenny, it's dangerous. The Outsiders.''

Jenny rolled her eyes. "I'm so sick of hearing about those Outsiders! How bad can they be when my own mother wants to burn my hands? No, I'm going to find that lady, because she's the only one who's ever helped me. Tommy Bivers said he's heard a voice too, from a woman who says that these people mean to hurt us and that we should get away.''

"My dad wouldn't hurt me.''

The sound of a closing door cut off Jenny's next words. Her father's voice was heard through the closed door. He had been in the city that day, on an assignment he wouldn't talk about, and Jenny hadn't expected him back so early. She shook her head at Michael, indicating the window. "Hi, Daddy!''

When she left the room, she didn't open her door wide enough for her father to see Michael scrambling through her window.

Outside, Michael ran through the Segals' back yard. He paused for just a moment at the street, wondering if he should go home or to his father's office. He needed his father now, so he headed toward his building. Once he was inside, he'd be safe . . .

A sudden movement up ahead made him stop short. Michael felt ice rushing through him and heard an inner voice commanding him to run. But he couldn't move. He could only stare at the familiar, terrifying figure that approached him. It was the young man Bambi had been so cruel to the other day. He walked slowly toward Michael, staring at him with those white-blue eyes, his expression unreadable.

Michael realized he'd been caught disobeying one of Dr. Adams' prime rules: no children outside at night. He wasn't certain if this teenager would tell on him. But he was certain the older boy meant no good. And suddenly, his sense came back to him, as did his muscle skills.

He broke into a run, not looking back to see if he was being pursued. Fear was a great source of momentum, and in less than two minutes he crashed through the front doors of his father's building. His sneakers thudded loudly as he raced down the hall, seeming to send a message: "Child outside! Child outside!"

Michael was crying when he reached his father's office.

Ralph dropped the pencil he was drawing with and hurried around the drafting table to take his son in his arms. "Whoa, Michael," he cried. "What's wrong, son?"

"Daddy, I'm scared."

Ralph hugged him, feeling the small body tremble violently. "Tell me what happened?"

"I—I got sick when I was doing my homework," Michael said. "A really bad feeling, like something bad was happening to someone I knew. I thought it was you, Daddy."

Ralph held him at arm's length. "I'm fine, Michael," he said. "Look at me. All in one piece."

Michael didn't reflect his smile. "Someone saw me outside," he said. "That big boy who wears the fringe jacket. He's gonna tell on me, I know it. They're gonna put me up in the watch tower, and—"

"Shh," Ralph soothed, hugging him again. "No one's gonna put you in any damned watch tower. Not as long as I'm around."

Someone knocked at the door. Panicked, Michael looked up at his father. Ralph leaned closer and whispered to him, "Go on in the bathroom and wash your face," he said. "Don't come out until you've calmed down, understand? I'll take care of this."

Michael did as he was told, listening to Dr. Adams' voice through the door. He couldn't quite make out the words, but knew the two grown-ups were arguing. Splashing water on his face and drying it with paper towels helped calm him. He took a few deep breaths, then carefully walked into his father's office.

"Hi, Dr. Adams," he said sheepishly.

"How long have you been here, Michael?"

Michael looked up at his father. Ralph tugged his ear a few times, and Michael immediately recognized the number two.

"Two hours, Dr. Adams," he said quickly.

"One of my staff said he saw you outside."

"Then he's mistaken," Ralph said. "Michael's been with me the whole time."

Dr. Adams nodded, but there was something doubting in his eyes. "Just make sure you always obey the rules," he said. He left the room.

Michael went to his father and hugged him. "Thanks, Dad."

"That was close."

"I don't like that man anymore, Dad," Michael said. "He scares me."

Ralph didn't express his own feelings, knowing Michael could read them very well on his own.

I'm scared, too, Michael.

29

JILL HAD REMAINED AT THE HOTEL THAT NIGHT, IN spite of the terrifying incident in the bathroom. It had been too late to go off in search of another place to stay, and she doubted anyone would be so bold as to invade her room again. Awake all night, she tried to figure out exactly how the intruder could have slipped out of a locked room without being seen. Finally, she came up with two possibilities. The first was that someone had slipped something to her in the restaurant, causing her to hallucinate. But the problem with that theory was that there hadn't been time to plant a suggestion in her head as to what she would envision.

Her second idea made more sense to her. Somehow, when she wasn't looking, the red-haired man—formerly a Wheaton, Michigan, cop—had set the intruder free. But whatever had happened, Jill understood now that Maureen had been right. "They" had been watching her all along.

She flipped the top of her suitcase back onto her bed and began to repack. Certain now that Ryan was at the LaMane Center, she would proceed to the next step in her plan: surveillance of the area from a safe distance, just as she'd told Maureen.

Jill checked out of the hotel and drove along Central. Every once in a while her line of vision would go to the rearview mirror, just to convince her no one was following her. She drove until she saw the huge, wood-framed stained-glass sun hanging from a sign-post outside a small shopping center. She had noticed it on her way home from Maureen's house the previous night, the orange-and-yellow flares of glass shining like a beacon in the moonlight, under a sign that said, SUNFLOWER MALL. She remembered seeing a large sporting-goods store here and had filed the stained-glass sun away as a landmark.

Although it was small, it was well-stocked, and within twenty minutes Jill had all the things she had been unable to pack in New York. She handed the clerk a credit card and waited impatiently while her order was tallied. Then the teller filled a huge shopping bag with everything she had purchased: a small camp stove, a lantern, a huge canteen, and a box of waterproof matches. There was long underwear, heavy socks, hiking boots, a wool hat, and numerous small items.

"Cold time of the year to be camping," the teller commented.

"But the best time of year for viewing certain constellations," Jill answered. She hoisted the bag up, grabbed her new, rolled-up sleeping bag by its cord, and left the store.

Jill then stopped at the grocery for provisions, packed the bags into her car, and drove away. One more stop now, she thought. The most logical place to find a camera store would be near the university. Sure enough, she located one between a shop specializing in stained-glass works and a place called New York Deli. She went inside and found a display of high-powered telescopes. She turned one toward the university grounds, then adjusted the guide scope until she found a letter on a far-off campus building. From this distance, she couldn't identify it. She peered into the eyepiece and adjusted the focus know until the letter came into perfect view: M.

"Perfect," Jill said.

After the order had been written up, Jill carried her new prize from the store and set it down carefully on the floor behind her seat. She knew Virginia would have fits to know she had spent money on something she had at least three of at the museum. But there was no time to have Virginia send her a telescope, and she didn't want her partner asking questions. It had been hard enough to lie about the trip to Albuquerque, saying a relative had passed away. She seriously doubted Virginia believed a word of it.

But now wasn't the time to worry about her partner back in New York. Jill turned back onto the highway and headed toward the mountains. She really wanted to go straight to the LaMane Center, but didn't dare, lest they recognize her. As much as she wanted Ryan back quickly, she knew this had to be done very carefully. There would be no soft hotel bed tonight, but the thick loft of a warm sleeping bag.

Over the past six years, Jill had become used to the seasonal changes on Long Island. Here in Albuquerque, the lack of water provided for very few trees, and most of what Jill saw as she sped along the highway was cast in shades of brown. But when she reached the Sandia Mountains, she was able to marvel at the deftness of nature's paintbrush. Driving deeper between them, rocks and flora changed from browns to greens to brilliant reds. Early snow dotted the upper cliffs, while small waterfalls spattered rainbows in the air.

Jill could not resist pulling off to the side of the road. She got out of her car and went to a chain-link fence, wondering why it was here among so much natural beauty. A moment later, she understood: it protected travelers from the depths of a dark ravine. Shivering, she went back to her car and continued up into the mountains. There was a sign marked SANDIA CREST, but Jill passed the turnoff. She knew the attraction faced Albuquerque itself and that even at this time of year there would be tourists there. What she needed was a place farther into the mountains, one that would give her a good view of the LaMane Center.

It took her half an hour to find it. Pulling her car into a clearing, she got out and walked through a thick growth of juniper and pine. There below her, some twenty miles from the base of the mountain, was an isolated collection of adobe-style houses. Even without the telescope, Jill could see the rectangular shape of Victory gardens. Twenty years ago, it might have been a hippie commune. But the presence of a long, low building dispelled any ideas that this was a place where people came to get back to nature. Jill suspected it was some kind of hospital or a research laboratory.

She went back to her car and unpacked her equipment, setting up the little stove to start a pot of coffee going. It wasn't until she breathed in its warm aroma that she realized she was famished. Jill prepared a quick sandwich for herself and ate it with one hand while she erected the telescope. Peering through the lens, she was able to make out the bent-over figure of a woman working in her cactus garden. Jill swung the telescope slowly on its tripod, seeing other adults, a corral of horses, a huge barn, and some stray dogs. But not a single child. Were they keeping them hidden? she wondered. Had Ryan been locked in a prison all these years, unable to see the sun?

The thought depressed her so that she closed her eyes and bent her head. She had to get a look inside the buildings, but that couldn't be done until nightfall, when lights would be turned on. Realizing this, Jill decided she ought to take a nap. After all, she hadn't slept a wink the previous night, and she couldn't afford to fall asleep when she was supposed to be spying on the LaMane Center. She would only sleep for an hour or two, then she would watch some more.

The name "LaMane" echoed in her mind as she drifted off, using her rolled-up sleeping bag as a pillow. The sun shone down through the branches of the trees, caressing her face warmly. LaMane . . . something familiar about it . . . she'd heard it before . . .

She was presented with a newborn Ryan, all wet with fluids from her womb and still attached to his umbilical cord. She cooed at him, gently consoling him as he protested his introduction to the world.

"Oh, Jeffrey, I can't believe it," she had cried. *"After all these years, a baby! I had almost given up."*

"A baby boy," Jeffrey said, beaming.

The doctor helped her deliver the afterbirth, then stitched up the episiotomy. At Jill's request, he got into one of the family pictures the nurse was snapping.

"Thank goodness for modern technology," he said. *"I told you not to give up hope."*

"But after all the tests," Jill said, *"and after trying Perganol and—"*

"That doesn't matter now," the doctor said. *"It was Neolamane that did the trick."*

"Great new discovery," Jeff said. Suddenly, he turned to Jill, his eyes darkening. He frowned deeply and spoke in guttural tones that echoed through the sterile room. *"Too bad Ryan won't live to tell about it . . ."*

Jill sat up with a gasp, jerking herself into wakefulness before her dream could turn into a nightmare. Shaking, she crawled over to the stove and poured herself another cup of coffee. Since she had only been asleep a short time, it was still warm, and it helped settle her nerves. As she sat against a tree sipping it, she went over the dream in her mind. Immediately, she understood the message that had been sent to her. LaMane—it was a pharmaceutical company, manufacturer of a fertility drug called Neolamane. It was this same drug that had helped Jill conceive after years of trying.

Was it possible that the drug had had some effect on the babies it produced?

"I have a lot of questions to ask," Jill said out loud.

But whom could she ask? Whom could she trust? It was just a chance she had to take, but she had to find out everything she could about the drug. It would be hours until nightfall, and no amount of viewing through the telescope had produced the sight of a child. With a new lead to follow, Jill packed the car up again and headed back down the mountain. She would return this evening, but in the meantime, she'd spend the day following up on the LaMane Center.

When she arrived back in Albuquerque, she headed into the campus in search of Maureen Provost Swanson. Perhaps the teacher had access to the school's computers, where she might find some information. She left her car in the parking lot, everything locked safely in her trunk. If anyone had followed her here, she didn't want to advertise her intentions by leaving the telescope and camping gear in plain sight.

Jill found Maureen in the teacher's lounge, grabbing a quick lunch between classes. The woman smiled to greet her, waving her into the room.

"What happened?" Maureen asked eagerly. "Did you learn anything?"

"You were right about my being followed," Jill said. "Someone broke into my room last night."

Maureen gasped. A couple sitting at the opposite end of the table turned to look her way, then refocused their attentions on each other. Maureen lowered her voice and spoke again. "Was anything stolen?"

Jill shook her head. "He didn't touch a thing. He was there for one reason only: to get rid of me, or at least to frighten the hell out of me."

Jill related what had occurred, watching Maureen's brown eyes grow rounder with each sentence.

"Thank God you're all right," Maureen said. "But what are you going to do now? Do you need a place to stay?"

"I'm as fine as I can be right now," Jill answered. "As to my accommodations, those are being provided by Mother Nature. I'm setting up camp in the mountains, right above the LaMane Center. Bought myself a fancy telescope and a good supply of camping gear."

Maureen grinned. "Good for you. But what brings you to the university?"

"I think I might have made a connection, at last," Jill said. "LaMane is the name of a company that produces a fertility drug called Neolamane. I took it before conceiving Ryan. So I need an 'in' at your science or math department, to ask if anyone knows about the drug.''

"I'll do better than that," Maureen said. "It just so happens that Steve teaches computer programming.''

When Jill was introduced to Steven Swanson, her immediate thought was that he looked like a young, slim Rod Steiger. But when he spoke, his mellifluous tones were more like Leonard Nimoy's. He was more than happy to help her. When Maureen left them to return to her classes, he led Jill to an array of humming computers.

"This one is on a bulletin board," he explained, sitting before a monitor. It was blank except for a blinking cursor. Steven punched in a code, and a menu began to scroll.

"Can you patch into the LaMane Center's computer?''

"If they have one," Steven said. "And if it is necessary. But first, this drug of which you spoke. Neolamane?''

"That's correct.''

"Aha! Here it is." He typed a few more letters, and an adjacent printer began to hum and click. Moments later, he pulled out a three-page report entitled "Neolamane—A five-year Market Study.''

"This is fantastic," Jill said. "How can I thank you?''

"Just get your child back," Steven said. "It will be the only thing to make my sister-in-law's death worth something.''

Eager to know the contents of the printout, Jill thanked Steven again and hurried outside to find a place to sit. A beautiful pond attracted her, filled with mallards and surrounded by trees and benches. She sat on one of them and began to read.

What she found was so shocking that she had to go over the paper twice. Neolamane had turned out to be a pharmaceutical nightmare, almost a reincarnation of the Thalidomide scare, but on a different scale.

She realized now that her beloved Ryan had been brought into the world by the work of evil.

30

"DID YOU SEE THAT?"

"What happened?"

"That crazy guy jumped right through that window."

The crowd that had disembarked a flight from Dallas/Ft. Worth suddenly took notice of the mayhem in the souvenir boutique. The window was cracked in a pattern of rays as if a bullet had gone through it, but instead of a bullet, a body hung suspended in the glass. The legs dangled grotesquely, like a pair of pants set into a wall for display. They were soaked with blood, dripping from the belt down to the shoes, down to the floor.

People shoved and jostled to get a closer look, but one woman stood frozen in the midst of the crowd. They had not seen what Lillian had just witnessed. Somehow, they had seen only the aftermath of Stuart backing out of the window, and it had appeared he was jumping through it. In the instant that Lillian had screamed, the crowd had come out of a strange kind of mass hypnosis.

"Well, for God's sake, get help," someone yelled.

"I already called the police," said Tito Puerto, the airport security guard on duty.

"Is he okay? Is he alive?"

Please let him be alive! How can I tell Beth her father is dead? And her grandfather! Oscar!

"Oscar," Lillian screamed. She pushed through the crowd, crying out her husband's name.

Gasps and cries of shock rang through the lobby as the bystanders wondered if it had been her husband who had acted so insanely. Up to now, no one had gone near the window. There was an underlying fear among the travelers, something keeping them back. But Lillian was beyond fear now. Oscar and Stuart had been hurt. She had to help them.

She reached out and touched Stuart's leg.

With a resounding *thunk* the lower half of Stuart's body fell to the floor. He had been bisected at the waist.

Lillian doubled over and began to retch. Screams raced through the crowd, cries of dismay rose up from children as their mothers quickly turned them away from the sight. There were shouts, the wail of sirens, and at last a group of uniformed police officers appeared.

"It's really bad, Chief Vermont," Tito said, his Hispanic complexion having gone shades lighter.

The young guard had graduated from the police academy only a year ago, and he had never witnessed anything like this. Even Chief of Police Lou Vermont, a seasoned veteran with thirty years under his utility belt, stiffened in horror at the sight. He'd seen terrible accidents—mountain climbers at the bottom of ravines, skiers who had landed headfirst in shallow snow—but nothing, nothing so nightmarish.

Still, he had to take control.

"George, get something to cover him up," he ordered, his voice taking on a steady, professional tone. He turned to the crowd and barked like the marine sergeant he'd once been: "All right, clear out. There's nothing here to see."

"What happened?" a woman in the crowd demanded.

"That's what I'm here to find out," the guard said.

Tito had found some garbage bags and helped George cover the remains.

The other half's inside. The half with his head.

The woman who'd asked the question tapped the chief's shoulder. She pointed to Lillian, who was crouched down on the floor, her arms wrapped around her stomach.

"I think that's his wife," she said.

Lou nodded.

Tito, happy to get away from the gory sight, went to help her up. "Is that your husband?" he asked gently.

Lillian shook her head, staring at the floor with tear-filled eyes.

"She says it's not her husband, Chief," Tito said. "Who is it then, ma'am?"

Lillian could only muster the faintest squeak of a voice. "Son-in-law."

"Sit her down and stay with her until help comes," Lou said. He opened the door of the boutique and stepped inside. From the corner of his eye, he saw a face staring across the floor, the mouth agape in a silent scream. He wouldn't look at it. Let the medical examiner's people take care of it.

Lou sidled over to the remains, squinting as he threw another garbage bag over Stuart's head. Now that the hideous thing was out of sight, he took a deep breath and went about his investigation. Within moments, he found Oscar's body.

Lou got to his knees and pressed his ear against the man's chest. There was only a thready whisper of a heartbeat. He jumped to his feet.

"Get that stretcher in here," he cried. "We've got another one in here, but he's alive. Heart attack."

The cop named George took off.

"Is this the store-owner?" a police woman asked Lou.

"I guess so," Lou said. "I'm still looking around."

As they lifted the man onto a stretcher, Lou continued his investigation. The boutique was a shambles. Toy animals had been thrown in every direction, some crushed or ripped. When he heard a wailing noise, he looked out to see the woman running to the stretcher.

"What in the name of God happened here?" he asked out loud.

Lou found the store-owner behind his counter. Four parallel lines of blood ran down the front of his shredded shirt. His head was thrown so far back it touched his spine, unhinged by a gaping, bleeding hole. Lou blinked and tried to understand what he was seeing. It couldn't be possible, and yet . . .

"My God," he said out loud, "he looks like he's been mauled by a wildcat."

There would be no way of knowing just what happened until the forensic team finished its work. Lou left the store to them and went out to start asking questions. One of his officers had already begun. He came to his senior partner, shaking his head.

"No one saw a thing," he said. "They heard glass breaking and looked up to see the guy halfway into the window. No one even saw him take the jump."

"How can you miss something like this?" Lou demanded. "That store looks like the end of the Third World War. And no one heard anything?"

The younger cop shook his head, as befuddled as his senior partner.

A few miles away, someone else was fighting confusion. With Dr. Adams gone now, Michael Colpan was better able to explain the strange feeling that had overcome him. He sat on the couch in his father's office, still wearing his jacket.

"I was doing my homework," he said. "Then all of a sudden I got this really bad pain in my stomach. It really hurt. And then I started hearing someone in my brain."

Quietly, calmly, Ralph pressed for more information. "What—what exactly did your brain tell you?"

Michael cuddled closer. "I heard a kid's voice. I think it was that little girl I told you about—the one they made me burn, even though she wasn't even there at the clinic? But you know what's weird? You want to hear what she called me?''

I don't think I want to hear this. The barriers are breaking down. He's making contact . . .

''What—what did she call you, Michael?''

''Peter,'' the boy replied. ''How come? My name is Michael.''

Ralph squeezed Michael tighter. ''Michael, let's go home,'' he said, helping his son to his feet. ''There's something we have to do.''

''What's the matter?'' Michael sensed his father was terribly afraid of something.

''We have to get away from here,'' Ralph said. ''Don't ask questions, Michael. Just trust me. Trust me, because *I am* your father and I love you.''

Michael frowned at him, wondering why he'd stressed the words ''I am.'' But he didn't say a word as his father led him home.

Because it was Emalina's day off, it was empty. Ralph left Michael in his room and went to retrieve two suitcases from his own bedroom closet. He opened one on his bed and took the other to Michael's room.

''Just pack a few clothes and some toys and books,'' he ordered. ''And don't forget a sweater.''

Michael just stood his ground. ''Where are we going?''

''Away,'' Ralph said. He looked terribly sad. ''Michael, I've made a horrible mistake. I realized that after your mother disappeared, but now I'm trying to make up for it.''

''Make up for what?''

''Michael, there's no time for questions,'' Ralph snapped. He steadied himself. ''Pack your things. I'll explain everything later.'' He turned to leave the room, but Michael stopped him with another question.

''How're we going to get past the gates? You know they don't let anyone out without a permit.''

A humorless smile cut across Ralph's face. Here, at last, was something over which he had control.

"Did you forget I'm the one who designed that fence?" he asked. "I know exactly where to turn off the alarm."

Michael nodded and went to his dresser. None of this made sense: not the frightening vision he'd had, not his father's sudden weird behavior. But he trusted his Dad, and if there was some reason they had to run away, he'd go along. Within five minutes, he had packed up everything.

He met his father out at the car, his backpack hooked around his shoulders and his small suitcase held tightly. The night was moonless and filled with stars, the autumn air so chilly he could see his breath. Ralph took the suitcase and put it in the trunk with his own. Michael climbed into the passenger seat, and his father got behind the wheel. Ralph handed him a blue folder.

"Hold this in your backpack," he said. "It'll explain a lot of things later, and it'll just slow us down if I have to drag my briefcase along."

He started the engine.

"First stop, back to my office," Ralph said. "I'll go into the cellar and cut a few wires. We'll be out of here in fifteen minutes, Michael. And then, when I'm sure we're not being followed, I've got a long story to tell you."

He drove ever so slowly along the dark road. When he reached the administration building, he left his son in the car and went inside. Two doors and a long flight of metal stairs took him down into the cellar. It was filled with crates of equipment and building materials. Drugs had been locked in a tall cabinet that reached clear up to the twenty-foot ceiling. On the mechanical end of Dr. Adams' experiment, Ralph had never really known what the drugs were for. But he'd heard rumors, whispers that medication had been given to the children over the years to keep them under control.

Except that now, some of them were building up a resistance. Michael had shown it ever since his mother vanished, in his visions of his real parents and his insistence that he felt close to someone outside the LaMane Center. Jenny Segal's invisible prison was starting to crumble away, too. From what Ralph had heard, she was also seeing visions of her real parents. And Tommy Bivers had fought back when forced to make a toy do terrible things. He hadn't blindly obeyed Dr. Adams and his colleagues.

Something was happening at LaMane. Ralph knew a rebellion was simmering, one that would certainly reach fruition when the pliable youngsters became defiant adolescents. He didn't have to be psychic to know there'd be bloodshed. And he had no intention of letting Michael get hurt . . . Letting Peter get hurt.

He shook his head vigorously, making his way around the shelves. Ralph had learned Michael's true identity long ago, when, unknown to Adams, he'd been working inside an air-conditioning duct. He'd overheard the doctor talking about a couple in San Francisco, demanding that their daughter be kept under surveillance.

"It seems she's trying to contact her twin," he'd said. "We can't let that happen. We can't let Stuart Morse know his son is still alive."

"He thinks Peter died in a plane crash," a female voice had responded.

"Let him go on thinking that," Adams said. "No one must ever know that Peter Morse is still alive, living here with the Colpans. The Colpans themselves must never know where the boy came from."

Ralph had felt angered and betrayed to hear the words. Michael had been no orphan. He'd been kidnapped.

Even now, three years later, Ralph's hands clenched into fists at the thought. He'd told Risa about it, but she'd insisted he was mistaken. To her, Dr. Adams was a god, the one man who had brought a child to her when no one else could. And the thought that Michael wasn't really hers was too much to even consider. She had spent every possible moment she could with the boy, playing games with him, teaching him to play the piano, drawing sketch after sketch of him.

Ralph peered through the darkness and saw the gleaming edge of a long metal box. Stepping over a coiled-up hose, he went to it and opened a door. Hundreds of switches were lined up, controlling the outflow of electricity to every section of the center. Without hesitation, Ralph flicked three of them down. He had just cut off power to the electrified fence. It was just a matter of opening the gates and . . .

From upstairs, he heard Michael's screams. Ralph broke into a run, taking the stairs two at a time and crashing through the doorway. To his dismay, he saw Dr. Adams and two of his technicians. One burly man had Michael tucked under his arm, oblivious to the way he kicked and fought.

"What are you doing with my son?"

Dr. Adams smiled. "What are you doing sneaking around here?"

"Sneaking around?" Ralph made himself taller, indignant. "Since when is it sneaking around to check the circuit box when the power was suddenly cut off in my house?"

"You had to bring your son for that?"

"I didn't want to leave him alone."

Michael went on kicking and crying until Dr. Adams gave the signal to put him down. The young boy gazed over at his father, confused. His eyes asked what to do, but Ralph could only give his head a slight shake in response. They'd been caught, and only lies might save them.

"Now that I've straightened things out," Ralph said, "may I take my son home? It's getting late . . ."

The front door opened, and another man entered. He held up two suitcases. Ralph felt his heart sink.

"Found them in the trunk," the man said.

Dr. Adams' eyes widened. "You were going to run away. You traitor! You were going to betray us."

"No, I—"

Adams silenced him with an uppercut to his stomach. Ralph doubled over with a gasp. Before he could react, Adams' other fist came up to his chin. He stumbled back against the wall.

"Traitor! No one leaves the center without permission. No one!"

Lines of red radiated the ice-blue eyes, and Adams' skin turned pale. As he ranted, he unwittingly gave Ralph a chance to catch his breath. Michael's father leapt forward, knocking the doctor to the floor. They rolled across the tiles, punching, kicking. Summoning all his strength, Ralph pushed his hands up against the doctor's jaw and started bending his head backward. Adams had him by the throat, shaking him.

"Stop it!"

No one heard Michael's cry. This must be what the little girl he had heard in his brain meant. His father really was going to get killed.

Unless Michael could do something . . .

He'd made that same little girl burn herself once. He'd made a wooden donkey kick an innocent cat to death. But he'd never controlled an adult. Michael didn't know if he could do it now, after years of failure. But he had to try. Dr. Adams was going to kill his dad.

Michael swung around and looked at the three technicians. They were motionless, as if waiting for Dr. Adams to demand their help. The boy found the smallest one and locked his gaze on the man's face.

Take out your gun. Take out your gun. Take . . .

To his surprise, the man began to reach for his holster.

Shoot Dr. Adams!

Instantaneously, the man raised his gun and pulled the trigger. The shot missed, richocheting off the stone wall and jetting through a window. The fight broke up as both men looked around in horror. The other technicians came forward, leaping at their partner and wrestling him to the ground. Adams leapt to his feet, but Ralph reached up and grabbed him around the knees.

"Run, Michael. Get out of here. Get out!"

Michael stood still for only a split second until his sneakers seemed to take on a life of their own. Then, in the confusion of the fighting grown-ups, he broke into a sprint and disappeared through the front doors. He heard them open up behind him, but he didn't stop to investigate. He just kept running, not knowing where to go, hardly able to see for his tears.

Then he saw Jenny Segal's house. Her bedroom light was still on. Maybe he could hide with her until his dad came. With a quick look over his shoulder to be certain he'd lost his pursuer, he scrambled over the Segals' fence. He crouched down low and pressed himself into the shadows beneath his friend's window. Carefully, his heart pounding, he raised himself up.

Jenny was alone. She was lying on her stomach, knees bent and ankles crossed, as she read a book. Michael tapped on her window.

Jenny's eyebrows went up when she saw him. She rolled off the bed and came to open the window, helping him inside. "What are you doing back here?" she whispered. "You sure do like to take chances."

Michael swallowed hard. "Jenny, something bad's happening. My dad and I were trying to run away, but Dr. Adams caught us."

Jenny shook her head. "Why were you trying to run away? I thought—I thought we were going to make plans."

"I don't know," Michael said. "But Dad said we had to go now. He was going to explain when we got out. But Dr. Adams has him now. He was trying to kill him. Jenny, remember when I told you I thought something was really wrong about this place?"

Jenny nodded.

"Well, I was right," Michael said. "I don't know exactly what it is, but I know we've got to get away, tonight. My dad told me to run and hide. Jenny, do you want to come?"

Jenny hushed him and went to her door. Opening it carefully, she looked down the hall and saw the reflections of TV lights flickering on the wall. She closed the door again.

"Climb back out the window," she said. "I'll get some things together. We can meet by the school. You know, that playhouse?"

"How're you gonna get out?"

"I'll tell my parents I'm walking the dog," Jenny said. "Go on, Michael. I'll meet you in a few minutes."

Michael went to the window, but stopped and turned.

"Tommy oughta be with us," he said. "If something bad is gonna happen . . ."

"Okay," Jenny said. "See if you can get him. We'll all meet at the playhouse."

Michael climbed out the window. The alley behind the Segal house was deserted and dark. Whoever had been chasing him had either given up or gone in another direction. But Michael kept to the shadows as he hurried to Tommy's house. He was not as lucky there as he'd been at Jenny's. Tommy's room was dark, as was the entire house. Michael was about to give up and leave his friend behind when he heard faint voices. Carefully, he walked around to the other side of the house. Tommy and his parents were sitting at a picnic table, illuminated by two glowing citronella candles. Tommy's father had set up a telescope, and they were all star-gazing at the autumn sky.

Michael had to get to his friend. He'd been successful in controlling one adult tonight, if only for a few seconds. Not knowing if he could do it again, he tried. He glared at the back of Mr. Bivers' head, commanding him to get up and go into the house.

Instantly, Tommy's father rose. "I'm thirsty," he said. "I'll bring out some pop."

Without Michael's influence, Tommy's mother also got up.

"Hot chocolate would be better," she said. "I'll make us some."

When the adults were in the house, Michael rushed over to his friend.

"Huh?" Tommy jumped.

"Dr. Adams tried to kill my dad."

"What're you talking about?"

"Something bad is gonna happen and my dad knew it," Michael said. "He told me to run and hide. You know those feelings you've been having. The ones we've all been having. We're right, Tommy. The grown-ups are going to hurt us; and we have to run away."

Tommy looked over at the back door. "How come you're going now?"

"I saw something in my head," Michael said. "And then it really happened. At least, I think it really happened, and—"

"Shut up," Tommy cried. "I believe you. What—what're we going to do?"

"We're going to meet Jenny at the playhouse," Michael said. "Can you come?"

"Sure," Tommy said, excited to be on an adventure.

With no further discussion, the boys ran out of the yard. By the time Tommy's parents returned, he was nowhere in sight.

The three children met as planned, hiding in the playhouse to discuss what had happened.

"I always knew Dr. Adams was a creep," Tommy said.

"I thought he was nice at first," Jenny agreed, "but lately he's been scaring me. Ever since I saw that lady with the brown hair in my mind."

"Some Outsiders are trying to make contact with us," Michael said. "I don't know who they are, and I don't know how they found us. But I do know we gotta get out of this place."

Tommy bent his feet up and fiddled with the laces of his sneakers.

"I know how they found me," he said quietly. "I

called for help. In my head, I mean. Someone must have heard.''

"Maybe it's a trick," Jenny said. "You know what we learned about the Outsiders, how they hate us. Maybe it's a trap.''

Tommy gritted his teeth. "And maybe that stuff about Outsiders is a big lie. I say we find out.''

"We sure can't stay here," Michael agreed.

"How're we going to get out?''

Michael stood up. "Gosh, I forgot something. My dad was trying to turn off the electric fence. Maybe it's still off. If we hurry, we can get out.''

"Someone'll be at the gate for sure," Jenny said.

Michael smiled at her. "Can't you climb?''

Jenny's head bobbed up and down. Picking up the satchel she'd filled with food, she swung it over her shoulder and followed the boys out of the playhouse. The school sat across the street from a long row of barns. Part of the fence ran behind them, hidden from view. Because all the lights along the fence were still out, Michael knew the guard in the watch tower couldn't see them.

"Power's still off," he whispered. "Let's go.''

With one last look to be sure the way was clear, the children scrambled over the fence. It was twelve feet high and the bars were slippery, but they somehow made it over. Jenny's food bag crashed to the ground, cans rattling loudly. All three froze to hear a grown-up's voice.

"Over here! I heard something!''

"Crud," Tommy whispered.

"Let's get going," Michael urged.

They helped Jenny gather up the food. Then, hidden by the darkness of the moonless night, the children started to run.

31

THREE SMALL CHILDREN WALKED ALONG A DESERT road toward distant mountains that reached far, far away from Kate Emerson. Two little boys and a girl: Joey, Chris, and Laura.

"Please come back. I'm your mother. Come home with me."

Only little Joey turned around, waving sadly, pouting. Then his mouth opened soundlessly. A puff of blue-black smoke poured from the small opening. Joey's skin went stark white, patches of black dotting him like a dalmation. Sparks flew from his fingers, and his hair stood on end. Then he collapsed, pulling Chris and Laura down with him. Kate started running, running as fast as she could, never reaching her children . . .

Kate woke from the nightmare with a jolt. She looked frantically around herself, taking in the flowered curtain hanging from a track in the ceiling and the three chrome rails that shimmered in the soft light. She was still in the hospital. What was she doing here when Joey and Chris needed her. She tried to stand up, but gentle, strong hands pressed her back down again. Kate blinked a few times to squeeze the tears from her eyes and focused her gaze on her husband. Danny was standing at the side of the bed, his hands pressed against her shoulders.

"Easy, Kate . . ."

"Oh, Danny," Kate whispered. "Something—something's happened to the boys. And Laura. I saw

Laura and she . . .'' She frowned. "Chris and Joey? What's happened to them?''

"Shh,'' Danny said softly. "I'll explain everything in time. But you have to rest now, Kate. You aren't strong enough.''

Kate frowned at him, the facial gesture sending searing pain through her head. She felt as if her bed were floating on water, rising up and down on slowly moving waves. The lights were too bright in here, and Danny's voice was too loud. No, it wasn't loud enough. She couldn't hear him at all.

What's happening to me?

"It's the medicine, Kate,'' Danny said, trying to reassure her. "They gave you some kind of sedative. The doctor said it'd take hours to wear off, so why don't you close your eyes and go back to sleep?''

"But my children,'' Kate protested. She tried to lift her head from her pillow, but it flopped back down again as if someone had tied a brick to the back of her skull. So tired . . .

"Go to sleep, Kate,'' Danny said.

She closed her eyes and almost instantly began to breathe in the even, slow way of sleep.

Danny waited with her for a few moments, waited to be sure she was really resting and not about to toss around in the throes of another nightmare. It had pained him to hear her calling out the names of their children. His fists had clenched at the thought of Chris and Joey, downstairs in pediatrics, their condition critical.

Someone was going to pay for hurting them.

But thank God they're alive.

Who had said that? he wondered. He couldn't quite remember. The past hours had been chaotic, one moment overlapping another. He vaguely recalled phoning for help, Kate screaming in the background and his mother-in-law numbly trying to lift the boys from the tub. Danny couldn't remember the EMTs arriving, but he could still hear one of them saying with loud relief, "I've got a pulse.''

Who had had a pulse? Chris? Joey?

Were his boys going to make it, or were those bastards going to rob him of his sons, too?

No! He'd never let that happen.

He felt a soft tap on his shoulder and turned to see the nurse.

"Why don't you go on now, Mr. Emerson?" she asked in her soft Irish brogue. "Perhaps you'll be wantin' to see the boys again? Mrs. Emerson will sleep just fine now, I'm sure."

"You'll call me if there's any trouble."

"You know that, sir," the nurse said.

Danny got up and walked from the room, biting his lip. This was all his fault, of course. His unwitting part in Laura's kidnapping—for he now believed that is what had happened—had never even occurred to him until he remembered the name of the place where Kate said Laura was being held: LaMane Center. It had taken a few minutes, but when he realized the implications of that name, a cold chill gripped his heart. LaMane Pharmaceuticals made a fertility drug called Neolamane. Kate's inability to have children had prompted Danny to obtain the drug for her from some friends. Ronald Preminger had insisted it was perfectly safe, and Danny was ready to believe him. Preminger was studying to be a doctor, after all, and Neolamane was available on the market with a prescription.

Riding down the elevator to Pediatrics, Danny was taken back to the day Ronald Preminger had handed him the small brown vial.

"Are you sure this stuff is safe, Ron?" Danny had asked. "I wouldn't want to do anything to hurt Kate."

"It wouldn't be on the market if it wasn't safe, Dan," Ron had insisted. "Look, I went to a lot of trouble to get this. If anyone found out, I'd be thrown out of med school. I'm doing you a real big favor here, Emerson. So, do you want it?"

Danny had stood chewing his lips, thinking of Kate. They'd been married a little over a year and had been trying to have a baby for almost as long. Each time Kate had her period, she'd walk around the house in tears. He couldn't see her go on like that. Her doctor insisted there was nothing to worry about, that they hadn't been trying long enough. But Danny wanted a baby as much as Kate did, and he had no intention of waiting until some specialist decided they were ready for fertility drugs. He'd read about Neolamane and had started asking questions. Eventually, he met the brother of one of his former classmates, Bob Preminger. Ron was in med school, serving his internship. A brief phone conversation resulted in this clandestine meeting, sitting in a restaurant in Ann Arbor.

Preminger sat tapping his spoon against his cup, impatient.

"All right," Danny breathed. "If it's available as a prescription, it must be safe."

He'd taken the drug home and he'd discussed it with Kate, and she'd agreed to try it. Miraculously, her periods stopped. Her doctor confirmed it: she was pregnant! Kate's joy overshadowed the strange stories Danny was beginning to hear about Neolamane, stories of minor deformities. He prayed and prayed the baby would be all right. Laura was perfect when she was born.

It wasn't until she started walking that he realized she wasn't really all right. Just as Kate had reminded him soon after Laura began appearing to her, the child had had the gift of precognition. She would sit babbling in her crib and would look up at Danny with big brown eyes and say, "I tell Grandma, 'Turn off stove!' "

Danny would call his mother and she'd tell him she almost burned a pot of potatoes. There were so many incidents like that, showing Laura's unique talents. Someone else knew of them. Danny wondered who had followed them here all the way from Michigan just to watch Laura grow? Someone who knew the effects of the drug, of course. He'd tried getting through to

Ron Preminger, with no luck. Wherever the bastard was, he knew what had happened to Laura.

Instead of stopping in Pediatrics, Danny went down to the main floor and out to his car. He had to find out just where the LaMane Center was. As soon as he was certain where Laura was, he would hop on a plane and go to her. Maybe those people had been smart enough to kidnap a three-year-old girl and make her parents believe she was dead. But they weren't smart enough to stop her father from getting her back again.

32

BETH KNEW THE POLICE WERE COMING LONG BEFORE Natalie heard the sirens. She saw the squad car in her mind, red light splashing over the stony lawns and brick facades of adobe-style houses. And she knew there was trouble, because she had seen Peter running in the darkness, a look of terror on his face. She'd tried calling out to him, but he hadn't heard her.

It wasn't until she heard the doorbell ring that Beth crawled out from under her grandmother's quilt and walked barefoot to her bedroom door. She heard mumbled voices, sensed questions being asked. Her mother's screams started her running toward the front door.

In the foyer, a red-haired policeman caught her by the arm. His pale-green eyes and the bright scar that ran along his hairline frightened the little girl. But his voice was soothing as he spoke to her. Beth gazed out the open front door, watching her mother being helped into a police car. Why hadn't her mother waited for her? What had happened?

"We're taking your mother to the hospital," the red-headed cop said. "I'm afraid there's been an accident and your father was badly hurt. You can come with me, and I'll take you to see him."

Basic childish instinct, having nothing to do with Beth's unusual talents, set off a warning bell in her mind. But before she could protest, he led her out the door to his own car. They followed the squad car that held her mother for several miles. But at the exit to the highway, the car Beth was in swerved off in a different direction.

"Where are we going?" Beth demanded.

"To see your father," the cop insisted.

"We are not. My mother's not in front of us."

The reflection of his eyes thinned as he looked up at the rearview mirror. Beth leaned back in her seat, her heart pounding. Something was wrong here . . .

Softly, in a voice almost too small to hear, she said, "You're taking me to Peter, aren't you?"

The "cop" shook his head. "No, kid. *You* are going to bring Peter back to *us.*"

33

IN THE WAITING ROOM JUST OUTSIDE THE IC UNIT OF San Felipe Hospital, Lou Vermont paced the floor. He had been waiting for an eternity for permission to speak with Lillian Blair, the only person who might be able to give him a clue as to what happened back at the airport terminal. After checking the ID of the victims, he sent a squad car to the Blair residence, only to find it empty.

"But something doesn't seem right, sir," the young

officer told him over the telephone. "There's food left out on the table, as if they'd been eating, and the television is still on. And none of the doors was locked."

Lou stopped at the window and peered through the vertical blinds at the nearby mountains. It seemed that Oscar, Lillian, and their son-in-law, Stuart, had left in a hurry for the airport. Someone had confronted them there, murdering Stuart Morse and the shop-owner, causing Oscar Blair to have a heart attack and sending his wife into such a state of shock that her doctor refused to let the cop talk to her.

Someone . . .

Lou pounded at the window, making the blinds clap against one another. He heard a heavy sigh and turned to see another woman waiting, her eyes brimming with tears. Lou whispered an apology, and the woman returned her gaze to the door, lost in her own private worries. Lou tried to keep his emotions under control, arguing with himself in the silence of his mind.

Just some*one*? The shop had looked as if a pack of wild dogs had gone at it. The doctor who arrived first said that the marks in the owner's neck were like snake bites, but that there was no trace of venom. Of course not! Who the hell would keep a poisonous snake in a public shop?

But, then, who the hell would bisect a man at the waist as cleanly and efficiently as if a giant scalpel had been used? It was almost as if the window itself had sliced through him. But the window was intact except for the small area where the man had jutted through.

Now, that was another oddity: if a man jumped through a plate-glass window, wouldn't it make sense that his face and arms and upper body would be cut to pieces? Other than the hideous mess of his waist, there wasn't a mark on him.

Grunting, Lou hurried through the open door to the nurses' station. "Is Mrs. Blair available yet?" he demanded.

"Dr. Simeone said—"

"I know what she said," Lou cried. "Don't you people realize there's a murderer on the loose?"

The nurse's eyes thinned. "Our immediate concern is the health of our patients," she said. "Mrs. Blair was in shock when she came in, and I doubt—"

"It's all right, Karen," a woman's voice said.

Devon Simeone walked toward the nurses' station, carrying a silver clipboard. She was barely a head taller than the top of the counter, though her fluffy brown hair added two inches to her height. Lou thought she looked about seventeen years old. But when she turned to him, there was such an air of authority about her that he backed up a step.

"Mrs. Blair wants to speak with you," Dr. Simeone said in a tone that indicated she thought better of the idea. "But I warn you, she's very agitated, and the slightest upset could be very detrimental. You have five minutes, Officer Vermont."

"Thanks," Lou said. He hurried through the heavy swinging doors to Lillian Blair's room. She was sitting up in bed, an IV running from her wrist, looking as pale as someone who'd been sick for months. Lou realized she must have seen everything, watched her son-in-law die and her husband's collapse. He breathed deeply to stay his own eagerness to pursue the matter and approached her as gently as he could.

"Mrs. Blair, I'm Officer Lou Vermont."

"I remember you," Lillian said, her voice small.

"Mrs. Blair . . . ." He took the liberty of sitting on the edge of her bed, taking her hand. There was no nurse in here to scowl at him and his germs, and he had found in his experience that a tactile approach often worked wonders. "Can you tell me what happened? Who hurt you?"

Lillian squeezed his hand. "I—I don't know."

"Were you going somewhere?" Lou asked. "Is that why you were at the airport?"

"No," Lillian said softly. "We were—were trying to remember something."

"What was that?"

Lillian was silent for a long time, staring up at the IV bag that dripped into her vein. What had she been trying to remember? She had gone to the airport with Oscar and Stuart because Stuart wanted her to recall something that had happened there . . .

When?

A picture of her grandson flashed in her mind, Peter Morse at age three.

"I know," she said. "I was retracing steps I took six years ago when I brought my grandson to the same gift shop."

She explained how Peter had come to visit, accompanied by his schoolteacher.

"But they never made it home," she said. "The plane crashed. Oscar and I couldn't clearly remember putting Peter on the airplane, so Stuart thinks something happened to him. He believes Peter never got on that plane. Beth thinks so, too."

Lou shook his head, befuddled.

"You've got me, Mrs. Blair," he said. "Who's Beth? Maybe you'd better start at the beginning."

But the mention of her granddaughter's name had resurrected some of the feisty Lillian Blair that Lou had never met. She jerked her hand away from him and met his gaze with a wild expression.

"Beth," she cried. "My granddaughter. They'll be after her, too. And her mother, my daughter, Natalie. We left them home when we went to the airport. You've got to get to the house. You've got to protect them. If those horrible people get—"

"What people?" Lou interrupted.

"I don't know who they are," Lillian wailed. "But Stuart said they were from that place called the LaMane Center. They're evil, Officer. They'll murder my grandchildren. You have to stop them."

Her words had risen to a shrill cry, bringing Devon Simeone and a nurse running. Lou jumped away from the bed and watched as they administered a sedative, trying to help the frantic woman calm down. Dr. Simeone dismissed him with a hard glance, but Lou had not planned to stay anyway.

Something had happened at the Blair house. Lou hurried down to his squad car and got on the radio to headquarters. They not only had a double murder on their hands, but unless he found that woman and child there would be two more victims.

34

JILL WANTED TO DRIVE UP TO THE GATES OF THE LaMane Center, to barge through them and demand the return of her son. But her training as a scientist slowed her down, making her follow every lead. After reading the paper given to her by Professor Juárez, she understood fully what Jeffrey's colleagues had wanted from her son. Those late-night meetings, the times he had insisted Ryan join his "friends" at their club, his almost-fanatical concern about Ryan's health—they were all indicative of the sick plans Jeff had for their baby boy.

Jill realized that she had been an unwitting human guinea pig, a woman so desperate to have a baby that she'd agreed to try a drug newly introduced to the market. Jill knew that all drugs had years of testing behind them before they appeared at the prescription level, and she had trusted her ob/gyn. In truth, Neolamane had not given her any troubles during pregnancy. Everything was normal, right up to the birth. And then, from the time Ryan was able to crawl, he began to show signs of being different.

Jill could remember him scooting over to the front door every evening, a few minutes before Jeff's car

turned the corner to their home. It was as if the baby
had a built-in clock and knew when his father was
going to arrive. Once Jeff had told a friend a joke, and
the baby had laughed out loud before the grown-ups
did, as if he understood. Then there was the extraordinary part—the stuffed animals that seemed to come
to life, dolls Ryan had made dance by themselves, and
a leather puppy dog with a sewn mouth who began to
bark. Ryan had had the ability to bring inanimate ob-
jects to life.

And Neolamane had given him the power.

Jill ran over the words of the medical report as she
drove back toward the mountains. It hadn't said a word
about psychic abilities, but it did lambast LaMane for
not pulling the drug off the market at the very first
signs of trouble. The trouble these doctors were talking about was physical—minor birth defects like sixth
and seventh toes, bones already fused in adult forma-
tions, missing eyebrows. Nothing life-threatening, but
the writers had said continued use of Neolamane might
very well lead to other, more tragic incidents. The
article had been written eleven years ago, and according to further research, the drug had been removed
from pharmacists' shelves a year later. Which meant
that Jeffrey had given her an illegal drug to help her
conceive.

Jill remembered the cold way Jeff had behaved toward her after Ryan's birth. He'd doted on the child,
panicking at the slightest sniffle, insisting Jill was either nursing too little or too much. Many nights, he
was off at his club, having secret meetings with his
colleagues. Jill knew what the bastards had been up
to, now. They'd realized that, in some cases, Neolamane affected the brain and caused it to develop su-
perpowers. That's why they'd taken Ryan away, killing
Jeff in the process. They'd wanted to study him, like
some specimen under a microscope.

And from the size of the LaMane Center, Jill was certain
there were many other children in the same predicament.

Jill glanced into her rearview mirror, planning to

change lanes. There was a car behind her, and when she crossed over the avenue, it followed her. Her fingers tightened around the steering wheel and her foot depressed the accelerator. That man was following her again.

She exited the main highway. The car behind her followed. At the first opportunity, Jill pulled to the side of the road and pretended to be busy with a map. The car passed her, and she sighed with relief. If the car was following her, the driver didn't have the nerve to make himself obvious by stopping when she did. If she tried, she could lose him again and make it safely back to the mountains without her lookout being discovered.

But as soon as she'd driven two blocks, the same car turned the corner and began following her again from about a half-block distance. Realizing there was no use in driving up to the Sandias now, she looked around for a way out. Then she saw a sign that read OLD TOWN. She decided she'd park her car, pretend to browse through a few stores, and leave the major tourist attraction of Albuquerque as soon as she felt it was safe.

Jill's mind was not so occupied that she missed the quaint charm of Old Town. There was a Spanish feeling everywhere, from the Church of San Felipe de Neri to shops selling everything from turquoise jewelry to rattlesnake eggs. On impulse, Jill went into a store and browsed through the souvenirs. She wanted to buy something for Ryan, something to celebrate their reunion. Jill reached for a set of hand-carved building blocks, each with a design of Mexican origin. Ryan had always loved building blocks . . .

She stopped herself. Somehow, she'd forgotten Ryan was ten years old now. Ten! The shock of seeing the change in him, when her mind was fixed with an image of a three-year-old, might be almost too much to bear. But she'd know Ryan when she saw him. She was sure of that. What would Ryan be interested in now? There would be so much to learn about him. Then she remembered how, even as a little kid, he loved building things. She spotted a kit for a model Conestoga wagon and took it to the sales counter. After paying for it, she walked across the road to the plaza that centered Old Town. She looked around and found no sign of the man who had been following her. Still, she couldn't take a chance. This was so damned frustrating. Every moment that went by was another moment without Ryan.

The aromas wafting from a nearby Mexican restaurant reminded her of how little she'd eaten since that morning. She left the plaza and went to have a late lunch. The restaurant was small, each table set with a terra-cotta candle molded in the shape of a dove. Jill ordered and sat looking out the window. In a few moments, she spotted the man who'd been looking for her. And he was headed straight for the restaurant.

She gazed at him through the wrought-iron gates that surrounded the windows. He stood on the sidewalk for a few moments, as if considering whether or not he would dine here.

Jill set her teeth hard. If he did come in, she'd confront him. She couldn't play the victim forever.

The waitress brought her order. "Are you Jill Sheldon?"

Jill's heart leapt. "Yes—yes I am. How—?"

"There was a message for you," the waitress said. "It was left at the front desk just a few minutes after you came in."

The woman handed her a folded piece of paper.

"Who left it?" Jill asked. "Do you know what he looked like?"

"I'm sorry," the waitress said. "The waiter who took the note just went off-duty."

Jill thanked her and tore open the envelope:

We know you are here. Stay away from the center and Ryan will be safe. You must give up your search, for your efforts will only result in the death of your son. And this time, it won't be a trick.

Jill crumpled up the note. When she looked out the window again, the man was gone.

Suddenly, she had lost her appetite. Asking the waitress to wrap the dinner for her, Jill paid her bill and quickly left the restaurant. Now was the time to get out of here, when her follower was certain she was still eating lunch. Maybe he was watching her right now, but he'd never get to his own car fast enough to catch up to her.

As she left Old Town and turned onto the highway again, Jill realized to her relief that she was right. No one was following her. She made her way back up into the Sandias again, ready to continue her vigil.

Upon arriving at her campsite, Jill hoisted the telescope from the trunk of her car and began to spread the legs of its tripod. Though there hadn't been much to see this morning, she hoped the aging day would bring more activity down in the center. She looked down into the valley, then trained the lens of the telescope in its direction. For a few moments, she gazed through the lens at a woman working in a desert garden. She was removing debris from the blanket of rocks surrounding her cactus plants, bits of feathers and twigs and dust that had rolled into her yard. Momentarily, the woman looked over her shoulder. Slowly, Jill moved the telescope. There was a child, at last! A girl with long, dark hair and a rather plain expression. When she came near to the woman, Jill saw she was as tall as her mother, but bore no resemblance at all to her. Jill wished she could read lips, aching to know what was being said. The telescope revealed two books held tightly in the child's arms.

"School," Jill cried, her voice sending a flutter of birds up out of a nearby juniper.

That was why she hadn't seen any children earlier. They were in school. Was it possible that the LaMane people were actually educating their victims?

"Educating them to do what?" Jill asked, speaking softly.

Jill took her viewing position again and began a

slow survey. Indeed, there were more and more children appearing on the streets. Some alone, some in pairs or clusters, just like normal schoolchildren at the end of a long day of classes. But there was something wrong here . . . Jill immediately saw that none of the children was running, that they moved in an orderly fashion down the main road of the center, branching off onto side streets to approach their homes.

Their homes. Did Ryan think of a house down there as his home? Did he remember at all that there had been another place, a farm in the Midwest? Was there even the vaguest memory of a mother who had loved him dearly?

Something suddenly occurred to her, and she sat back so abruptly that she sent the telescope swinging on the tripod in a wide arc. Ryan had been an active boy, and as talkative as any three-year-old. He wouldn't have just gone off with someone without a fight. The fact that they'd been successful in taking him suggested something so horrible that Jill thought she could feel her flesh icing over. Brainwashing! They must have done something to make Ryan completely forget his home and family. And Jill had no doubt Jeffrey had just handed their son over to these bastards—probably walked away from them, thinking he was home free, unaware they'd booby-trapped his car.

But there was another question, one more on a pile of questions reaching sky high. Witnesses to Jeffrey's accident said they had seen a child in the car. Jill knew now that the child wasn't Ryan. Then who was it?

Or had there ever even been a child at all? Craig Dylan had said the whole investigation was suspicious to him. If only she could have spoken further with him! Everything he'd said had been true. Someone had gone to a lot of trouble to get Ryan. How many people had accepted bribes to look the other way? How many witnesses changed their story about what they saw in Jeffrey's car after unclean money entered their pockets? It was unfathomable to Jill that anyone could be so full of hatred toward an innocent little boy.

She looked up at the sky, fighting angry tears. A silent vow was made under the majestic pines: no matter what it took, she would get Ryan back.

35

JENNY, MICHAEL, AND TOMMY HUDDLED TOGETHER in a small cave, listening to the sounds of shouts and running footsteps. They were hidden by more than the darkness of the alcove. Their own special talents went to work for them now, in a way they never could when each was trapped in the green chair at the clinic.

Tommy rustled bushes to make their pursuers move in certain directions.

Michael woke a sleeping lizard and sent him scurrying, so that the grown-ups would think someone frightened it.

And Jenny, recognizing voices outside, put her mind to picturing exactly where everyone was. But she'd been doing it for several hours now, and she was exhausted. Her head hurt, she was cold and hungry, and she really wanted to go back home. She stretched a little in the darkness, accidentally kicking Michael.

"Hey!"

"Shh!"

Jenny mumbled an apology. "How long do we have to stay here?" she asked in a whisper.

"Until my dad comes to get us," Michael said. "He knows I ran away, so he'll be looking for me."

"Sure, so he can take you back to the center," Tommy grumbled. "Just like those other grown-ups out there."

"Not my dad," Michael insisted. "He was trying

to get me out of that place. He said there was a lot of stuff he had to tell me, but before he could, Dr. Adams got him.''

Jenny shivered. She could just barely make out the outlines of the boys' faces. There was an odd shape behind Michael's head, and it took her a moment to realize he was using his backpack like a pillow.

"Maybe Dr. Adams locked him up," she suggested worriedly. "Maybe he can't come to us. You said they were really fighting.''

"My dad's strong," Michael insisted, though there was a hint of doubt in his voice. "He can get out of anything. And he'll come for us. I know he will.''

"But he doesn't know where we are," Jenny said.

There was a long silence, almost heavy enough to mask the sounds outside—a coyote howling, wind blowing, human shouts.

"Did you try calling him with your mind?" Jenny finally asked.

Michael nodded, the movement of his head making the backpack rustle. "He didn't answer me," he said. "I don't know why. I never called him like that before, so maybe he can't answer me. I mean, not like that lady with the brown hair always answered you.''

"I wish she was here now," Jenny said. "I'm sure she'd help us.''

"She is an Outsider," Tommy pointed out.

"Big deal," Michael cried. The other two shushed him in unison. He whispered, "So, what's an Outsider? Something Dr. Adams made up. We know the guy's a creep, so why should we believe anything he said to us? Jenny, even if I can't find my dad, maybe you can get that lady. Maybe she can help us.''

"I don't know—"

"We sure can't stay here forever," Tommy insisted. "Listen, they're moving farther away. I say we make a run for it. Head through the mountains and head for the city.''

"Albuquerque," Michael said. "My dad's been there. I think that's where we were go—"

Unexpectedly, the reality of what was happening hit the little boy full force. His voice cracked and soft squeals filled the darkness.

Jenny put her arms around him. "It's okay, Michael," she said. "We'll see your dad again. As soon as we can figure out what's going on at the center, we'll find a way to contact him. I'll picture him in my mind and tell you where he is."

Michael shivered in her arms.

"Why haven't you done it yet?" Tommy demanded. "That'd be a good idea."

"I did," Jenny said softly.

Michael pulled away from her. The wall of the cave felt cold as he pressed his back against it.

"You didn't tell me."

"I—I didn't see anything," Jenny answered. "I tried to picture him, but I could see only darkness. I don't know what that means, Michael."

"I do," Tommy said. He felt a push in the darkness.

"No," Michael snapped. "My daddy's okay. I know he is."

"Well, look," Tommy said, "whatever's happening, we gotta get out of here. I'll see if the coast is clear, then we run for that bunch of cactus and yucca plants over there. See them?"

Jenny and Michael said they did. Tommy crawled to the cave's opening and peered out. The moonlight washed yellow-white over the bare land, casting sharp-lined shadows of cactus and rock. There wasn't a sign of the grown-ups.

"They've gone on to someplace else," he whispered. "Come on!"

In a flash, the children were running across the brightly lit ground, not letting themselves think how vulnerable they were. They grouped behind a huge boulder to catch their breath and to listen with both ears and minds.

Jenny pictured one of the grown-ups down at the roadside. She gasped.

"What?" Tommy hissed.

"My mother," she said. "My mother's in the search party. Why?"

" 'Cause she's your mother, dummy," Tommy said.

Jenny shook her head. "No. There's something bad there, I can feel it. She's angry. Not worried about me, angry!" Jenny shuddered, making a disgusted face and rubbing quickly at her upper arms. "I—I don't like what my mind is telling me about her. I don't understand it."

"No time to figure it out," Michael said. "Let's go."

Michael was first to move out from behind the boulder. Jenny went next, all the while praying her mother was out to help, not harm her. Somehow, she couldn't believe it. Thoughts of her mother's anger frightened her, and as she ran, she searched her mind for her father's presence. He wasn't there.

Both children reached the cactus grove and turned to look for Tommy. But their friend was still back at the boulder, frozen. Jenny grabbed Michael's arm and squeezed it tightly, pointing.

Michael was being held at bay by one of the center's guard dogs. The hunkering rottweiler paced slowly back and forth, blocking Tommy's path to his friends. A deep growl started in the animal's barrel chest, so soft it could hardly be heard above the wind.

With all his might, Michael tried to send a thought message to his friend.

Kill it, Tommy! You've got to kill it, before it barks. If the grown-ups hear. . . .

Kill it, Tommy!

The little boy stood solid, unmoving, his eyes fixed on the snarling beast. Kill it? Michael sounded just like the grown-ups in the lab, who made him do things he didn't want to do. He didn't want to kill the dog. He didn't want to hurt anyone. He wanted . . . he wanted . . .

He wanted his mother. His eyes squeezed shut and an image came to his mind. Not of the woman he knew

as his mother, strangely, but of another woman: a
pretty one with red-brown hair and green eyes and a
heavy plaid coat. She was standing in front of him—
no, kneeling. She was kneeling, but he was looking
right into her eyes, as if he were very small. He wanted
her.

Who was she?

The dog let out one bark.

"Tommy!"

Tommy's eyes snapped open. Without another moment's thought, he glared hard at the dog. The animal's next bark was cut in half. The broad body jerked
left, then right, then clunked to the ground. It began
to slither across the dirt, leaving a trail of drool and
wild scratches where its toes clawed the ground. It
started to hiss, snakelike, tongue darting in and out of
its mouth.

Tommy rounded it on cardboard legs, racing toward
his friend. He hadn't killed the dog, but with his powers he had made it behave like a slow-moving snake.

36

THE FIRST THINGS RALPH COLPAN WAS AWARE OF
were the taste of blood on a badly swollen lower lip
and a thumping pain behind his left eye. Slowly, sniffling through a broken nose, he got onto his hands and
knees. He groped around in the darkness for some
sense of where he was. Because he had designed the
building himself, Ralph immediately recognized the
room behind the examination area. It was the one
where "victims" were placed, at whom the children
were instructed to direct their powers.

Carefully, he got to his feet, reaching out for support. His hand touched the cold glass of the window. It was a one-way mirror through which the children could be observed. Ralph's head felt like a rock, his forehead falling heavily against the glass. They'd drugged him after the beating, he knew. He remembered the needle . . .

The light came on in the examination room. Ralph's head jerked up so quickly that screaming pain shot through it and he was forced to steady himself against the mirror. Blood stained the cold glass.

Adams had returned. He was dragging a red-haired kid by the back of his neck.

"Mich—ael," Ralph croaked.

But when the child looked up, he saw that it wasn't Michael at all. It could have been Michael, with shorter hair and ten pounds skinnier. It could have been Michael . . . if it hadn't been a girl.

Michael's twin.

Ralph's mouth dropped as far open as his injuries would allow. He tried to call out, but the drug was still too much a captor to let him. He realized, somewhere in the fog he was in, that Adams had never expected him to wake up so soon.

The speaker. He had to hear what the little girl was saying. The buttons on the control panel were like colorful tropical fish, swimming in every direction. By sheer will he poked his finger at a black one. Static filled the darkened room, then a child's voice.

"You'd better let me go, mister. My daddy'll put you in jail. All of you."

Dr. Adams laughed. "Your daddy isn't going to do anything to anyone, little girl. Dead people don't cause trouble."

"No," Beth cried. "You're a liar. And when my mom sees I'm not at the police station . . ."

"Oh, but that's another mistake. Elizabeth," Dr. Adams said.

Elizabeth, Ralph thought. Her name is Elizabeth. What's Michael's real name?

"Your mother isn't at the police station. We took her for a little ride, even gave her something to calm her down. But we can kill her, Elizabeth. We can kill her as easily as we killed your father and grandfather."

Beth's lower lip began to quiver.

"You—you didn't kill them!"

"Oh, I'm afraid we did," Adams said.

Ralph had never noticed it before, but there was something maniacal about the man. Not just mesmerizing, as he'd been when Ralph first met him, but downright evil.

"But you can save your mother, Elizabeth," Adams said. "You can save her, and Peter, too."

Peter! That's my son's real name.

"Just call him back here, Elizabeth," Adams ordered. "Use your telepathic powers and tell him you're being held prisoner. He'll come to you."

Beth glared at him. "I won't do it. You go to hell, you jerk."

The slap was so hard that even Ralph stumbled. Beth gaped at her captor, unbelieving. Then she burst into tears, wailing so loudly that Ralph turned down the speaker's volume. If only there were a way out of this room . . . If only he could get to the little girl without being seen . . . Adams' talk had given him hope, because he realized now that Michael had somehow gotten away. He could use this child's help.

Adams' hand went up again. "Stop that confounded crying."

Beth wailed more loudly.

"Damn you," Adams screamed.

The door swung open and one of the technicians popped his head in.

"What do you want?" Dr. Adams demanded.

"Sorry to interrupt, sir," the man said. "But the mother's waking up. I thought you should know."

Adams waved an impatient hand to dismiss him. He turned and poked Beth's chest with his finger. "I'll be back," he said. "And if you want to get out of here

alive, you'll do as you're told. If I can't get Peter back,
I'll kill him. No one screws up my operations. No
one!" He left the room.

Beth sat in the big green chair, crying softly. Anger
at the child's mistreatment and an overwhelming desire to get to his son sent adrenaline through Ralph's
body, which counteracted the drugs. He lifted his fist
and began to pound on the glass. A look of confusion
passed over Beth's face as she tried to find the source
of the knocking. She looked directly at Ralph, seeing
only her reflection.

With a quick look at the door, she got out of the
seat and walked toward the mirror. Pressing her cheek
against the glass, she called, "Is someone there?"

"Unlock the door," Ralph cried.

The twisted remains of his mouth and the barrier of
glass made it impossible to understand him.

"What?"

"Op-en door!"

Beth hurried toward the door. She twisted the lock
and pulled it open. When Ralph stumbled into the
room, the child stopped a gasp with both hands.

"Who—who—"

"No t-time," Ralph whispered, his swollen mouth
struggling with the words. "I know how to get outta
here. We can find M-Michael together."

"Find who?"

"Peter," Ralph corrected himself. "I—I call him
Michael. He's my son."

"Peter's my brother," Beth said, staring round-eyed
at this bloody, battered stranger.

"I rec'nized you," Ralph said. "I'd know that red
hair anywhere." He looked toward the door; Lincoln
Adams could appear at any moment.

"No time to talk. We can crawl through the air-
conditioning ducts."

"How will we know where to go?" Beth asked,
frightened by the idea of being caught in some dark
hole.

"You follow me," Ralph said. "I designed this

building. I know ev'ry twist and turn. I'll get you outta here, I promise.''

37

JILL TRIED TO FORCE THE ZIPPER OF HER JACKET FUR-ther closed than its teeth would allow, shivering in the icy darkness. The fire in the camp stove offered just a little warmth. She had set it up near the telescope, and now the mix of heat and cold kept frosting up the lenses. For what seemed like the hundredth time, Jill wiped away condensation and peered through the eye-piece.

She had hoped to get a good look at the center, but she had never expected anything as clear as this. It seemed as if every street, porch, and flood light was on. The whole thing had the effect of a prison yard, completely devoid of shadows.

But why had she expected anything different? Wasn't LaMane Center, in reality, a prison?

A short while earlier, she had seen a man running down the middle of one of the roads. She'd watched as he stopped and turned, beckoning someone else to follow. The two men turned a corner and disappeared from her line of view. Then she saw a woman and another man hurrying in the same direction. It seemed they were looking for someone. Jill's notebook, illu-minated by the light of the fire now, held an entry at six-thirty P.M., her last sighting of anyone in the streets until the four people she'd spotted half an hour ago.

8:10 P.M.: after nearly two hours, signs of life. One man running, then another. What are they running af-ter? Or from? Or are they chasing someone?

Her pen was still open, waiting for the next entry.
But it was nearly nine o'clock now and she hadn't seen
another soul. Shivering, Jill sank back and crossed her
legs. She picked up her mug of coffee and cradled it
in her gloved hands. She wondered if this whole
damned thing wasn't futile. Hours peering through the
telescope had revealed only two children, both of them
girls. Jill still had no doubt that Ryan was down there
somewhere. But when she saw how tightly locked up
everything was in the center, she began to wonder how
easy it would be to just walk right in and take Ryan
home with her.

But she'd do it, she was certain. She hadn't come
this far to give up, and . . .

A fluttering in the bushes. Jill cocked her head and
listened. Crunch, crunch, crunch. Something walking.

"Deer," Jill whispered.

She wasn't certain if deer came up this high in the
mountains. Zoology hadn't been one of the sciences
she'd studied back at Michigan State.

Crunch, crunch, crunch . . .

Jill put her mug down and slowly got to her feet.
Someone was out there, someone moving slowly toward her. She thought of the man in the hotel bathroom, of Deliah's murder, of Craig Dylan in his
wheelchair.

She'd been smart enough to buy camping equipment
and a telescope. Why the hell hadn't she been smart
enough to arm herself? Those ravines she'd passed on
the way up were deep and dark enough to hide a body
forever.

Crunch, crunch . . .

"Who's there?"

The scream came from Jill before she could stop it,
an involuntary scream in anger. She looked around
herself quickly, searching for a branch or rock. Her
eyes locked on the telescope and she quickly un-
screwed it from its tripod. She held it up, ready to
strike the dark shadow that was emerging from the
nearby road. It swung down, skinning only the edge

of the silhouette. When he came into view, she saw to her horror that it was the man in the dark glasses.

"Christ Almighty," a man's voice shouted. "Lady, don't!"

Overcome by fear and exhaustion, Jill didn't wait for him to finish. She swung the telescope again, the heavy instrument hitting the man across the shoulder. He stumbled back, his glasses falling off to reveal wide, terrified eyes. For a split second, he seemed frozen against the starry sky, arms and legs flailing. And then he was gone, nothing left of him but a long, horrible scream.

Jill let the telescope drop and slowly walked toward the edge of the cliff. Numb, she searched the shadows of scrub brush and cactus below. She was too shocked to think of using her telescope.

"Oh, my God . . ."

Her words were a choked whisper, barely louder than the wind. And the wind seemed to answer her, stirring up icily, rushing at her face as if to slap her. The cold air shocked her back to her senses, and the reality of what had just happened struck her like a brick.

Moving rapidly, she worked her way down the steep slope. "Let him be alive," she cried. "I didn't mean to kill him." Desperately, she searched for signs of a body. By the time she found him, her face was soaked with tears. If he was dead, that made her a murderess.

And if he was alive, you'd probably be the one who was lying down here.

Jill ignored the practical side of her brain. Carefully, she knelt beside the body. By the unnatural twist of its head she knew the man couldn't harm her again. Slowly, she reached out and turned him over. His face was a frozen mask of horror, eyes and mouth opened wide. It was a young face.

"Oh, dear Lord," Jill whimpered. "He can't be more than twenty. Those bastards used another kid to go after me."

An idea came to her, and without forethought she

began to go through the young man's pockets. At last she found what she was searching for—evidence this kid was connected with the LaMane Center. Though he was a perfect stranger, he carried a picture in his wallet of Ryan and her. It had been taken when Ryan was a baby. Someone had given him this to help identify her.

So he could kill you, Jill . . .

That was right. It was exactly what he had intended to do, what he'd been paid for, judging by the five hundred dollars she found in his wallet. His driver's license identified him as Wilson Barnes, a resident of Albuquerque. There was no other information on him.

Jill tried to calm herself down, but found it impossible with those eyes staring sightlessly at the stars. She turned away, her fists clenching and unclenching. The mix of fear, anger, and horror was almost too much to take. She breathed deeply, forcing herself to deal with the situation. Somehow, she had to let the people at LaMane think Barnes succeeded in killing her. But how? She could fake a phone call, but they'd know it wasn't the young man's voice. But if he didn't check in, they'd think that he'd either taken off with his pay or that she'd gotten to him first. She decided she'd take the chance and make the call. There were a lot of other things to do, but first . . .

Jill turned back to the body and stuffed the wallet in Barnes' pocket, including the money. She'd killed this man by accident, but she wasn't a thief. Still, she was grateful for the gloves she wore. There would be no prints. It was doubtful much of an investigation would be made anyway. Someone would think he'd fallen from the cliff by accident.

Washed by a calm that came from shock rather than acceptance, Jill climbed back up the hill to her campsite, wanting nothing more than to get the hell out of there.

38

FOR A LONG TIME, DANNY EMERSON WAITED OUTSIDE the ivy-covered brick building. He sat in a rented car picked up when he'd landed a little over an hour ago in Detroit. He'd moved quickly from the airport, unburdened by luggage, and headed north of the city toward the suburb of Wheaton. Though it had been several years since he'd been to his hometown, he could have driven the streets blindfolded. The energy that had begun to smolder back at the hospital was burning furiously now, and he gripped the steering wheel tightly to steady himself.

He recalled the one and only time he'd ever been inside that building, a small colonial on the edge of the campus grounds. It was the night he acquired his prescription of Neolamane from Ronald Preminger. Now, seven years later, he hoped to find Preminger again. No matter what it took, he'd have the truth about Laura's whereabouts before he returned to Massachusetts.

He watched as younger men walked in and out of the building, some dressed in hospital whites and burdened with fat textbooks. Preminger was a full-fledged doctor now, but a phone call to the clubhouse confirmed that he still came here several nights a week to unwind.

At last, the vigil paid off. Danny's heart started thumping inside his barrel chest when he saw the familiar face. Preminger had a touch of premature gray around his temples, but he was still as fit as he'd been years ago. Danny watched as the doctor walked up the steps of the building, disappearing through the big white door. Then he got out of the car and followed him inside.

He was stopped by an armed security guard.

"I'm here to see Dr. Preminger," Danny said, glaring at the old man.

"Dr. Preminger just came by and didn't say anything about a visitor," the guard said, eyeing him suspiciously.

"He's not expecting me," Danny said. "But he'll see me. Tell him Danny Emerson is here."

The old guard shrugged, then turned his back to Danny and picked up a phone. He turned back a moment later.

"Dr. Preminger says he doesn't know—"

Danny never could have explained where his next move came from, for, despite his size, he was a gentle man by nature. But he suddenly swung out and knocked the old man to the ground. For a moment, he was so stunned by the action that he only stared at his victim. But when he realized the old man was okay, that he'd only had the wind knocked out of him, Danny rushed by him and down the hall behind the foyer. Looking into one room after another, he finally found Ronald Preminger hurriedly shoving papers into a briefcase.

"Got plans?" he asked.

"I'm going to—" Preminger's mouth dropped open at the sight of his old acquaintance. "How did you get in here?" he demanded.

Danny stepped forward, and with one shove from his big hand he pushed Preminger into a chair. "I will ask the questions," he said, his tone dark. "And you will answer them."

"I'm going to call the—"

Danny stopped him, his grip like a vise. "You aren't going to call anyone," Danny said. "What good would it do, Preminger? Once I told the police you kidnapped my daughter, they'd have your ass in jail so fast your tailbone would bend."

Preminger laughed. "Is that a threat? Don't bother.

Who do you think the police would believe, a doctor with a reputation like mine, or some weirdo who doesn't even live in Wheaton?''

Danny didn't waste another moment. ''Where the hell is my daughter?''

''She's dead.''

''She's alive, and you know where she is,'' Danny said. ''And if you want to walk out of this room in one piece, you'll tell me.''

''She's dead,'' Preminger said again. ''They killed her.''

''Who?'' Danny pressed, refusing to be taken in by Preminger's cruel words. ''The LaMane people? I don't think so. Laura was too valuable a prize. You see, I figured out why they took her, Ron. That stuff you gave me to help Kate conceive had a bizarre side effect. My daughter can see into the near future, Ron. And she can read people's minds and talk to spirits. Neolamane did that to her. It turned her into a freak.''

''You're crazy,'' Ronald hissed, though his face had gone several shades paler during Danny's tirade.

''I may be just that,'' Danny said. ''But you people are downright sick. Now, are you going to tell me where to find my little girl or am I going to show you just how crazy a father can get?''

Preminger stared up at the former football player, having no difficulty imagining what those massive hands could do to him. But worse was the thought of being caught by his superiors, the higher-ups in a long chain of deceptive, evil characters. When they'd thought Ken Safton might reveal too much, they'd murdered him. Preminger realized he was stuck between a rock and a hard place. Death at the hands of the people who'd been paying him to keep his mouth shut, or something far worse from an innocent child's loving father. The fire in Danny Emerson's eyes was almost supernatural, so full of hate at that moment that there was no telling what he'd do.

''Christ,'' Preminger choked. ''You're as bad as that Sheldon woman.''

"Sheldon?" Danny asked. He shook his head a little. "Jill Sheldon, right? I remember now. She was trying to get pregnant, too, about the same time as my Kate. She and Kate used to comfort each other, but then Kate got pregnant and we moved away. You gave that stuff to Sheldon's wife, too? Did he know what you were up to?"

"Jeff was much more cooperative than you've been," Preminger said. "I almost regretted he had to be destroyed. But we do what we have to do, Dan. No matter what you learn from me, you're a dead man. You know that, don't you?"

"If I die," Danny said grimly, "I'll take you with me, but not before I learn what I came here to learn." He took a menacing step closer to his captive. "I'm tired of talking . . ."

39

IN THE CLOSE QUARTERS OF THE DARK AIR SHAFTS, Ralph Colpan's wheezing sounded like a struggling car engine. Beth crawled before him, praying each time they passed a vent that no one would hear them in here. He had not said a word since he helped her inside and pulled the vent cover closed behind them. She was full of questions, but the fact that these shafts could carry her voice easily to any given room in the building made Beth bite her tongue to keep silent.

If only the man behind her could stop breathing like that . . .

Someone had hurt him real bad, she knew. Maybe that creepy guy with the light-blue eyes. Ralph got hurt because he was trying to stop that man from doing something terrible. He had said Peter was his son. No, he called him Michael. Beth didn't know why her brother had been with this man, or why Ralph insisted he was Peter's father. But something made her believe he would not hurt her, and her desperation to find anyone willing to help kept her wariness in check.

Every once in a while, Ralph would tap her on the ankle, and he'd stop to catch his breath. Moving through the shafts was a tight-enough squeeze for a ten-year-old girl. Beth couldn't imagine how a grown-up was managing to do it. Especially a grown-up who was all beaten up.

Beth felt as if she'd been crawling on her stomach for hours, though in reality she had only been moving a few minutes. She came to a dead end and felt a turn to the left. It was the first time she dared to speak.

"There's a turn here," she whispered, her voice unusually loud. Only the presence of Ralph's body kept it from bouncing down the shaft.

"Okay," Ralph said. "We're almost there."

"Where are we going?"

"A lab at the back of the building," Ralph said. "There's a way out. Once we get away from here, we'll get away from the center and go for help."

"But what about my mother?" Beth asked. "That man said she's here."

"And he said she was sedated," Ralph pointed out. "We can't risk looking for her."

Beth started to whimper.

"But I want my mother," she cried.

"I know, I know," Ralph soothed, patting her awkwardly on the back of her calf. "But we can't help her now. We have to get out of here first. You've come this far, Beth. Can you make it farther?"

"Are they gonna kill us?"

"Not if I can help it," Ralph growled.

Beth was silent and unmoving for a few moments. Then she asked, "Why did you say Peter was your son?"

"That's a long story, Beth," Ralph answered. "We don't have time for it now. Ready to go on again?"

"Okay," Beth said softly.

She turned the dark corner and started making her way along the new path. Whenever light shone through a vent, Ralph would tap her ankle and she'd stop to listen. Now, she felt his signal and paused about three feet back from the next beam of light.

She recognized Dr. Adams' voice at once and backed up another foot, nearly kicking Ralph in his injured face. He grabbed hold of her ankle to steady her. Silently, they listened.

"No one sleeps until those three are brought back," Adams was yelling. "I don't care if we have to wake up the whole damned center. How in the hell three children can escape from two dozen—"

"I have a suggestion," a woman said. Ralph recognized Alice Segal's voice, cold and calculated. He had always hated that woman, with her probing eyes and grim expression. Unlike Ralph, Alice Segal knew exactly what she was getting when Jennifer was given to her years ago. She didn't love that little girl the way Ralph loved Michael. She saw Jenny as a lab specimen, part of a horrible, grand experiment.

"Why not employ some of the telepathic children?" Alice said. "Surely they could find Jennifer and the boys quickly enough."

So, Michael isn't alone, Ralph thought.

"Get on it, then," Dr. Adams said. "I'm going back to the sister. If anyone can lure Michael Colpan back here, it's her."

In the dark, Beth shook her head. A few moments later, the light from the vent was cut off, and they knew it was safe to go on.

"He'll be in the room in a minute," Ralph said. "And he'll be looking for us then."

"Will he think about the vent?" Beth asked as she crawled forward.

"Not right away," Ralph told her. "I fixed the door

lock to make it seem we broke out. We'll be free before he thinks to look here."

"God, I hope so," Beth whispered.

40

THE GROWN-UPS WERE GETTING CLOSER. THE THREE children knew it, not only by their gifts but by the way sleeping birds would suddenly shoot up into the darkness, or by the pounding hooves of startled deer. Even in the moonlight, junipers and pines fashioned dark shadows that slowed their progress. Worse than that, none of them had any idea where they were going. They'd been running for nearly three hours now, and all three were exhausted.

"Please, Tommy," Jenny said, since Tommy had taken the lead after his confrontation with the dog. "Can't we hide and rest? It's so cold."

"We have to move as far as we can before daylight," Tommy insisted. "They're right behind us, Jenny. You know that. And you know what's gonna happen if they catch us."

Michael shook his head. "But my dad would never let—"

"I wouldn't count on your dad doing anything," Tommy said coldly, shooting Michael an angry look. "None of us was able to reach his mind. Come on, stop being scared. It was your idea to run away, so let's run."

They hadn't walked another ten yards when Jenny suddenly stopped, bringing her hands up to her face. She moaned softly, standing like that for a few moments. Michael and Tommy watched her in bewilder-

ment, teeth chattering loudly. Then she said firmly,
"No!"

"What's going on, Jenny?" Michael asked.

"Voices," Jenny replied, bringing her hands away
from her face. "There are voices in my head."

"That lady with the brown hair?" Tommy suggested.

"No," Jenny said. "I'm not sure who . . ." She
gasped, a thick cloud forming in front of her mouth.
"Bambi," she cried. "And some other children. The
grown-ups are making them find out where we are.
Michael, Tommy, they'll be able to catch us if the
other kids help."

"Then shut off your mind," Tommy ordered.
"Don't let them in."

"Don't be so stupid," Jenny snapped. "I don't
know how to do that."

"We're doomed," Michael groaned. He cocked his
head. "You hear that? More dogs! And I hear grown-
up voices. They can't be that far away."

"What're we gonna do?" Jenny asked. She thought
of her mother, and how much anger and hate she felt
when she had sensed the woman as part of the search
team. How could a mother hate her child so much?
She did not want to confront Alice.

"We're gonna move faster," Tommy said. "Maybe
they have kids working against us, but our powers are
pretty strong, too. Jenny, maybe you are right. Maybe
we should find another cave to hide in. But instead
of resting, we'll figure out a way to fight back. We'll
concentrate on pushing Bambi's thoughts someplace
else."

Michael nodded eagerly. "Trick 'em. I get it,
Tommy. We'll make them go someplace else."

"Will it work?" Jenny asked.

"I don't know," Tommy said. "But we'll try. Let's
get going, okay?"

Silent again, they pressed forward, ducking through
low-hanging pine branches and between crevices
where no adult could possibly maneuver. In a short

time, they found another cave. The sight of bones at the entrance made them stop, and Michael whispered to Tommy, "Can you handle a bear or a mountain lion?"

"I don't know," Tommy whispered back. He peered into the darkness. "Can either one of you guys sense if there's something in there?"

Jenny and Michael stared at the cave opening for a few moments. Then they turned and said in unison, "It's empty."

Thus informed, Tommy led the way into the blackness. They groped along the cold wall, turning into countless passageways, until they saw a shaft of moonlight beaming from the cave roof up ahead. It illuminated a good-size room.

And a huge, hunkering bear.

Tommy signaled to his friends to be quiet, but Jenny let out a cry of dismay. The bear turned, eyed them for a split second, then turned and climbed up on a rock shelf. It roared, lumbering around the cave in search of a way out. Frightened, trapped, it turned from flight to fight instinct. It started toward the children . . .

"Tommy, do something!"

. . . reared up on its hind legs . . .

"I can't. I'm too scared."

Jenny screamed, backing away. In the darkness behind her, she couldn't find her way out of the cave. She heard the boys crying out behind her, heard the bear's deafening growls.

"Tommmeeeeee!" Michael's scream made something snap in Tommy's mind. He had never tried using his powers to their fullest, but in a moment of sheer panic, when his own self-defense mechanisms set in, he imagined the bear to be a cloud of dust.

The great animal's roar stopped halfway in its throat, because suddenly there was no throat to emit the sound. There was no bear. In its place stood a thick brown cloud, smelling strongly of bear for a moment,

then of fish, then honey, then blood. Then, nothing
but the smell of a dirt cave. The cloud was gone, too.

Michael turned to Tommy, ready to congratulate
him. But his friend had collapsed to the ground and
was curled up like a newborn baby. Tears streamed
from Tommy's dirt-smudged face, and a strange keen-
ing noise came from behind his clenched teeth.

"Tommy, what's wrong?" Michael looked behind
himself for Jenny, but the girl wasn't there. Forgetting
her for a moment, he sank to his knees and put a hand
on Tommy's arm.

"Tommy, you okay? You saved us, you know."

"I—I never killed anything," Tommy said. "It
hurts. My head, my whole body, everything hurts."

"Oh, geez," Michael whispered, not knowing what
to do. "Maybe Jenny's got something in her bag." He
jumped to his feet and ran to the dark passageway,
calling Jenny's name.

Trapped by the blackness, Jenny hadn't gone very
far, and she came immediately. When she saw that the
bear was gone, she looked at Michael questioningly.

"Tommy turned it into a dust cloud," Michael said.
"But it hurt him really bad to do it. I guess none of
us knows how much power we really have."

Tommy moaned all the more loudly.

"Maybe a cold drink," Jenny suggested. "And rest.
I don't care what you say, Tommy. We can't get away
from the center if we're worn out. And you can't go a
step farther."

She opened her bag and pulled out one of the drink
boxes she'd stolen from her parents' refrigerator. Un-
wrapping the straw, she stabbed it into the little silver
circle at the box top and handed it to Tommy. It wasn't
medication, but the juice was refreshing. Tommy realized his friends were right. They were exhausted—
and, Tommy suddenly noticed, absolutely famished.

"Have you got any food in that bag?" he asked
Jenny.

"Sure I do," Jenny said. "A couple of apples, some
raisins, some cheese slices."

Tommy managed to sit up. "Gimme a piece of cheese."

The boy ate the small orange square as if he were half-starved. Jenny turned to offer some to Michael.

"That's okay," Michael said. "I have a candy bar in my backpack."

"A candy bar," Jenny snorted. "That isn't nutritious."

Michael shrugged, not really caring about nutrition at this point. They didn't even know if they'd ever leave this cave alive. He unbuckled the straps of his backpack and rummaged through his clothes for the candy bar. Instead, he found the file folder his father had asked him to pack at the last minute.

"What's that?" Tommy asked.

"I don't know," Michael said, opening it. "My father gave it to me." He started reading, turning so that the shaft of moonlight gave him the best illumination. Once in a while, Jenny or Tommy would interrupt him, but he'd hush them irritably. By the time he'd finished with the papers, tears were streaming down his cheeks.

"Michael?" Jenny asked very softly.

Suddenly, Michael pulled back his arm and thrust the folder forward with all his might. Papers scattered everywhere.

"They lied to us," Michael cried. "My dad, my mom, your parents, Dr. Adams, they all lied." He threw himself flat on the ground and began to pound the dirt, sobbing so uncontrollably that neither Tommy nor Jenny could get through to him. They moved nearer each other, hugging against the cold and the fear that Michael had discovered something very, very sinister.

41

DANNY CAUGHT THE LAST POSSIBLE FLIGHT FROM DE-
troit to Boston. Within an hour, he had arrived home.
The house seemed so cold now, so full of Kate and
the children that every room reminded him that his
beloved family was not there. He picked up one of
Joey's stuffed animals and clutched it tightly. Blood
had congealed on the knuckles of both hands, some of
it his own, some of it Ronald Preminger's.

Danny let the animal drop and left his sons' room.
A quick stop in the bathroom to freshen up after his
long trip, and he was on his way out again. He knew
that visiting hours had been over long ago and that
he'd have to sneak into Kate's room. He knew exactly
where Laura was now, and Kate was the only one who
could communicate with their daughter.

When he reached the hospital, he found a parking
space in the almost-empty lot. Gull's Flight was such
a small town that there was no hope of the reception
area being crowded enough for him to slip by unnoticed. But miracles do happen, and by some chance
tonight there were five people standing in front of the
desk: two very pregnant women, one leaning against
her husband with her eyes closed, the other standing
between what seemed to be her mother and sister.
While the receptionist busied herself with signing them
in, Danny hurried toward the elevator banks and up to
Kate's floor. He wasn't certain how he'd get by that
nurses' station, but luck was still with him, and at the
moment it was empty. Quickly, he went to Kate's

238

room, thanking God for the additional luck that she didn't have a roommate.

She was sleeping, but Danny could tell by her pained expression that there was no peace in that sleep. Did she dream of Laura? Or was she thinking of their two boys, sleeping downstairs in Pediatrics, waiting for the results of tests done on them? Did nightmares tell her that she would lose her sons the way she lost her daughter?

But we didn't lose our daughter, Kate. She's alive.

Gently, he kissed her on the mouth. She stirred, frowned, and wriggled deeper into her pillow.

"Kate?"

Danny's whisper brought a shuddering sigh from her. A moment later, she opened her eyes. Recognition opened them even wider and she sat up abruptly.

"Danny, what are you doing here? It must be past midnight! Oh, my God, it's the boys, isn't it? I was dreaming that they were with Laura, running away from me. What happened to them?"

"Shh," Danny hissed. "You'll bring the nurses running. The boys are fine, Kate. Well, I mean that I haven't heard anything bad. But I've got some news for you."

Kate pressed a button, bringing the back end of her mattress up to a comfortable position. "News?" she echoed. "Is that why you didn't come during visiting hours? Where were you, Danny?"

"Wheaton," Danny replied simply.

Kate opened her mouth to question him, but he hushed her with a finger placed to her lips. "I went to see Ronald Preminger," Danny said. "I thought he might know something of what happened to Laura. After all, he was the one who gave me the Neolamane for you."

"Neolamane," Kate said. She nodded, remembering. "We called it a miracle, didn't we, Danny? Is that what happened to Laura? Did that drug do something to her?"

Danny nodded, surprised at the perception Kate was able to show despite all that had happened to her.

"Neolamane is—I mean, was—manufactured by LaMane Pharmaceuticals," Danny said. He went on to explain the strange side effects that had occurred with the drug and how it was quickly pulled from the market. "Of course, no one mentioned the mystic side of the drug, how in some children it fostered supernatural talents. Our Laura was one of those, Kate."

Kate's green eyes slitted. "And those people took her to study her," she said, "Like some lab specimen. A three-year-old girl. Those slimy—" She stopped herself, looking up at Danny again. "Did Preminger say anything?"

"After I blackened both his eyes and did some other damage to him," Danny answered, holding up both his bruised hands.

"Oh, Danny!" Kate took the hands and kissed them.

"I know where Laura is, Kate," Danny answered bluntly. "When you had dreams that she was in a desert, you were almost right. Actually, she's in a place called the LaMane Center, a few miles outside Albuquerque, New Mexico."

"Then let's go there and get her," Kate cried.

"It isn't that simple, Kate," Danny said. "Not after all these years. Preminger confessed those children were brainwashed to forget their pasts. There's no doubt that Laura has a new family, even new parents she's very fond of. She may not want to come with us, even if we could prove she was our daughter."

For a few moments, Kate stared at the floral pattern on the curtain by her bed. Almost imperceptibly, her lower lip began to tremble. Then, tears streamed down her face and she brought her fist to her mouth. "She can't love a new mother," Kate cried. "I'm her mother. *I* am! And she must sense something about that or else she wouldn't be calling me in my dreams."

"Then that's the way we have to get to her," Danny

said. "Through your mind, Kate. You have to try to call her."

Kate shook her head. "The last time I tried, she denounced me and ran away. I don't want to scare her again."

"Someone made her talk that way, Kate," Danny said. "There's only one hope, and that's if you can convince her to at least meet with me. I don't know how she'll get away from that place, because Preminger says its well-guarded. But somehow, we've got to arrange it. There's a seven A.M. flight to Albuquerque, and I'm going to be on it."

"Danny, I have to come with you," Kate said.

"You can't," Danny insisted. "Kate, there's no time to argue about this. You have to stay here with the boys."

Kate thought for just a moment, then nodded. Danny was right, of course. What would Joey and Chris think of her if she wasn't there for them when they woke up?

"I should arrive about ten A.M. their time," Danny calculated. "Meanwhile, you've got to work on getting her back again. Call her Jenny if it makes her more comfortable, but convince her that we're her friends and that we want to help her."

Kate rubbed the tears from her eyes. "She must want help, if she's been contacting me."

"That's right, Kate," Danny encouraged. "So close your eyes and call our daughter back to us."

42

IMPATIENTLY, JILL DRUMMED HER FINGERS ON THE counter of the Rent-a-Car desk.

"You say there's a strange noise under the hood?" the woman behind the desk asked.

"Three times," Jill repeated in a monotone. God, this was tiresome. "The car was fine until about an hour ago, and then it started making this odd *ka-lunk, ka-lunk* sound. Look, I'm really pressed for time. Do you have a car or don't you?"

"We don't," the woman answered. "But I've been on the phone to other rental agencies, trying to find one for you. It's been difficult. Not only is there a furniture convention in town, but the Balloon Festival starts tomorrow."

Jill sighed, realizing the woman was doing the best she could. Still, it was frustrating to know how close she was to Ryan. If she dared to use the same car she'd been driving for the past two days, she could find him. But part of her strategy was to get an entirely different car, one they wouldn't be looking for. She hadn't yet made a phone call to the LaMane Center because it was only twelve-fifteen in the morning.

She walked across the hall and plunked down onto a bench. By all rights she should have been tired enough to fall asleep, even here. But the thought of being without a car was like a powerful stimulant. Fidgety, she got back up and walked over to a newspaper rack. There was only one copy left, and since it was past midnight, this made it a day old. She took it without paying for it and brought it back to the bench.

Shuffling through the pages without really seeing them, she was suddenly stopped by a four-color spread depicting hundreds of brilliant balloons. The caption explained that this was taken at last year's Balloon Festival and that the next one would commence tomorrow. It was a beautiful shot, but what caught Jill's attention was the small map drawn in one corner. The field being used was almost halfway between the city and the LaMane Center.

Wheels began to turn in Jill's mind, ideas forming even as her eyes started to droop closed. With the thought that the Balloon Festival would be the perfect place to hide when she escaped with Ryan, she fell into reluctant sleep.

43

AFTER WHAT SEEMED LIKE AN ETERNITY IN THE AIR shafts, Ralph and Beth found themselves in a darkened, empty laboratory. Beth had come to trust this stranger, though she couldn't understand what he had to do with her brother, and she let him take her by the hand to lead her through the darkness. When she accidentally brushed against a rack of test tubes, she gasped, waiting for the door to open. Ralph pulled her forward with a reassuring squeeze from his warm hand.

Slowly, stopping each time the sash creaked, Ralph opened one of the windows. The yard behind the clinic was completely deserted. He helped Beth out, then followed himself. Just as carefully, he closed the window. The darkness behind the glass created a mirror effect, and he saw that his beaten face had swollen even more. But after being cooped up in the air shafts, the burst of cool autumn air was invigorating. They'd gotten this far, and nothing, not even the severe pain behind his eye, would stop them.

He motioned toward a copse of trees about ten yards ahead of them. Beth looked all around, opening her arms. Softly, Ralph said, "They wouldn't be looking this close, I think. If my son—if your brother ran away, he's far gone from here."

He took her hand again, and they began to run. Beth thought the security lamps made her shadow stretch so far that someone else was sure to spot it. She did not take a single breath until she was hidden in the darkness of the trees.

"How are we going to find Peter?" she asked worriedly. "And my mother? What will they do to my mother?"

"To both questions, I don't know," Ralph whispered. "But the first thing we have to do is get you back to your family. They can call the authorities and we'll get some help. I'm hurt bad, Beth. I don't think I could make it through these mountains, even if I did know exactly where Michael—Peter might be."

God, it was hard to call his son Peter. But Peter wasn't really his son . . . Ralph cut the depressing thought short and leaned down to Beth again.

"We have to scale the fence," he said. "I cut the power off to it hours ago, and I made such a mess of the circuits I don't think they could have fixed them by now."

When she came to the tall fence, Beth thought it looked like the sides of a cage at the zoo. Ralph said he'd cut the power off. That meant there was electricity going through it. Was every part of the fence cut off? Or would she fry to a crisp once she touched it?

She heard the back door of the clinic slam and threw herself into Ralph's arms. He pulled her back into the shadows, feeling her body trembling. They both listened.

"I swear I saw someone back here," a voice shouted.

"You're wasting your time," another man answered. "We already looked here, and those kids would never come back. Adams is gonna have fits if he catches us chasing shadows."

Shadows, Beth thought. My shadow was so big! "Let's go," the first voice said. "They think they've gone off toward St. Marta's Ridge, so we oughta look there, too."

When he felt it was safe to talk again, Ralph whispered, "St. Marta's Ridge is about six miles from here," he said. "I could never walk that."

"I could," Beth said, her mouth set hard. "And if Peter's there, I'll know it. I'll feel him."

"Feel him?"

"I can talk to him with my mind," Beth said. "That's how I knew he was here."

Ralph looked down at the pretty little red-haired girl who hugged him tightly. Of course, it made sense. If Michael had been born with powers, then his twin sister would certainly have them, too.

"Lead us to him, then," Ralph said, starting toward the fence. A quick check proved it hadn't been turned on again, and a minute later they were both on the other side. Ralph had to pause a moment until the pounding stopped in his head, and then he motioned Beth toward a trail that led between two huge boulders.

The night was silent except for the hiss of the wind and occasional howl, telling Ralph the search was not going on in this area. If he could just get to St. Marta's Ridge, if he could just hold out that long . . .

In his mind, he spoke words of encouragement to himself, trying to drive away the pain he felt. He was so deep in this self-bargaining that he did not realize half an hour had passed without Beth saying a word. In fact, he had almost forgotten her presence until she let out a small scream.

From the hissing sound, Ralph was certain the little

girl had come across a snake. "Don't move," he said. "That snake's probably as scared of you as—"

"It's a dog," Beth cried.

Ralph came closer and looked down with horror and awe at the monstrosity at their feet. He recognized one of the guard dogs from the LaMane Center by the blue collar around its neck. But even though this animal physically resembled a dog, its mannerisms were those of a snake. Its feet were tucked very close to its body, its neck was stretched out as far as possible, and its tail waved in a way that would have normally been impossible. The animal's tongue flicked in and out, and instead of whimpers of pain, it was hissing. A trail of multiple Ss had been made in the dirt.

"One of the kids did this," Ralph guessed.

"Would—would Peter hurt an animal?" Beth wanted to know, unable to tear her eyes from the freakish sight.

"I don't think so," Ralph said. "But it wasn't meant to be done cruelly. I'm sure the dog was about to attack, and they had to defend themselves. Come on, Beth. There's nothing we can do for this poor mutt until we find the other children."

Leaving the snake-dog behind, gazing at him over her shoulder, Beth followed Ralph as he limped deeper into the mountains.

44

OVER THE NEXT HOURS, UNTIL THE SUN ROSE AT dawn, each group involved in the LaMane Center crisis pushed itself toward an unforeseeable future. Jill finally obtained a car, but she was so exhausted she couldn't trust herself to drive it. And there would be no finding Ryan at this early hour anyway. She fell back into fitful sleep in the airport lobby.

Danny caught snatches of unbidden sleep on the airplane, though he tried to stay awake and make plans. Beth and Ralph pushed forward in their quest, following Beth's instincts and subtle clues left behind by the runaways. But the pain behind Ralph's eye became so bad that he collapsed against a tree at one point and begged his small companion for a moment's rest. Tired and cranky herself, she agreed, and she fell asleep with her head on his shoulder. Whether she shivered from the wind or from fear was hard to tell. As for the runaways themselves, they slept fitfully in their cave hideout. Each one took a turn keeping watch, while the other two slept and dreamed of a monster who bore a remarkable resemblance to Dr. Adams.

Only Lou Vermont's and Lincoln Adams' teams kept at work. Armed with information from Lillian Blair, Lou had gathered a posse of sorts and headed toward the LaMane Center. But when he approached the gate, no amount of bell ringing or yelling brought any signs of human life. Lou couldn't know that Adams was still leading a search party through the mountains and that he had left word behind that no one was to leave his or her home until word was given. The LaMane Center might as well have been a ghost town.

"Screw it," Lou snapped. He turned to the young man behind him. "John, get those bolt shears and get this chain open. We're going inside."

While John went for the shears, another cop said, "Doesn't look like there's anyone in there. Maybe they've flown the coop because they suspected we'd be coming."

"Maybe so," Lou said. "But they had to have left clues." He shifted impatiently from one booted foot to another while John worked at snapping off the chain that locked the gates. When it came free, he pushed both of them out of the way and entered the confines of the center.

"I always was suspicious about this place," he said. "The way they'd never let anyone in, the way they never came out. Something sick's going on in here, you mark my words." He came to a turn in the roadway and looked left, then right. Seeing a long, low building in the distance, he pointed. "Let's look there first."

"We don't have a search warrant," John said. "Aren't we gonna get in trouble?"

"Who's gonna know?" Lou asked. "The place is deserted, isn't it? And even if we do find anyone, I'm sure we can convince them to be cooperative."

There was such an air of assurance, of sheer menace, in Lou's voice that the younger officers exchanged glances of wonder. But they followed him to the building. A small sign over the door was crammed with the legend: ADAMS CLINIC FOR THE STUDY OF PARAPSYCHOLOGICAL AND PARANEUROLOGICAL BEHAVIOR.

"What the hell does that mean?" someone asked.

"We'll find out," Lou said. He wiggled the door. To his surprise, it opened easily.

The group moved into the building, where Lou signaled them to split up to either end of a long hallway. John remained with Lou, heading toward a door marked LAB A. Other than the soft steps of their own shoes, there wasn't a sound to be heard. Lou pushed open the door and looked in at a room that reminded him of his high-school chemistry class. Nothing unusual here. Lab B was a duplicate of the first, although this one had two large refrigerators. In the third room, they found a green chair like the kind used in dentists' offices. Monitors and electrical equipment that Lou could not identify surrounded the chair. A mirror lined the back wall, ending with a double-bolted door. Right now, the locks were open.

John pulled the door open to investigate. "Look at this," he said. He turned to Lou, showing bloodstained fingertips. "It's fresh."

Lou hurried around the green chair, taking hold of

the door himself. Carefully, not wanting to think what he might find in there, he yanked it open.

He found a viewing room. Eight chairs had been set up on stairlike platforms, facing the large window at the front. There were three large cabinets along the back wall, secured with padlocks.

"One-way mirror," he said. "They must be doing some kind of psycho experiments here."

"Where did the blood come from?" John wanted to know.

Lou shook his head. The two men combed the room, but there was nothing to be found. No body.

John tapped his shoulder and pointed up toward the ceiling. There were a number of cameras suspended from heavy chains, each one aimed at the window. Their darkened lights told Lou they hadn't been running during his search.

"There have to be tapes somewhere," he said. "If we find them, we may find answers. Nothing else is turning up."

"Maybe they keep them in those cabinets," John suggested.

"Let's find out," Lou said, pulling his gun.

"Lou?"

Without answering and without even trying to pick one of the locks, Lou shot through its shaft. Adams had never expected anyone outside the center to ever be in this room, and so he used simple locks just to keep curious kids from getting their hands on his videotapes.

They were lined up like books, each one bearing a numerical code that didn't give the slightest hint of content.

"What, now?" John asked. "We can't look through every one of these. There must be two hundred in this cabinet alone."

"We'll take a random sample," Lou said, pulling four tapes out. He handed them to John, then took out four more. The younger officer watched in bewilderment as Lou unzipped his black leather jacket and stuffed the videos inside. The jacket's cinched waist created a natural pouch, and its thick lining prevented any bulges from showing. Understanding, John did the same.

"There's nothing more we can do here," Lou said. "Let's get the other guys and get out. Once we've viewed these tapes, we'll decide what to do next."

When they walked back out into the hallway, they heard the sounds of a heated argument. The other two officers were standing outside a pair of double doors, hands raised. A third man had his back to them, but they knew by his stance that he was holding a gun. Silently, swiftly, Lou and John pulled their own weapons and sneaked behind the man.

"Put it down," Lou said. "We don't want any trouble here."

The man turned around and, seeing the two revolvers pointed at him, let his own gun drop to the floor. One of the other cops immediately picked it up.

"What are you doing here?" the man asked. "You have no right to come in here. You don't have a warrant, do you?"

"Why? Do you have something to hide?" Lou asked sarcastically. "We received a distress call about a half-hour ago, a report that there was some trouble here."

The man looked around himself. "The only trouble I see here is four crazy, trigger-happy cops. You guys are in a lot of trouble, you know. Searching this place without a warrant—"

Lou put on an innocent face. "Searching? That would mean tearing open doors and breaking locks, wouldn't it?"

The man shrugged.

"None of you gentlemen did anything like that, did you?" Lou asked.

His fellow officers responded negatively.

"We were only trying to find the source of trouble we'd been told about," John put in. "Something about a little girl being hurt."

The man paled visibly, and when he spoke again,

there was a tremor in his voice despite his reassuring words. "If any child was being hurt here," he said, "I—I would know about it. I'm the night watchman, and I've been on duty since eleven P.M. I haven't heard a sound."

He's hiding something, Lou thought.

"Would you mind if we had a better look around?" he asked politely. "Just to be sure, you know. After all, we've come all this way, and if a child was being hurt, it's our duty to put a stop to it."

"But I told you—"

"Be a lot easier than coming back with a warrant and tearing the place to pieces."

Again, the man paled. "All right," he said. "I'll show you around. But please, don't touch anything. We're working with some delicate equipment here."

As Lou and the others followed the man, Lou pressed for more information. He really wanted to get home, to view the videotapes that lay hidden beneath his and John's coats. Other than the blood John had found on the viewing-room door, nothing in this place seemed out of order, nothing indicated someone here had planned the murders of three people and the kidnapping of at least two more.

While he was playing the nice policeman, cooperating with the security guard, the real murderers were still on the loose.

"What exactly do you do here?" he asked.

"I'm a security guard," the man said. "I told you that."

"I don't mean you personally," Lou said, impatient. "I mean, in this place. What do they do in this place?"

The security guard shook his head, opening a door. It was a sparsely furnished office. A huge oak desk sat against the back wall, beneath an oil rendering of the Grand Canyon. Six oak file cabinets stood in threes to either side, and a computer was set up on a metal table to Lou's right. The cabinets were locked tight, as was a door at the back of the room which appeared to be a closet. He thought he had never seen so many pad-locks in a building.

But his study of the office was giving the guard time to forget his question. He asked it again.

"I don't really know," the man said. "I'm not one of the doctors. But I do know they work with brain-damaged kids, trying to rehabilitate them. Dr. Adams does remarkable work."

"Dr. Adams."

The guard looked down at his shoes. Had he re-vealed too much? Just showing these men around would get him into big trouble, but what choice did he have? Throwing them out would only arouse suspi-cion.

"Lincoln Adams," he volunteered, finally deciding they could find this out easily enough themselves. "He's the head of this place. If you want to know anything, you'll have to ask him directly."

"And where is he?"

"Home, I suppose," the guard said. "Sleeping. It's five o'clock in the morning, for God's sake."

Lou nodded. "I know. I'm beginning to think the call we received was a crank. Nothing seems out of order here."

"Then you'll be going?" There was a hopeful tone in the guard's voice.

"I'll be back this afternoon," Lou promised. "You can forewarn Dr. Adams that I'm coming and that he'd damned well better be here."

Lou saw the guard's shoulders sink down about an inch and realized the man had been walking with tensed muscles. Now that the police were leaving, he probably felt he could relax.

"I'm sure he'll want to talk to you," the guard said, leading them from the room.

Just as he was about to close the door, he heard a series of taps from the locked closet. He started to cough, covering the noise. He shut the door quickly and started talking. "Can't get used to this dry air," he said. "I'm from Washington, originally. Came here to visit my cousins and fell in love with the place. I've been working for Dr. Adams for three years now.''

He was practically shoving them toward the hall that led to the front exit. Lou wondered why he was suddenly so agitated. Had he missed something?

"I'll tell Dr. Adams you were here,'' the guard said.

"I'll be back,'' Lou promised. He opened the door, and the four cops walked out to their squad cars.

None of them could have known the office was just a front, set up in case something like this ever happened. The guard hurried back to it, grateful the cops hadn't asked him to open up the closet. It wasn't a closet at all, but a small room complete with a toilet, a cot, and a sink. A prison cell with no windows.

The guard pulled a key from his ring, unfastened the padlock, and opened the door. From the mussed-up bed, Natalie Morse gazed up at him with huge, bloodshot eyes. She struggled to say something from behind the gag she wore, struggled to move in spite of the tape that bound her wrists and ankles.

"Looks like you didn't get enough of this,'' the guard said, pulling a hypo from his pocket. "You almost gave us away, lady, and we can't have that. No, we can't do anything to make Dr. Adams mad.''

As Natalie made strange noises behind the gag, the guard plunged a needle into her arm. It hurt like hell—he was no professional—but within moments pain didn't matter. Natalie slumped back into darkness.

Carefully, the guard shut and locked the door again. Then he went to see what damage the police might have done and how much he had to cover to keep himself on Adams' good side.

45

A SHAFT OF LIGHT POURED THROUGH THE HOLE IN the roof of the cave, warming Michael's face. Still asleep, he tightened his eyes until something in his brain told him he couldn't shut out the light and forced him to wake up. Groggily, he pulled himself to his feet, scratching his head. His skin itched from the fine layer of dirt that had come to rest over his body, and his mouth had a disgusting taste. For a few moments, he just stood there, not really thinking and hardly seeing the other two sleeping figures. In spite of all their efforts to keep watch for the grown-ups, they had finally fallen asleep.

As he became more wakeful, Michael was aware of an urgent need to relieve himself. He moved toward the far wall and started to unzip his jeans. Then he remembered Jenny's presence. Worried she might wake up and see him, he crossed the room to the passageway. Even though he hadn't had a thing to drink since last night, he peed as if he'd taken in quarts of water. His stomach hurt and he wished there was something for breakfast. Michael thought of the great pancakes his mother used to make and of the French toast his father learned to prepare after his mother disappeared. Tears rose in his eyes, making them sting. He rubbed them away, determined not to cry. Crying wouldn't change things.

Because his mother and father weren't really his mother and father. They had lied to him.

Jenny was stirring, and her moans started Tommy

waking up. In a moment, they were both sitting, looking up at Michael.

"I feel gross," Jenny said.

"I'm starving," Tommy put in.

Michael frowned at them. "Is that all you guys think
about? After what we read last night . . ."

Jenny crawled over to her bag and took out a comb.
Tommy shook his head, supposing that only a girl
would think to run away with a comb. As she worked
it through her hair, she said, "Michael, we don't understand everything we read in those papers. You didn't
even see our names."

"Oh, yea?" Michael answered. He picked up the
file folder, now neatly put together again, and opened
it. He read, "Subject: Male, Age three. Signs of possible telepathy, pyrokinesis. Quick response to treatment. Surrogate parents number 23517. Subject:
Female, age four. Telepathy, telekinesis. Stronger
treatment needed. Surrogate parents number 58672.
Subject: Female, Age three—"

"Okay, already," Tommy snapped. "So we're part
of some weird project? I never did feel my mother
really loved me, and now I know why. It's kind of a
relief, you guys. This may be weird, but I'm glad she's
not my mother. Then at least I know it wasn't my fault
she treated me like that."

Jenny nodded solemnly. "Me, too. Alice was just
too mean to me, and even though Daddy was nice, he
never stopped her being that way."

Michael put the folder down on a rock and sat beside it. "I guess if my parents had been like that," he
said, "I'd feel the way you guys did. But my mom and
dad were really good to me. My dad was the best,
only now I found out he lied to me. He never told me
I was adopted."

"Maybe he couldn't," Jenny said. "Maybe he was
afraid."

Michael looked over at her. Now that she'd combed
her long dark hair, she looked neat and clean despite
the dirt smudges on her face.

"He did try to get you out of there," Jenny went on. "And since he gave you that file it means he was going to explain everything. Maybe he was even going to tell you about your real parents."

"I don't think I want to know mine," Tommy growled. "They gave me up."

Jenny shook her head. "I'm not sure. Do you remember that lady I told you about? I saw her again last night, when I was dreaming. I mean, it felt like a dream, but it felt real too. The way it is when I see someone or hear voices. I tried to ignore her, but she kept calling to me. She said that a man was coming to help me and that I should keep listening until she could tell me where he would be. She said the man would look a lot like me because . . ." She drew in a deep breath. "Because he's my real father."

Michael's eyes rounded. "That lady is your mother?"

"I don't know," Jenny said. "But I know she'll help us."

"She's an Outsider," Tommy warned.

"There aren't any Outsiders," Michael snapped. "It's just a big lie Adams made up. Jenny, where are we supposed to meet this guy?"

"She didn't tell me," Jenny said. "I think he's on an airplane, coming here. I keep trying to contact the lady, but there's nothing there."

"Maybe she's asleep," Michael suggested.

"I think so," Jenny agreed. She looked up at the hole in the roof. "Sure do wish we knew what time it was."

"Time for us to get out of here," Tommy said. "We've stayed too long for this hideout to be safe. Jenny, Michael, can you sense if anyone's nearby?"

Both children closed their eyes and concentrated. Jenny shook her head, then Michael.

"It's clear, as far as I can tell," Jenny said. "But you can bet there'll be another search team out. We'd better go while we can."

Gathering their things, the three children walked

single-file through the passageway and out into the valley. They saw now that they were facing a roadway, about sixty yards ahead of them. It was lined with a Cyclone fence, and when they drew closer, they saw a sign on it that read: ST. MARTHA'S RIDGE. Cigarette butts and an occasional crushed can littered the otherwise peaceful scenery. None of the children could be sure it was left behind by tourists or by the search team. They followed the road for a while, sensing there was no one nearby, until Michael stopped and said, "Someone's calling me."

"I don't hear anything," Tommy said.

"In my head," Michael said. "It's that girl, the one with red hair like me. She's really nearby."

"She may be with someone from the center," Jenny warned.

Michael stopped and closed his eyes. In his mind, he saw the red-haired girl, looking as dirty and disheveled as he. What had happened to her? he wondered. And with her was a man he hardly recognized for the bruises on his face.

His father!

"My dad got away," Michael cried. "He's coming to look for me."

"And Adams is probably following him," Tommy said. "Come on, Michael, let's get off this road. It isn't safe. That sign over there says Albuquerque is in that direction, so we should make our way there."

"But my father."

"If your father is looking for us," Jenny said, "it'd be safer to meet him in the city. Dr. Adams wouldn't dare try anything with other people around."

Michael hesitated, but Tommy pulled on his arm. "Come on! Your dad and that other girl will find us easy enough, but we can't walk into a trap. We've got to get to the city before Adams starts looking for us again."

Nodding in reluctant agreement, Michael followed his friends into the crevice between the huge boulders.

A moment later, there was no sign at all of the three children.

46

At precisely eleven a.m. Mountain Time, the wheels of Flight 444 from Boston bumped hard on the ground, waking Danny Emerson from a deep sleep. He gazed out the window as the plane taxied to its final destination. The airport was washed with a mellow, soft light, beaming down from a sun that hung in a clear blue sky.

Danny didn't have Kate's sense of ESP, but somehow he could feel Laura's presence. She was there, somewhere, in those mountains. Locked up in a horror town called the LaMane Center. But he'd get her out as soon as he could, even if it meant storming the place and taking her forcibly. As long as Kate was able to contact their daughter, Laura would know he was coming and she'd be ready.

When he disembarked the plane, burdened with only a large overnight bag, he hurried toward the exit. He paused at the coffeeshop, thinking he might need sustenance. But it was just a moment's pause. Laura was waiting for him, after all.

He noticed, but hardly registered, the souvenir shop two doors down from the cafeteria. There was a strange hole in the middle of the glass window, with cracks radiating from it. A yellow police banner blocked off the area.

He was passing the Rent-a-Car desk when he casually glanced at a young woman sitting on a nearby bench. He wouldn't even have given her a second thought if the woman didn't stir suddenly and sit up, stretching her arms. Danny stopped in his tracks. Could that be who he thought it was?

He went to the woman and leaned forward a little, looking down at her.

"Jill? Jill Sheldon?"

For a moment, she didn't recognize her old schoolmate. Then a big smile spread across her face. "Danny Emerson," she cried. "What on earth are you doing here?"

"I could ask you the same question," Danny said.

"It—it would be hard to explain," Jill said. "I've been waiting on a rental car and haven't had any luck yet."

Danny studied her for a moment. Was it only coincidence to find a friend here? A woman who had also lost a child when she was living in Wheaton, Michigan? He ventured a guess. "We're both looking for our children, aren't we?"

Jill gasped.

"I'm right, then," Danny said. Jill moved the overnight bag she'd used for a pillow last night and Danny took a seat. "What do you know so far?"

Jill told him all that had happened, ending with the incident up on the mountains the previous night.

Danny whistled softly. "These people aren't kidding around," he said.

"We could have figured that out already," Jill grumbled. "They kidnapped our children."

"We'll get them back, Jill," Danny vowed. "Now that we aren't alone, we'll be stronger."

Jill nodded in agreement. Danny Emerson had gone to school with her back in Wheaton, a member of the football team who had been taken in by a pro team. She wondered why he'd quit, and guessed it had something to do with Laura's death. But she didn't ask, realizing it was all a moot point now. Laura was no more dead than Ryan.

She stood up, stretching. Her muscles felt like frayed rubber bands. "I don't know about you," she said, "but I can't do a damned thing if I don't have another cup of coffee. It's my fourth this morning. We've got a big day ahead of us, so we'd better fortify ourselves and make some definite plans."

"I'm all for that," Danny said.

In the coffeeshop, Jill said, "You don't know how happy I am that you're here, Danny. But where's Kate?"

Danny explained what had happened to the boys and how his wife had a breakdown.

"Two boys," Jill cried. "Are they . . ." She paused for the right words, but Danny filled in.

"They aren't like Laura," Danny said. "Chris and Joey were born after Laura disappeared. By God's hand, that is. I'm afraid I rushed Kate into taking that horrible drug because I was so anxious to have a child."

Jill nodded, understanding. After four years of trying, she was an easy target for Ronald Preminger herself, although it had been Jeff who recommended that she see him.

"How we could have been so stupid—" she began.

"We weren't stupid," Danny said. "We were two young couples with a normal desire to have a family. And no matter what we say about Neolamane, it did give us our children. It was the lab people who took them away."

Jill drank some coffee. "So, where do we start today?" she asked.

"I'll give Kate a call," Danny said. "She's been trying to keep in contact with our daughter, to tell her I'm coming. If she was able to reach her, then we'll have an idea where the children might be."

"The pay phone is right across the hall," Jill said. She opened her purse and handed him a roll of quarters. "Ten dollars ought to give you a few minutes."

She wouldn't listen to Danny's protests about taking the money, so he got up and went to the pay phone. When he reached it, he instinctively began to dial his home number. Then, remembering where Kate really was, he made a call to the hospital. A recorded voice asked for more money, and he deposited quarter after quarter until the call went through.

Kate's voice was so clear that he knew she was wide awake, and probably had been for hours.

"Kate, you're not going to believe this," Danny said, "but Jill Sheldon is here. She says she got messages from her son the way you heard from Laura."

"Thank God you're not alone," Kate said. "There's safety in numbers, and I think you're going to need to take all the precautions you can get. I reached Laura last night."

"Where is she, Kate?" Danny asked anxiously.

"She isn't exactly sure," Kate said. "And I'm not certain I convinced her of our sincerity. But this morning I saw her again. She didn't acknowledge me, but I saw a sign that might help. She's in the mountains, Danny, near a place called St. Marta's Ridge. At least she was an hour ago. Danny, she's run away from the center. She's stranded in those mountains with two little boys."

"Keep trying her, Kate," Danny urged. "I'm going to hang up now and get a map. I'll call back in two hours, okay?"

"I love you, Danny," Kate said. "Please, bring our baby girl home to me?"

"I won't leave here without her," Danny said. He hung up and went back to the coffeeshop. Jill had already paid the bill and was waiting at the door. Danny relayed Kate's message.

"They ran away?" Jill gasped. "Now what do we do? How are we ever going to find them out there?"

"Kate says she thinks the children are near a place called St. Marta's Ridge," Danny reported. "Do you know where that is?"

Jill shook her head, then bent down to pull her map from the pocket of her overnight bag. Carrying it to a wooden bench, they spread it across their laps and studied the territory around Albuquerque.

Jill was the one to find it, and she pointed. "Look,

it's right next to where the Balloon Festival is taking place,'' she said. ''I bet we could use that to our advantage.''

She told Danny about the festival taking place that day. Then she glanced at her watch. ''It's early still. If we hurry, we can get there while the balloonists are still setting up. I'm sure we can convince someone to give us the first ride. Once we're up, we'll have a good view. And this''—she took out her telescope—''will improve our view.''

''This,'' Danny countered, stealthily opening his wallet to show it was stuffed with money, ''will help us bribe one of the aeronauts.''

As they passed the shattered window of the boutique, curiosity got the better of Danny and he stopped to question the young security guard.

Tito shook his head. He had related this story many times over and still hadn't gotten tired of the attention it brought him.

''Craziest thing I ever saw,'' he said. ''This guy had somehow jumped through the window, and it cut his body right in half.''

Jill shuddered and Danny felt something ice up in his big chest.

''There were two other guys inside,'' Tito said. ''One of them was dead, but the other one had had a heart attack. I don't even know if he's alive.''

''What in the name of God happened?'' Danny asked.

''There was a woman here who said she was the dead guy's mother-in-law,'' Tito said. ''She said some crazy people were after them, that they took their granddaughter. I don't doubt it, if you just look at the place.''

Something about his words set off an alarm in Jill's head.

''Someone took their child?'' she asked. ''Could you—could you possibly tell us the woman's name?''

''Sure,'' the young security guard said. ''It's been in all the papers. Lillian Blair.''

It didn't ring a bell, so Jill pressed on. "How about her son-in-law?"

"Him?" Tito thought a moment. "I think his name was Morrison, or Morse. I'm pretty sure his first name was Stuart."

"Stuart Morse," Danny repeated.

"We aren't alone, then," Jill said.

They quickly thanked the guard for his information and went on their way. As they exited the airport into the clean, cool morning air, Jill had a stern reminder.

"Those people murdered our friend," she said. "Hideously, and in view of witnesses. Yet no one seems to know what happened. It should give us pause and make us think what these creeps are capable of pulling off."

They crossed the parking lot to where the rental cars were waiting. Jill's was easy enough to find. Other than the one she'd brought back last night, it was the only car in this part of the lot. She realized how lucky she was to have it.

"We have to trick them," Jill said. "We have to call the children to us, but in a way that they won't be discovered until it's too late. The LaMane people are still looking for my original rental, and we can't let them find out we switched cars until we have those children on board a flight out of here, safe."

Jill glanced across the parking lot at the spire of the airport chapel.

"I wish we had time to say a prayer," she said. "I have a feeling we're going to need it."

47

Lou Vermont's wife blocked the view of the television set, snapping the screen off and setting her hands on her ample hips. She wore a bright-red apron over her dress, decorated with a dozen child-size hand prints. It was the one she wore every Saturday when her grandchildren came to have dinner with her.

"You are not going to sit in front of the TV set," she said. "Hilary and Davie are bringing the kids today. And Julie and Sam said they may come, too. You'll be so tired you won't be able to pay attention to them."

Lou rubbed his eyes with a thumb and forefinger. How long had he been watching those films? He looked at his watch. It was nearly eight o'clock.

"You didn't go to bed when you came home from night-shift duty," Beatrice said, reading his mind. "That means you've been awake for almost twenty-four hours."

"I can't sleep," Lou said, though he could have passed out right there in his blue La-Z-Boy. "This is one of the strangest cases I've ever come across. Somehow, those murders at the airport are connected to the LaMane Center, and I'm determined to find out."

"You couldn't possibly think straight without sleep," Beatrice said. "Why don't you go in the bedroom and lie down? You have a few hours before the kids will arrive."

Lou nodded and pulled himself from his chair. Funny, he could command a whole department of

264

tough young men and women, but there was no doubt Beatrice was the real boss here at home. Not in a nagging way, though, but in a way that showed she loved him. He kissed her warmly, then shuffled off to bed.

But he couldn't sleep. He kept thinking of the films he'd been watching since he came home, the videos stolen from the center. Most of them involved experiments with animals—monkeys taught to press certain buttons for treats, for example. Since there was no cruelty involved, Lou couldn't build a case on that alone. The last two films had been progressively stranger, though. There was a horse that managed to get itself up onto a balance beam to walk as stealthily as a cat. Lou swore he even heard it meow instead of whinny, but decided it was probably the poor quality of the tape. Stranger still was the line of G.I. Joe dolls that seemed to walk across a floor. Trick photography, no doubt, but why?

Somehow, Lou felt the answer lay in the sound of childish voices he always heard in the background. Whoever they were, they spoke little and very often pleaded not to be made to do something. Child abuse in that place was another possibility. But as long as the kids were off-camera, what could he prove? He had to get back to the center, get more information, even if it meant hauling Dr. Lincoln Adams in on some trumped-up charges.

Agitated, running on a fresh supply of adrenaline, Lou jumped from the bed. He was still fully clothed. He slipped his feet back into his black shoes and reached for his utility belt. Beatrice would scold him like a mother hen, but he couldn't let this rest until the mystery was solved.

He went to the mirror that hung on the bedroom door, to make certain his uniform didn't look rumpled. No matter what Beatrice thought, he couldn't let go of this case. There were a couple of kids missing out there, and a young mother. Lou didn't let himself think what a maniac like Lincoln Adams might do to Natalie Morse. He desperately needed more facts be-

fore he could pursue the case, and he decided he'd
defy visiting hours at the hospital to have another talk
with Lillian Blair. Maybe today she would enlighten
him as to her daughter's involvement with Adams and
how the doctor came to be in possession of her grandson. Somehow, he hoped, the information would also
lead him to Natalie Morse's whereabouts . . .

48

CLUTCHING HER SUITCASE IN HER SMALL HAND, KATE
boarded the elevator and pressed the button that would
take her to Pediatrics. She had been both surprised
and pleased when Dr. Wilson released her that morning, and all she could think of was getting downstairs
to see her boys. Even Laura was forgotten at the moment. When the doors slid open, she went over to the
nurses' station.

"Oh, yes, Mrs. Emerson," the nurse said, a green-
eyed, red-haired girl who couldn't have been more than
nineteen. "Dr. Wilson told us you'd be down. I'm sure
Chris and Joey will be happy to see you."

"But I was told they aren't aware of anything," Kate
said. Had there been any new developments?

The nurse smiled a little sheepishly. "I'm sorry. It's
just that I believe people in comas can sometimes hear,
and I think the boys will be comforted to hear their
mommy's voice."

Kate nodded, understanding. "Then take me to
them."

In the time she'd been upstairs, she hadn't been allowed to visit her sons. No amount of information from
either Danny or the doctors prepared her for the sight

of those two little bodies, in adjacent beds with high steel rails that looked like futuristic playpens. They looked so tiny. . . .

She rushed between the beds and reached either hand out to touch them. The children were being fed intravenously; Kate thought the tubes looked bigger than Joey's arm. She wondered what Joey would do when he woke up. Probably ask a question. Probably dozens of questions.

Kate bit her trembling lip.

"Mrs. Emerson."

The voice was deep, soothing. Kate turned to see Nicholas Somers, the head pediatrician.

"How are they doing?" Kate asked. "Has anything new happened?"

Dr. Somers shook his head sadly. "I'm afraid not. This case baffles me, Mrs. Emerson, and I'm not usually a man to admit to such a thing. I haven't had much of a chance to talk with you. Dr. Wilson wouldn't let anyone near you." He noticed her bag. "Going home today?"

She nodded. "I wish my babies were coming with me. Dr. Somers, can you give me any bit of hope?"

"That would be unfair," Somers said. "And cruel. But if you could answer a few questions, it might help us."

"Of course."

"My office is—"

Kate's grip tightened around the little hands to either side of her. "I'm not leaving my babies."

"All right," Somers said, understanding. He often wondered if parents felt that being near their children kept the specter of death away. But these boys weren't going to die. He was sure of that.

"Mrs. Emerson," he said, "when the boys were brought in, your husband told us they'd been electrocuted. That a cord connected to a live socket had fallen in the bathtub."

"I saw it, too."

"But the strange thing is that neither boy showed

signs of having been electrocuted," the doctor said. "The very fact they were alive makes me wonder if there wasn't a mistake.

"The horror of seeing your boys hurt so might have clouded your vision," Dr. Somers added. "Is it possible the cord wasn't even plugged in? That the whole thing was a setup?"

Kate glowered at him. She pushed her glasses up her nose with a quick, angry movement.

"Some setup," she growled sarcastically. "It's a pretty convincing trick, isn't it? Doctor, my boys may be dying."

It was so hard to fight the tears.

"No, no," Somers said. "I don't think so. That's the other strange thing. Both these boys are strappingly healthy. We can't find a thing wrong with them other than the fact that they're comatose."

He went to Joey's crib and reached through the bars. Gently, he brushed back the soft blond hair. Kate noticed for the first time that the nurses had taken the time to wash it.

"I've spoken to both you and your husband," Somers said. "Neither of you seems to remember a thing. But there's one person I haven't been able to contact—your sitter, Mrs. Ginmoor. She was the third witness to this strange phenomenon, and she may be able to help us."

Kate thought a moment. She'd been so busy thinking of Laura and worrying about the boys that she hadn't even realized that Mrs. Ginmoor did not come to visit her.

"She didn't come to see the boys?"

"Her name is not on the sign-up sheet," Dr. Somers said. "And though I've tried calling her several times, she doesn't answer. On the day you were brought in, you were mumbling something about someone hurting your boys. Could it have been Mrs. Ginmoor? Could she have tried to kill them and is hiding because of her crime?"

Kate's green eyes widened. "Not in a million

years,'' she cried. ''Mrs. Ginmoor was like a grand-mother to those boys.''

Dr. Somers' question was blunt. ''Then why hasn't she come to visit them?''

Kate opened her mouth, but only a strange gulping noise came out. She could not answer the doctor's question.

49

RALPH AND BETH STAYED ON THE MOUNTAIN ROAD AS long as they felt it was safe—that is, as long as Beth didn't pick up feelings of other people in the area. She could still sense her brother's presence, but no matter how hard she tried to contact him, he didn't answer. It frustrated her, because she didn't know if he was ignoring her or if he was unable to respond. She also tried to think of her mother, and she felt that she was very frightened, locked in a dark place.

She didn't let herself think of her father. When she did, nothing was there.

They came to a turn in the road that sloped at a deep angle. On one side, the craggy mountain face worked toward the sky like a staircase. The other side, protected by railings only at its curves, dropped sharply into thick greenery.

Ralph glanced over the edge, felt the pounding be-gin again behind his eye, and moved quickly toward the relative safety of the other side of the road. Now that they'd turned another corner, he asked, ''Are you getting closer? Do you feel anything?''

''They just keep moving farther and farther away,'' Beth said. She was tired and hungry, her legs hurt terribly, and she was scared. But she didn't say so. Poor Ralph looked so hurt, and she had come to like him very much. She still didn't understand what he had to do with Peter's disappearance, but she could feel that he had loved her brother very much and was trying to do the right thing by him now.

They plodded on, silent for the next half-hour. At the base of the slope, Ralph finally let out a sigh of exhaustion. He was willing to admit what a ten-year-old wouldn't.

"I'm beat," he said. "We'll never find them this way. My head is pounding and I can't think straight. We have to get help, Beth."

"But I don't think we can trust anyone," Beth said worriedly.

"Not here, of course," Ralph said. "But I'm pretty sure we're heading toward a highway. We'll hitch a ride into the city. I'll bet the police have been looking for you."

Beth shook her head wildly, her red hair flying. "No! We can't go to the police. They still have my mother and I'm sure they're looking real hard for Peter. If they even suspect we went for help they might—they might . . ."

Ralph put his arms around the little girl, but she only shuddered a little bit and didn't let fresh tears fall. Pulling away from him, she had an expression of determination on her face that reminded Ralph of Michael. He felt a chill rush over him and turned quickly.

"Let's go," he said. "I think I can hold on for a little while longer. How about you?"

Beth nodded.

They took a shortcut through a path that had been cut by a long-extinct river, and to their surprise found themselves on the main highway. Dozens of cars whizzed by, ignoring Ralph's outstretched thumb. But at last a man and woman who seemed to be in their fifties pulled over. The woman gasped.

"Hiram, they've been in an accident."

"What happened to you?" Hiram asked. He

reached across his wife and unlocked her door. She slid close to him and Ralph and Beth squeezed in beside them.

"We were camping," Ralph said. Even in his battered state, he was somehow able to think quickly. "I—I fell into one of those ravines. My little girl here stayed all night with me, but in the morning I insisted we try to get help."

"I told him to lie still," Beth put in, picking up on the story line. "I was going to get a doctor myself."

"Can you imagine a little girl wandering through this area alone?" Ralph asked.

"Well, you aren't alone now," Hiram said. "Let's get you to the hospital."

When they arrived, Beth was surprised to see so many policemen in the lobby. She looked around warily, and when one of them pointed to her, she jumped into the safety of Ralph's arms.

"That's her! That's the kid!"

A dozen people rushed toward her.

"Are you Elizabeth Morse?"

She nodded.

One of the cops eyed Ralph suspiciously. "Who are you? What are you doing with this kid?"

It had been a long ordeal. Not just the flight from the LaMane Center, but all the previous six years. He did not put up a fight.

"It's a long story," he said. "You've got to help us, please . . ."

Suddenly, dozens of questions were being shot at him. Some were from police, some from reporters. It was so overwhelming and so sudden that Ralph's brain could not take the pressure. He let out a soft moan, then fainted into darkness.

Beth screamed, kneeling down next to him. "You bad people! Look what you've done to him! He was going to help me find my brother, but now he can't."

"What happened to your brother?" a woman asked.

"No questions," Lou Vermont's voice boomed across the lobby. The crowd parted and the police chief made his way toward the little girl. He lifted her gently by the elbows and whisked her away from the crowd.

Looking back over her shoulder, Beth saw doctors and nurses working with Ralph. She was taken to a room, where a lady doctor came in and quickly looked her over.

"She's suffering from exposure," the woman said. "Lots of bug bites, some bruises . . ."

"Where've you been all night, honey?" Lou asked.

The doctor called a nurse and asked that Beth be admitted. As Lou talked to her, the doctor continued to examine the little girl.

"Some bad men came and took my mom and me to a weird place," Beth said. "I don't know where my mom is. Ralph and I got out and we were trying to find Peter."

"Peter?"

"My brother," Beth explained. She saw the look of doubt over the police chief's face and was put on the defensive. "My brother didn't die. My mom and dad didn't believe me either, even when Peter kept appearing to me."

"Appearing to you?" Lou was growing more confused. Was the kid delirious?

But the doctor negated this possibility. "You seem fine, Beth, but we'll keep you for observation."

"What do you mean, he was appearing to you?" Lou pressed after the doctor had left.

Beth shook her head. She could sense Lou would never understand. "My mom and dad didn't believe Peter was alive, at first," she said. "But then my mom saw him, too. And my dad checked with a friend at the airport and found out Peter never got on the plane. So we all came to stay at Grandma's. Daddy and Grandma and Grandpa went back to the airport to see if they could remember anything. I don't know where they are now."

Lou felt a clump of ice forming at the bottom of his stomach. God, how he hated times like this. But Beth seemed like an intelligent child, and if he wanted her to answer his questions, he had to be honest with her.

"Beth, your grandma and grandpa are in two rooms upstairs," he said softly.

Beth eyed him. "And where's my daddy?"

Lou took a deep breath. "I'm afraid your daddy died last night, Beth."

He expected her to scream, to protest. Instead, she simply stared at him blankly. Her head moved slowly up and down. "I thought so," she said. "I kept trying to think of him, but there was only black in my head. I knew he was—I guessed he was prob—probably . . ."

And now the tears began to flow. As Lou held her in his arms and comforted her, he let the child let go of her grief. He was surprised how quickly she pulled away. Her expression which had been bland at first and then bewildered, was full of anger now.

"They killed my daddy," she seethed. "They took Peter from us a long time ago and they have my mommy locked up somewhere."

"Who are they?" Lou pressed. "Do you know who kidnapped you?"

"I think the guy with the scary blue eyes was named Dr. Adams," Beth recalled. "Ralph would know. He helped me get out of that place."

Lou felt excitement growing in himself. "Was it the LaMane Center?"

Beth nodded eagerly. "That's what Ralph called it."

"And who exactly is Ralph? Why was he there?"

Beth did not answer right away. It seemed that Ralph had cared very much about Peter, even though he called him Michael, but if he was at the center in the first place, was he also a bad man? But he helped her to escape, to get to the police. She couldn't get him into trouble.

"I—I don't really know," she mumbled.

It was only a little lie. She didn't really know exactly why he was there.

"Well, we're going to head right over there," Lou

said, straightening up. "If your mom is still there, we'll find her. In the meantime, maybe I can arrange for you to see your grandma before you go to your own room. Would you like that?"

Beth nodded eagerly. When she was taken to Lillian's room, the older woman burst into tears of joy. Beth was momentarily stunned by her grandmother's appearance. She wore no makeup or jewelry, and instead of a brightly colored outfit, she wore the bland colors of a hospital gown. But Beth saw so much love in Lillian's eyes that she ran to her and held her tightly. Together, they cried, mixed tears of relief and sorrow.

50

Peter! Peter, please wait for me. Don't run away, we won't hurt you.

Michael couldn't see the red-haired girl as he followed Tommy and Jenny. But her voice was so loud in his mind—louder than the brook he was crossing over precarious stones—that he could almost believe she was right there. But that was impossible. Whoever she was, he had always sensed she was very far away. There was no way she could be here in the mountains.

Peter, don't ignore me. You can hear me in your mind, I know it. Please, please try to remember me. Stop, close your eyes, and picture me.

Michael stopped short, on a large flat rock in the middle of the brook, and closed his eyes. Yes, he could see her. Red hair like his own, freckles. And all around her, white.

Who are you?

He made the demand more furiously than ever before.

I'm your sister, Peter. Your sister, Beth. Do you remember me?

No. I don't have a sister. And my name is Michael.

Your name is Peter! They messed up your brain and tried to make you forget who you really are, but you can remember if you try. I know you can.

The girl's words brought the file in his backpack to mind. Yes, she was right. The grown-ups at LaMane had lied to all the children. But his real name? Nothing in the files indicated that. The numbers on those papers gave no word as to identities.

I don't know who I am.

The girl moved and a grown-up came into the scene playing in Michael's mind. He gasped, but did not open his eyes or move from the rock. His father! Lying in a bed with white sheets, a bandage over half his face.

Daddy! You—you're in a hospital?

He can't hear you, Peter. He doesn't have the gift we share. I can hear because I'm your twin. We got away, Peter. Just tell me where you are and I'll send help.

I don't really know. I'm so tired. There's a brook, and . . .

"Michael!"

"What are you doing? You'll fall in."

The sounds of Jenny's and Tommy's voices snapped Michael out of his reverie. He opened his eyes and realized he had taken a step forward. He was ankle-deep in the icy water.

"I saw my sister," he cried. "In my mind. She's with my father."

Balancing on a fallen tree, Tommy grabbed Michael by the arm and pulled him to shore.

"You don't have a sister," he said.

"How do you know?" Michael demanded. "Who knows what kind of families we really have? She was with my dad, and they're trying to find us."

Tommy shook his head, holding Michael so tightly by the upper arms that the smaller boy winced. "It's a trick, Michael," he said sternly. "Don't believe it. Adams is using the other kids to get to us, and someone's making you see things that aren't there."

"But she—"

"Don't fall for it," Jenny said. "We can't be safe. We can't trust anyone yet."

Michael studied his friends. Tommy's blondish-brown hair stuck out in all directions, a shade darker for the layer of dirt that had settled on it during their hike. Even though she had brushed it, Jenny's hair was still full of junk from the floor of the cave. Both their faces were smudged, and Jenny's eyes were bloodshot from crying. All three were exhausted, hungry, and frightened. But Michael believed Tommy was right. Even if that girl really was his sister, it was too weird to imagine her here with his father.

He nodded. "All right," he said softly.

Miles away, at Ralph's bedside, Beth wailed in frustration as she lost contact with Peter once more.

"He was going to tell us where he is."

"He's afraid," Ralph whispered, a bit groggy from the painkillers he'd been given.

"Don't worry," Lou Vermont said. "We'll find him. I have a team going through those mountains now."

"What about the center itself?" Ralph asked.

"Got myself a bona-fide warrant and sent my best men there," Lou said. "I'll be going there myself, but I wanted to talk with you first. This business about kids with powers, it's the screwiest thing I ever heard of."

"But you saw Beth," Ralph protested. "You can't say you think she was faking that!"

Lou shrugged. "She's his twin. Maybe they have some kind of connection, I don't know. But a whole community of kids like that? It's like that movie, *Village of the Damned.*"

"But it's the adults who are evil this time," Ralph

said. He closed his eyes wearily, not even wanting to think of the price he'd pay for his part in Lincoln Adams' bizarre experiment. They could throw him in jail forever. But that wouldn't hurt as much as losing Michael.

The phone rang and he jumped. Lou reached for it before Ralph could make a move. Both he and Beth looked up at the cop, watching his expression change from interest to surprise to anger as he spoke. When he hung up, he was pale.

"It's empty," Lou said. "The LaMane Center is empty. There isn't a single person in the whole complex."

"Adams knew you were coming and moved them out," Ralph said.

"They took the files, books, tapes, everything," Lou went on in amazement. "Left all the furniture and most of their clothes, but my team says the houses look as if people went through their belongings in a hurry. This can only have happened in the last few hours."

"They could easily be on various flights out of Albuquerque," Ralph pointed out. "I'm afraid you've probably lost him."

Beth shook her head. "But what about my mother?"

"I'm afraid there was no sign of her," Lou said softly.

Beth was too numbed by the events of the past day to react. She simply asked another question. "And Peter?" she said. "Wasn't Dr. Adams mad about Peter and his friends escaping?"

"She's right," Ralph said. "He'd still be after them."

"But where?" Lou asked. "Where do we start looking so we can get to the kids first?"

Beth looked down at her worn sneakers.

"I'll try calling Peter again," she said softly.

But no matter how hard she directed her thoughts toward him, he did not answer.

It wasn't that Peter didn't hear her. But he was so

afraid that Dr. Adams and the other adults—even the kids—were trying to trap them that he forced himself to ignore her pleas. He felt like crying again and chewed his lips to stop the tears from flowing. The sound of Jenny's gasp made him look up. The sight before him pushed all thoughts of the red-haired girl from his mind.

They had come out of the mountains and were standing several hundred yards from a long ribbon of sun-grayed blacktop. Cars were whizzing by in either direction, the chain broken by an occasional truck. But it was what they saw beyond the highway that made the children gaze in wonder.

Against the backdrop of a clear blue sky hung countless hot-air balloons, colored brightly with red, white, and blue, the oranges and reds and yellows of sunsets, green and white, purples, pinks, and dozens of other combinations. There was even a flag shaped like the head of a cartoon character.

"Wow," Tommy whispered.

"What do you suppose is going on?" Jenny asked.

"Hot-air balloons," Michael said. "It's the Balloon Festival. They have it every year at this time. My dad told me about it . . ." He cut himself off, afraid memories like that would start him crying. But there would be no time for self-pity, for Tommy was urging them toward the road. They ran out in the open for the first time since leaving the center, forgetting their fears in the excitement of reaching the festival. At the road, they waited for an opening in the cars and dodged across. Within minutes they were mingling with the crowds.

"This is a safe place," Tommy said. "Adams would never try to hurt us in front of all these people."

Jenny looked around warily at the strange faces. "But what if someone from the center *is* here?" she asked. "What if they just try to sneak us out?"

"If any of you feel someone touching you," Tommy warned, "scream like crazy. Now, I don't know about

you guys, but I'm starved. Let's see if we can get ourselves something to eat.''

The children weaved their way through the crowds,
passing lines of people waiting for balloon rides,
walking around huge ovals of nylon lying flat on the
ground. They were unaware they were being watched.
Weary from a long plane ride, the woman hardly had
the energy to keep up with them. But she stayed close
behind, knowing she had a job to do and determined
to carry it through.

51

AS THEY DROVE TOWARD THE SANDIA MOUNTAINS,
Danny was at the wheel while Jill navigated, a map
spread across her lap. She had circled the area where
the LaMane Center was located, as well as St. Marta's
Ridge. From these points, the two had decided the
children were heading toward the city. For a long time
neither one of them said a word, lost in similar
thoughts of the dangers they were facing. The possibility that they might not succeed, that they might end
up as dead as Stuart Morse, was not allowed to grow
beyond the vaguest of uneasy feelings. Worried as she
was about what lay ahead, Jill thought of the Conestoga wagon kit she'd bought. The package said, Age 9
and up. Once more she wondered what Ryan would be
like at age ten, how similar to the angelic little boy
she remembered. She finally spoke to Danny.

"Did you ever wonder what Laura looks like now?"

"A bit," Danny said. "But Kate tells me the child
she sees in her visions looks a little like me. Poor
kid!"

Jill couldn't help a smile. It was hard to imagine a feminine, youthful version of this bear of a man. He wasn't homely by any means, but his heavy dark brows and deep-set brown eyes would be overpowering on a little girl.

"I'm sure she's charming," Jill said.

"With enough of her mother's genes to get her by, I hope," Danny said. "I don't care what she looks like. I just want her back again."

Jill pointed off the road.

"There, that exit," she said. "That will take us back to the center."

Danny veered off the highway and followed the dusty mountain road for about fifteen minutes. When the mammoth wrought-iron fence around the LaMane Center came into distant view, Jill was struck by how its dour appearance contrasted with the gentle reds, browns, and greens of the surrounding mountains. But at the sound of Danny's gasp, she turned away from the view and looked to where he was pointing. There was a roadblock up ahead.

Two police cars were parked sideways on the road, headlight to headlight. Behind them was another one marked SHERIFF.

Jill sat back and looked at Danny with wide eyes. "What's going on?" she asked.

Danny only shook his head. Had the LaMane people been caught? Had something happened to one of the children?

"Looks like we're going to have the police helping us after all," Danny said.

Jill thought of the scarred man who had posed as a cop after Ryan and Jeff's accident, and later as a guest at her hotel.

"I don't think . . ."

Danny stopped the car and rolled down the window.

"What're you folks doing here?" the policeman asked, his eyes hidden behind dark glasses.

Danny made no attempt at pretense.

"We're looking for our children," he blurted.

"Those bastards at that LaManc Center kidnapped my little girl and I've come to get her back."

"Danny," Jill gasped.

The policeman took off his glasses and squinted into the back seat. "You better come with me."

Jill glared at Danny for a second, wanting to berate him. How could he be so trusting? But before she could say a word Danny was already out of the car. They were introduced to a man in a uniform the same sandy color as his hair. Lou Vermont wasn't quite as tall as Danny, but his barrel chest and thrown-back shoulders gave him the appearance of being every bit as strong. Lou did not waste time with preliminaries.

"Either of you folks know Stuart and Natalie Morse?"

"We went to school together," Jill said. "I—we heard about what happened at the airport."

"We're looking for our kids, too," Danny put in. "What's going on in there?" He cocked his head toward the cluster of adobe-style buildings beyond the black fence.

"That's what I mean to find out," Lou said. He studied the pair before him. "Your kids, huh? Damn, but this whole thing gets messier by the minute. What makes you think they're here?"

Jill and Danny exchanged glances.

"I doubt you'd believe—" Danny began.

"Oh, I'm sure I would," Lou drawled. "But you're too late. The whole complex is empty. Whatever's been going on in there, they've packed everyone and everything up and left in a hurry. I've got my men searching the place for a clue as to where they went, but I don't think they're gonna find anything. So if your kids really are with them—"

"My daughter isn't," Danny said. "I'm sure of that. She ran away from this place, along with two other boys. Sheriff, have there been any others who claimed their children were brought here?"

"Why are you here at all?" Jill wanted to know.

Lou held up his hands, his stubby fingers spread

wide. "Slow down. No, nobody's said anything about
their kid being here. I'm here to investigate a murder."

"A murder?" Jill asked.

"You heard that that fellow was killed in an airport
coffeeshop," Lou said. "The most bizarre thing I've
ever seen. His mother-in-law was also a victim, and
when I went to talk to her, she mentioned this place."
He took off his cap and scratched his head. "Damn
but I wish I could figure this out!"

"We may have another clue," Danny said. "Stuart
Morse was an old friend of mine. Y'see, Jill, Stuart,
and I went to school together back in a town called
Wheaton, Michigan."

Jill watched him with a mix of annoyance and fear
as he told their story, of the illegal fertility drug, of
the "deaths" of their children, and how Laura had
been in contact with his wife.

Lou heard all this without saying a word, and when
Danny was finished, he took in a deep breath and blew
it out slowly.

"If you don't believe this," Danny said, "I'd understand."

"Look, I got a murder on my hands no one can
explain," Lou said. "A woman and her daughter are
missing, and now you two strangers come out of nowhere telling me details of this case that fit in like they
were die-cut. I don't know what to believe, but if
you've got any suggestions I'm open-minded."

"Danny, don't . . ."

But Danny was so delighted to have the help of the
police that he ignored Jill's attempts to quiet him.

"When I last spoke to my wife," he said, "she told
me she had a vision that Laura and two boys were near
a place called St. Marta's Ridge. We've decided they
must be heading toward the city. What we hope is that
they'll cross paths with the Balloon Festival and that
we'll be able to rescue them there."

"Several questions," Lou put in. "Okay, so maybe

this is all for real and that is your daughter. But how do you know it's your boy, Mrs. Sheldon?''

"I didn't, at first," Jill said. "But the fact that Ryan had tried to make contact, too, tells me he might be one of the children. Call it a mother's instincts, it's just something I believe."

"And if it isn't Ryan?"

Jill turned away from the sheriff to hide the look of fear on her face. She hadn't allowed herself to think of that possibility . . .

It was Danny who spoke for her.

"If it isn't Ryan, then it's another scared little kid who'll help us find the boy."

Jill swung around, her eyes rimmed red with tears she hadn't allowed to fall. "If you really are here to help us," she said forcefully, "then what are you going to do to get our kids back?"

"Well, this is all really unexpected," Lou said. "Normally, there'd be a missing-persons report to be filed—"

"Screw that," Danny grumbled. "Some maniac is after our children."

Lou stared at him. "I've got people working on it. They're looking for a large group of people, either on the road or at the bus station or airport."

Jill listened to this while staring at the mud-caked tops of her boots. In the sunlight, she thought she saw the reddish-brown remains of blood and she closed her eyes in horror to remember what had happened the night before. She was terrified to think what might happen if the sheriff knew what she'd done—not of the price she'd pay for the crime, but of the delay in getting to Ryan. The LaMane people were on the run, too. And they'd be searching for the runaways to stop them from revealing too much.

Slowly, she looked up and spoke in a voice so soft it could barely be heard. "I know where there's a crowd," she said. "The Balloon Festival. What if they've gone there after the children? How easily could

they mingle with the crowds in search of Laura and
the boys?''

She was wide-eyed, imagining now a shuffling of
people, moving in unison and unaware of what was
happening to any one individual. How easily a knife
could be slipped between small ribs . . .

She swayed a little and Danny reached out to put an
arm around her shoulders.

"We don't have time to talk," he said. "Just trust
me that the kids are in danger. Are the phones still
working here? I want to call my wife."

Lou turned and called to one of the other cops. A
petite woman with dark skin and huge brown eyes hurried over.

"Officer Maizi," Lou said, "show this gentleman
to a phone. You're lucky they didn't have time to cut
if off.''

Danny followed the policewoman inside a nearby
building. In a nearly barren office, he picked up a
tipped-over chair and sat at the empty desk. The draw-
ers had all been pulled open and emptied; the files
across the room were in the same condition. He dialed
the hospital. He was surprised to hear Kate had been
released, since there had been no indication of this
when he spoke to her. Dialing his home phone number
only resulted in incessant ringing. Despondent, Danny
hung up. Where the hell was Kate now? Had she forgotten he'd be contacting her?

Kate, at that moment, was busy with an investigation of her own. When Dorothy picked her up at the
hospital, she was curious to find out why Mrs. Ginmoor hadn't paid a visit to either her or the boys. Kate
insisted on driving to the old woman's house. On the
way, she explained everything to her friend.

"I wish you had told me this earlier," Dorothy said,
sounding offended. "How could you bear such a burden alone?"

"I wasn't alone," Kate said. "I had Danny."

"Who didn't believe you at first," Dorothy said.

Kate looked at her. "Would you have? Or would you have thought I was a hysterical, overly hopeful mother?"

"I don't know," Dorothy said. "But I would have stuck by you."

Kate pointed. "That's her house. Pull in the driveway, will you?"

A moment later both women were standing on Mrs. Ginmoor's porch, knocking at her door.

"I just had a terrible thought, Kate," Dorothy said. "What if the same people who hurt Chris and Joey got Mrs. Ginmoor, too? What if that's why you haven't heard from her?"

Taking in Dorothy's ominous suggestion, Kate regarded her friend for just a moment. She took out her own keys and found the spare one to Mrs. Ginmoor's house. The old woman had given it to her in the event something happened while the boys were in her house.

Kate led Dorothy through the familiar rooms, quiet except for the droning noise of the furnace below and the hum of the refrigerator.

"We'd better check every room," Dorothy said. "If she's hurt somewhere . . ."

Or dead . . .

A thorough investigation proved the house was empty.

"She's just out for the morning," Dorothy said.

"No, I don't think so," Kate said. "Something's wrong. I'm telling you, Dorothy, Mrs. Ginmoor was crazy about our children. It just doesn't make sense that she'd have neglected them."

They were in the kitchen now, a small room of glimmering tile and cheerful yellow appliances. All signs of the exploded pie had been removed, though a faintly acrid smell still hung in the air.

"I think I've found something, Kate," Dorothy said. She had crossed toward a counter, near the wall phone.

Mrs. Ginmoor had left a phone book open on her counter, to the Yellow Pages listings for travel agents.

Kate moaned a little and pointed to the notes scribbled hastily in the margins.

"ABQ. TWA. Flight 200."

"ABQ?" Dorothy repeated. "Short for Albuquerque?"

"Where Danny went to find Laura," Kate said, disbelieving. "Why would Mrs. Ginmoor be there, too? How could she know?"

She stopped herself, her mind a boiling kettle of questions.

"Kate, I think your sweet old Mrs. Ginmoor was working for these LaMane people," Dorothy said.

Kate shook her head. "No. She loved our children."

"It's too much of a coincidence that she's in Albuquerque, too," Dorothy said. "Kate, I knew nothing of this until a few minutes ago. So I can be objective. Listen and think—you needed a sitter when you arrived in Massachusetts because both you and Danny worked. Along comes Mrs. Ginmoor, who conveniently agrees to stay even after Laura disappeared, thinking you'd need help. And who had no reason to leave because soon after you gave birth to Chris. But convenient for whom?"

"Mrs. Ginmoor was a godsend," Kate protested lamely. It couldn't be true.

"It wasn't God who sent her," Dorothy said. "She was planted with your family, Kate, to keep an eye on you. I wouldn't be surprised if she arranged the details of Laura's kidnapping. And she stayed on to be certain you never got too suspicious."

"It's so crazy," Kate said. "I never told her about Laura appearing to . . ." She let out a cry. "Oh, my God, the pictures!"

Her fingers squeezed Dorothy's arm like a talon as she told about the pictures she had had altered to look like Laura might today.

"She must have reported it," Kate said. "And when the boys were alone with her in this house, she arranged to have them hurt. That witch! I'll kill her when I find her. When I think that I left my babies alone with her!''

"Kate, she must be after them now," Dorothy said. "I don't know why she was called down there, but it may be that Laura will remember her, even subconsciously. Your daughter may trust her enough to go anywhere with her.''

Kate looked at the phone. "I've got to call Danny! But how? I don't even know where he is. Last we spoke, he was at the airport.''

"Then, let's get back to your house," Dorothy said. "We'll wait for him to call us. And as hard as you can, Kate, send Laura a warning to stay away from Mrs. Ginmoor.''

52

"THE CORNDOGS ARE A BUCK FIFTY EACH," THE MAN at the concession stand said, looking down from his perch at three grimy faces. "Drinks are seventy-five cents.''

Jenny, Tommy, and Michael gathered in a circle and emptied their pockets and bags of all the coins they could find. In their haste to run away, none of them had taken the time to bring very much money.

"Three dollars and ten cents," Tommy sneered. "We could split up two dogs, I guess.''

"I'm thirsty," Jenny said. "Walking in that hot sun—''

Both boys shushed her.

"We can find water somewhere," Michael suggested. "But we can't move on without energy from food. Those snacks we brought, they aren't enough. I say we go for the corndogs.''

Jenny felt a tap on her shoulder and swung abruptly. An elderly woman was gazing at her with sad eyes, her face so kindly that Jenny was speechless for a moment. There was something about her, something strangely familiar. An alarm went off in the little girl's mind, warning her that this might be someone from the center. But in the few moments she studied the woman's face in silence, she realized she hadn't seen her at LaMane. Still, she felt as if she knew her, as if she had met her long ago.

"I couldn't help overhearing," the woman said. "I'd be happy to treat you children."

Tommy shook his heard, his expression grim. "No way, lady. We don't talk to strangers."

"But—"

The woman's words were cut off when Jenny pulled Tommy a little farther away. Michael stepped over with them.

"We could use the help," she said.

"Are you nuts?" Tommy asked. "What if she's with Adams?"

"She isn't," Jenny said. "I'd know it if she was. And if you two boys would open up your minds, you'd know it, too. She's just a nice old lady who wants to help us."

Jenny didn't report the strange familiarity she'd felt.

"Buying those dogs is gonna wipe us out," Michael said. "We can't go anywhere without money, Tommy."

"It isn't like we're going to leave the fair with her," Jenny added. "Tommy, just let her buy us the food. It'll give us time to find out if she really is a nice person. And if she is, she can help us."

"We don't need help," Tommy growled.

"Don't be a jerk," Michael said. "How long do you think we're gonna last, three kids alone?"

Jenny and Michael turned back toward the old woman, who was already holding a box with three corndogs and three sodas. Ravenous, even Tommy accepted the food, which disappeared in minutes.

"My, but you're very hungry, aren't you?" the old woman said. "And filthy, too. Where have you been that you got so dirty? Where are your parents?"

The children exchanged glances.

"We—we ran away," Michael said quickly. He felt Jenny and Tommy's astonished gazes, but he went on. "Last night, we decided to try to camp out in the mountains. It was terrible. Really cold."

"And we kept hearing growling noises," Jenny put in, though she didn't quite understand Michael's game. She only knew he was smart enough not to get them into more trouble.

"You poor things," the old woman said. "But your parents must be terribly worried. No matter what the reason you ran away, you must let them know you're safe. If we could find a phone . . ."

Michael shook his head. "No! See, my dad was gonna work with one of the balloonists today. But this place is so big and there are so many people, I just can't find him."

The old woman smiled. "You leave that to me. How about a balloon ride? You'd be so far up you could see the entire grounds."

Jenny and Michael nodded eagerly. Tommy held back, still not trusting the woman. But Michael leaned and whispered to him, "We won't find my father, of course. But we will be able to tell if anyone from the center is here."

Tommy finally nodded, understanding what Michael had been up to all along. All three children followed the kindly old woman until she found the shortest line, leading to a balloon decorated with alternate panels of red and white. She pulled a small, beaded wallet from her black handbag. Jenny and the boys went agape at the sight of two crisp hundred-dollar bills.

"Wow," Tommy cried. "What's that for?"

The old woman smiled at him. "For the ride, of

course. You don't think these balloonists work for nothing?''

"But it's too much," Jenny protested. "You can't spend money like that on us. We don't even know you.''

Oh, but you do remember me, Laura. Don't you know my face? Think back, think long back . . .

Jenny froze, staring at the old woman. Where had the thoughts come from? Why had she heard the name "Laura," the same name the woman with glasses and brown hair used?

"What—what's your name?''

"Mrs. Mira," the woman said.

Nothing familiar about that. And nothing in the woman's expression revealed that the strange message had come from her own mind. Jenny was more confused than ever. But before she could ask another question, they found themselves at the beginning of the line.

Mrs. Mira paid the ticket man and climbed into the wicker gondola with the three children. "We're looking for someone," she said. "One of the other balloonists.''

"What's his name?" the man asked, readying the balloon for another trip.

Mrs. Mira looked at the children.

"Ralph Colpan," Michael said, able to think only of his father's name.

"Haven't met him," the aeronaut said, busy working the controls at the dashboard. "I know most everyone here. I've been into aerostation for ten years.''

"Aerostation?" Michael echoed.

"A fancy word for ballooning," the man said with a smile.

The slack in the tether line was released and the variometer began to measure in feet per second the balloon's lazy climb toward the sky. Tommy and Jenny clung to the padded leather edges of the huge basket, gazing in awe at the bright colors around them. Jenny pushed back the hair that had been blown into her face

by the wind. Soon, the noise of the burner sending
heat up into the throat of the balloon drowned out the
sounds of the people below. Jenny clung to the side,
afraid the basket would shake in the wind, but she was
surprised at how sturdy it felt.

"How come it isn't jiggly?" she asked the balloonist, who wore a name tag that said he was called Max.

"The cables hanging down from the balloon are
very strong," Max replied, "and they provide a re-
markably stable base. Do you know, movie-makers can
get steadier air shots from a balloon than from a plane
or helicopter?"

Michael could see for himself that the gondola was
sturdy, and he knew a strong tether line held them
anchored to the ground below. But his fear of heights
kept him from going to the edge. He sat on one of the
large, lightweight fuel tanks stored at one end of the
gondola. The higher up they went, the more he was
reminded of the watch tower at the center. If anything
happened, it would be a long fall.

"I can't see anyone's face very well," Jenny said.
"How will we find Mr. Colpan?"

"Lots of people want a good look around," the
balloonist said, speaking loudly over the roar of the
burner. He opened a door under the control panel and
pulled out a pair of binoculars. "Try these."

"Neat," Jenny cried.

"Let me look," Tommy insisted.

"You should really take turns, children," Mrs. Mira
said.

Michael looked at the binoculars. He wanted them,
too, wanted the illusion of being closer to the ground.
But he was frozen, terrified to go too close to the edge
of the balloon carriage. He couldn't move a muscle.

"You go first, Jen," Tommy said. Mrs. Mira was
nice, he decided. If she wanted to bring them back to
the LaMane Center, she wouldn't be bothering to
spend so much time and money on a ride.

Jenny put the binoculars to her eyes and scanned
the crowds below. None of the faces looked familiar,

she saw to her relief. If Dr. Adams was still looking for them, he hadn't gotten this far. She decided to ask the boys to leave as soon as the balloon landed again. They obviously had a head start on their adversaries.

"I don't see him," Jenny said.

Tommy realized this was her way of telling him there was no one familiar below. He looked for himself and saw this was true. But when he tried to hand Michael the binoculars, he saw that his friend was sitting stiffly on a fuel tank, as white as a ghost.

"What's the matter?" he asked.

Michael shook his head with small, jerky movements.

The balloonist smiled.

"Didn't realize how high up we go, did you?" Max asked. "Don't worry, I haven't had an accident yet, and I don't intend to start now. We'll be descending in a moment and you'll be on good old terra firma before you know it."

Mrs. Mira opened her purse again. "We aren't going anywhere," she said.

"What're you talking about, ma'am?"

The balloonist's cry of protest and Jenny's scream were both drowned out by the roar of the burner overhead. No one below could know the drama taking place hundreds of feet in the air. The man at the end of the tether rope saw the basket above jerk a little, and he swore under his breath at the ornery kids who were shaking it. He couldn't know that Mrs. Mira had pulled a hypodermic needle from her purse and had jabbed the balloonist in the neck with it. Max fell to the floor of the basket in a heap. Mrs. Mira picked up his walkie-talkie and threw it over the edge.

"Why did you do that?" Jenny asked.

"I told you we shouldn't have trusted her," Tommy cried. He leaned over the edge of the carriage. "Help! Help!"

But Mrs. Mira jerked him back quickly before his words could travel to the ground below.

"You trusted me, Laura," Mrs. Mira said.

Jenny backed up a step, bumping into Michael. She felt his hand take hers and squeeze it tightly.

"Why—why did you call me that? My name is Jenny Segal."

"Your real name is Laura Emerson."

She knows the thoughts that have been in my mind. She's saying the same things as that other woman.

"Don't you remember me, dear?" Mrs. Mira said. "It's been a long time, I know, since I last saw you. You were waving good-bye to me from the ferry on Great Gull Bay."

Jenny shook her head. Great Gull Bay? Ferry?

"Oh, I'm certain they've erased much of your memory, sweetheart," Mrs. Mira said. "But if you dig back into that amazing brain of yours, you'll find my face. A younger face, of course. Six years younger. I was your nanny, Laura. I took care of you until the center was ready for you."

"You're nuts," Tommy growled. "Her name isn't Laura. You're working for Dr. Adams and you just want to get Jenny upset so she can't read your mind and learn what you're really up to."

The old woman smiled. "No need to read my mind. My real name is Mrs. Ginmoor. Ring a bell yet, Laura?"

"My name is Jenny," the little girl protested weakly. There was something so comfortable to her about the name "Laura." The more she heard it applied to her, the more it began to fit. Like a shoe worn until it almost molded to the shape of the foot. And there was something equally familiar about Mrs. Ginmoor, an even stronger feeling than the one Jenny had sensed when she first saw her in front of the concession stand.

No! Stay away from her. Stay away.

The voice cut so sharply into Jenny's mind that she squeezed her eyes shut. She envisioned the younger woman with brown hair and glasses. The woman was shaking her head like crazy, her fingers entwined as if in beseechment. Jenny realized she was being sent a warning, and she tried hard to send her own thoughts back.

Who is she?

Someone who once cared for you, but someone who will hurt you now. Get away from her!

I can't. We're up in a balloon. What do I do?

"What do I do?" Jenny spoke the words aloud without realizing it.

"No," Mrs. Ginmoor cried. "I won't allow it. You can't talk with Kate."

Jenny felt something strike her hard across the face, and she tumbled to the floor, against the prone form of the balloonist. She opened her eyes to see Mrs. Ginmoor's arm drawn back and Tommy jumping on the woman. As if possessed by supernatural strength, she shoved Tommy to the floor, too, and turned to challenge Michael. The red-haired boy had leapt to his feet, but now he stood frozen.

"I came all the way from Massachusetts because Dr. Adams called me here," she said. "He knew where you children were heading and he needed someone you didn't know to finish his work. Well, it isn't exactly that you don't know me, Laura. You remembered enough of me subconsciously to trust me. And now I've got all three of you trapped. Won't Dr. Adams be proud of me when he learns I've got you? That I've prevented you from revealing the truth about his experiments?"

"Ex-periments?" Michael whispered in a choking voice. He thought of the files in his backpack.

Tommy flew at the woman, knocking her to the ground. "You aren't going to kill us," he roared. "We aren't going to die."

Mrs. Ginmoor laughed maniacally, kicking him away from her. She reached into her purse yet again and pulled out a glimmering kitchen knife. Jenny screamed as the woman headed toward her . . .

But Mrs. Ginmoor did not thrust the knife toward the child. Instead, she began to cut away at the knot of the tether rope.

Down below, the balloonist's partner saw the basket jerking crazily again. The next people in line were complaining about the wait, and he realized this group had been up there an unusually long time. Maybe something was wrong . . .

He picked up the walkie-talkie, which allowed him to communicate with his partner.

"Max? Max, Neal here. Come in, please."

Nothing but static.

"Max?" the man's voice was more urgent now. He was about to call his partner again when a young boy on line pointed skyward with a shout.

The balloon had broken free!

Everyone on the ground gazed upward in amazement as the wind carried the balloon off. It seemed to be moving lazily, but Neal knew it was moving with unusual speed. And heading straight toward another one. If a crash ripped the gore seams open . . .

He wouldn't let himself dwell on that possibility, but ran off to get help.

In the balloon, Tommy cried out. "We're gonna crash. You gotta steer us. You gotta move us in between the other balloons."

Mrs. Ginmoor laughed. "How silly! I don't know how to steer a balloon."

"But we're gonna die," Tommy screamed.

Jenny was still on the floor, wailing. Michael hadn't budged from his spot.

Tommy looked at his friends, an expression of disgust coming over his face. "Quit acting like babies," he demanded. "Don't let her do this to us. We gotta help ourselves."

"You're going to die," Mrs. Ginmoor shouted. She began to saw away at one of the suspension ropes.

Tommy understood immediately that she intended to free the gondola from the support of the balloon above.

"No," he shouted, racing toward the control panel. He recognized a compass, but the other gauges were completely foreign to him. Wasn't there something here he could use to bring them down? The next balloon was coming closer and closer. The people in it were on the opposite side, unaware of imminent disaster. If only he could warn them, make them move . . .

He scanned the next balloon frantically. Its gores were orange-and-black-striped, emblazoned with the graphic of an eagle. Tommy's eyes caught a small stuffed eagle hanging from one of the burner supports. He was taken back to the clinic, to the animals he had brought to life. He stared at the toy, willing it to move into the basket. The platform of his own gondola jerked a few times as the first of the suspension ropes was cut free.

As she moved to another, Mrs. Ginmoor saw the little creature open its beak and spread wings that should have been sewn to its plush feathers. It broke free of its string, reared up, and curled its talons like a real eagle in search of prey. Mrs. Ginmoor knew what Tommy was up to and jerked him away before the spell could be completed. Halfway to the back of the balloonist, the little eagle became a toy once more and thumped to the floor of the carriage.

"You won't stop me. We'll fall to the ground, and you'll die."

Michael had suddenly found his voice. "If we crash, you'll die, too." His tone was as matter-of-fact as if he were reciting arithmetic tables.

Mrs. Ginmoor let go of Tommy and turned to the smaller boy. "I know that," she said. "I have known I might be called to the ultimate self-sacrifice since the day I agreed to join Dr. Adams' team. Yes, I'll die. But I'll go down in the glory of his magnificent work, knowing I prevented you from stopping its progress."

"Yeah, you'll go down," Michael said, his tone dark. "But you'll go down alone."

Jenny and Tommy looked up at their friend. Somehow, he had come out of his trance of fear. What was he going to do?

Michael stared at Mrs. Ginmoor, his eyes seeming to grow dark. Or was that just the shadow of a cloud passing overhead?

"Go to the edge, Mrs. Ginmoor."

Something about his voice sent chills through his friends. Jenny sidled over to Tommy and put her arms around him. Michael's was a voice that could not be disobeyed, it seemed.

"Don't do that," Mrs. Ginmoor said. "I know all about your powers and they won't work on me."

"Go to the edge, Mrs. Ginmoor."

She was backing up in spite of her protests. She stopped abruptly at the back end of the basket, grabbing hold of a rope.

"Climb over and jump, Mrs. Ginmoor."

The child's voice had a deep, almost guttural quality. Jenny watched in amazement as Mrs. Ginmoor lifted one foot up. Tommy looked behind them at the ever-nearing orange-and-black balloon.

"Climb over. Climb over and jump."

"No! No!" Mrs. Ginmoor was fighting with all her might.

"I told you to jump, you stupid old witch."

Michael was suddenly running toward the old woman, arms outstretched. Just as he reached her, she obeyed the command she could not have ignored anyway. She threw her leg over the side, leaned far forward, and flew from the edge of the basket. Michael slammed into the wicker side, grabbing hold of the padded-leather rim, watching dizzily as Mrs. Ginmoor grabbed desperately for the basket handle, then the scuff leather around the bottom. In less than ten seconds her body was whirling down into the screaming crowds below.

And he saw himself falling, falling from the watch tower, spinning like an airplane out of control, spinning around and around . . .

My name is Peter Morse. My name is Peter Morse. It's not Michael Colpan. It isn't!

Say your name is Michael or I'll drop you.

Peter Morse!
Michael Colpan!
I don't wanna fall. I don't wanna fall.
"I'm not Peter Morse," Michael screamed. "I'm Michael Colpan."
Jenny and Tommy leapt to their feet and pulled him away from the side. His screams had alerted the balloonist, who worked with lightning speed to open the rip panel and duck his balloon down. Word spread through walkie-talkies and soon a path cleared for the runaway balloon. As if they'd been synchronized, dozens of colorful balloons sank to the ground to give way. And now the wind was carrying children's balloon toward the massive walls of the mountains, toward the top of trees that could easily rip the balloon to shreds . . .
Tommy knelt down beside the unconscious balloonist and began to slap his cheeks in a desperate attempt to wake him.
Michael tried to will the balloon to open air, finding to his frustration that his talents did not work.
Jenny closed her eyes and began to call out to the brown-haired woman, using words she sensed all along but hadn't had the courage to believe in.
Mommy? Mommy, help us. We're going to crash and I don't want to die.

53

KATE'S KNEES BUCKLED AS IF THEY'D BEEN SNAPPED in two, and she sank to the floor of her kitchen. Dorothy helped her into a chair, feeling the violent trembling of her friend's body. Kate was as pale as a ghost, her green eyes wild.

"Laura's going to die," Kate cried. "Mrs. Ginmoor's trying to kill my little girl."

"How do you know?" Dorothy demanded, beyond questioning the reality of what was happening. Kate's distress was no game. "Can you see her? Do you know where she is?"

Kate nodded. "She—Laura said she's up in a balloon. Some kind of hot-air balloon, I think. She said the old woman is trying to kill her. Dorothy, why doesn't Danny call? Why doesn't he call?"

Her voice was so panic-stricken that Dorothy had to hold her firmly by the shoulders to calm her. "Kate, if you believe this so strongly," she said, "we'll contact Information and get the number of the police down there."

"No," Kate cried. "They won't believe us. It's just too crazy a story. Even Danny took a long time to believe I was really in contact with our little girl, that she was alive." She gazed at the phone. "Call me, Danny," she whisper-cried. "Please call me."

If only she could contact her husband the way she contacted Laura . . .

Like a miracle, as if Danny really had received her message, the phone rang and he was on the other end. He started telling her about the deserted LaMane Center, but she cut him off.

"Danny, I had contact with Laura a few minutes ago," Kate said breathlessly. "She's in a hot-air balloon somewhere. Danny, Mrs. Ginmoor was one of them. They planted her here to spy on us."

Thousands of miles away, Danny closed his eyes in disbelief at his own gullibility. But there was no time for that now.

"Kate, I know where to look for her," he said. "There's a balloon festival in Albuquerque right now. Kate, I swear to you when I call back, I'll have our little girl."

Without waiting for a good-bye, he hung up and

went to find Lou and the others. "We've got to get to the balloon fair," Danny said. "The kids are in a balloon somewhere, with a crazy woman who's trying to kill them."

"How do you know?" Lou demanded.

"Don't ask," Danny said. "It's too complicated and we don't have time to waste."

Lou nodded, having come to the point that he just accepted anything these people said. The whole thing was insane. Quickly, followed by the others, he went to the squad car and put in a call. When he came back, his ruddy complexion had gone pale.

"There's a report of a runaway balloon, all right," he said, gazing at Danny in awe and fear. "Fellow at the end of a tether line said an old woman and three kids got on board. The—the old woman fell over the side of the basket and ended straight up and hip-deep in the mud. She's dead."

"What about the balloonist?" Jill asked. "The children can't be alone up there."

"They might be," Lou said. "No one can establish radio contact with the balloonist."

Jill closed her eyes, feeling the heat of tears behind them. Had she come this far only to see her son die in a freak accident? It couldn't happen that way. None of this could be such a waste. "Come on," she said. "Let's get to that field."

"Follow me," Lou said. "I'll give you an escort."

Red-and-blue beacons flashing, the sheriff's car roared down the mountain road and onto the highway. They were at the fair in moments, where Lou received a report of what had happened from the security team assigned to watch over the crowds.

"Do you know where the balloon is now?" Jill asked, looking up at the colorful gathering in the sky. "Is there any way to stop it?"

"Of course there is," said a man who had joined the group. It was Max's partner, Neal. "You've got to pull a rope that leads to a rip panel. Trouble is, landing may not be so slow and smooth without the tether line.''

"It won't be smooth at all if they crash," Danny growled.

"Aerostation accidents are rarely serious," Neal reassured.

Danny scratched his head. "I'd feel better if that 'rarely' was a 'never.' ''

"But where is it?" Jill asked again.

"Heading eastward," Neal said. "We've got people monitoring it."

"I'll put in a call to those helicopters I've had searching for Adams and his crew," Lou said, heading back to the squad car.

Danny had a sickening thought. "What—what happens when the burner is empty?"

"The air already in the bag will hold them up," Neal said. "They'll go down at parachute speed. But it isn't the descension that's dangerous. It's finding a safe place to land. On a clear day like this, you need about sixty feet of clear space for the empty bag. But if the winds pick up, you need much more. The gondola drags a bit before it stops."

"What if they hit trees?" Jill asked.

"If they're going slow enough," Neal said, "not much harm will be done. But if they hit something at high speed, or if they land too fast . . ." He let the other imagine the rest.

Jill shivered and moved closer to Danny. He put his arms around her. "If only there was some way to contact the children," he said.

Now Jill pulled away again, her eyes wide. "But there is! Danny, you can call Kate and have her send a message to Laura. Neal here can give you instructions over the phone on landing that thing."

Danny nodded eagerly. "It could work."

"It has to work," Jill said. "Six years ago, we thought our children had died. We can't sit by and make it really happen. Not after all we've gone through to get them back again."

Danny turned to Neal. "Where can I find a phone?"

"We have a trailer set up at the back of the field," Neal said. "Just follow me."

They raced toward the crowds. Danny was so nervous when they climbed into the van that his big fingers fumbled with the phone dial. Jill took it gently, asked Danny's home number, and dialed. Only half a ring sounded when Kate jerked the phone off the hook.

"You found her?" she asked hopefully, remembering Danny's earlier promise.

"In a way," Danny said. "Kate, you were right. Laura is up in a balloon and there's no one to land it. The only way we can help is if you contact Laura and instruct her. There's a fellow here named Neal who'll show you how."

"I understand," Kate said. "Give me a few minutes to get in touch."

"I'll wait," Danny said, though he wished Kate's gift was as fast as a telephone.

Every minute that went by put his daughter, and the other two children, in greater danger. And this time, it wouldn't be a trick.

54

THE BALLOON FLOATED LAZILY ON CURRENTS OF mountain wind, carrying its four passengers farther and farther from the crowded fairgrounds. The din of the burner as it shot heat into the mouth of the balloon was loud enough to drown out the cries of the people below, but Jenny could sense their horror as easily as she had picked up other voices and thoughts throughout the past years. She searched her mind for the woman with brown hair and glasses, a woman she now believed to be her real mother. Even if Michael hadn't found those files, she would have come to this conclusion. Alice Segal had never shown her any love. She had always treated Jenny like a . . .

Jenny tried hard to think of a word. Like something under a microscope, she decided. Her father had been nicer—her pretend father, that was—but he never did anything to stop the hurting. And he'd taken her away from her real parents.

The girl looked over the rim of the basket at the mountains. Fortunately, the wind was blowing them away from the Rockies, but if it turned, or if the burner stopped . . .

She shook her head hard, not letting herself think such things. There had to be a way out of this. The boys were trying to come up with a solution. Tommy was busy patting the balloonist's face, trying to revive him. Michael, forcing himself to overcome his fear of heights, was studying the control panel. Jenny caught a flash of his thoughts and realized he had figured one of the gauges, labeled VARIMOMETER, was measuring their ascent in feet per seconds. But then she became so caught up in her own search for her real mother that she shut Michael out completely.

Tommy looked up from Max, seeing Jenny staring out at the mountains. "What're you doing?" he asked. "I need help here."

"I'm trying to get us help," Jenny said. "I've been trying to reach my mother, to call for help. But she's cut me off, for some reason."

The truth of the matter was that Kate Emerson had channeled all her mental energies into memorizing the instructions Neal was giving her over the phone. Before she could relay them to Laura, before she could risk the lives of three children, she had to be certain she knew exactly what she was doing.

From thousands of miles away, Neal's voice was tinny and crackling. Kate jotted down notes with a nervous scribble as Dorothy read them over her shoulder. Guide the balloon down through telepathy? It seemed impossible, but it was the only chance the children had.

"Okay, I'm ready," she said. "Put Danny on the line." When Danny got on, she said, "Say a prayer this works. I've had tentative cooperation from Laura in the last day, but I still think she's skeptical."

"She'll listen," Danny says. "She'll feel how much we love her and she'll know we want to help."

"I'm giving the phone to Dorothy now," Kate said. "If there's any trouble, she'll let you know."

"Good luck, Kate."

Kate didn't respond. She gave the receiver to her friend and pulled out a chair. Sitting at the kitchen table, she closed her eyes and rested her head in her arms. Over and over she called her daughter's name, begging her to answer, telling Laura how much she loved her.

The response was so immediate that Kate sat up with a jolt, her eyes open but glazed.

"Kate?"

She didn't hear Dorothy's voice. Her friend reported Kate's condition over the phone and kept watching her. The eyes were blank, as if Kate's soul had fallen through some kind of hole into another dimension. Dorothy wondered if Laura was there, too.

To Laura, it wasn't like falling through a hole into blackness, but like having a brilliant light suddenly flicked on when you'd spent days in darkness. Darkness. They'd locked her in a dark room and told her she could have light only if she said her name was Jenny Segal. But when the brown-haired woman with glasses started appearing to her, she'd sensed joy and light. It was only now, in the terrifying situation she was in, that Jenny/Laura could let herself accept that light.

"She's here," Laura cried. "My mother is here and she's going to help us."

Tommy looked up at her. He wasn't telepathic like

Michael or Jenny or some of the others, so he didn't really understand what was going on. But if Jenny was in touch with someone who was going to get them the heck down to the ground, he was all for that. He glanced over at Michael, who still stood bent over the control panel. Tommy felt helpless, but still he continued to prod the balloonist.

"I can hear her calling me," Jenny said. "I've got to—to answer." She closed her own eyes and sat on the fuel tank.

I knew you'd come, Mommy.

You called me mommy! Oh, Laura, my baby . . .

I don't want to die, Mommy.

You won't, sweetheart, Oh, no, you won't. I'm going to tell you how to get that thing down. Can you listen to me and talk to your friends at the same time?

I guess I can. What do you want me to do?

Who's at the control panel?

Michael Colpan. He's real smart.

All right, tell him to keep watch on the variometer. You want to lower the balloon very slowly, no more than five hundred feet per minute to start. When you get closer, you'll be going as slow as a hundred feet per minute, okay? And then, even slower than that.

Jenny looked up at Michael. "We have to go down slow, Michael," she said. "The variometer's not supposed to say more than five hundred feet per minute."

Michael nodded. Right now, the wind was carrying the balloon upward.

How do we get it to go down?

What's the other boy doing, Laura?

He's trying to wake Max up.

Tell him to forget Max right now. Tell him to look at the cables and find one that goes right up into the top of the balloon.

Jenny relayed the message. Tommy left Max and went to peer up into the throat of the balloon. He quickly spotted the rope that Jenny had described to him.

He's got it, Mommy.

Tell him that's the rip line. When you pull it, a panel opens on top and lets air escape. It's the way you lower the balloon. But tell him not to open it yet.

"That's a rip line," Jenny said. "It opens the top of the balloon so we can go down. But you aren't supposed to pull it yet."

"Then when can I?" Tommy asked impatiently. "I want to get down from here."

Jenny ignored his outburst and turned her mind back to her mother.

He's got it. What now?

Now look out around you. What do you see?

Mountains, but they're getting farther away. I see a lake, and a big, big ranch. There's cows there.

How far away is the ranch?

I don't know. It looks really far.

In her kitchen, Kate sighed deeply. She didn't feel Dorothy's hand on her shoulder. If only she could see what Jenny was seeing! Was the area big enough to land the balloon? Was it far enough away to give them the right amount of time for descent? Neal had said they'd need sixty yards of clear space for the deflated bag. Well, if it was a cattle ranch, then they certainly had the space. She only hoped the landing didn't startle the animals into a stampede.

But there was no time for speculation. She had to guide those children down the best she could, using the instructions Neal had given her.

I'm back, Jenny. I was thinking. Now listen, it should take you about ten or fifteen minutes to get down. Is there anything in your way? Any tall trees or electrical wires?

It looks pretty clear.

Great! Now, tell Tommy to slowly, slowly open the rip panel.

"She says you can open it now," Jenny reported.

Eagerly, Tommy yanked the rip cord. Michael saw the needle of the variometer swing toward DOWN. The numbers climbed higher and higher until they read five-hundred feet per second. When the balloon began

to accelerate even more, Michael cried out, "No!
Close it. We're going too fast."

Tommy let the rip line go. The heat from the burner
right above him had brought a pink flush to his cheeks,
and he wiped his arm across his sweat-covered forehead. Whoever said it was freezing up in the sky had
never ridden in a hot-air balloon.

How close are you to the ground?

I don't know. I'll ask Michael.

"How far do we have to go?"

"About 375 feet," Michael reported, never taking
his eyes from the gauges.

Three hundred seventy-five feet.

Then slow down to a hundred feet per second.

Jenny relayed the orders and Tommy opened the rip
panel ever so slowly. The balloon moved so lazily, so
carefully, that it seemed the danger was past them. Jenny
could see the field was clear. This realization, combined with the strength of her mother's guidance, gave
her a sense of confidence.

What, now?

Just keep coming down, very, very, slowly. When
you touch ground, you'll drag about ten to twenty feet
as the remaining air is released. Laura?

Yes, Mommy?

Are you afraid?

I don't know. You make me feel so safe, Mommy.
I never felt that way with Alice.

Alice?

The lady I thought was my real mother.

Kate's response was muffled by ominous words from
Michael.

"Something's wrong."

Tommy, still holding the rip line, turned and looked
at him. Jenny gazed up from her seat on the fuel tank.

"What do you mean?" Jenny asked. "We're so
close to the ground. What could possibly happen
now?"

"The wind's picked up," Michael said. "Can't you

feel it? It's pulling us along, back toward the mountains.''

''We'll land before we go too far, won't we?'' Jenny asked.

The wind's blowing really hard, Mommy. What's going to happen?

Just tell Tommy to keep tight hold of that rope. And watch the speed.

''How fast are we going, Michael?''

''Three hundred feet per second,'' Michael cried. ''Tommy. Close the panel, now!''

Tommy had been so caught up in the conversation between his friends that he'd forgotten to open and close the rip panel to regulate the speed of their descent. They were going down too fast.

''We're gonna crash,'' Michael cried. ''The wind is blowing too hard and we aren't slowing fast enough.''

Mommy, Mommy, we're going to crash.

No! Oh, no, Laura. You won't crash.

But the ground is so close and it's so windy and the field is really bumpy, and . . .

Kate's mind went blank. She opened her eyes and turned to Dorothy, her face completely pale. ''Oh, dear Lord, Dorothy,'' she said, ''I've lost contact.''

Dorothy spoke into the phone. ''Danny, she doesn't have Laura anymore.''

The two women hugged each other, praying the cutoff wasn't caused by the child's death.

But, in truth, it had been caused by the impact of the gondola on the rough ground, so swift that Jenny was thrown from her seat on the fuel tank. Michael flew backward with a scream. Though he tried to hold on fast to the rip line, the rapid vertical speed of their landing and the high winds caused him to lose his grip. He fell to the floor of the gondola, too. In a heap, thrown over one another as the gondola turned, the children watched in horror. They were being dragged across the field by a balloon in almost full sail.

''Oh, no!''

The three children barely registered the sound of the male voice. Max's voice! Jolted out of his drugged sleep by the impact of their landing, he scrambled toward the ropes, climbing right over Michael. Because he was still light-headed, Max saw the ropes not as taut lines, but as sinewy waves. As the basket tumbled, his befuddled mind raced to find the right cable. He pulled one line, unsuccessfully. Another, then another . . .

And finally caught the rip line. With a jerk, he opened it and released the rest of the air in the balloon. The gondola slowed very gradually, finally coming to rest. Max turned off the burner, then collapsed against the side of the carriage. For a few moments, no one said a word, though the air was filled with the sounds of heavy gasping and the lowing of startled cows.

Then Tommy whined, "My arm! I think I broke my arm."

Slowly, Max pulled himself to a sitting position. He studied the three children, bloodied and bruised but alive. There had been a woman, hadn't there? He couldn't quite remember.

"I'm gonna throw up," Jenny whispered.

"Not on me," Tommy cried. "Owwww! My arm!"

Michael breathed in deeply and felt a stabbing pain in his chest. Had he broken a rib? He looked at Jenny and saw blood trickling down her face. She rose unsteadily to her feet and stumbled out of the basket, retching.

"We're alive," Michael whispered.

Tommy kept on crying about his arm. But Jenny, finished being sick, turned to look at her friends. Michael was right. By some miracle, they were alive.

She burst into tears, sinking to the ground.

We're alive! Can you hear me, Mommy? We're alive.

Kate let out such a scream that even Danny heard it over the phone wires. She didn't respond to her daughter. Instead, she grabbed the phone and cried, "They're alive! They're okay, Danny."

She heard strange noises and realized her big, strapping, former linebacker husband had burst into tears. She could imagine the scene in New Mexico. Hugging, kissing, tears. Now all they had to do was get the kids . . .

"But we don't know where they are," she said.

"Yes, we do," Danny reported. "Lou Vermont, the sheriff, had a team of helicopters out. One of them's landing right now."

And in the field, Max and the children watched with relief as a team of paramedics came racing toward them. The children let themselves be taken to the helicopter, Michael and Tommy on stretchers. Jenny made no attempt to contact her mother again. She knew it would only be a matter of hours before they were reunited.

55

EVEN THOUGH HIS YOUNG PATIENTS WEREN'T AWARE of his presence, Dr. Nicholas Somers attended to them with as much loving care as he would give his own children. He examined Joey and Chris Emerson as he had done before, thoroughly and gently. No amount of research would solve the baffling mystery of their accident. Nicholas had concluded that they really hadn't been electrocuted—none of the symptoms was present. The very fact they were alive made the doctor suspicious. He hated to say they were comatose, although it seemed that way. To Dr. Somers, the boys were in a very, very deep sleep.

He folded his stethoscope in half and stuck it in the pocket of his coat. The nurse stayed behind a few minutes to move the boys to another position, so that they would not get bedsores.

"They're so beautiful," Martha Parks said.

"I am not."

Somers stopped in his tracks, his hand on the lever of the door.

"Doctor?" the nurse's voice was tremulous.

"I am not be-yoo-ful," Chris Emerson said. "Boys ain't be-yoo-ful."

Nicholas swung around so fast his shoes squeaked across the tile floor. He hurried to Chris's bedside.

The little boy stared up at him with huge green eyes. He frowned deeply, then asked in a quiet voice, "Where's my mommy? Where's Daddy? What happened to Mrs. Ginmoor? Who're you? What's that?"

"Shh! Shh," Nurse Parks hushed.

In a flash, Nicholas was looking the boy over. As if he'd wakened from a deep sleep, he was perfectly fine. Somers shook his head. "This is one for the record books," he said. "How do you feel, Chris?"

"I'm hungry," Chris said. "Where's my mommy? How come this bed has a cage around it?"

The nurse and the doctor laughed. Danny and Kate Emerson had mentioned their son's never-ending questions.

But it was a day for multiple miracles. Across the room, a shrill scream came from Joey Emerson's bed. They raced to him, doing their best to soothe and examine him at the same time.

"I don't understand it," Dr. Somers said. "I've never seen anyone snap out of a coma like that. And both of them at the same time."

"They're going to be okay, aren't they?" the nurse asked.

Dr. Somers shrugged. "Looks good to me." He smiled at the boys.

Joey was crying his eyes out, gazing at these

strangers in terror. Chris frowned and studied his surroundings.

"You know what, guys?" Dr. Somers said. "I'm going to bring a telephone in here. There's someone who's gonna want to hear your voice."

Nurse Parks went off and found a phone. Once it was connected, Nicholas tried to call Kate's home. It took a few minutes to get past the busy signal, but at last he got through. He handed the phone to Chris.

"Hi, Mommy! Where are you? Are you gonna come get me?"

For a moment, Kate was silent.

Somers took the phone from the little boy. "It's Dr. Somers, Mrs. Emerson," he said. "I can't understand what happened, but both Joey and Chris are awake. And they seem fine."

Kate said something the doctor couldn't understand, then let out a whoop. He could hear sobbing on the other end of the line, but he understood what was happening. Kate's were the tears of relief, the release of tension after being in the dark about her boys for so long.

"Dr. Somers, this is the most incredible, wonderful, marvelous day of my life," Kate said. "We've found my daughter, too. Your suspicions about Mrs. Ginmoor were right."

"Kate, you come and tell me all about it," Dr. Somers said. "But not on the phone. There are two little boys here who are very anxious to see their mother."

"Tell them I'll be right there," Kate said. "I'll be there as fast as I can drive."

56

NATALIE STARED UP AT THE MAN WITH THE SCARY blue eyes, her own eyes and nose a glaring red contrast to the gauze around her mouth. She was sitting in what, by its simple furnishings, appeared to be a hotel room. From the moment she woke to find herself tied to a wooden chair, Natalie had been trying to free herself of the ropes that tied her. Even though she couldn't see them, the soreness in her wrists indicated they were raw and bloody. But the pain there was nothing compared to the searing fire in her heart. Dr. Adams had been going on for hours about her husband and children being dead. No matter how much she tried to tell herself this Dr. Adams was a maniac, she couldn't convince herself his cruel taunts weren't true.

"The boy's dead by now, too, you know," he said. "I must say I'm sorry to lose Michael. He was a boy of remarkable genius and might easily have stood at my right hand when he grew up."

His name is Peter, you bastard!

Adams ignored the flash in Natalie's eyes. He paced around the room, speaking to her, and yet speaking as if she weren't there.

"Some of the children are almost grown up, you know," Adams reported. "You see, I saw the potential of Neolamane long before any others, because I had given it to my wife in its earliest stages. Our baby was much like these children. He could make things happen. You wouldn't want to give him something, but suddenly you found yourself doing it anyway. I knew Lincoln Junior was forcing his mother's hand through his mind. He couldn't do it with sounds, you know. Not crying, not talking. He didn't have a mouth.''

Something congealed in the pit of Natalie's stomach, and she closed her eyes in disgust.

"He only lived a few months," Adams went on, his voice faraway. "When he died, my wife committed suicide.''

He stopped abruptly, staring off into space as if seeing something from his past. If Natalie had been able to know his thoughts, her terror would have expanded beyond the point of sanity. Adams was correcting himself silently, remembering exactly how his wife *really* died.

Lincoln Jr., twisted and frail though he was, had mind powers beyond anything his father could have imagined. Power enough to force his mother's hand to pull the trigger on a gun.

Natalie saw Adams jump, but couldn't know he had actually heard the gunshot. She watched in silence as he stood trancelike, off in his own world, unaware of her.

Lincoln Jr. had died a few hours after his mother. But his father saw at once the potential of Neolamane, already being taken off the market due to the birth defects it had caused. If he could perfect it, working in his father-in-law's laboratory at LaMane Pharmaceuticals, he could create a race of beings so powerful they could use mind power alone to control their subjects. And if he did everything right, he would be in control of these magnificent beings.

Adams buried his wife in a private family ceremony, claiming she had died in childbirth. He set Lincoln Jr.'s birthday back several weeks, making everyone believe the child had died because of his deformities. Perfunctory tears were shed for Helen Adams, but in the back of his mind he was already wondering where to find a new woman to carry on his plans.

It was easy enough. Adams only had to spend a few days at the bus terminal to pick up a runaway girl. Her name had been Victoria—aged eighteen, she claimed, and the victim of child abuse. She'd been wary at first, but Adams had won her over, finally taking her into his beautiful home and caring for her as no adult ever had.

It was only a matter of time before he got the Neolamane into her, in the guise of vitamins. How naïve she had been! So naïve that she believed his promises of marriage after she became pregnant.

"But I must make certain everything is settled with my affairs," Lincoln had told her. "After all, it's only been a year since my wife died."

"I'll wait, Lincoln," Victoria had said, her eyes wide with admiration.

Adams tried to remember if she'd been pretty, but could see only a pale face, frizzy brown hair, and a big belly. She'd meant nothing to him, other than her importance as an incubator. When Gregory was born, a perfectly beautiful little boy, Adams turned completely cold. Months passed with no sign that the child was different. Hurt by Lincoln's hardness, confused by his complete obsession with the baby, Victoria had finally snapped.

"Now I see what you wanted me for," she had screamed one day. "You only wanted a child. Not me. You don't love me. You used me. You stupid old man, you used me!"

Lincoln had only smiled at her. He was cradling the three-month-old baby in his arms.

"Old man?" he'd said. "I'm barely forty. Although, I suppose to a child like yourself I am an old man."

"I'm not a child," Victoria had cried out. "Lincoln, I gave birth to a baby. I'm no longer a little girl, but a mother. Why are you always taking Gregory away from me? Why can't you let me be his mother?"

Lincoln stared at her for a few moments. Then he said, very evenly, "You are not capable of caring for this child. He is special, more special than you can realize. He requires more care than a spoiled, incompetent little brat can give him."

Victoria had let out such a scream that Gregory began to wail. Ignoring her, Lincoln clucked at the baby, trying to soothe him. He didn't see the vase come hurtling at him . . .

. . . until it burst into flames midair and then vanished.

Victoria had gasped, staring at the puff of smoke that hung in the air. Lincoln had looked at it, too, then at the baby. It had finally happened. His experiment was a success!

Gregory was a miracle.

And there would be more miracles, more power, and finally, the prestige that was rightfully his.

Adams blinked, snapping out of his reverie.

He turned now to Natalie and took her by her bound shoulders. "I've worked so hard," he cried, his blue eyes reflecting his madness. "I'm a genius, a god! Those children will never stop me."

Adams let her go and started to pace again. The room was dark except for one small light on the night table beside the double bed. All the curtains were drawn.

"The first subject was my own son," he said. "My second son, I mean. His name is Gregory. His mother was a runaway, but she's dead now. I took care of that." He looked at Natalie. "Strychnine in her cola. Very simple. No one missed her, either."

Natalie felt a cold sweat break out over her skin. Why was Adams telling her all this when she could easily tell it to the police? Easily? Natalie reminded herself she was tied up, at the mercy of a lunatic.

He doesn't care what you know. He's going to kill you.

"I raised the boy on my own," Adams went on. "Remarkable child! He could completely destroy something, then reassemble it before your eyes. It took me a long time to realize it was all illusion. He actually tricked your mind into believing what you saw. That's how he killed the boy's father, you know. Made him think the window was broken when in truth the glass was intact. When your husband tried to climb through, the glass cut him in two. Oh, it must have been a remarkable sight.''

He spoke in a tone of such sheer delight that Natalie couldn't suppress the belief it was all the rantings of a madman. Stuart was alive, of course. He was alive and he was going to find her.

Wherever she was . . .

''My boy has other talents as well. Telepathy, pyrokinesis. Imagine the power I felt to have such a being at my command. I began to work even further with Neolamane. Of course, all drugs are heavily tested before they appear on the market even at the prescription level. In every test performed, none of my son's unusual gifts was indicated. I thought Gregory might have been a freak. Neolamane seemed a safe means of inducing pregnancy. And in many cases, it was. But then the mutations began and I knew the potential for another like Gregory was still there. Oh, they tried to take Neolamane off the market, but that didn't stop me. With the help of a few med students—students who would have failed their courses anyway—I managed to get the drug to a select few. You were lucky enough to be one of those women, Natalie Morse. You see, your husband mentioned to one of my med students that you'd been trying for years to have a baby. Stuart was more than happy to try Neolamane. Since it was off the market, he had never heard of it, but he had trusted Ken Safton because the med student was a good friend.''

Natalie closed her eyes, remembering Safton's frequent visits to the house during her pregnancy. She'd thought it was unusual when the young man transferred to a medical college in California, soon after Stuart and Natalie moved there from Ann Arbor, Michigan. But she'd been so caught up in her twins that she didn't dwell on the topic.

As if he'd read her mind, Adams said, ''Twins! More than I could ever have hoped for. I so wanted to have both of them, but you know I was only able to get the boy. He's been a fascinating study, Natalie. You should be proud of him. But you won't have time to be proud, will you? Because you're going to die. I only have to ask one of my children and I'll have a whole slew of executions at my disposal. But I was talking about Michael, wasn't I? It's only a shame he's dead now. I can't imagine what kind of money I would have made if I'd been able to sell him. When I think what the army could do . . .''

Adams stopped abruptly once again and came closer to Natalie. Disgust at what this man had done had overwhelmed her, and she found herself losing control. To her chagrin and anger, the corduroy upholstery of the seat felt damp beneath her.

"Look at that," Adams said in a scolding voice. "And you're an adult. Well, I suppose I have had you confined for a long time. For God's sake, get up and clean yourself in the bathroom."

Natalie glared at him.

He frowned, then his eyes widened. "Of course," he said. "You can't move, can you?" He began to untie her.

Natalie brought her arms carefully forward and looked in horror at the raw, bloodied skin on her wrists.

Adams began to untie the gauze bandage he'd used to gag her, but paused a moment. "By the way," he said in a matter-of-fact tone that belied the monster inside him, "don't bother screaming. There's no one else here but my own people. We're at a retreat I had built especially for an emergency like this one."

With that, he untied the gag. Natalie worked her mouth and tried to speak, but her throat was so dry she could only emit a strange little croak. She stood up, shook the kinks out of her legs, and gazed at the doctor. He indicated the bathroom with a chillingly pleasant smile.

"You'll find towels and a robe," Dr. Adams said. "I had them set up especially for you. You do want to be presentable at your execution."

Safe within the confines of the bath, Natalie flicked on the light and went to the sink. Her hair was a rat's nest, her skin ghostly pale in some spots and bruised in others. Dry, cracked lips welcomed the cool water she carried to them in cupped hands. Tenderly, numbly, she began to wash the dirt from her sore wrists. The shower was so inviting, but Natalie wondered if she dared to put herself in such a vulnerable situation, naked and at the mercy of Dr. Adams.

"Stop—stop calling him 'doctor,' " she whispered. She had serious doubts about his medical degree.

Still, she needed to revive herself if she ever planned to get out of here. Natalie reached for the door and locked it. Then she undressed, turned on the shower, and got in. The water was icy cold, but it shocked away the last of the drug that had been used to sedate her. Fearful that Adams would burst in on her in spite of the door's lock, she got out quickly and dried herself off. Then, to make him think she was still busy, she turned the sink on. Almost completely revived now and not letting herself wonder why she was allowed the luxury of a shower, Natalie climbed back into the tub and peered out the small window. Adams hadn't been lying. She seemed to be in a large house in the middle of nowhere. From this direction, she could not see the mountains. Natalie tried to get her bearings, but couldn't decide which direction she was facing.

There was a knock. "Are you almost finished?"

"I'm –I'm sick," Natalie said. It was only half a lie.

"Let me take care of you," Adams said congenially. "I'm a doctor."

You're a goddamned devil, that's what you are!

Natalie didn't answer him. Instead, she glared at the battered face she saw reflected in a mirror. If he'd done this to her, it was frightening to think what he'd done to her children. And to Stuart—God, let him be alive!—and her parents. She'd make him pay, somehow. If it killed her, she'd take this bastard down with her.

She looked all around the bathroom in the hope of finding a weapon. The medicine cabinet was empty, as was the cabinet beneath. There had to be something here, anything she could use . . .

Her eyes came to rest on the shower curtain. It was held up by wire rings, some of them rusted after years of use. Working quickly, Natalie pulled one down, then rearranged the curtains so it would not be noticed, Long ago, an old boyfriend had been a magician who specialized in sleight of hand. He'd shown her a trick called palming, where the magician kept something hidden in the palm of his hand. Natalie untwisted the ring as best she could, then fitted it into the slightly bent heel of her palm. To others, it would seem she was holding her hand in a relaxed position. As long as she didn't turn it, no one would notice. The wire wouldn't kill anyone, but it could inflict enough pain to give her a moment's advantage.

At last, she opened the door. Natalie was surprised to see another woman standing with the doctor. She had dark hair pulled back in a severe bun and she wore a nurse's white uniform.

"Come with us," Alice Segal said without introduction. "There is something we want you to see."

Silently, her hair still dripping wet, Natalie followed them down a dark hall. Adams opened a door at the end to lead them into what might have been a ballroom at one time. The floor was patterned in concentric circles of red and azure, each circle directly beneath a heavy crystal chandelier. Natalie barely had time to register the tall windows at the back before noticing the rows of seats to her left. There were more than fifty, each occupied. Almost a third held children. She noticed all of them were about Beth's and Peter's age.

"These are my children," Dr. Adams said, indicating them with a sweeping gesture. "The children I took from parents who could not appreciate them. Of all those who took Neolamane, only these select few possess the gifts I am about to demonstrate. Through the years, I have not only been training them, but I have been trying to find out why they reacted so differently to the drug.''

"But—but their real parents . . ." Natalie whispered. She studied a few of the children's faces. They looked just like regular kids.

"I'm so tired of explaining," Adams said. "Do sit down."

With more force than necessary, the dark-haired nurse pushed her into a chair. Natalie held fast to the wire hidden in her partially opened hand.

For the next half-hour, she sat spellbound as the children demonstrated their talents to her. Peter and Beth had been telepathic, but these others went far beyond that. Their potential for destruction was immense. At last, she blinked a few times and looked over at Dr. Adams. The maniacal gleam had gone from the man's ice-blue eyes. She saw now the warmth that had caused all these people to trust him.

"I'm impressed," she said. "You really have done something important here."

The awe in her voice was the result of horror, not the admiration she hoped Adams would read into it. She was not disappointed.

"Then you understand why I did it?"

"I do," Natalie said. She stood up. The Gestapo-like nurse tried to hold her down, but Adams signaled that she be allowed to approach.

"Imagine what you could do if this didn't have to be secretive," she said. "If the children could have been kept with their real parents and the medical community had continued the manufacture of Neolamane."

"Yes, you do understand!" Adams was as delighted as a child. The others watched him, but kept silent. They'd been ordered not to say or do a thing without his orders.

"Oh, I understand," Natalie said. She was standing right in front of him now. Her voice was a monotone. "I understand that you're a brilliant, gifted . . ."

The wire-weapon came out of nowhere and plunged into the man's neck.

". . . Blood-crazed bastard!"

Natalie screamed her words of anger even as Dr. Adams reached for his neck with a wail of dismay. The previously orderly room went helter-skelter as children cried and grown-ups ran to see what happened. In the ensuing chaos, Natalie was given the few moments she needed. She bolted for the door.

Alice Segal was after her in a flash. But in those few seconds, a strange feeling came over one of the children. A feeling that all of this was very wrong. Without really understanding what she was doing, a ten-year-old-girl reached out her foot and tripped Jenny Segal's mother. Her actions gave Natalie a chance to escape.

The halls were only dimly lit, but in a few moments Natalie found herself in a kitchen. She heard doors opening behind her. Not stopping, Natalie jerked open the back door and ran out into the cold, moonlit night.

"Get her! Don't let her get away!"

She heard a woman shouting and imagined the dark-haired nurse in pursuit of her. Breathless, pebbles and pine cones cutting into her bare feet, Natalie raced toward the distant mountains. The doctor's mansion was built on a slope, leading into a copse of juniper trees. Natalie headed for these and did not stop to catch her breath until she was safely hidden in the shadows. She heard shouting.

And something else. A steady, roaring noise. Natalie moved toward its source and realized she was near a road. All she had to do now was flag down help.

Overwhelmed at the prospect of being saved, Natalie let the wall she had built to protect herself from what was happening crumble. Like a wild woman, she bolted through the woods and headed out to the street. Two pinpoints of light were heading toward her. She waved her arms, screaming "Stop!" A horn bellowed at her, but she didn't move. Her own injuries and exhaustion had muddled her sense of depth perception.

Though the driver had slammed his brakes, the pickup truck was on top of her before she realized how close he was. From somewhere far away she heard a young man's voice swear loudly, then the sound of a slamming door.

"Oh, my God! What're you doin' jumpin' in fronna trucks like that, lady? Oh, my God!"

And then other voices. Natalie couldn't move or respond, but she could hear every word.

"It wasn't your fault, young man." This was Dr. Adams speaking. "She's one of my patients. Now, if you'd just help me get her into the back of your truck, you can help me take her home."

"But—but aren't you going to call the police?"

"As I said, it wasn't your fault," Dr. Adams replied.

No! No! In her mind, Natalie's screams were the loudest noise around. But no one else heard her.

"Just help me get her back and we'll forget the whole thing."

"Sure," the young driver said, overwhelmed and relieved that nothing was going to happen to him.

Natalie felt hands all over her, lifting her. Cold on her breasts told her the robe had blown open, but she could not move to cover herself. Seconds later, someone closed the robe for her. She was lowered ever so gently onto the bed of the truck.

"Okay, follow us back to the house," Dr. Adams said. "Slowly."

No! Oh, God, don't let them take me back there. They're going to kill me. I know they're going to kill me.

Slowly, bumping up the rocky slope, the truck made its way to the house.

57

LOU VERMONT TOOK OFF HIS SHERIFF'S CAP AND scratched his head. Across the room, Danny Emerson sat on Jenny's bed with his arms around his daughter.

"I'm still having trouble figuring this all out," Lou said. "But I know one thing: it isn't going to take any blood test or prints to prove Jenny Segal is really Laura Emerson."

Danny gave his daughter a bear hug, about the hundredth since their reunion, and Laura giggled. Lou had noticed right away that they both had the same dark hair and eyes, the same large bones and heavy brows. Now he heard they had very similar laughs, although Danny's was much deeper in tone than his daughter's.

"It's like a miracle," Danny said. "Laura, your mommy will be arriving in a few hours. And when you go home, you'll meet your brothers."

Lou put his cap back on and stood up.

"Did you hear anything more about them?"

"I called Kate while they were checking Laura over," Danny said, grinning. "Joey and Chris are fine. The doctors are still wondering what happened, but just about the same time Laura told Kate she was alive, the boys snapped out of their comas. It's as if a spell had been put on them and it was broken."

Lou sighed. "I'll never understand this. Well, I better go check on the others."

He left the room and headed toward the one where Michael, really Peter, and Beth would be. Lou felt weary, anticipating the difficulty of his next task. Now that he'd heard as much of the story as possible, he realized it was his duty to place Ralph Colpan under arrest. He knocked at Peter's door. The little boy was sitting up in bed, holding a pair of binoculars.

"Look what my dad bought me," he said. "Aren't they neat?"

Beth frowned, looking at her feet. Ralph cleared his throat.

"Well, I still think of him as my dad," Michael said. "Maybe I really am Peter Morse, but he took good care of me and I love him."

Ralph shook his head. There was a heavy bandage over one side of his face, but the throbbing pain behind his eye had been eradicated with medicine. The doctor had said he'd be fine in a few weeks, but Ralph couldn't agree with that.

"What I did was wrong, Michael," Ralph said. He coughed. "I mean, Peter. That's your real name, you know." He looked at the sheriff. "I only learned about it recently," he said. "But I suspected a long time ago that Michael was no orphan."

Lou nodded sympathetically. "There are mitigating circumstances here. I'm sure any judge will understand you were almost as much a victim of Adams as Peter was."

"What about Adams?" Ralph asked. "Have you found him?"

"We're still looking," Lou said. "If a man could disappear from the face of the earth, it seems he's done it."

Peter looked at his sister, then back at the sheriff.

"What do you mean about a judge?" he asked. "You aren't going to arrest my dad, are you?"

"He's not our dad," Beth cried. "Our real daddy is dead."

Her face screwed up and she began to sob. Ralph hesitated a moment, then put his arms around her. In their ordeal together, they had become friends.

"It'll be okay," he said. "When we find your mom, it'll be okay."

Beth pulled away. "That Dr. Adams is going to kill her, too. I know it."

"No," Peter cried. "We can't let him. Beth, Jenny's real mom used her mind to help us down from the balloon. Maybe we can use our minds to call our real mother."

Ralph shook his head vigorously. "Nothing doing, you guys. You've been through enough."

"Mr. Colpan is right," Lou agreed. "You kids need to rest. Leave this to the police."

"But she's our mother," Beth protested. "We've got to—"

The door opened and a nurse popped her head in. "Sheriff Vermont? There's a disturbance down in the emergency room. Could you help us out?"

Lou followed her down the hall to the elevator. When they reached the emergency room, he heard the sounds of a woman's screams. One of his officers, John, hurried up to him.

"We think we found the Morse woman," he said. "Fellow over there brought her in unconscious, but when she woke up, she started screaming her head off."

There was sudden silence. Lou guessed the woman had been given a sedative. He went up to the triage nurse and asked permission to see her. When he was led into the room where she was now sleeping, Lou studied the haggard woman under the white sheets. Despite her strawlike hair and pale skin, he knew from pictures he'd seen that she was, indeed, Natalie Morse. The thing to do now was figure out how she'd gotten here. He left the room and went to talk to the man who had brought her in.

The fellow John was talking to now was more a boy than a man, dressed in faded jeans and an embroidered western-style shirt. He wore his long blond hair back in a ponytail.

"This is Simon Fisher," John said.

"I'm Sheriff Vermont," Lou said. "Want to tell me what happened, Simon?"

The young man nodded. "I was driving my pickup. See, I deliver bundles of newspapers to different stops in the county. All of a sudden this woman comes running out in front of my car, screaming. I couldn't stop fast enough, and I—I hit her." He shuddered.

"What happened next?"

"Well," Simon said. "There were other people who came out of the trees next to the road. It's pretty foresty in that area. Anyway, one of them said he was her doctor. I believed him, 'cause she did look pretty spacey. So I helped load her into the back of the truck to take her up to the house for them. I thought she might be hurt, but the doctor guy said he'd take care of her. You gotta realize I was really happy not to be in trouble. But I felt bad for the lady, too. So I took one good look at her before I climbed into my truck. Something about her face was real familiar, you know? Then I remembered where I saw it—on page two of the newspaper yesterday. I had a copy on the seat next to me. I checked it and it was her!"

"So what did you do?"

"I was halfway back to the house, following the people who were walking. One of them was in the back of the truck, but I had to take a chance. I spun out and turned back to the road. I guess the other guy jumped off when he realized what I was doing 'cause he wasn't on the truck bed."

"Can you tell me where exactly you hit her?" Lou asked.

"Sure," Simon said. "I can even take you there. What's going on, Sheriff?"

"I can't say," Lou answered. "But I'll tell you this. You're a hero, Simon, if ever there was one." He put his arm around the young man's shoulders. "Come on, show me where this doctor is hiding."

Lou and Simon left the hospital. The sheriff followed the younger man's pickup truck, all the while hoping this was the end of this whole insane mess.

58

DOWN THE HALL FROM THE ROOMS WHERE MICHAEL and Jenny had been reunited with their real families, Jill waited outside her son's room with tears streaming down her cheeks. They were not just tears of joy, or even relief. They were tears of confusion. When she arrived at the hospital, Danny Emerson was called right in to see his daughter. She was happy for him, and she was happy to hear that the other little boy's mother and sister had been found. But Ryan didn't seem to want to see her. When a nurse exited his room, Jill hurried toward her with a look of hope on her face. The woman smiled and Jill felt every muscle in her body relax.

"He wants to see me?"

"He sure does," the nurse said. "I know it was hard to wait, but he's been through . . ."

Jill didn't hear a word she was saying. For a few seconds, she stood frozen, staring at the closed door. Ryan was in there. Ryan! But in spite of her eagerness, she was still worried about facing her son. She hadn't seen him yet and had no idea what to expect. In her heart's eye, Jill was still seeing Ryan as a bright-eyed three-year-old.

She held her breath as she opened the door.

And she knew it was Ryan the moment she laid eyes on him. The baby fat was long gone from his cheeks, and the bouncing curls had softened to waves. But there was still a bright twinkle in his eyes, and the smile was as mischievous as ever. Jill hesitated, unable to say a word. Her tears had been spent out in the hall.

"I was thinking," Tommy/Ryan said. "If you came all the way from Long Island to get me, you might just be my real mom. I know I don't belong to those people. I'm sure of that."

"Oh . . . oh, God!"

Jill was too flustered to say more. She crossed the room in one long step and landed on the side of Ryan's bed. She hugged him and kissed him until he groaned in protest. But he wouldn't let her go, as if trying to make up for all the years of coldness at the hands of his foster parents. He still wasn't sure if she was really his mother, but it was obvious she cared a whole lot about him. And for Tommy Bivers, to be known from now on as Ryan Sheldon, that was enough.

59

WITH SIMON AT THE LEAD, A CONVOY OF POLICE VE-hicles headed toward Lincoln Adams' private retreat. When they arrived, they circled the building and climbed from their cars with weapons at the ready. Opened doors were used as shields. Lou held a bull-horn up and called to the doctor.

"This is the police. Dr. Lincoln Adams, and any individuals present in this building are asked to come out peacefully, with your hands in the air."

He waited a moment. Only the sound of the night wind answered him. His breath turned to steam in the icy October air. One of the officers near him shifted uncomfortably. It was so quiet . . .

Lou raised the bullhorn again. "This building is

surrounded. Come out peacefully with your hands in the air. No one will be hurt—you have my word.''

Lou guessed, from all he had heard about the LaMane Center, that there were children inside. He half-expected to hear them crying. But there was still nothing but cold silence.

''Sheriff, I don't think there's anyone in there,'' John said.

''It's too quiet,'' another officer agreed.

Lou shook his head. ''Could be a trap. Cover me.''

In spite of the bulletproof vest he'd taken the time to put under his khaki shirt, Lou's heart was thumping in anticipation of what might happen in the next few seconds. But he held his head up and walked with confidence toward the front door of the house. He pulled out his gun, raised a booted foot, and kicked the door open.

''Freeze!''

His gun aimed into an empty hallway.

Slowly, ever alert, Lou walked inside. His deputies waited impatiently, worried about their chief. Lou reappeared at the battered door a few minutes later.

''Place is deserted,'' he called.

Simon was the first to stand up. ''But this is where we were heading with that woman. I'm sure of it.''

''And you're probably right,'' Lou reassured when he came to the circle of cars. Guns clicked into holsters as the other cops began to stand up. ''Bastard's given us the slip again. John, Kim, you take a good look upstairs. Bill, Pat, and Steve have the main floor. I'll take the basement. I want every inch of this place searched for clues. We'll catch that child-snatching son of a bitch if it takes us forever.''

But more than an hour of tearing the deserted house apart brought no clues to the investigation. Lou called his men in and headed back to the station to file a report. It was the most difficult thing that he had ever written. The kidnapping part was easy enough. But how could he explain the unusual way the children were able to contact their parents? And that was another task to be carried out—getting positive proof that the grown-ups really were parents to these children. No problem there; it would just be a matter of checking footprints and thumbprints taken when the children were born.

As far as finding Lincoln Adams and the rest of the families was concerned, Lou guessed the FBI would be busy for years. And if these kids were all as gifted as he'd been led to believe, it wouldn't be long before other children were searching out, albeit subconsciously, their true relatives. The sheriff was confident Adams would be caught someday.

60

Ten Days Later

RYAN SHELDON FLIPPED A SWITCH AND WATCHED model planets orbit around a glowing sun. He wore a pair of earphones and listened as a recording told him of the solar system. It was amazing. There had never been anything like this at the LaMane Center. He was almost totally absorbed in the recording, but aware, too, of his mother standing across the room with her friend. He knew they were talking about him, but he didn't mind. Lou Vermont had found a really good lawyer who worked very hard and found the prints taken when Ryan was a baby. It was positive proof that Ryan Sheldon, born ten years ago, was the same child as Tommy Bivers, for whom there were no records prior to his fourth birthday.

"I still can't believe he's your son," Virginia said, her elbow resting on the glass top of the souvenir stand. "How could you have kept such a secret?"

"As I told you already," Jill said, "I had no idea

Ryan was even alive. And when Deliah Provost set my investigation in motion, I thought it too impossible, and then too dangerous, to discuss with anyone.''

Virginia nodded. ''Well, thank God in heaven he's home again. What a gorgeous kid. Those LaMane people must have been ogres to hurt such a beautiful, sweet child.''

''They were monsters, all right,'' Jill said. ''But you can't really blame LaMane Pharmaceuticals. It turns out Lincoln Adams' father-in-law owned the company, and he only named his own division after it.''

''That Adams fellow gives me the creeps,'' Virginia said. ''He must have been insane.''

''From what Natalie Morse said,'' Jill replied, ''he certainly was. I only hope to God they find him and hang him. He shouldn't be allowed to live.''

Virginia saw a spot on the glass and rubbed it with her cuff. She understood Jill's anger and let her friend rant for a few moments to let off steam. Then she said, ''What about the others? Have any other families been reunited?''

''That's the other mystery,'' Jill said. ''No one knows where they are. But a full-scale FBI investigation is being started. Adams can't go very far. And if other children start seeking the truth through their powers, the whole thing is going to come crashing down on him.''

She gazed across the empty room at her son. He looked so forlorn, with his tousled hair and his arm in a sling. So much love welled up in her that she wanted to run across the room and smother him with kisses. But Ryan had shown himself to be the kind of kid who balked at such displays of affection. It was enough for now, the psychologists said, that he accepted her as his mother. Jill prayed the counseling he was receiving would help him on the road to a normal childhood— the normal childhood that had been denied him.

''I hope things are going to be all right,'' Jill said. ''I just want to hide away somewhere here on Long

Island for a while, to enjoy the holidays with my son. I don't know how easy that's going to be with all the investigations going on.''

''Well,'' Virginia said with a sigh, ''at least you got to bring him home. I really feel sorry for that other family you told me about—the Morses. Imagine losing a father in such a hideous way. This whole thing is crazy, and I don't think I'll ever understand it.''

''I don't want to understand it,'' Jill said. ''I just want my life, and my child's life, back again.''

Across the room, Ryan had moved out from under the solar system to a scale model of the moon. He pressed a button, and a small figure of a man began to wave an American flag. The recording told him about Neil Armstrong's walk on the moon. And then the man's voice began to change, to grow fainter. Ryan winced as static filtered into his ears. He started to take the earphones off, but stopped.

Someone was calling his name.

Tommy? Tommy? I see you but I don't know where you are!

Ryan looked across the room at his mother. She was staring at him with sad eyes. He didn't like the way she looked at him, but the doctor he'd been given to help him get through this said that she only gazed at him because she couldn't believe he was there. He smiled a little. She smiled back. Ryan turned his back to her.

Who are you?

The thought travelled from his mind as easily as a voice over a phone wire.

It's Cissy Critchfield.

Tommy frowned. Cissy had been such a spoiled brat, and he had never liked her friend, Bambi Freed.

If you're trying to trick me, you can forget it. The police know all about Dr. Adams and no one's going to take me from my real family again.

Tommy . . . Tommy this isn't a trick. I'm so scared! Dr. Adams made us all split up and go different places. I don't even know where Bambi is, and I miss her.

And then I hear my parents talking and saying what a mess they're in because of me. They want to get rid of me, Tommy.

Is that what they said?

Through the earphones, Tommy heard what sounded like sniffling.

My father said he hates me and he wishes they'd given him a boy! Who? What were they talking about?

Cissy, I don't think you're going to like this . . .

With his mind, Ryan tried to explain what had happened. When he finished, there was silence. Then, softly, like a bad connection, No . . . no . . . no . . .

And a sudden scream so loud that Ryan ripped the earphones from his head.

"Ryan? What is it?"

Jill and Virginia raced across the room. The earphones had dropped to the floor and Ryan was grimacing as he rubbed his ears.

Jill took his head in her hands. "Ryan?"

He shook his head and looked at his mother's concerned face. "I heard from one of them," he said softly.

"Who?" Virginia asked in confusion.

"One of the other kids," Ryan said. "Cissy Critchfield. Dr. Adams made everyone split up, and now her parents want to get rid of her. I told her those weren't her real parents. I told her what Dr. Adams did to all of us. She didn't like it very much, and she started screaming."

Jill bent down and picked up the earphones. "You heard her through these?"

Ryan nodded. "She sounded pretty clear, too, so maybe she's somewhere nearby."

"I'll contact Lou Vermont," Jill said. "He's working with the FBI on this case. Ryan, try to keep your mind closed to those other children for now. I know you want to help them, but I'm afraid the strain will be too much for you."

"Maybe you should sit down," Virginia said. "Does your arm hurt you?"

"I'm okay," Ryan insisted. "Maybe I could have a pop?"

Virginia looked at Jill. Her friend smiled.

"He means soda," Jill said.

"Oh! Well, come on, Ryan. We've got a refrigerator full of all sorts of interesting things."

While they were gone, Jill went to the phone and dialed Lou's number in Albuquerque. After greeting him and answering his questions about Ryan's progress, she told him what she'd just learned.

"Ryan's had contact with another child. She told him Adams split the group up and sent them in different directions."

"Then that means one of two things," Lou said. "Either he's given up the whole project, or he plans to rendezvous at some point. I'd opt for the former. Once his face is plastered on the walls of every post office in America, he wouldn't dare start trouble again."

"Is there any word of him?"

"Not a thing," Lou said. "It's as if he dropped off the world. But they've taken a few people into custody—including that Ronald Preminger fellow our friend Danny Emerson beat up—and that's going to help. We'll find him, Jill. Don't worry."

"I can't help worrying," Jill said. "I look at Ryan and I'm so terrified someone's going to take him away again. I don't want to let him out of my sight, and we can't live like this. I'm so frightened."

There was a long silence, as if Lou was considering something. "My wife has relatives in Queens," he said, "and we're due for a visit. Would you feel better if I came up there?"

Jill smiled. She shook her head even though Lou couldn't see. "That's sweet," she said, "but I can't have protection forever. All I ask is that you guys keep working on finding that man. Find him and put an end to all this!"

61

LAURA EMERSON WALKED BAREFOOT ACROSS THE
sandy beach behind her new home—her *real* home,
she reminded herself—carrying a big bag of potato
chips. Her little brother Joey came running up to her,
grabbing for it. She laughed and held it up higher.
Then she broke into a run.

"Who wants chips?"

"Me, me," Chris yelled.

Beth and Peter Morse looked up from the sand castle they were building. Laura handed the bag to Peter.
As he took a handful, she thought how funny it was
to call him that name. Sometimes, when her daddy
called her Laura, she didn't answer. Sometimes, she
was afraid to answer, as if she would be hurt if she
did. She had a doctor lady who was helping her push
away the bad thoughts Dr. Adams had planted in her
mind. Peter had one, too, but his doctor had agreed
with Kate and Danny Emerson's suggestion that the
Morses spend a few weeks at their house on the beach.
It was really crowded inside, with so many children.
Beth and Peter's grandparents had come, too. Oscar
Blair didn't talk at all—Laura's daddy explained that
he had been sick—and Lillian wore black with lots and
lots of jewelry. They talked a lot about Stuart and how
much they wanted to kill Dr. Adams for murdering
him. Laura didn't want to hear about it. She just
wanted to forget.

"Peter, here's a feather for the top of your castle,"
Beth was saying. "You sure built it nice. Did you have
sand at . . . ?"

Beth cut herself off. It was an unspoken rule among the children never to talk about the LaMane Center.

But Peter straightened himself up. "I remember we had a sandbox," he said. "My dad—I mean, my foster dad—and I would build all sorts of neat things. I sure miss him."

Laura went to her friend and put her arms around him. "It'll be okay, Peter. Mr. Colpan is helping the police find Dr. Adams. And Sheriff Vermont was sure he'd be let off easy. Dr. Adams tricked him."

"I know," Peter sighed.

He put his shovel down and started to stand up, very carefully, taking care not to jerk around too fast and hurt his sore ribs. He'd fractured them in the balloon accident. Then, without a word, he started to walk down the beach. When he reached the jetty, he climbed over and sat down on its opposite side. He had been here in Massachusetts for three days, and all this time he'd been trying to locate Dr. Adams. He was perfectly willing to accept that Beth and Natalie were his family. But he couldn't give up hope of being reunited with Ralph Colpan. And he would never, ever rest until Dr. Adams paid for what he did.

Whenever he was completely alone, Peter would close his eyes and shut off awareness of everything around him. He would control his own mind as he had never demonstrated at the clinic. He guessed that a lot of the children kept the extent of their gifts hidden. If the other kids would fight back, Dr. Adams could never win. So today, hiding behind the jetty with his bare feet in a tide pool, Peter tried to contact one of the other children. After a few moments, an image flickered quickly, then disappeared. Peter thought it was a face, but whose?

Ralph had once told him that Dr. Adams thought there was a mental link between all the children in the LaMane Center. Peter didn't know how far the link would hold, but in his efforts over the past two days he'd picked up bits and pieces of information. The faces were always vague, so he couldn't be sure they belonged to anyone from LaMane. But he kept trying, obsessed with carrying out a plan he had conjured up from the moment the police took his father away from the hospital.

Today would be the day his wish was fulfilled.

The face came back into view. Peter recognized one of the boys from the LaMane Center—Bobby Whitelock. Bobby was standing near a fence of some kind . . .

No, it was a corral. A horse came up to the boy, and Bobby backed away a little. Then he carefully approached the Apaloosa and reached up to run a hand along his hide.

Bobby?

In his mind, Peter saw his friend jump a little.

Who is that? Mom, is that you?

It isn't your mother, Bobby. It's Peter—I mean, Michael Colpan. What happened to everybody? You're the first person I've been able to contact.

The image of Peter's mind was as clear as the picture on a movie screen. Bobby turned in a circle, looking very frightened. When Peter heard him speak, his mouth didn't move.

Where are you, Michael?

Can't tell you that. You tell me where you are.

I—I don't think we're supposed to talk to you guys. What happened to Jenny and Tommy? What did you guys do? Dr. Adams was really mad—he said you screwed everything up.

Where is Dr. Adams?

I don't know.

You're lying!

I can't tell you. He told my family to hide somewhere, so now we're on my aunt's farm in Iowa.

The mind-image of Bobby's face went pale.

I shouldn't have said that!

I won't tell on you, Bobby. But why can't you tell me where Dr. Adams is? I just want to contact him, to let him know we're okay.

He said you're devils. He said we'd be punished if

we ever told what happened. If he finds out I'm talking to you, he's going to take me to the middle of the lake and knock me overboard. I don't want that to happen.

Peter cringed. So, the fear they'd put in Bobby's head had been drowning. For Michael, it was falling from the tower.

Dr. Adams will never know. Is he there with you?

He—he comes here sometimes.

When's he gonna—

Shhh! Someone's coming.

With his eyes closed, Peter watched a scene that was taking place a thousand miles away. Two men were approaching Bobby, but he could only see from the back. When they stopped and turned, Peter gasped. Bobby made the very same sound. It was Dr. Adams.

Through Bobby's mind, Peter listened to the conversation.

"Bambi tells us you are in contact with Michael Colpan," Dr. Adams says.

"I am not," Bobby insisted.

"Bambi Freed does not tell lies," Dr. Adams said. "She's my most promising subject. You know she can read minds best of anyone. If she says you are in contact with Michael Colpan, then you must be. Don't lie to us, Robert. You wouldn't want to be punished . . ."

"The lake is mighty cold this time of the year," another man said.

Bobby's face went pale. "What—what do you want me to do?"

"Find out where he is," Dr. Adams said.

Tell him I'm in a place called Gull's Flight, Massachusetts. I'm staying at the Emersons' house. It's Jenny Segal's real family.

You're kidding. You really want me to say that?

Tell him to come here and get me.

You're crazy, Michael!

I'm waiting for him. You tell him that! You tell him.

Peter broke contact with the boy in Iowa. He didn't know if his plan would work, but he was willing to wait. Slowly, he stood up and shook a kink out of his leg. Then he climbed back over the jetty and walked toward his friends. He didn't say a word of what had happened, but the look on Laura's face told him she had somehow picked up bits on his mind-talk with Bobby.

"Michael," she whispered, "what are you up to?"

"I'm up to fixing things," Peter replied. "I don't want to talk about it."

Then he walked up to the house to have dinner, go to bed, and wait for Dr. Adams to walk into the trap he had set.

The doctor arrived in Gull's Flight the very next day. Peter felt his presence growing stronger and stronger. Though he did not have direct mind-contact with the doctor, he could almost imagine him on the flight from Des Moines to Boston. No doubt he would be checking into a hotel, then driving a rented car into Gull's Flight. Knowing the name of Jenny Segal's real family, the Emersons, he would only have to look up their address to find him. But even though Dr. Adams was a maniac, he wasn't stupid. He wouldn't just walk up to the doorbell and ring it. Somehow, Peter had to lure him to the house.

Danny Emerson got all the children, and most of the adults, involved in a game of touch football. Peter's habit of staying alone prevented them from becoming suspicious when he insisted upon staying inside. He went to the phone book in the Emersons' kitchen and turned to the Yellow Pages listing of local motels. It wasn't hard to find—Gull's Flight boasted only one small inn. Peter dialed the number quickly, afraid someone would come into the kitchen and catch him.

Within minutes, he was talking to Dr. Adams.

"It's awful here," he said. "You were right about the Outsiders—they all hate us. Please come and get me, Dr. Adams. I'm scared and I want to go home."

"Calm down, Michael," Adams said. Peter could almost see the evil smile on his face. "I can't just come and take you away—not with all the adults that are there. Can you meet me?''

"Sure," Peter said. "There's an abandoned boat house right down the road. You take Main Street out of town and get off at Saltwater Lane. Then you drive to the third stop sign and make a left turn. The boat house is a little ways down the road. How fast can you get here, Dr. Adams? I really want to leave.''

"I'll be there in half an hour," Adams said. "You wait for me, Michael. I'll take care of you.''

Dr. Adams hung up the line.

Peter hung up his own end, smiling wickedly. If anyone was to be taken care of . . .

His sister walked in through the back door at that moment, her cheeks flushed and bits of leaves in her long red hair. She went to the sink for a drink of water, then turned to look at him.

"Peter, what's that weird smile?" Beth asked.

Peter looked at his twin, seeing almost a mirror image of himself. He'd always thought he was kind of goofy-looking, with his messy red hair and freckles. But on Beth, the features made her really cute. Having her with him filled a void he had lived with for years. He wanted to share his secret with her, and with Laura, but he didn't want to risk their getting hurt.

"I've just been thinking," Peter said.

"You do a lot of thinking," Beth retorted. "I just wish you'd talk to me.''

"I will," Peter promised, "when I'm finished. Beth, if our mother is looking for us, I've gone for a walk down the road.''

Beth watched him go to the hall closet and pull on his jacket. It was strange how he referred to their parent as "our mother," as if to stress Natalie was someone they shared.

Outside, Peter began to walk down the road to the boat house. With Halloween just a day away, almost all the Cape Cod homes along the road were decorated with scarecrows, pumpkins, and ghouls. Halloween was something new to Peter, since they rarely celebrated holidays at the center. Ghouls, on the other hand, were quite familiar.

After the last house on the road, there was a twenty-yard stretch of foxtails, and then the remains of a long-abandoned boat house. Its roof was almost completely gone, the windows had been shot out with slingshots and BB guns, and the big doors hung crookedly on their hinges. When they had passed it for the first time on their way to Laura's house, Danny had warned the children that it was a dangerous place and they were never to go inside.

Peter looked left and right down the road, and once he determined he was alone, he pulled one of the doors open. He walked inside and studied his surroundings by the sunlight that seeped in through cracks in the rotted wood walls. The floor was cement, sloping down into the water that still sloshed into the house from the bay. Peter went to its edge and watched clumps of debris move gently back and forth. There was a strong smell of rot in here; it was icy cold and dark.

It was a perfect place to kill Dr. Adams.

There were hooks along several of the walls and shelves that had once held boat equipment. But what interested Peter the most was an old staircase that led to a three-foot ledge. A rusted clamming rake explained what had been stored up there, out of the way. Carefully, Peter climbed up the stairs. He was light enough so that they wouldn't break under his weight, but still he held fast to hooks he found on the wall as he walked out to the end of the ledge. He wouldn't let himself look down, even though the water was barely ten feet below him. Memories of being hung upside down from the watch tower tried to crowd his mind. He forced them away and sat down, rolling himself into a ball.

What happened in the next half-hour was not done by the little boy Ralph Colpan had loved so much and Stuart Morse had died for, that Natalie and Beth Morse adored. It was done by a child who had suffered years of subtle torture at the hands of a madman whose twisted mind helped him justify all his crimes. It was done by a child who saw no end to his nightmare other than this.

The door creaked open and sunlight poured into the boat house. Peter stiffened—and looked down at the shining white hair of the doctor. His stark eyes seemed to glow in the dark.

"I'm up here, Dr. Adams," Peter said.

The doctor looked up at him, the pale eyes going wide. He opened his arms and beckoned the child down. But Peter shook his head vehemently.

"I'm scared," he said, a tremor in his voice. "I think they might come looking for me, and I don't want them to find me."

"Then we must hurry," Dr. Adams said. "Let me take you back with the others and we'll start all over again."

Peter stared down at him. "Come up and get me, Dr. Adams."

"You can walk down by yourself," the doctor insisted. "Those stairs won't support me."

"Yes, they will," Peter insisted. "They're sturdy. I want you to come up here, Dr. Adams. I want you to help me down. I'm afraid of high places, you know."

The doctor's eyes thinned now and his jaw set firmly. "Yes, I suppose you are," he said. "We'll have to work on eradicating that, won't we?"

Peter nodded.

"Come up and get me, Dr. Adams."

The voice was different this time, strangely deep for a young boy. Almost guttural.

Dr. Adams started toward the stairs, then froze. "What do you think you're doing, Michael?" he demanded.

"Walk up the stairs."

Deep. Guttural. Unable to be ignored.

Dr. Adams felt his feet lifting up. He tried to resist, but before he knew it, he was at the top of the stairs. He gazed down the ledge at the small boy on the other end. None of the children had ever used their powers to control him. He was stronger. He had perfected Neolamane and had complete power over its subjects. He had to resist.

"Walk over to me, Dr. Adams. Come and get me. Come here . . . c'mon . . ."

In his mind, the doctor fought the child's demands. But his body obeyed and he walked slowly across the ledge. How had Michael become so powerful? Was it because he had left the center? Suddenly, Adams smiled a delighted smile. What exciting possibilities for study—letting the children infiltrate the real world. Perhaps their powers were boundless, and if he could turn them over to the armed forces when they were of legal fighting age, what formidable weapons they would be. Oh, it was almost too exciting to . . .

Adams jerked his head up, looking into Michael's eyes. The boy had said something, but he hadn't heard. He stopped short to find a rusted lobster trap in his way. Its wooden handle was broken in half, and many of the tines were missing or rusted. Adams started to kick it away, but Peter called out in his strange voice: "Pick up the rake, Dr. Adams."

The doctor obeyed without question.

"Now, stand there and listen to me. Don't talk and don't move."

In an instant, Peter's expression changed from one of grim coldness to the twisted features of a heartbroken child. Tears welled up in his green eyes, and his lower lip quivered. His voice was his own.

"I hate you, Dr. Adams," he said. "I hate you for taking me away from my real parents, for killing my mom from the center, and for killing my real dad. I hate you 'cause now my dad Ralph is in big trouble and he'll never get out of jail no matter what anyone says and I'll never see him again. You hurt me with those stupid wires and tests and that stupid big green chair and making me hurt other people and animals and telling me I was bad if I didn't and telling me you were gonna take me to the watch tower and making my friends do bad things, too.''

After the rambling sentence, he gulped in a shaky breath, then went on.

Dr. Adams remained silent and frozen.

''You took children from their real parents because some medicine you gave the mothers made weird babies. Kids like me. My dad gave me a file he stole, Dr. Adams. There weren't any names, but I could guess who was who. Most of us are telepaths, aren't we? Well, I'm gonna send thought messages to the other kids, and Laura and Ryan are gonna do it, too. You know who Laura and Ryan are, Dr. Adams? That's Jenny and Tommy's real names. And the other kids are gonna know their real names, too, and you aren't gonna stop me because you're gonna die. I'm gonna kill you.''

And suddenly, the child's voice turned diabolical. ''Pick up the rake, Dr. Adams. Pick it up.''

In jerking movements that showed he was fighting every step of the way, Adams picked up the rusted rake.

''Turn the points up to your chest. Stab the rake into your chest, Dr. Adams. Kill yourself the way you killed my real father and my mom. Kill yourself. Kill yourself!''

The doctor pulled the rake back, gazing at the quivering tines, his mouth dropped open in a silent scream. This was impossible. He was too brilliant a scientist to have been tricked by a ten-year-old boy. A boy who was one of his subjects. He wouldn't let it happen. He couldn't!

''Peter!''

At the sound of Beth's voice, the spell was broken. In an instant, Dr. Adams jerked around and lost his footing. With a long scream he plunged into the mucky, icy water below the ledge. There was a splash, then silence. Peter moved toward the wall, covering his face. He didn't want to look.

But Beth looked; she screamed and screamed.

Dr. Adams had fallen onto the rusted tines of the clamming rake. He floated facedown in the dark water, his body resting over the length of the rake as if it were a float. The tines pointed up toward the neck, where blood began to gush out with the flow of the water.

Beth's screams brought the adults running. Natalie, without thinking of danger to herself, rushed up to her sobbing child and took him in her arms. Kate kept the other children out of the boat house while Danny went to look at the man floating in the water. He walked down the cement ramp until he was waist-deep, then pulled the body back with him. When he turned him over on the cement, a sick feeling congealed in his stomach. The rake had shoved up under his chin, deep into his head. With his mouth still open, one of the tines was visible. Danny jerked off his coat and covered the body.

But before he did, Natalie took a look at it and let out a cry. "That's Adams. That's Dr. Adams."

Danny looked up at the woman, holding her son tightly. "We—we'd better call the police," he said softly. "Peter, come down now. Come down and tell us what the hell just happened here."

Epilogue

One Year Later

WITH HER ARM AROUND HER SON, JILL WAITED AT THE entrance to Disney World and watched for their friends to arrive. In the year since Adams died, there had been no contact with others from the LaMane Center. To the frustration of everyone involved, the case was put on the back burner for lack of evidence. When Adams died, it seemed the whole sickening affair died with him. It would only live on in his victims, in the innocent children who had suffered at his hands, until another child came forward in search of his real past. But the past of three particular children—Laura, Peter, and Ryan—was something that the adults in their lives were trying to deal with. In spite of the memories, the children insisted upon keeping contact with one another. They had grown too close during their ordeal to forget their friendship.

There had been an investigation after Dr. Adams' death. Peter had insisted he killed the doctor, but the police concluded from Beth's eyewitness testimony that the man had intended to use the clam rake to kill the boy. Beth told them she saw him fall off the ledge. No matter what Peter said, no one would let him believe he had actually murdered the doctor. Peter, Beth, Natalie, and the Blairs had gone home to put their lives back together. Frequent letters and occasional phone calls convinced both the Emersons and Jill Sheldon that Peter was coming along as well as their own children.

"Wait until Peter sees the surprise we have for him," Jill whispered.

Ryan broke his hand free and pointed. "There they are! There they are!"

He waved both arms over his head, and Laura Emerson came running. Beth and Peter followed, but the little Emerson boys were held back by their father. There was a lot of giggling and hugging until Beth said, "I can't believe you guys are here."

Kate and Danny and Natalie reached the group and hands were shook all around.

Once they were inside the park, Chris tugged at Danny's leg and asked, "Where's Mickey and Donald? I want to see Mickey! Is Goofy here? Are we gonna go on rides?"

Jocy squealed with delight. "Mickey Mouse!"

The adults laughed and a knowing look was exchanged between Jill and Natalie.

"Let me ask someone," Jill said. "There's a man over there." She walked through the crowd, making Peter ask why she had to talk to that man in particular. When he turned around, the answer became obvious.

"Dad! Dad!" Peter yelled so loudly other people turned to stare curiously. But he was unaware of their presence as he raced toward Ralph Colpan's open arms. Ralph, who had not seen his child since he was taken from the hospital in New Mexico, gathered the boy up and covered him with kisses. Tears brimmed in the women's eyes, and Danny gazed at the scene in amazement.

"How . . . how . . . ?" He couldn't choke out the question.

"It took a lot of work," Natalie explained. "But since the FBI was not pursuing the case, and since the Morses refused to press charges against Ralph Colpan, there was little reason to keep him locked up. With Lou Vermont's help and influence, we were able to have him released on probation. The judge was able to see that Ralph was as much a victim as the others, and he let him go on the stipulation that he come forward to testify if ever the other members of the LaMane Center are found."

"You kept this a secret from Tommy?" Kate asked.

"From Peter," Natalie corrected. "I was afraid to say anything in case Ralph wanted to cut himself off completely. You can see what a fool I was to believe that."

"This is an incredible day," Kate said, shaking her head.

Beth and Laura and Ryan hugged one another and jumped up and down. "It's the best, best day ever," they cried out in unison.

The adults nodded. Maybe, just maybe, things were going to be all right.

As the happy group walked into the park, a man turned and walked away from the door of a gift shop. He wore a fringed suede jacket and tattered jeans. His face was plain, except for one startling feature—blue eyes that were so pale they seemed colorless. He followed the group for a while, but when they stopped at the gate to one of the rides, he ducked back into a crowd.

His mind was full of sick thoughts.

I'll get them, Father. I'll get them back again, and I'll continue your work, no matter how long it takes.

Gregory Adams, son of the late Lincoln Adams and his most successful experiment, stared at the children, especially the red-haired boy who had murdered his father. Michael Colpan would pay for that.

Gregory listened to the children's laughter, hating the sound of it.